"Do not put words into my mouth, Helene."

Cam answered in a voice that was suddenly low and rough. Swiftly, as if to force her to his will, his hand came down to cover hers, squeezing her fingers far too hard.

A wicked stubbornness took hold of her then and Helene moved to grab the books. Cam sprang like a cat, slapping his broad hands on top of the stack, and anchoring it to the desk.

"Stop it, Helene," he said, a little too softly. "Look at me. *Look at me, Helene!*"

Helen lifted her eyes in a bold challenge, stubbornly locking them with his. "Let go of my books, if you please," she coldly enunciated. "You are hurting my fingers."

"I want you to stay," he demanded.

"Do you indeed?" She lifted her chin a notch higher. "But what of my lax morals? My wicked French blood? And let us not forget that carefree Continental lifestyle I've been living!"

Cam looked at her coldly. "That is your business, Helene."

As he leaned over her, Cam's face drew so near that she could feel the warmth of his breath. In the implacability of his grip, she sensed a ruthless energy which she did not recognize. She did not know this man. And yet, if she looked up at him now, her forehead would almost certainly brush is chin, and their lips would be far too close. . . .

PRAISE FOR NATIONAL BESTSELLING AUTHOR LIZ CARLYLE

"Hot and sexy, just how I like them! Romance fans will want to remember Liz Carlyle's name."
—*New York Times* bestselling author Linda Howard

"Carlyle delivers great suspense and . . . sensual scenes."
—*Publishers Weekly* (starred review)

Acclaim for her romantic fiction . . .

A DEAL WITH THE DEVIL

"Sinfully sensual and superbly written . . . nothing short of brilliant."

—*Booklist*

THE DEVIL TO PAY

"Intriguing . . . engaging . . . an illicit delight."
—*New York Times* bestselling author Stephanie Laurens

THE DEVIL YOU KNOW

"Sweep-you-off-your-feet romance, the sort of book that leaves you saying, 'More, please!' "

—Connie Brockway, award-wining author of *My Surrender*

"Rich and sensual, an unforgettable story in the grand romantic tradition."

—Christina Dodd, *New York Times* bestselling author of *Close to You*

NO TRUE GENTLEMAN

"One of the year's best historical romances."

—*Publishers Weekly* (starred review)

"Carlyle neatly balances passion and danger in this sizzling, sensual historical that should tempt fans of Amanda Quick and Mary Balogh."

—*Booklist*

A WOMAN OF VIRTUE

"With *A Woman of Virtue,* Liz Carlyle shows she deserves fan support from mystery aficionados as well as romance lovers."

—*Affaire de Coeur*

"A beautifully written book. . . . I was mesmerized from the first page to the last."

—*The Old Book Barn Gazette*

"I can't recommend this author's books highly enough; they are among my all-time favorites."

—Romance Reviews Today

A WOMAN SCORNED

"Fabulous! Regency-based novels could not be in better hands. . . ."

—*Affaire de Coeur*

MY FALSE HEART

"*My False Heart* is a treat!"

—*New York Times* bestselling author Linda Howard

Also by Liz Carlyle from Pocket Books

THE DEVIL TO PAY
A DEAL WITH THE DEVIL
THE DEVIL YOU KNOW
NO TRUE GENTLEMAN
TEA FOR TWO
A WOMAN OF VIRTUE
A WOMAN SCORNED
MY FALSE HEART

Beauty Like the Night

POCKET STAR BOOKS
New York London Toronto Sydney

This book is a work of fiction. Names, characters, places and incidents are products of the author's imagination or are used fictitiously. Any resemblance to actual events or locales or persons, living or dead, is entirely coincidental.

An *Original* Publication of POCKET BOOKS

A Pocket Star Book published by
POCKET BOOKS, a division of Simon & Schuster, Inc.
1230 Avenue of the Americas, New York, NY 10020

ISBN: 1-4165-1061-3

First Pocket Books printing November 2000

10 9 8 7 6 5 4 3 2 1

Illustration by Alan Ayers

Manufactured in the United States of America

to all the Boadiceas in this world
who do not have
a warm hearth,
a soft bed,
or a kind master

and to all those
who so tirelessly give of themselves
on behalf of
homeless and abused animals

Beauty Like the Night

Prologue

In Which the old Devil comes to a Bad end

An early October mist still lay heavy in the vales of Gloucestershire when the Honorable Mr. Camden Rutledge rose before dawn to partake of his customary morning repast, black coffee and two slices of bread, lightly buttered. Therefore, by the time the blood-chilling screams commenced, he had been miserably but diligently occupied in reviewing the estate finances for well over an hour, whilst ensconced in what was—or only moments earlier had been—his father's study.

As a matter of old-fashioned civility, the room had always been called "his father's study," despite the fact that the wicked old devil had never troubled himself to study anything save games of chance, and had certainly never gazed upon the inside of an account ledger. Indeed, Chalcote Court's elderly housekeeper had often sworn that the Earl of Treyhern had never poked so much as a toe inside the room during her tenure—though he had reputedly poked a rather saucy parlormaid in the corridor just outside the door one raucous New Year's Eve.

His father's lack of scholarship aside, Cam's rather formidable concentration was abruptly severed when the aforesaid screaming began at precisely a quarter past seven. The shrieking was unmistakably feminine in origin, for Cam found it loud, shrill, and unremitting. The racket echoed down the ancient corridors of Chalcote, bounced off the tapestried walls, and sent a bevy of curious servants scurrying up from the pantries and kitchens and cellars, all of them eager to see just what mischief the old lord had wrought this time. And all of them—or so it seemed to Cam—bolted past the study door en route to the commotion, their boots and brogans pounding on the hard oak floor.

Hopelessly distracted from an already impossible task, Cam jerked from his chair with a hiss of frustration, and started toward the door just as the butler floated in, looking rather paler than usual. "I fear it's the new governess, Mr. Rutledge," Milford explained without preamble. He knew that the young master preferred to take bad news the same way he took his whisky; smooth, neat, and infrequently.

Cam threw his new pen onto the desk in disgust. "Good *God—!* What now?"

The ashen-faced butler hesitated. "She's in the corridor upstairs, sir."

Cam elevated one straight black brow. "As I plainly hear, Milford."

"And she—well, she's in a rather revealing state of dishabille, sir."

Both Cam's brows shot up. "Indeed? Cannot someone fetch her a wrapper?"

The screams were lessening a bit. Milford cleared his throat decorously. "Yes, Mr. Rutledge. Mrs. Naffles is seeing to it, but the more pressing concern, sir, is . . . is his lordship. I greatly fear that . . . well, the governess was in . . . in his . . . your father's . . . bedchamber and—"

"Oh, devil take it, Milford!" Against his will, Cam's hands flew to his temples. "Please don't say it—!"

"Oh, sir," said the butler mournfully. "I fear so . . ."

Blood pounded in his head as Cam tried to dredge up a measure of apathy. Given his father's ribald predilections, this embarrassment had probably been inevitable. "Well, he's a damned ugly sight, seen bare-arsed," he remarked flatly. "I should scream, too, I daresay."

"Yes—well, I mean no . . ." Milford shook his head as if to clear his vision. "Indeed, Mr. Rutledge is—or I should say—his lordship is perfectly bare-ars—er, naked, sir. But in addition, I fear he's . . . he's—"

"Christ, man! Spit it out!"

"Dead."

"Dead—?" Cam looked at the servant incredulously. "Dead, as in . . . ?" He made a vague motion with his hand.

"Ah . . . just dead, sir. In the regular way. 'Twas overexertion, I daresay, if you'll forgive the impertinence." Milford looked obviously relieved that the news was out. "Mrs. Naffles says 'twas apoplexy for sure, since his lordship's gone an even darker shade of red than usual, sir. Rather like bad burgundy. And the eyes are even more protruding than . . . well . . . never mind about that. Nonetheless, a man of his advanced years . . . and the governess, Miss Eggers . . . er, rather lively and all that—"

"Yes, and apparently possessed of exceptional lungs," interposed Cam dryly. The screams had subsided into heaving, hysterical sobs.

"Yes, sir. Quite good . . . *lungs*, sir."

Cam picked up his pen and balanced it in the palm of his hand. "Where is my daughter, Milford? Dare I hope that she has been spared this debacle?"

"Oh, yes, sir! Miss Ariane is still abed in the schoolroom wing."

"Good." Cam sat back down. "Well, I thank you, Milford. That will be all."

"Thank you, sir. I mean . . . *my lord.*" The butler began to back out of the room, then paused. "By the way, my lord . . . what, precisely, ought we to do now? About the, er, young lady? Miss Eggers?"

Cam scraped his chair forward and snapped open the next ledger. Without looking up from his task, he began to etch neat, uniformly shaped numbers into a perfectly straight column down one side of the page. "Precisely how long, Milford," he finally replied, "had Miss Eggers been warming my father's bed? And was she willing?"

The butler did not bother to feign ignorance. Hands clasped behind his back, the thin, angular servant looked up at the ceiling, calculating. "Above two months, the housekeeper says. And by all accounts, she had every expectation of becoming the next Lady Treyhern."

"Well, that rather settles it then, doesn't it? *I* certainly shan't be marrying her, so best put her on the next mail coach to London."

"Yes, my lord. And the . . . the corpse?"

Elbows propped upon the desk, Cam heaved a weary sigh and dropped his head into his palms. "Just send for the priest, Milford. I can do no more for my father. He is in God's hands now, not mine. And I do not envy God the task."

Allowing a glint of a challenge to light her eyes, Helene de Severs lifted her chin and stared confidently across the burnished mahogany desk, studying the elderly gentleman who leaned back in his chair with such a condescending indolence. Outside the open window, the clatter of passing carriages and the rumble of drays in Threadneedle Street mingled with the strident cries of a morning costermonger as he made his way toward Bishopsgate and the old city walls.

By comparison, the bustling London traffic in the street below made the heavy, protracted silence inside the oak-paneled office seem all the more discordant. Finally, the elderly solicitor leaned forward, splaying his long, thin fingers upon his burnished desktop, as if perhaps he had decided to rise and escort his young visitor to the door.

Instead, the old man cleared his throat sonorously and began to tap one spindly finger as if to emphasize his warning. "Miss de Severs, you really must understand the full circumstance of this position," he explained, his thick white brows pulled gravely together. "I am afraid Lord Treyhern's child is, er, rather . . . how shall I put it? *Peculiar.*"

Already remarkably rigid in her chair, Helene de Severs nonetheless managed to draw herself up another inch or two. She was a tall woman, not easily cowed, so the motion was usually effective. "I do beg your pardon," she said archly. "You say the child is *what—?*"

"Peculiar. As in abnormal," the solicitor returned coldly.

Helene suppressed her rising ire. "I am accustomed to challenging assignments, Mr. Brightsmith," she said with a tight, uncomfortable smile. "I collect that the difficult nature of this assignment is precisely why I am here today, is it not? But *peculiar* and *abnormal* seem rather harsh words for any child."

The solicitor shrugged. "In point of fact, I am given to understand that the girl may be hopelessly dim-witted. We simply do not know, and indeed, there may be little that you can do. But apparently, Lord Treyhern remains . . . hopeful. He wishes to engage someone with special experience to work with the child."

Helene held both her breath and her tongue for a long moment. Life in London had been abysmally dull since her return from abroad. Moreover, another three months of this indolence would severely press her meager savings. She needed this post rather desperately, and not just for the money. Given poor Nanny's age and health, Helene needed to remain in England just now. But most of all, Helene needed the challenge, for try as she might, she had found that she could not be happy without her work.

Nonetheless, she most assuredly would not obtain the position by angering Lord Treyhern's rather unenlightened solicitor. She was trained to educate children, Helene reminded herself, not pompous old men. So resolved, Helene tossed her neatly gloved hand dismissively, then bestowed upon old Mr. Brightsmith her most charming smile. It was a look, Helene knew, which could soften the most hardened of men, for she had seen her late mother use it often, and to merciless advantage.

"My dear Mr. Brightsmith, I have every confidence that I can be of help to his lordship," said Helene. "Pray give me the benefit of any insight you may have regarding the child. A man of your experience can but be of help in such a difficult situation."

The solicitor seemed mollified. He shuffled through a few papers on his desk, then drew out a long sheet of foolscap. "Well, Ariane is about six years old. She resides in Gloucestershire with her widowed father, Lord Treyhern, who has directed me to find a . . . a special teacher. Highly qualified, and experienced in these sorts of cases." He faltered a little. "I fear, Miss de Severs, that I know little more than that."

"And the child's disorder—?"

"Her disorder?" The solicitor shot Helene an indeterminate look. "Well, the child cannot speak! She is mute!"

Her ire flashed again, and Helene forgot to simper. "Mute?" she archly replied. "Do you mean, sir, that she cannot speak? Or that she *will* not speak?"

The old man bristled a bit. "Indeed, Miss de Severs, is there some difference which escapes me? It is simple enough; the child cannot talk."

There was often a great deal of difference, but Helene would not trouble herself to cast pearls before swine. Instead, she slumped back against her chair, unaware until that moment of how intently she had been leaning forward. "I see," she said softly. "But has the child never spoken? Not even when she was younger?"

At this, the white brows shot up. "Why, er . . . yes! Exactly so! The child did begin to jabber on a bit when she was a babe. But she no longer seems capable."

"Ah!" murmured Helene knowingly. "I have studied a few such cases."

"Have you indeed?" The old solicitor looked fleetingly impressed, then no doubt recollecting that she was a mere female, quickly squashed it. "The child looks well enough. I've seen her myself. But she does appear a bit . . . *wild* about the eyes."

"And are you at liberty to tell me what happened to her, Mr. Brightsmith?" she asked rather sharply. Then, seeing his haughty glare, she dropped her eyes deferentially. "You see, sir, I cannot very well help the child without some understanding of her circumstance."

"Circumstance?" he answered vaguely.

"Indeed. You asked me here today because I have had some experience with children who have, as you say, *difficulties*. Moreover, I have read and studied many such cases. And in my opinion, such abrupt losses of speech, or similar aberrations in what have previously appeared to be normally developing children are often precipitated by some sort of accident or crisis."

Momentarily absorbed in thought, Helene furrowed her brows. "It could, of course, be a cranial tumor bearing pressure on something . . . or perhaps there was a blow to the head? And of course, an emotional trauma can disrupt normal childhood devel—"

"Thank you, Miss de Severs!" interjected Mr. Brightsmith, his thin hand extended, palm out, as if to forestall her extemporary lecture. "Rest assured, the child has sustained no injury. Moreover, I am already convinced of your qualifications for this post. As you must know, the letter from your German baroness in Passau is glowing, as were your earlier references."

Helene had been interviewed often enough to know when the dice had finished tumbling. "You are too kind, sir," she said graciously, then settled back to wait.

As if he had read her mind, the old solicitor pushed a sealed letter across the glossy desk. "I must say, Miss de Severs, you do come rather dear for . . . for a governess, or for whatever it is you are."

"Indeed, a governess," echoed Helene compliantly.

"Yes, well. Against my judgment, his lordship has agreed to your extraordinary salary demands of £90 per annum, half payable in advance. However, I shall require a signature here," he paused to thrust forward another document, "to signify your intent to remain in Treyhern's employ for the duration. He has had difficulty retaining staff, and he wishes for consistency in his daughter's life."

"That is both wise and fair." Helene scribbled her signature, and with a little prayer of thanks, picked up the envelope. This advance was enough to repair her ancient cottage, and keep Nanny supplied with coal for the coming winter.

"Moreover, if it eases your mind at all, sir," she added, tucking the envelope into her reticule, "I am perhaps just a little more than a governess. His lordship shall have no cause to regret this." She spoke with more confidence than she felt.

"A bold claim, Miss de Severs." Brightsmith took up his quill and began to scratch out an address.

Helene smiled again. "I have always thought Virgil said it best," she answered crisply. "*Fortune favors the bold.* I think I have the translation aright, do I not?"

"You do indeed," he answered dryly, folding, then sliding the paper toward her. "Your traveling directions, ma'am. You are expected in Cheston-on-the-Water, Tuesday a week."

Helene felt her throat constrict. "Ch-*Cheston*?"

The solicitor's keen eyes flicked up at her from his desk. "Is there a problem?"

"No." Helene swallowed hard, tightly gripping the paper. "Not at all."

"Excellent." Brightsmith stood. "And Miss de Severs?"

"Yes?" she answered, glancing up a little uncertainly.

"Do take your black fripperies. Ribbons and such. His lordship's household is in deep mourning."

Helene nodded dumbly, and as if in a trance, walked out of Mr. Brightsmith's office, through the reception room, and down the long flight of stairs which led to the street below. Weaving her way through the late morning pedestrians, she braced an unsteady hand against the door of her hired carriage, oblivious of the driver who leapt forward to assist.

Blindly, she stared down at the folded slip of paper Mr. Brightsmith had pressed into her palm. *Surely not Cheston-on-the-Water? So very near to Chalcote* . . . It could not possibly be so, could it? Over a decade had passed. Gloucestershire was a vast county; its wolds scattered with fine estates. Moreover, Helene had never heard of the Earl of Treyhern.

As she tried to reassure herself, an empty tumbrel spun past, crowding her carriage and spraying a filthy arc of water across her hems. "Hey, look lively, miss!" insisted the driver. "I ain't got all day."

Helene finally flipped the paper open to scan the crabbed, sideways scrawl. *Camden Rutledge, Lord Treyhern. Chalcote Court, Cheston-on-the-Water, Gloucestershire.* A deep buzzing began somewhere inside her head.

"Miss? What's all this? You ill?" The driver's voice,

urgent now, came as if from a deep, black well, and Helene was only dimly aware that he had jerked open the carriage door and was pressing her into its shadowy depths. *Camden Rutledge, Lord Treyhern* . . . the words began to whirl through her mind.

"Best get you back up to Hampstead quick-like, aye?" added the driver uneasily, slamming shut the door.

"Y-yes," agreed Helene. But the driver was already climbing onto his seat.

1

Miss Middleton goes Home to Gloucestershire

The newly invested Earl of Treyhern stood at his bedroom window, absently sipping tepid coffee, and pondering the state of his life, when his black traveling coach spun merrily into the long drive, returning from its errand in the nearby village of Cheston. An ancient dray, which the earl did not recognize, rumbled along in the coach's wake. Lord Treyhern gazed wearily across the perfectly manicured lawns of Chalcote Court, watching as the faint November daylight reflected off the carriage roof, and wondering what next he ought to do.

He did not care for life's uncertainties, for he was a precise, controlling sort of man. And yet, the preceding month had been a difficult one; harder somehow than he had expected. It had brought home to him the stark realization that while his father's death had removed an undeniable burden from his life, it had been by no means the only one.

Indeed, following the sudden departure of her most recent—albeit incompetent—governess, Ariane had crawled ever deeper into her dark silence, and he was at a loss as to what should be done for the child. In all of his twenty-nine years, the earl had never felt so alone, nor so old.

As his valet moved quietly about, neatening his room, Camden studied the carriage, its yellow wheels spinning inexorably toward the front door as it trundled beneath the blazing oaks which lined the drive. And as his eyes followed its progress, Cam began to fervently pray that it held at least a part of what his life so desperately needed right now. Oddly enough, he had the most fanciful feeling that it did, and he was not a man much given to optimism or prognostication.

He could hear the crunch of gravel as his coachman neared the steps which led down into the sweeping circular drive. In a flash, a liveried footman trotted dutifully down to open the door, a second following to unload the luggage. Through the open carriage door, Cam saw an arm extend gracefully; saw the flash of white skin just where her cuff met her glove. Surprisingly, both sleeve and glove were a deep, rich shade of purple, like a well-cut amethyst viewed by candlelight. Subdued, but nonetheless opulent.

At a glance, neither her attire nor her bearing looked quite like that of a governess, and yet, Cam could not have said precisely why that was so. She stepped down into the drive, her burnished black tresses swept tightly up in what Cam always thought of as "governess hair." But once again, on this woman, the arrangement looked strangely paradoxical, particularly so when topped by a dark purple hat, trimmed with a rakishly tilted black feather.

The footmen were unloading her luggage now as she stood beside the dray, gesturing her instructions to them in a decidedly bold, Gallic way. Good God! Had the woman come to stay forever? A veritable heap of boxes and trunks seemed to be accumulating in his driveway. Cam was taken aback; he had never known a governess to own so many things, let alone to travel with them.

Somehow, it seemed inappropriate. This was the

country, and she would have little need of such fripperies and fineries, if that was what her luggage held. Indeed, what else could it be? Cam recollected that Miss de Severs's decidedly French name had initially given him pause when Brightsmith recommended her. Perhaps his hesitation had been justified. What Cam had wanted was a sturdy, stoic Englishwoman, yet as the pile of baggage grew, he began to be very much afraid that was not at all what he'd got.

Damn his luck to hell.

"Crane!" the earl called sharply to the valet who was busily brushing his frock coat. "What sort of luggage do you make that out to be, eh?"

The portly valet stepped up to the glass and peered down at the drive. "Well, my lord . . . 'tis mostly packing crates, I should say. Four o' them." He squinted mightily. "Aye, with two trunks, a dressing case, a small leather valise, and a portmanteau. All trussed up with a length of rope, that one is."

"Good eye," mumbled Lord Treyhern. His gaze left the mountain of luggage to study his new employee. He could not help himself; Helene de Severs was fascinating, even at a distance. She was a tall woman, yet she moved across the drive with an almost athletic grace. Not the mincing steps and rigid hips of most women, but a leggy, confident stride, her shoulders back, and her chin up.

Her cloak was of the severest black, her gown suitably trimmed for a house in mourning, and yet she seemed to glow with inner radiance. He could not help but wonder at the color of her eyes. Something exotic, most likely.

Then, just as Cam lifted the lukewarm cup to his lips, the new governess looked up to smile beatifically at the helpful footman, and Cam sucked in his breath with an audible gasp, very nearly choking on his coffee.

Bloody hell, it *was* Helene!

Not Helene de Severs. *Helene Middleton.* What the

devil was she doing here? Despite the passage of eleven barren years, and the utter destruction of all his youthful fantasies, Cam truly believed that he would have known her anywhere. His first thought was that his elderly coachman had taken up the wrong passenger; that somewhere in the dust and disorder of the Rose and Crown stood a bewildered and abandoned governess. The real governess. A plain, sensible, middle-aged woman in proper, wrenlike attire. But there was no mistake. He knew it with a certainty.

Dear God! Cam had prayed hard for a miracle, advertised repeatedly for a governess, and yet what had the Good Lord and old Brightsmith conspired to send him? *Helene!* The unusual name had immediately drawn his eye when first he had skimmed her letter of introduction, the very sight of the word submerging him in warm memories of his nascent sensuality. Inexplicably, he had not slept well since. Perhaps his subconscious had held fast to those same memories this sen'night past. Perhaps he had even been hoping to see her.

Hoping?

Oh no. He had hoped never to see Helene Middleton again.

Helene found herself ushered into a vast but simply furnished gentleman's study, then offered refreshment, which she summarily declined. Left alone to await his lordship's pleasure, she cast her eyes about the room, taking in its obviously masculine warmth. In one corner, a fat ginger tabby snoozed peacefully, her impressive breadth taking up the better part of a stout leather armchair, one white foot hanging over the edge.

"Ah, le chat botté," murmured Helene, kneeling down. *"Bonjour!"*

The desultory cat greeted her with a wide, toothy yawn, extended one leg in a tremulous stretch, then returned to her nap, leaving Helene to her own devices. She strolled through the room, which was broad and deep, and filled with sturdy, simple furniture. This was a room she had never seen before, of that she was certain. More of a library, really, for a huge desk sat in its center, and massive bookshelves ran from floor to ceiling along three walls. In the center of the rear wall was a deep, Jacobean window with a tattered cushion laid across its seat.

It was the first tattered thing she had seen at Chalcote Court, beginning with the elegant stone gateposts which flanked the drive, to the obviously new Turkish carpets which warmed the massive entry hall. Quite a contrast to the crumbling manor house she remembered from her youth. Obviously, the new Lord Treyhern had gotten the whip hand on his dissolute sire before the place collapsed into the pile of Cotswold rubble from whence it had sprung.

Helene's gaze traveled across the walls as she paced the room's length. Books of every type were methodically shelved, apparently by subject, then size. Adjacent to the window seat, one entire bookcase had been given over to poetry, some of it of very recent origin. She pulled a well-worn volume from one shelf, and it fell easily open. To her surprise, the poem was one of her favorites, "Beauty Like the Night" by Lord Byron.

Thoughtfully, she slid it back and let her eyes skim across the titles. How very odd it was. The late, and probably not too lamented Randolph Rutledge had never given the impression of having literary inclinations. But then, if Helene's memory served, his lordship had inherited Chalcote Court from his Camden in-laws, hence his eldest son's name. Perhaps these finely bound books were theirs? Perhaps they were even Cam's.

Inwardly, Helene laughed at her foolishness. Of course, they were Cam's. The new Lord Treyhern had always been heir to Chalcote, under the terms of his mother's marriage settlements. But somewhere along the way, old "Randy" Rutledge had got himself an earldom, then passed it along to his eldest, too. The title had come from an ancient great-uncle, or so Nanny had learned. But Rutledge had held it less than two months before keeling over—probably from celebratory excesses, Helene did not doubt. Oddly enough, Helene had no recollection of a title hanging about in the Rutledge family tree, but she would have bet her last sou that *Maman* had been keenly aware.

Despite the passage of time, however, Gloucestershire, and indeed Chalcote itself, seemed very much the same, and Helene was struck by how . . . well, how comfortable it felt to return. Not at all as she had feared. And why should she be afraid? She had been only seventeen when last she had come to Chalcote. Cam had been young, too. And they had been the best of friends. He would be glad, perhaps, that she had come.

Yet that optimistic thought had barely taken root when the study door flew open as if propelled inward by an unholy power, squashing all of Helene's tenuous hopes against the wall as it jarred the adjacent picture frame. The tabby sailed off her perch and pattered across the carpet with a throaty trill of greeting.

And suddenly, there he was. A man grown. And a fine specimen of manhood, at that. Not that Helene had harbored any doubt whatsoever on that score. As a boy, he had been lean and graceful. As a man, he was large and overpowering. Indeed, even her sudden fear could not obliterate the sheer physical presence of Camden Rutledge in a foul temper. And unless she missed her guess, such was his mood. Well! *C'est la vie!* Helene gave him a muted smile.

Clearly dressed for the country, Cam paused to stare heatedly at her for a moment, his broad shoulders filling the doorway. His long, booted legs were set wide; his stance rigid. Obviously, Lord Treyhern had come down in some haste, for he had not paused to don his frock coat, and stood before her now in his rolled linen shirtsleeves and plain waistcoat. He looked for all the world like an irate young squire who had just discovered a vagrant poaching his pheasants.

The effect of this intimidating entrance was somewhat diminished, however, when the ginger cat began to purr resonantly, twining herself sensually back and forth around his topboots in a gesture which clearly belied his cruelty.

"Welcome to Chalcote, *Miss de Severs*," he said, ignoring the cat. "Or is it not Miss Middleton? You look so very much alike, I vow, I cannot make it out."

"You were ever a wit, my lord." Helene gave a light, casual laugh as she dropped into a smooth curtsey. "Can you forgive the confusion? For in truth, I have always been Helene de Severs."

"Indeed?" he replied, strolling into the room. "I never heard you called so."

"*Maman*'s first husband, my lord—? That rather obscure Frenchman who lost his head in the September massacres? I'm given to understand that he was my father, but perhaps *Maman* thought the pretense made her seem younger. Too many husbands, you know . . . not very *bon ton.*"

"Ah!" he answered sharply. "And your mother . . . ?" Cam lifted one hand in the barest gesture of civility, then flicked it toward the desk to show that she might sit down. "Mrs. Middleton is, I hope, w—"

"Dead, my lord," interjected Helene, sinking gratefully into the proffered chair. "After the war she died in Paris. Cholera. Since then, I have rarely come back to England. Which is to say, only if Nanny needed me."

Cam took a seat behind the wide mahogany desk and

laid his hands flat against the desktop, pressing down as if the act might restrain his own emotions, which were plainly in turmoil. "I knew none of this," he said at last. "I'm sorry for Mrs. Middleton's death. I am sure you feel her loss very deeply."

"Yes, much to my amazement, I do," Helene admitted. "And allow me to extend my condolences on the death of your father, my lord. I pray your brother and sister are well?"

Something which looked like exasperation flared in Cam's eyes. "Catherine married too young, and Bentley is floundering at Oxford," he answered with a curt half-nod. "But I suppose they are well enough."

Helene bowed her head deferentially, pausing to gather her scattered wits. Despite the fact that she had had ten days in which to prepare herself, it was difficult to maintain the semblance of professionalism while in the presence of this man. This *man*.

The word shocked her still. For Cam was more than a man grown; he had a hint of silver glinting at his temples. The boyishly attractive face was gone, too, the skin now drawn taut and closer to the bone, and darkened by the shadow of a heavy beard. No less handsome, but far more intimidating.

In her own mind, Helene supposed, she had irrationally fixed him forever in time. There, in her daydreams, and sometimes in her nocturnal fantasies, Cam would always be her gentle, laughing beau. Nonetheless, it took but one quick glance at the harshly drawn lines of Cam's face, and just a scant few moments of conversation, to see that the love of her life had grown dour, distant, and humorless.

"It has been rather a long time, my lord," she said quietly, lifting her eyes to his. "I feel the passage of it most keenly." And there, for the briefest moment, she saw his gaze soften.

"Yes, a very long time," he murmured, then set his hands firmly down on the desktop again. Surprisingly, her heart lurched when he then absently lifted one up again, raking his fingers through his thick, black hair in a boyish, achingly familiar gesture. The awkward cowlick which had always plagued him was still there, she saw. Inwardly, she smiled at the memory, and tried not to permit the familiar wave of bitterness to surge forth.

He stared at her blankly for a long moment. "I—well! Indeed, Helene, I cannot think how this has happened."

"How what has happened, my lord?"

"Your returning here. To Chalcote. After so many years."

"It is a rather simple matter, I collect," she answered dryly. "I am a particular sort of . . . of governess. And you required a teacher of children who are—"

"You, Helene?" he interjected. "A *governess?* I vow, I never could have dreamt such a thing."

"Really, Lord Treyhern?" she asked archly, emphasizing his title. "Whatever did you fancy would become of me?"

She watched the muscle in his jaw harden and twitch. "Why, I am sure I had no notion," he said at last.

Oh, but I think you did, she responded, but with her eyes, not her lips. "Rest assured, my lord, that I am relatively untarnished by my mother's reputation," she coolly returned. "I am respected in my field. Indeed, your money has bought you rather more than a governess. I believe my training and experience speaks for itself, but if you do not wish to avail yourself of it, someone else will be glad to do so."

Cam swallowed hard. She watched the movements of his throat with fascination. "Yes, yes! To be sure," he admitted vaguely.

Suddenly, Helene found herself a little angry at her new employer's veiled remarks and pregnant silences. In the years since she'd left Gloucestershire, Helene had learned to govern her wild exuberance and passionate nature, but her temper was far less obliging. "Forgive me, Lord Treyhern. I grow weary of having my past suspiciously poked and prodded. Might we discuss your daughter?"

Cam took an obvious exception to her tone, jerking from his desk chair and crossing to the wide bow window. He stared silently through the glass, one hand set at his narrow hips, the other absently massaging the muscles in the back of his neck. In the weak morning sun, a sprinkling of dark hair was visible across the corded tendons of his raised forearm.

"I do not believe, Helene, that this is wise." His voice was thick with some emotion she could not identify. "Indeed, it just won't do. I think you know it as well as I."

"*Quelle sottise,* Cam!" she exploded, rising from her seat to stride after him. "Particularly when your daughter is in want of help! What do you think really matters here? Your pride? My sensibilities? I like this no better than you, but there is a child who must come first."

"I am only too well aware of that, Helene," he snapped.

Helene softened her tone. "The child requires a teacher—and a good one, from all I have heard. Moreover, I accepted your offer and signed your contract, all without knowing who you were. But upon learning it, I have kept my word. I will go, and gladly, if you will release me from our agreement. But if you wish me to stay, I want to see Ariane now."

Cam turned to look at her, his straight dark brows drawing taut across his eyes. "No, Helene. I am afraid it is out of the question."

"Why?" she demanded. "Because of my mother's reputation?"

"No. But Helene—after what has passed between us, I cannot—you cannot possibly think—"

"Think *what,* for God's sake?" Helene's voice took on a

bitter edge. "I can assure you, my lord, that I think of nothing but your daughter's welfare. You and I were naught but friends. At worst, we were two forsaken children, thrown together by selfish parents. I was fond of you, and you of me. Is that such a bad thing?"

Almost of its own volition, her hand reached out to rest lightly upon his shoulder. Despite her height, she had to reach up to do so. As if under her command, Cam sunk down into the window seat, and pressed the heel of one palm against his brow.

"No," he answered at last. "For the most part, it was a very good thing, our friendship. And it came at a time when I needed a friend. Rather badly, perhaps."

Helene's knees turned to pudding at his frank response, and she realized how close she had been standing. Stepping slightly backward, she let her hand slide away. "Perhaps you need a friend now, my lord. It is no small matter to bury a parent, no matter their failings. No one understands that fact better than I. And your daughter, she concerns you greatly, does she not?"

Cam stared at her, unblinking. "I have changed, Helene," he said simply.

She laughed unsteadily. "My lord, we are none of us what we once were. You and I, well, we are all grown up now. We may do as we please, just as we always wished. And yet, for my part, I feel decidedly old."

"You do not look old," he answered gruffly. "You look the very same. I would have known you anywhere."

When she made no further response, Cam rose and pulled the bell. "I must think on this, Helene. Milford will show you to your room. Please make yourself—" His words faltered for a moment. "Please make yourself at home here. We'll speak again tomorrow."

As she stood to leave, the cat rose, stretched languidly, then crossed the room to leap up onto a folded newspaper which had been left atop the desk. Cam followed

Helene's every move as his butler ushered her from the room.

"Damn it, Boadicea!" he growled to the ginger cat after the door thumped shut. "What the devil was I thinking? Why did I not simply send her away?"

Boadicea stared at him, blinked her eyes slowly, then stretched out a coppery leg and began to nibble between her toes. It was probably the most sagacious response one could expect, given the sheer stupidity of his behavior. Perhaps, Cam inwardly admitted, Helene was an excellent teacher. Nonetheless, he was not sure he could bear to have her beneath his roof. Helene enticed a man to live his life as if it were meant for laughter and pleasure. A tempting but treacherous illusion, that.

Violently, he shoved his chair back from the desk, much to his cat's disapproval. Ignoring her glare, Cam told himself to get a grip on his thoughts. He was no green lad now. The woman was just a damned governess, for pity's sake. But she was right about one thing. His overriding concern had to be Ariane's welfare, and if Helene was as gifted as her references would have one believe, could he in all fairness to the child send her away? Life's challenges, which had seemed merely plentiful a quarter-hour ago, now seemed innumerable.

"And there are Bentley and Cousin Joan to sort out, as well," Cam murmured to Boadicea. "Bentley, I fear, will soon come to a bad end. And Aunt Belmont! God preserve me from her! I feel perplexed by it all."

The cat stretched out on the desktop with a low rumble of contentment, but otherwise had little to offer. Nor did Cam, for that matter. His young brother, Bentley, was an eternal font of misfortune. Although the boy had returned to Oxford after the funeral, disturbing rumors of his progress, or lack thereof, had already reached Cheston-on-the-Water. Not even Cam's wealth would be able to buy his brother another chance this time.

As to his Cousin Joan, she would shortly be eighteen, and Cam could sense that Aunt Belmont was anxious for him to announce their betrothal, and save her the expense of a London season. Cam kept telling himself that he was glad; that his aunt's zeal would help propel him forward into the future, for he had been too long mired in the past.

And yet, he did nothing. It was time to stop waiting, always waiting. And what the devil was he waiting for, anyway? For the hole in his heart to be filled by something greater than himself? Perhaps Joan was up to the task, though he was hard-pressed to feel much enthusiasm.

Nonetheless, he would do his duty. A Belmont match had been his mother's dearest wish, for her father had had no sons, so he had divided his land between his two daughters, with the vague hope that it might be reunited by a marriage between cousins.

But over the years, those dreams and many more had been tossed to the wind like so much cold ash, with Randy Rutledge hefting the shovel.

Now, however, things had changed. Cam was a wealthy widower, and Joan was of an age for marriage. There was an understanding. And no one could deny his cousin's suitability as a wife, for she was quiet, subtle, and delicate. Indeed, Joan would never challenge a man's opinion, poke her nose into his business, or leave him tossing and turning in his bed until dawn. And Joan would never wear purple, nor set such a rakish feather in her hat.

In the darkness, she listened. The pretty lady with the lilting voice was gone now. But Papa was still talking to his cat. Papa was perplexed. *Per-plexed*. She liked the sound that word made in her head. She shaped it with her lips, careful to let no noise escape.

Her leg was numb now. It was squashed against the

door of Milford's service pantry. Quietly, carefully, she twisted about in her tiny cubbyhole beneath the shelves. *Ooh, ooh! Pins-and-needles!* She rubbed her leg, waiting for the pain to go away. She wanted out. She wanted to slip away, to follow the lady upstairs. But Milford was rumbling about in the parlor now, and Papa was still in his study. She was trapped between them.

She knew why the lady had come. Oh, yes. The lady was here to make her talk. They would sit together in the schoolroom, and the lady would show her the pictures on paper. The lady would say words, and scratch them with chalk, like little white birch twigs, onto the slate.

Anxiously, she shifted her weight again. Why, oh, why did Milford not leave? She wanted to follow, to see the lady up close. Miss Eggers had been bouncy and round like Mama, with . . . sunshine hair. The new one was like Milford. Like Milford but not like him at all. Tall and . . . and willowy, yes. But pretty, not ugly. Papa called her . . . not Miss something, but . . . Helene.

Hay-leen. Hay-leen. She said the word in her head, just as Papa did, with a little lilt at the end.

Well, well! Papa was *per-plexed* by *Hay-leen.* She wondered if that was a good thing or a bad thing. She did not know. But she would find out. In the dark, Ariane suppressed a giggle.

In the dead silence which remained in the wake of Helene's departure, Cam could hear a mouse scrabbling about in the walls of the service pantry. There seemed to be rather a lot of them in the house lately. He pushed back his chair and glared at Boadicea, who now snoozed lazily atop his morning paper.

Abruptly, he rose from his seat to pace about in the oppressive stillness, letting his indignation fill the emptiness. Crossing the rug with long strides, Cam seized the poker and jabbed viciously at the coals until they sprang into full flame. Helene's flashing dark blue eyes had always been able to heat a room, and her departure had seemingly stripped all warmth from this one.

Abruptly, he was roused from his introspection by a loud, rapid knock.

2

The Perennial Spring of all Prodigality

Before Cam could turn from the hearth, the door was pitched open to admit a whirlwind, in the form of the Honorable Randolph Bentham Rutledge, who stalked into the room, then hurled his lithe frame into the chair Helene had just vacated. A bitter smile made plain the boy's mood, even before he spoke.

"Do your worst, my lord brother!" announced Bentley without preamble, stretching his long legs out to cross them carelessly at the ankles. "I'm out on my ear, and they'll not have me back." He spoke with an indifference which stripped any semblance of apology from his words.

The earl stared at his seventeen-year-old sibling in amazement. Given what had already been a disconcerting morning, Cam's comprehension was sluggish, but catch up it finally did. "Bentley," he began ominously, "we are but a few scant days into Michaelmas term. I pray, for your sake, that you have some mitigating explanation for your presence here . . . ?"

"No," said Bentley. Through a spreading haze of anger, Cam watched as what appeared to be his late father's handsomely carved chin and jaw went rigid, solidifying into stubborn, arrogant lines.

"Just *no* . . . ?" The earl's voice dropped to a cold whisper.

"No, *my lord?*" responded Bentley, slipping fractionally lower in his chair. "I have no explanation. Or none, I daresay, which you would care to hear."

"How exceedingly perceptive!" Cam wanted to throttle the boy. Instead, he sat down, picked up his pencil, and began to beat a violent tattoo on the opposite palm. He found the pain strangely satisfying, and settled back to study his young brother's ashen but willful face.

"Oh, blister it, Bentley!" he said, after a time. "Cards or dice?"

"Neither."

"Drunkenness? Whoring?"

Bentley shrugged equivocally.

"Cut line, my boy," cautioned Cam. "How bad? What's it to cost? Or perhaps more to the point, will I even pay it?"

"Sorry to put it to you, Saint Camden, but I'm not *your boy,* and I've no dearth of funds." Bentley managed a snide grin, then drew a tattered letter from his coat pocket and sent it sailing through the air with a casual flick of his wrist. "Here, then, if you've nothing better to read. I believe you'll find that the vice chancellor 'regrets my enduring lack of scholarly interest, and feels I might better be occupied in some less intellectually demanding endeavor.' At least, that's what I recollect it said. Wasn't there to receive the official dressing-down, don't you know. Had to tool down to London to watch a little turn-up and to play hazard with some chaps at the Cocoa-Tree." The chin came up again. "And I won, too."

Cam suddenly snapped, raking the note and half the contents of his desktop onto the floor with a sweeping right arm. "Damn you to hell and back, Bentley!" he raged as Boadicea bolted for cover amidst the clatter. "I swear, you're no better than Father. The pair of you could bring a nobleman to a ninepence in a fortnight."

"Why, one does what one can for the family," murmured Bentley tauntingly. Then in a mockingly seductive whisper, "Good Lord, Cam, I do love to make you lose that infernal self-control. Reminds me of the good old days when Cassandra was still alive. Glad you've still got a temper underneath all that ice."

Cam came out of his chair. "My dead wife is none of your concern, Bentley! My God! Have you no notion of what is due your name? Do you believe us to be made of money? Do you imagine our reputation so unsullied by scandal that it can bear your going on this way?"

Bentley snorted derisively. "Our name? Our *reputation?* Indeed! Father cared little enough for either, so why should I be troubled with them? I hold one saint in this family to be piety enough. And as to money, if we've been caught short—which I doubt—then perhaps you might just thaw out that whacking great cock of yours and marry us another merchant's chit, eh? But Joan would never serve that purpose, would she?"

Cam's fist came down on the desk, rattling the drawer-pulls. Bentley did jump then, his first show of real fear. "You will leave my intended bride out of this, Bentley! Do you hear me? I'll not have you impugn your cousin's good name."

Bentley was out of his chair in a flash. He strode to the window, arms crossed over his chest and fists wedged beneath his armpits, as if he could barely restrain them. "Damn you, Cam," he whispered, staring out into the sun-dappled gardens. "You know I'd never hurt Joan! It is you whom I scorn! I am so damned tired of bowing and scraping to the savior of our reputation, our fortunes, and indeed, our bloody self-righteousness! Yet all the while, you go on trampling over all of us and doing what you presume to think best. Father never plagued me. It has always been *you.*"

Cam opened his mouth, then clapped it shut again. He

wanted to say *"Yes! Because Father never gave a damn about you!"* But it was clear, even to him, that this confrontation had nothing to do with scandal or school or funerals. Indeed, Cam was hard put to explain just what was wrong. But it obviously ran cold and deep inside Bentley's heart, and Cam was struck with the impression that this time his whelp of a brother was truly spoiling for a fight. Damn it, he bloody well would not give it to him.

Cam exhaled slowly and forced his temper under control. "Very well, Bentley," he responded tightly. "I collect that you plan to seek your fortune without benefit of education, then. Moreover, you have no further wish to live under my guardianship. Do I understand that aright?"

Bentley still refused to face him, but he watched suspiciously from the corner of his left eye. "I . . . no. I . . . that is to say, I have not yet decided."

"Then by all means, let me help you," answered Cam, his voice laced with deceptive softness. "Law . . . or the church?" He laid one finger against his lips for a moment. "No, I fancy not. If you cannot finish Oxford, those methods of earning one's bread would never do, would they? But perhaps you would like a pair of colors? Or does the navy hold some attraction?"

"Oh no—!" said Bentley, snapping around. "I shan't leave England, and you cannot make me!"

"Yes, very true! Very true!" said Cam in a contemplative tone. He was beginning to have a vague suspicion as to what this latest outburst—indeed, perhaps the last several—were all about. But there was nothing to be done for it.

"Then I shall send you down to our seat in Devonshire," he said at last. "Old Hastings shall require a bit of assistance with winter coming soon. You may go in my stead, and learn something about estate management in the bargain."

"Don't plan my future, Cam!" cautioned Bentley. "You have no notion of what is best for me."

"True enough," admitted Cam softly. "But if you think to piss away your life, you'll not do it here." He paused in thought, drumming his fingers upon the desktop. "Very well, Bentley. I shall look to you to decide what is best done with your future. I shall give you until the New Year, at which time you shall have three options: you may beg—without my help—for admission to Cambridge, or you may go down to Treyhern Castle and help old Hastings. Thirdly, if those do not suit, you must seek your fortune by whatever means you think best."

Bentley's brown eyes widened in shock. "You cannot—why, you *cannot* send me away from Chalcote!"

"*Can* and *will*," countered Cam dryly. "It is time to wake up, bold fellow! You'll be eighteen soon. If life under my roof holds such thwarted opportunity, then go and seek it where you may."

For only a fraction, Bentley looked crestfallen, his arms dropping loose at his sides. Then just as quickly, the impudent grin was back. "Right, then," he said, bouncing eagerly up onto the balls of his feet. "Since I have until the New Year, I'd best pass the time in some pleasurable pursuit. I fancy I shall spend it seducing that rather fetching governess you've just hired. Older women are so experienced, and God blind me if she ain't got a rack of tits to put old Miss Eggers to sha—!"

But Bentley did not get a chance to further elucidate. Cam had hold of his cravat and was pounding him mercilessly into a bookcase. A hailstorm of books rained down around them as Cam yanked taut the fabric, then hoisted him ruthlessly upward by the coat collar, leaving Bentley's booted feet dangling aimlessly above the Oriental carpet.

"*Aahk! Ugghk!*" gagged Bentley, his face flooding with red as he clawed impotently at his brother's fists.

Cam slammed his brother's head roughly back against the bookshelf. "So you want to see me lose my infernal self-control, Bentley?" he hissed, hitching the cravat a notch higher. "You touch so much as her gloved hand, and by God, see it you surely shall. I'll relieve you of your ballocks with my own blade."

Abruptly, he let go, and Bentley collapsed onto the jumble of books which were scattered about on the carpet. "And reshelve my bloody poetry collection," he added, striding toward the door. "I'll not be cleaning up after you ever again."

From behind him, Cam heard Boadicea drop to the floor. She darted forward to precede him from the room, haughtily waving her bright orange tail, as if she were the herald of an invading army.

Cam strode toward the stables, still shaking with rage. A part of him was all too aware that he could have hurt his brother. Cam was physically powerful, and he too easily forgot it. For many years, he'd had to work side by side with his retainers like the lowliest yeoman farmer, just to ensure the estate's survival. It had given him a strong back and powerful arms. Yet his self-discipline had always been far stronger.

What in heaven's name was wrong with him? First Helene Middleton, and now this! Look what the mere mention of the woman had done to him. He'd very nearly throttled a seventeen-year-old boy! In truth, he loved Bentley, and wanted only the best for him. As he did for Ariane and Catherine.

Yes, the family's name was still a bit tarnished, despite the fact that Cam had forced his father to restrict his antics to the country these past few years. But now, with their father finally at peace, Bentley could throw off the bad influence and yet make something of his life. He was Cam's heir, for pity's sake. Was that what so rankled his brother? Did the thought of Cam's remarriage remind Bentley that he might easily be supplanted?

By the time Cam reached the stables he had calmed marginally. He strode past the box stalls and into the tack room, then hefted his saddle onto one shoulder.

"Beg pardon, m'lord," came a voice from the shadows. "Would you be in need of a mount?" Shreeves, the groom, stuck his head out of a stall and into a shaft of sunlight. Dust motes danced about his head like a rustic halo.

"Ah, Shreeves!" said Cam, shifting the weight of the saddle. "Be so obliging as to bring 'round that new bay stallion. I've a mind for some exercise."

The groom's face split into a grin as he strode into the corridor. "Aye, if it's exercise you're wantin', you'll get it. That devil's a trifle ill-tempered today."

Cam smiled grimly. "Aye, well, we'll make a fine pair, then."

"Oh ho! Like that, is it?" The grin widened to reveal a broad gap in his teeth. "Looked as though 'twas young Hell-Bent's gear being unloaded this morning. Right after that new governess arrived, it was."

Cam inwardly smiled at the staff's nickname for his brother. "Yes, Shreeves, it's like that. Now fetch me the bay so I can die in style."

He carried the saddle out into the daylight, and in another ten minutes, Cam was well on his way to breaking his neck. The stallion was worse than feisty, he was outright spiteful, and it took Cam the better part of half an hour to work the devilment out of the both of them. Soon enough, however, the horse settled down for a long, hard ride, and Cam settled down to decide what to do with Helene. What a task that had always been!

Cam had first laid eyes on her as a wide-eyed, leggy adolescent, and even then, she was a dark, coquettish beauty in the making. And she had learned from the best. Her mother, Marie Middleton, had been a beautiful

French émigré of uncertain origin. The lovely widow had taken London by storm when first she had arrived in England. Before long, she had buried two more marginally respectable English husbands, and only God knew how many lovers.

Cam's mother had died a few months after Bentley's birth, when Cam was in his teens, and Catherine but a child. Randolph Rutledge had cast off his mourning early, and with relish. In truth, the short charade of grief had suited him very ill, for he had never loved his wife.

Mrs. Middleton had run with a raffish crowd which moved on the fringes of Polite Society. In hindsight, it seemed perfectly natural that such a woman should soon become fast friends with his father. Throughout the gay autumn which followed, Chalcote had buzzed with house parties and hunting, country weekends and picnics. And through it all, Cam had watched the dashing, hoydenish Helene with an inward fascination, for she was everything he dared not be.

Soon Marie Middleton was his father's paramour, and because they were so frequently thrown together by self-absorbed parents, Cam and Helene became friends, and partners in crime as well, for no one could ferret out adventure like Helene unleashed on an unsuspecting countryside. Serious even as a child, Cam was shocked to discover his own penchant for mischief under Helene's wayward influence.

Their friendship deepened over the course of many months, and soon, a more dangerous sort of attachment began to take root. The years drifted past, until eventually, Helene had bewitched and bedeviled poor Cam to the point that his young cock was incessantly rigid, like a Maypole stuffed into his breeches. He had been utterly humiliated, utterly charmed, and utterly lost in the depths of her blue-black gaze.

In the end, Cam had been so maddened by desire, he

had been unable to help himself. They were close; too close. And ultimately, he had been unable to stop himself from compromising her, by even the most liberal of English standards. Had Marie Middleton wielded any influence among the *ton,* there would have been a parson's mousetrap for Cam, and never mind his tender years.

But what, then, would his life have been like?

If he were honest, he'd admit having been haunted by that question all too often throughout the years. But the answer was always the same: damned difficult. Certainly, there would not have been his wife's marriage portion to save Chalcote from his father's excesses. There would have been no money to fund his sister's dowry, nor to educate Bentley. In those respects, at least, Cam's marriage had been worth something. But it was of cold comfort to him now, when he looked back over the last decade of his life, and felt a timeless hunger gnawing at his gut.

And now . . . and now Helene had come back. And to his eye, though she would soon be eight-and-twenty, she had not changed at all. There would be all manner of trouble if he allowed her to stay. His argument with Bentley was but the first instance.

But bloody hell, the woman invited such remarks! That seductive smile! That saucy hat! That bold, assessing stare! Still, Cam was admittedly hard-pressed to blame her for this one. How dare the boy even dream of bedding Helene? Or any other member of the household? Damn it all, it just was not done.

Well, it *was* done, and Cam was shrewd enough to know it. But by thunder, not in his house.

Already Bentley was too much like their father for Cam's comfort. Just short of eighteen, the boy was a handsome charmer who looked far older than his years. Bentley had already managed to breach the portals of London's hells, and Cam knew for a fact that the boy consorted with Haymarket whores and village barmaids every chance he got. Cam just prayed that his brother would not carry out his threat to trifle with Helene.

Fleetingly, however, he wondered what Helene's reaction would be. Would she be flattered by the attentions of a younger man? Bentley was handsome enough, and in a few years' time, he would come into a decent independence.

Cam remembered with perfect clarity what he had been like at Bentley's age. He had wanted to bed Helene, and he was quietly determined that nothing was going to stop him. Her mother had barely done so. He had tried to tell himself afterward that it was not his fault. That Helene had been more temptation than any young man could have been expected to resist.

But in truth, it was no more her fault than his, and the attraction had been more than her body. Cam was alternately angry at their parents for separating them, and angry at himself for compromising her. Often, he had even been irrationally angry with Helene for making him want her.

Beneath him, the horse set a steady course along a familiar bridle path, its powerful muscles rolling under him in a smooth, flowing motion, but Cam had all but forgotten where he was.

Standing on tippy-toes until her feet hurt, Ariane Rutledge watched the new lady through the crack in the dressing room door. She could barely see. It was just too, too bad! If not for Milford, she could have been under the lady's bed by now.

The lady walked all about the room, her forehead wrinkled like Papa's, and her arms crossed over her . . . her front. But Bentley called it something else . . . a *bosom*. She almost let a giggle escape. Uncle Bentley was funny.

"Gad's me life!" she had once heard Grandpapa say to Bentley. *"If that ain't a fine rack o' tits."*

"Why, that bosom could pretty nearly smother a fellow!" Bentley had answered.

And then they had laughed and laughed. But they had been talking about Miss Eggers, not this pretty new lady. And now Miss Eggers was . . . gone.

And Grandpapa was gone, too. From what she'd heard Milford say belowstairs, she rather thought Grandpapa had been smothered by Miss Eggers's tits or bosoms or something, which made no sense at all. Anyway, he was gone. Like Mama was gone. Gone forever, which was different from gone away, like Miss Eggers. They did not think she understood the difference. But she was not a baby anymore. She knew a lot of things.

Suddenly, the lady came closer. She walked to the window and pulled away the draperies with one fingertip. She stared out through the glass, then went to her dressing table and began lifting up the bottles and jars. Now she was back at the window, peering out again, and nibbling at her thumbnail. Slowly, she lifted her hand and let her fingers rest upon the glass, as if studying someone beyond.

Perhaps the lady was restless. She knew about *restless*. Papa used to say it a lot. *"Your Mama is just restless,"* he would say. And then, he would hold her in his lap, because Mama was usually too busy walking around, being restless. Staring out the window and making gloomy faces. And soon, she was gone forever.

Suddenly, the lady made a little gasping sound, then let the draperies drop again. Well! Ariane knew what *that* was all about. She knew that look. She knew what the little sound meant. The watcher was out there. Perhaps he was watching the new lady, too. Ariane shivered. She would not think about him. Not at all. She would not let herself. She would think about the new lady.

She wondered if the new lady was about to become gone. She sure looked as if she wanted to be. That would be all right, she supposed. If the new lady—Helene—stayed, then Helene would just want her to talk. Talk, talk. That was what they always wanted. They wanted to ask her questions.

But she would say nothing.

Mama had said *"Do not ever tell!"* And *"Shh! shh!"* she would whisper. *"It must be our little secret, Ariane! Don't answer their questions!"* Ooh, it all made her head hurt now. And the worst thing was, she could no longer remember exactly what it was that she was not supposed to tell. She could not remember the secret anymore, no matter how hard she tried.

Suddenly, something soft and warm touched her leg. Boadicea! Oh, no! But Papa's cat was very quick. She darted past, and pushed open the door to run across the lady's bedchamber. *Damn and blast and bloody hell!* That is what Uncle Bentley would have said! But she did not have time to think about silly Bentley. She moved fast, too. Back through the passageway, toward the schoolroom.

"Le chat botté!" she heard the lady say in her pretty, lilting voice. "Wherever did you come from?"

Filled with restless unease, Helene paced the length of her bedchamber, staring at her unopened trunk and wondering what next to do. How dare Camden Rutledge insult her so! Five minutes into their meeting, Cam had leapt to some less than flattering assumptions about her character, and what had she done? She had offered him her friendship, when she ought to have slapped his face and stalked out.

Helene caught herself up short. She was not being entirely fair. Cam had always been an honorable person, and in Helene's experience, people changed little. And, really, what would most people have expected her to become? Certainly, Helene had not been brought up in the most respectable of environments.

And despite Cam's being her elder, Helene knew perfectly well that throughout their adolescence, she had tormented him—yes, even manipulated him—beyond human bearing. Helene had enticed quiet, responsible Cam into capers that hauled him through hell and back. They had painted all the village weathervanes blue on May Day, replaced all the prayer books with Methodist hymnals on Palm Sunday, and burnt down Mr. Clapham's hayrick on Guy Fawkes' Day—accidentally, of course—in a veritable calendar of misadventure.

And as they got older, matters become far more serious than a few childish pranks. Ah, yes. More serious indeed. Little wonder Cam thought her unfit to teach his daughter. And from the outset of their friendship, neither of them had been, figuratively speaking, an innocent. Helene had been unduly influenced by her mother's devil-may-care attitudes. Marie had believed that life was short. That life was for the taking. That life was for pleasure. These were the lessons taught her by the guillotine. For a very long time, Helene had known no better.

Abruptly, Helene threw back her shoulders and pushed aside the memories. Resentment seemed like a safer emotion. And she very much resented being sequestered in this bedchamber, instead of being permitted to see her intended pupil. For what seemed like the tenth time in a quarter hour, Helene strode to the window, drew back the draperies, and stared dully across the rear gardens of Chalcote. This time, however, as she turned away, her eye caught a flash of motion in the distance. She looked again.

Someone—a man—was walking rapidly along the public footpath which ran from the village proper along the wall of Chalcote's rear garden. Abruptly, he stopped, then turned to stare. Indeed, he seemed to look quite deliberately at the rear of the house. Helene gasped when his gaze, almost methodically scanning the row of windows, caught and held hers for a long moment. Or at least, it seemed that it had done so.

An ugly, unpleasant chill ran up her spine. But how fanciful. She was just weary and distracted. The stranger was some five hundred yards away, and on a public path, no less. Indeed, she could not even see his features; just his size, his long, open greatcoat and black hat. She blinked, and looked again. He was continuing on his way, perfectly disinterested in Chalcote and its occupants. Still, the chilly unease lingered. Helene wrapped her arms about her shoulders and shivered. Good heavens, her nerves were overset!

Suddenly, the door to her dressing closet creaked inward, and Cam's ginger tabby darted around the bed. How odd. She was quite certain she had shut that door. Nonetheless, Helene greeted the cat, then knelt down and offered her fingertips. But the huge beast did not deign to be scratched, choosing instead to lazily circle Helene's trunk and portmanteau, pausing to sniff every hinge and handle. And then, as if she had done what she had come to do, the cat turned about and strutted from the room, apparently satisfied.

Well! It would seem Helene had passed inspection, at least as far as Cam's cat was concerned. As to the lord and master himself, that was another thing altogether. With a weary sigh, she flopped down onto the wide bed and let herself sink into its thick, downy depths.

Idly, she let her gaze roam over the furnishings of her chamber. The room was of a good size, and conveniently connected to a passageway that led through a dressing closet, into the schoolroom, and on to Ariane Rutledge's room beyond. Like all of Chalcote, Helene's chamber was decorated in a style that was elegant yet comfortable. She found the contrast rather disconcerting, for without, Chalcote was solidly beautiful, the perfect country house. But within, despite its grace and symmetry, there was a bleakness, a sense of melancholy she did not remember from her earlier visits. She doubted it had much to do with Randolph's demise. Perhaps Cam grieved for the loss of his wife? And he was quite obviously worried for his child.

Her feet dangling off the bed, Helene toed off her shoes and let them fall, then curled up in the center of the elegant woolen coverlet. She pressed her nose into the pillow, realizing that she, like Cam's tabby, was searching for a comforting smell, for some sense of the familiar. Though she had lived more or less alone for years, it suddenly occurred to Helene that she felt terribly lonely in this vast, rambling house. Any sense of homecoming had vanished.

Yes, returning to Chalcote had been impetuous, she decided, picking aimlessly at a loose thread in the pillowcase. In that, at least, Cam had been entirely correct. Nanny had been right, too. Helene remembered every detail of the argument which had followed her dazed return from Brightsmith's interview. After gossiping amongst her network of former servants to confirm Helene's fears, the old woman had been beside herself with worry. Her remonstrations had continued until the day of Helene's departure.

"Are you perfectly sure, m'dear, that this is wise?" Nanny had said for the fifth time that morning.

Helene had felt her exasperation begin to battle the anxiety she had been trying so hard to hide. "Nanny, please!" she had begged. "Have we not been over this time and again? I want to be near you! And I must have a job—"

"Aye, and a job's what you'll get, but o' what sort, there's no knowing," the old woman had insisted with a wag of her gnarled finger. "Now mind me! That Camden Rutledge is his father's son, and blood'll tell! Aye, and rich now, too. A man don't rise up that high—not from where *he's* been—with easy ways and a gentle tongue."

In frustration, Helene had yanked fast the buckle on her portmanteau, ripping it off and nearly ruining the bag. "I am no longer a child to be nursed, Nanny," she had insisted, pitching the torn leather strap into the cold hearth. "And I am no longer so easily felled by a shy smile and a pair of smoldering eyes. Moreover, I've dealt with men far more sophisticated than the new Lord Treyhern."

Nonetheless, as she had stood in Cam's study this morning, Helene had begun to question the truth of her words. A lifetime had passed since she'd seen him. And in that time, the pain of her loss had lessened, and then numbed, until at last she had thought of him rarely.

Well, perhaps a little more often than that. But what she remembered was no more than a young girl's infatuation. And so it had seemed, all the way to Gloucestershire, across the Coln, over the wolds, and right up the twisting lane which led to the gates of Chalcote Court. With every mile, Helene had been increasingly confident that what she felt for the new Lord Treyhern was nothing more than a warm fondness for an old friend.

Even when Cam, dark with rage, had stepped into the study, Helene had believed herself to be in control of the situation. In the past, she usually had been. It had taken her all of about five minutes to realize that the tables had turned. No one controlled Camden Rutledge now. Helene saw it, as surely as she could see that the soft-spoken youth had grown into a dangerously quiet man.

And a stunningly handsome one, too. At seventeen, Cam had seemingly reached his full height, a lithesome six feet; yet now, he seemed far taller. Moreover, he was clearly possessed of that kind of silent, solid strength that quiet young men so often carry into adulthood. When Cam had set his hands stubbornly upon the desk and leaned toward her, Helene had watched a man's strength ripple through his wide shoulders. She had seen a man's anger—and yes, perhaps even a man's lust—flash across his face.

Drawing an unsteady breath, Helene turned her face into the pillow, her hand fisting tightly in the soft wool of the coverlet.

3

Thou turn'st Mine eyes into my Very soul

Before Cam realized just how far he had ridden, he looked up to discover that he had traveled the width of Chalcote, and now stood at the high wold which overlooked his Aunt Belmont's adjoining estate. He reined his horse about and went back down at once.

A dutiful nephew would have dropped in for tea, but he'd been avoiding his maternal aunt and cousin since the funeral. That delicately inquiring look which lingered in Aunt Belmont's eyes nowadays made him break into a sweat.

Cam accepted the fact that he had a duty to marry someone of unassailable character and exemplary breeding. And Joan more than met those lofty standards. Cam agreed that the old idea of reuniting the estates held some merit. Still, he delayed.

But today, Cam did not want to think about his plaguing, prodding female relatives. Someone else was still on his mind, despite the heart-pounding ride across the meadows and through the forests. How unwise it was to think about his youthful indiscretions at such a time.

But Helene had been his only indiscretion. Youthful or otherwise. Ever eager to vex his sober-minded son,

Randolph had once joked that Cam was so boring, trifling with Helene Middleton had been his only lapse in judgment. But in truth, Cam had not been trifling. He had foolishly meant to marry Helene.

At the time, it had not seemed so wildly out of the question. Despite all his earnest promises to his mother, Cam had been eldest son to a dissipated ne'er-do-well. There had been no title, just a ramshackle estate which Aunt Belmont had disdained to so much as visit. Yes, life had been simpler before he'd been thrust into the role of family savior.

With a sharp sigh, Cam reined in his horse and dismounted beneath a tree. He'd been but eighteen when Helene's mother had taken her away. Some black, desperate void—it had felt frighteningly like madness—had begun to swallow him up. For many months, Cam had been unable to control, and very nearly unable to bear, the swells of grief and rage.

And it was then that he had truly realized how very like his father he must be; governed by his appetites, filled with a raging desire for something he ought not have. Eventually, he had realized the value of control. He had seen the truth of his mother's oft-repeated warnings; that he, like the proverbial acorn, would never fall far from the tree if he could not govern such wayward desires.

And now, those old emotions were as newly familiar as the bitter taste of blood in his mouth. Perhaps Joan was the solution. A young, compliant bride beneath his bedcovers could ease his infernal needs and give him an heir. But he'd tried that once, had he not? And found himself shackled to an amoral hellcat. But Joan was nothing like Cassandra. Joan would be a faithful wife, a dutiful mother.

Nonetheless, duty and breeding aside, Joan would never warm his bed the way a woman like Helene would. Cam could not help but wonder how many men had enjoyed Helene's temptations. A woman of such potent emotions could not long remain alone. Could she? How well he remembered her inability to keep her hands off him. In the tilt of her chin, the turn of her wrist, even in the way she moved through a room, Helene exuded more overt femininity—no, *sensuality*—than most women did when stark naked and tangled in satin sheets.

Ruthlessly, Cam hurled himself into the saddle. He had been too long from home, and there was much work to be done. He would be glad when this nightmarish day was over, and he could retreat into the solitude of his bedchamber with a good book and a goblet of cognac.

Helene always rose early, often before dawn. Moreover, last night she had not slept well. Yesterday's meeting with Cam had disturbed her far more than she had expected. It was far better to rise, have a quick breakfast, then gather up her things quickly.

It was time to go back to Hampstead, and begin her employment search anew. Ruthlessly, she shoved one last hairpin into her plain chignon, and glanced at her reflection in the mirror.

The eyes which stared back looked honest enough. But Cam undoubtedly believed that she had returned to Chalcote under duplicitous circumstances, an opinion that was not wholly without merit. Helene had had almost a fortnight in which to write to Cam and ask what he would have her do. Yet she had not. Instead, she'd taken it upon herself to come, knowing that their past would be a painful embarrassment to him now.

Cam was now a wealthy nobleman, a widower with a child and at least two fine estates. Moreover, as a result of his marriage, Cam had received a tidy fortune in banking interests. Money that, by all accounts, he had aggressively parlayed into vast wealth. The title had been but icing on an already rich cake. Amongst the *ton*, according to Nanny's sources, the Earl of Treyhern was considered an ill-tempered anomaly: ruthless, reclusive, and unfailingly conservative. Had Helene really believed such a man would be pleased to acknowledge their past friendship?

She should not have come to Cheston-on-the-Water. Oh, she'd been bored to tears in town, but in time, she could have found another position. And despite her inward excuses about Nanny's health, there was Ireland, Scotland, even Brittany, any one of which would have been close enough. But she hadn't looked in those places, had she?

She had chosen to return to Chalcote. She had wanted to see Cam. She had to accept that horrid truth. Helene shoved her feet into her slippers and headed toward the door. Perhaps there was another, uglier truth to accept. Perhaps she was more like her mother than she had hoped. *"Blood will tell,"* Nanny had sworn. Well, old saws cut both ways.

Despite a sleepless night, Cam went down to the dining room for his coffee and buttered bread promptly at six o'clock, just as he did every morning of every day. And he choked it down, too, trying to ignore the fact that it tasted like ashes in his mouth, and that his eye sockets felt as if they had been scrubbed out with a brick. Pensively, he stared through the broad Jacobean window that gave onto Chalcote's front lawn. The murky world beyond lay cold and silent, seemingly frozen in time, eagerly awaiting morning's life-giving light.

Cam, too, felt edged with the same sort of anticipation. He was conflicted, at once deeply anxious, yet filled with eagerness, a little like a child at Christmas. Not a man given to disorderly emotion of any sort, the earl took great umbrage at such inner turmoil. As he swallowed the last dry crumb, Cam pulled out his watch and glanced at it.

Did Helene take breakfast in her room, or would she come downstairs? He had not thought to inquire. Or would Mrs. Naffles have taken care of it? Cam felt utterly bewildered, just as he always did when he thought of Helene. He needed to stop thinking about her, and more importantly, to stay away from her. Worse, he was now required to keep Bentley away from her.

The solution was simple, as he'd known all along. Helene must be sent away. And with a deep measure of regret, that was precisely what he meant to do this morning. Cam had always prided himself on being a man of purpose, one who was certain, swift and uncompromising in his decisions. He wouldn't be swayed—not that he expected Helene to argue. He would insist she keep the salary advance, and send her back to Hampstead in his own carriage.

His plan thusly decided, he rang for Milford, who slid into the room like a long, thin specter. "Yes, my lord?"

Cam drew a long, unsteady breath. Even his ghoulish butler, whom he could usually ignore, was making him ill at ease today. "Milford, when Miss de Severs has had her breakfast—"

The butler cut him off. "So sorry, my lord. Miss de Severs has already left."

"Left—?" Cam erupted, jerking from his chair. His empty dishes clattered precariously. "Good God! She cannot possibly have gone so soon—!"

Milford stabbed upward with one bloodless finger. "Left, as in left the dining room. Miss de Severs is, I must say, a remarkably early riser."

Cam found her in the schoolroom, standing amidst what looked like the aftermath of a windstorm. Apparently, very few of her boxes and trunks had contained clothing, for he now saw that most had been carted up to the schoolroom. Some had already been emptied, as evidenced by a dozen thick, well-worn tomes and a stack of notebooks which were scattered across the desk. Halfway down the long schoolroom table, a crate had been pried open. A wooden flute and small drum sat perched atop the jumble of playthings which spilt from it.

Well! It seemed Helene was unpacking. It was just like her to take the bull by the horns. Folding his arms over his chest, he leaned one shoulder against the frame of the open doorway and stared at her. At first, she did not see him, for she was rummaging in the tattered portmanteau which sat in the floor, her perfect rear end tilted up invitingly. Immediately, Cam felt his physical discomfort of the previous night threaten.

Age had merely enhanced the classic lines of her figure and the fine bones of her face. Today, Helene was dressed in a shade of dark amber. Just as yesterday's gown of deep purple had not been quite black, the amber of her morning dress was not quite brown. Apparently, Helene danced on the edge of propriety where her wardrobe was concerned. And in some other ways as well, he did not doubt.

Well, that was none of his business, was it? Helene was somewhat past the first blush of youth, and no longer an innocent, though the latter was partly his fault. Of course, his father had cavalierly explained to an enraged Marie Middleton that had her daughter's ruin not been Cam's doing, it would soon have been someone else's, given Helene's bold nature.

Was that true? Cam's blood still ran cold at the thought, but he had to believe it was. Otherwise . . .

Suddenly, Helene straightened up from the portmanteau, one hand pressed into the small of her back, the other clutching a bedraggled doll. She looked exasperated and pink-cheeked as she puffed upward at an unruly bit of hair which had tumbled down to tease at her nose.

"Unpacking?" he asked softly.

For only the second time in his life, he saw Helene blanch. "Unpacking?" she asked, aghast. "Indeed not! I am *repacking*. Mr. Larkin or Mr. Stoots must have pried open these crates. To be sure, I did not!"

Helene stared across the room at him, unblinking yet obviously anxious, and Cam was struck by a hailstorm of dissimilar thoughts. The first was that her distress heightened her beauty. The second was that she fully intended to leave. And thirdly, that Helene had still taken it upon herself to remember the names of his footmen.

How very like her. No doubt she already knew that Crane was plagued by a bilious liver, that Stoots gambled a little more than was prudent, and that Emmie, the scullery maid, was hopelessly in love with Shreeves, his groom. Helene, who made friends easily, had always been inappropriately warm.

And as for himself, Cam had broken into a sweat just looking at her. Suddenly the room seemed close, hot, and filled with Helene's fragrance.

Pulling himself away from the doorframe, he forced himself to smile. "Do not trouble yourself about the open crates. No harm has been done."

She gave a little half curtsy. "I thank you, my lord. I shall have these remaining things collected in a trice."

Stepping into the room, Cam tried to draw a deep breath. "You . . . you mean to go, then?" He kept his tone light, but something seemed caught in his chest.

"Indeed, yes." She hesitated, her dark, finely arched brows drawing inward in confusion. "I thought that was your wish." Cam opened his mouth to reply, but Helene did not pause. "And you are perfectly correct."

"Correct?" he echoed, his hands on his hips.

Helene bent down to shut the portmanteau and set it

upon the worktable. "In truth, I am not as . . . as comfortable here as I had hoped I might be."

"Not comfortable?" Inexplicably, alarm shot through him. "Is your room unsatisfactory? Is there something I can—"

"There is nothing, I thank you," she interjected, turning toward the desk and beginning to gather up the books that had been uncrated. A box sat nearby, and she dropped the first few into it.

From the corner of her eye, Helene watched Cam advance toward the desk, his expression masked. Nonetheless, she had the impression that he was displeased. *But by what?* Had he not told her to go? Yet as he came closer, she could feel the strength of some tightly controlled emotion vibrating in the air around him.

Cam halted on the other side of the narrow desk, his hands clasped behind his back. "Miss de Severs, I think I must insist—" He stopped abruptly and swallowed hard. "That is to say—I wish you to remain here. As you said, I must put Ariane's needs first."

Helene dropped another book into the box. "But my lord," she protested despairingly, "you've already said my staying would be imprudent. And quite rightly! Your housekeeper, Mrs. Naffles, has recognized me—and inquired after *Maman,* too! In time, someone may even mention our—"

"Nothing will be mentioned, Miss de Severs," he coldly interrupted. "No one here knows anything, and if they did, they would not dare speak of it."

Helene felt a flash of prideful anger. "Nonetheless, my *questionable* background—"

"—is my business. I do not suffer gossips or mischief-makers amongst my staff."

"Yes, my lord, but as we discussed—"

"And as for Mrs. Naffles, given my father's escapades, all else pales by comparison. This household is all but inured to scandal."

"I . . . but you said—"

"Never mind what I said, Miss de Severs," he snapped. Helene watched his mouth pull into a tight, thin line as he folded his arms across the wide plane of his chest. "Just do the job you've been employed to do, and we shall all be well pleased."

Helene braced her fingertips lightly on the desk, intently studying Cam's expression. She could feel her face beginning to flood with color. Again, she felt confusion war with humiliation. She was not this man's dog, to be ordered to go or sit or stay at his whim! Certainly she did not want his charity. As for her reputation, he had been the first to voice his concern about it. And it still hurt.

"My lord, I would have you suffer no embarrassment on my account," Helene answered stiffly. "I came only because I had agreed to Mr. Brightsmith's bargain." She moved as if to turn away from the table.

Swiftly, as if to force her to his will, Cam's hand came down to cover hers, squeezing her fingers far too hard. "Do not put words into my mouth, Helene," he answered in a voice that was suddenly low and rough. "I did not say that I was embarrassed by our . . . friendship. You will refrain from using that word again."

Abruptly, Cam lifted his hand away, only to reach into the box and draw out the books. One by one, he began resolutely stacking them atop the desk, as if the matter were resolved. A wicked stubbornness took hold of her then, and Helene moved to grab the books once more.

Cam sprang like a cat, leaning into her, slapping his broad hands on top of the stack, and anchoring it to the desk. "Stop it, Helene," he said, a little too softly. "Look at me. *Look at me, Helene!*"

Helene lifted her eyes in a bold challenge, stubbornly locking them with his. "Let go of my books, if you please," she coldly enunciated. "You are hurting my fingers."

"I want you to stay," he demanded.

"Do you indeed?" She lifted her chin a notch higher. "But what of my lax morals? My wicked French blood? And let us not forget that carefree Continental lifestyle I have been living!"

Cam looked at her coldly. "That is your business, Helene. I have not thrown it in your face. I want you to stay."

His acceptance further angered her. "I am a servant, my lord, not a slave."

"Damn it, stop parrying words with me, Helene!" Cam hissed through gritted teeth. "I am no longer your biddable swain, to be led about at your whim. It would be unwise to press the issue."

Helene still grasped the books, her fingers squashed beneath them. She should have pulled away, leaned back from him, but her fingers were trapped beneath the stack. Or so she told herself. Yet Cam would not break his gaze from her own. He looked so different now, far more hardened than she had ever remembered. "I am not parrying with you, sir!" she retorted, dropping her eyes to the stack of books.

As he leaned over her, Cam's face drew so near that Helene could feel the warmth of his breath as it stirred the wisps of hair around her forehead. And she could smell him, too. Cam, and the heat of his anger, mingled with the sharp, clean scent of shaving soap. In the implacability of his grip, Helene could sense a ruthless energy which she did not recognize. She could feel the intensity of his stare. She did not know this man. And yet, he was so near, she knew that if she looked back up at him now, her forehead would almost certainly brush his chin, and their lips would be far too close.

"I apologize," he said stiffly. "I wish you would stay."

Angry at the path her thoughts were taking, Helene yanked her hands free from the books, raking a little skin off one knuckle. Turning to face the wall behind the desk, she drew the wounded hand to her mouth. She was beginning to suspect just what this might be about, and it sickened her.

Cam wanted her. But he was ashamed of the wanting.

Men had often desired her. And Helene had had to learn that a man's reaction to his physical desire was a complex thing. Now Cam was angry. With her. With himself. And in response, he was perfectly willing to issue tyrannical demands, then drive her mad by arbitrarily changing them. *And by standing too close to her, touching her, and breathing softly just next to her ear.*

But how silly she was! It wasn't as if Cam were trying to seduce her! Perhaps he found it satisfying to exert his authority over her, to use his masculine strength to intimidate her just a little. But what did she care? She was required to earn her way in the world, and would always be accountable to someone. What did it matter if it were Cam—or some other arrogant nobleman?

Yes, he was judgmental and wrong, but at least Cam had always been a good man at heart. More important, there was work to be done. A child to be nurtured and comforted. Indeed, Helene was already here—at Chalcote—one of the few places she'd ever felt true happiness. Was that not part of the reason she'd come?

Suddenly, a faint, muffled sneeze fractured the precarious silence.

Cam's stern gaze swiveled toward a wide, old-fashioned corner cupboard that appeared to have been built into the walls of the schoolroom. Helene stepped back toward the desk, but Cam seemed not to notice her now. The whole of his attention was focused elsewhere. "Ariane," he said, in a surprisingly gentle voice. "Come out of the cupboard, sweet."

Immediately, all thoughts of what had just passed between them fled from Helene's mind. With a sharp sigh of exasperation, Cam strode across the schoolroom and tugged open the lower half of the door. Inside, a fair-haired, wraithlike child was curled up in the empty bottom, her knees tucked neatly beneath her chin. The girl made no sound whatsoever. And indeed, she hardly needed to, so grim was her expression.

Without further comment, Cam leaned down and offered his hand. Blinking against the sudden light, the child reached out obediently to take it, then with obvious reluctance, clambered out. Helene was surprised to see that her tiny feet were bare of shoes or stockings. Her hair was in wild disarray. In her empty hand, she clutched a tattered stuffed animal of uncertain breed.

Quietly, Cam knelt down to gather the child into his arms, then stood up, staring over the girl's tousled blonde hair to catch Helene's gaze. The unguarded pain in his eyes pierced her in a way his angry words could never have done. Cam loved the child; his affection was obvious for anyone to see. And in his simple but telling expression, Helene could see the torment—and the multitude of unanswered questions.

Her heart went out to Cam, as it had done to others before him. And suddenly, she saw him not as an old lover or an arrogant lord, but as a father who feared for the welfare of a child whom he struggled to understand. At last, he broke Helene's gaze and walked across the room toward her, his lips pressed lightly to the top of the child's head.

The little girl turned her face into her father's starched neckcloth, refusing to look at Helene. "Ariane," said Cam in a calm, matter-of-fact tone, "this is your new governess, Miss de Severs."

"Good morning, Ariane," said Helene brightly, taking her cue from Cam.

Urging her face deeper into the folds of her father's cravat, the child tightened her grip on her father.

"Sweetie," said Cam softly, "please look at Miss de Severs. Give her just a little smile, hmm?"

After a long moment, Ariane half-turned to look at Helene through one narrow eye, but no smile was forthcoming. Helene studied the child, pleased to see that the little girl appeared physically healthy, even tall, for her age. Her fine, curling hair was so blonde as to be very nearly white, and her eyes—at least the one Helene could see—was a startling shade of blue against her pink, almost translucent, skin. Her face was round, sweet, and utterly beautiful. The whole effect was ethereal, as though she were an angel instead of a real child.

Helene stared at the girl's white-knuckled grip on her father's lapels. Cam's affection for his daughter was as obvious as Ariane's discomfort, and for the first time, Helene felt the momentous weight of the task which she had so blithely accepted. What if she should fail? For if she did, she would be failing Cam, someone whom she already acknowledged would always mean more to her than just an employer.

"Don't worry, Ariane," she said, placing one hand lightly on the girl's thin shoulder. "I am sure you must be weary of training new governesses. I shall try to learn quickly."

The girl gave Helene what might have been a weak smile, but at that moment, a young servant materialized in the open doorway, a pair of tiny slippers clutched in her hand. "Oh, beg pardon, m'lord!" She bobbed perfunctorily. "The child got away from me. I went to fetch her shoes, and when I turned me back, she disappeared."

"I understand, Martha," Cam said calmly as he bent forward to put Ariane down. Fondly, he gave the girl a fatherly swat on the rear. "Go with Martha, imp! Finish dressing so that I may see you with your shoes and stockings at luncheon!"

Helene watched as the pair left the room and disappeared down the corridor. In the emptiness which remained, it felt as though a cold breeze had swept into the room, returning with it the uneasiness which had previously lingered between them. Behind her, she heard books sliding back and forth, as if Cam was sorting through the pile on the desk, but she did not immediately turn around.

"Well," he said at last, his voice sad. "You see how . . . how *unwell* she is, Miss de Severs."

Helene spun about to face him. "What I see is a very frightened child, my lord. Whether there is anything more to it than that I cannot yet say."

Cam seemed to be watching her carefully. "I have always been gentle with her," he said, his voice soft, and a little bitter. "I cannot but think it is more than simple fear which plagues the child."

Helene nodded, and chose her words carefully. "I apologize, my lord. My words were not ill-meant. And fear is rarely simple, particularly at Ariane's young age, when one cannot so easily discern the difference between an imaginary terror and a real danger."

Cam looked down at the desk and kept shuffling aimlessly through the pile of books. "Can you help her, Helene?" he asked at last, his voice inordinately weary. "Will you stay? Please?"

Helene slowly nodded. "I will stay," she finally answered. "But as to helping her, I pray that I can. Yet I never promise . . ." Weakly, she let her words trail away.

Cam made a dismissive gesture with his hand, then picked up one of her books. "What the devil is this, anyway?" he asked abruptly, as if hoping to break the pained intimacy between them. Slowly, he pronounced the book's title, as if pondering the words in his own mind. *"Medical Inquiries and Observations Upon the Diseases of the Mind—?"*

Helene stepped toward the desk. "The author, Dr.

Rush, was an American who studied at Edinburgh, my lord. He wrote about a special sort of medicine. It concerns the diseases which can affect one's mental processes, as opposed to one's physical body," she hesitantly concluded.

"I daresay I have some passing knowledge of the sort of medicine you mean, Helene," he responded tightly, "though I'll grant that I may look like the veriest rustic to you."

Helene refused to rise to the bait. "Well, then," she answered briskly, "you can see that Rush's work is a textbook on mental diseases. Already a bit outdated, I'm afraid, but many have furthered his research and I find it helpful in my . . . my governess work."

Cam's sadness, which had first shifted to arrogance, suddenly looked like anger. Ruthlessly, he slammed the book back down. "My daughter," he gritted out, "is *not* mad!"

Helene forced a light laugh. "Well, my lord, having just met her, I'd certainly be reluctant to apply the term *mad*," she coolly retorted. "However, if her moods are as mercurial as yours—"

"As *mine?*" he interjected archly, his eyes narrowing. Then slowly, and much to her surprise, his mouth quirked at one corner. "Yes! Very well! Devil take it, you've made your point. Perhaps I am mad." He drove his long fingers rather roughly through his hair. "But Ariane is not—and I shan't have her treated as such."

Ashamed of her sarcasm, Helene softened her tone. "Of course she is not, my lord. Indeed, the very term *madness* is somewhat *passé*. I have worked with such physicians and their patients for years, and have never seen above a half-dozen people one could accurately call *mad*. Why, once I attended a lecture at the University of Vienna—"

"At the medical school, do you mean?" he interrupted, his tone doubtful. "Surely they do not permit women to study such things nowadays, do they?"

"Well, not really," Helene hedged. "However, if one has the right sort of friends, one can occasionally visit hospitals, and discreetly observe lectures, and that sort of thing."

"Humph!" said Cam noncommittally. He paused to flip through the pages of another text, his eyes lighting with curiosity. "And what is this?" he muttered, struggling with the title. *"Rhapsodien üher—"*

"A Discourse on the Application of Psychotherapy," Helene translated, her tenuous enthusiasm growing. At least Camden Rutledge had not yet pitched her books out the window as one previous employer had done. "And that one—" Eagerly, she pointed to a third, a dog-eared manuscript, "—is by my countryman, Monsieur Pinel, the director of the *Bicêtre* hospital. He rejected bleeding, purging, and blistering as ineffective therapies for the treatment of mental disturbance."

Cam winced, then looked at her, his slashing, straight brows elevated. "I must confess, Miss de Severs, you do amaze me. How, precisely, does one go about diagnosing a mental disturbance? Indeed, I begin to fear I have been suffering from one these past two days!"

Helene shot him a quelling look. "I merely hope, my lord, that you will concede that *mental disturbance* is infinitely preferable to the term *madness*."

"Ah! Can one not suffer from both?" He shot her a grim smile.

Fighting down a laugh, Helene tried to ignore him. "A mental disturbance is, in fact, what Ariane likely suffers. I cannot say, for I am not a doctor of any sort. But if she is intelligent—?"

Cam gave a bark of laughter. "Like a fox," he answered, returning to his usual seriousness. "But that is my layman's opinion. The learned doctors insist that she is simple-minded. Nonetheless, a year ago, I engaged her first governess, in an attempt to teach her a little reading and arithmetic."

"Do I correctly understand that she began to speak as a child?" Helene asked, remembering Mr. Brightsmith's remarks.

"Yes, her vocabulary was initially advanced for her age."

"Certainly she appears physically well," mused Helene. "Can she learn? For example, can Ariane obey verbal commands? Play simple games? Does she ever show anger or happiness? Does she appear to think logically?"

Cam hesitated, looking perplexed and wounded by Helene's verbal barrage. "Why, yes, of course. I am persuaded that Ariane is not simple, just fearful. But when one cannot speak . . . ?"

"Yes, just so," agreed Helene sympathetically. "It is difficult to know why, is it not?"

She decided not to press Cam further until after she had spent more time with the child. Clearly, the issue was painful for him, and it would prove more productive to study and learn from Ariane herself.

4

But Love's a Malady without a Cure

Unexpectedly, Cam pulled up a chair and sat down beside the desk, motioning for Helene to do likewise. To maintain her distance, Helene took the precaution of choosing the seat behind the desk. As if they had been old friends forever, which was near the truth, Cam propped one elbow on the desk and rested his chin on his fist.

"Listen to me, Helene," he finally said, his haunting gray eyes distant and despondent. "I want only the best for my daughter. Can you understand that? I wish for her a happy life. I won't have Ariane doing without, either emotionally or materially. Nor will I allow her to be ashamed of herself, or of her family. I refuse to allow Ariane to grow up as Catherine and Bentley did—always on the edge of social humiliation, their futures constrained by society's opinion."

Helene was confused. "I am not sure, Cam, just what you want of me."

Cam colored slightly. "Ah, I badly digress, do I not?" he said with a grim smile. "It has fallen to me to repair my family's fortunes, both literally and figuratively. All I ask now, on Ariane's behalf, is that you help me to determine what's best done to ensure her happiness. I refuse to believe that my child is beyond help!" He pounded his fist on the desk. " I simply refuse!"

Helene leaned urgently forward. "Cam, I will do everything within my power. I promise."

As if embarrassed by the intensity of his own emotions, Cam grew silent for a long moment. "I am sorry," he finally said, "that I hurt your finger."

Helene spread out her hand on the desktop and ran one fingertip across the scraped knuckle. "Perhaps I should ask another ten pounds for hazardous duty?"

Cam lifted her hand and twisted it to one side to better view the damage. His touch felt analytical, not physical. "Oh, I fancy you will survive, Helene," he said dryly, and put her hand down again.

Helene drew her hands into her lap and folded them neatly. "I daresay I shall. I have suffered far more serious wounds."

Cam let that comment pass unanswered for a long moment. "You promise to stay, then?"

"If that is your wish, yes," she said slowly, knowing full well how unwise her decision was. "I shall stay—at least for the six months you've paid for."

Cam seemed to breathe a long sigh of relief, then looked across the room at the empty cupboard, its door still hanging open. "Sometimes, Helene, I cannot help but wonder if all this is somehow my fault. That Ariane is so withdrawn because I am . . . Well, I daresay you know how I am."

Helene leaned back in her chair and studied him. "I once knew you quite well, but no longer," she admitted softly. "As a young man, you were rather taciturn, yes. And altogether too serious for your own good."

"That, you see, is just what I mean," he admitted softly.

Helene shook her head. "I doubt that is it." She

spoke as much to herself as to him. "Though it seems that a few types of disturbances are inherited, a lack of speech is rarely so. Ariane's problem is more likely a manifestation of an internal fear. Perhaps a reaction to some sort of trauma? But not likely something passed through the blood, like a hooked nose, or blue eyes."

Cam seemed to stiffen, and his voice grew incrementally cooler. "No, I speak not of an inherited problem. I am sure that is not the case. Perhaps the fear that you refer to is simply her fear that she will grow up to be like me; too solemn, too introspective. Certainly with her mother dead, she has no one to whom she may look for an example of normalcy."

He was, she saw, quite serious. "Oh, Cam!" She gave a soft, reassuring laugh. "Why, that is perfectly absurd! A child could do no better than to emulate your ways, for there is nothing wrong with you. Indeed, I always thought you very nearly perfect."

"Good God, Helene!" He sounded genuinely shocked. "I hope you did not do so."

Helene's face sobered. She was not sure when they had resumed the use of given names, but for the moment, it seemed right. "I used to think of you as utter perfection, Cam. As I said, a little too sober-minded, perhaps, but you've always been burdened by duty."

His brows went up in surprise at that, and he looked at her intently. "Heavens, Cam! Did you think I could not see that?" she continued. "I may have been young, but I was far from stupid. However, now that you are older, I do think—" She paused abruptly.

Cam's color heightened. "Oh, go on, Helene!" he grumbled. "Say it."

She shook her head. "It would be improper."

Cam sighed melodramatically. "Helene, I can scarce think of you and propriety in the same sentence," he responded, a wry half-smile tugging at the corner of his mouth. "Say it and have done!"

"I beg your pardon, Lord Treyhern," she retorted. "I have cultivated quite a sense of propriety, and at great cost. Indeed, I am now excessively dull. But I shall say it: you have grown . . . cold, I think. And a bit irascible. But I cannot see how that could cause Ariane's problem. There! I'm done."

Cam really laughed then, his eyes crinkling mischievously in the corners. Unlike most men his age, he did not have laugh-lines around his eyes and mouth, and yet, his good humor sounded perfectly natural. Helene's heart gave an unexpected lurch at the fondly remembered sound.

"Irascible and cold? Only two adjectives, Hellie?" he retorted, using his old nickname for her. "You shall explode from restraint, I fear, if you do not tell all." Cam's eyes softened with mirth, and suddenly he looked so young, and so gentle.

Abruptly, Helene rose from her chair, scraping it hard on the oak floor as she pushed it back. "Another time, perhaps," she answered with false lightness. "I . . . I need to unpack. I must be ready to work with Ariane as soon as she begins to be comfortable in my company."

"Yes, of course," Cam responded, coming smoothly to his feet near the worktable. Pensively, he smoothed one hand around the side of her old portmanteau, his fingers momentarily catching on the length of rope she'd secured it with. "There is a very good saddler in the village, Helene," he said absently. "Give this bag to Milford, and he shall gladly see it repaired."

Helene watched his hand caress the ancient leather. "No!" she said, suddenly jerking herself to attention. "I mean . . . no . . . I thank you. But I should like to leave it just as it is. A reminder of . . . of something I particularly wish to remember."

Cam grinned again. "Like a string tied around one's finger?"

"Yes, just so," she returned. Then, to busy herself, Helene grabbed up the first stack of books she saw and carried them to the far end of the long worktable. "Did you say that you would see Ariane at lunch?"

"Yes, I try to take my noon meal with her whenever time permits." Cam looked at her uncertainly. "Why? Would you care to join us?"

Helene shook her head firmly. "Thank you, not today. It will be best, I am persuaded, to let her grow slowly accustomed to my presence in the house."

"Yes, of course." Cam's tone was a little formal now.

Helene busied herself by beginning to empty out the tiny musical instruments from the wooden crate on the table. "Tell me—was she overly attached to her last governess?"

"No," answered Cam bluntly, strolling down the length of the table. "She was not. Moreover, Miss Eggers was but one in a string of failures who have been unable to teach her anything. I've hired three governesses in the last twelve months. I daresay we are all rather weary of all their comings and goings."

Helene smiled rather stiffly. "Let me know when you feel she is comfortable enough to be alone with me. Until then, I will simply observe."

Cam made her a neat little half-bow. "By all means," he answered politely. And then he turned and abruptly quit the room.

Helene worked eagerly through luncheon, unpacking her crates and then rearranging the schoolroom. Having now glimpsed Ariane Rutledge, Helene was increasingly anxious to befriend the child, and to make a closer assessment of her potential. Moreover, she was fast becoming equally anxious to avoid Ariane's darkly handsome father.

After a morning spent first arguing, and then laughing, with Cam, she felt unaccountably wary, and more than a little disconcerted. He seemed strangely unpredictable, his moods swiftly changing in ways which seemed most uncharacteristic. Unable to still such troubling thoughts, Helene strode down the hall to her bedchamber. Outside, the late afternoon was cool but sunny. She put on her wrap and her half-boots, deciding on a long tramp through the countryside. The air would help clear her head, and she longed to be out-of-doors.

Exiting through the back of the manor house, Helene paused just long enough to study the footpaths which led away from Chalcote and toward the nearby villages. Having no wish to make the acquaintance of strangers just yet, Helene set off on the lane which circled behind the estate, through the lower pastures, and onto the high wold beyond. From there, she could take in the pleasant prospect of the house and the village below.

After a half-hour of strenuous walking, Helene found the perfect spot high atop the bluff behind Chalcote, and sat down in the grass to rest. In the distance, she could now view the three-story manor house as it rose gracefully—but by no means majestically—from the surrounding countryside. At a distance, with its sharply angled rooflines, jutting wings, and deep, multipaned windows, the Jacobean house looked almost magical. True to its name, Chalcote Court was enclosed by a courtyard framed in a warm, buttery stone to match the house, but its lawns were merely graceful, not vast, for just outside the walled gardens lay the estate's true purpose; miles of rolling farmland and forest.

Helene knew that Chalcote had been a serious agricultural enterprise since the Conquest, but that the house itself had been built much later, around 1620, by one of Cam's maternal ancestors. She shuddered at the toll Randolph Rutledge's dereliction must have taken on the land, and she had been pleased to see that the house itself had escaped unscathed.

To the west, the view of Cheston-on-the-Water made for another pleasant prospect. An ancient, twisting road made its way down the hill from the manor house, then undulated through the tiny hamlet's neat gardens and once verdant trees, which were rapidly shedding their fall foliage of red and gold. The village consisted of little more than a narrow lane of shops, one humble inn, the rectory, and about two dozen cottages of varying size, all built of the same butter-brown stone as Chalcote Court.

Of all the travels Helene had been forced to endure as a child, Gloucestershire had been the only destination she had truly looked forward to. Perhaps it was because of Cam. But no one could deny the beauty, indeed, the utter serenity, of the Cotswold countryside. In the cottage gardens below, heaps of late summer flowers still spilled over the ancient stone walls, often tumbling onto the cobblestoned paths below.

In the foreground, not far from Chalcote's western wall, Helene could see St. Michael's, with its squat, Saxon tower rising from the southeast corner of the village proper, just as it had done for almost nine hundred years. Despite her many visits to Chalcote, Helene had only once stepped foot inside St. Michael's—for the ignoble hymn-book escapade. Holy Eucharist at the local parish church was not precisely the sort of entertainment Randolph Rutledge had included in his country-house parties.

As a child, Helene had attended church only on those rare occasions when Nanny had taken her. But inexplicably, she now felt a very strong urge to go down to St. Michael's. And why shouldn't she? She was a member of the established Church—though not, perhaps, an especially constant one. Nonetheless, she had as much right to go inside as anyone.

From a distance, the old stone church looked peacefully inviting, nestled in its sheltering vale and washed in autumn sunlight. Instinctively, Helene was sure she could find balm for her chaotic thoughts inside St. Michael's. That was what she needed just now. A small measure of peace. Once inside, perhaps she could sit quietly and count her many blessings. Perhaps she could focus on what really mattered, such as Nanny. She could even say a little prayer for the old woman's rheumatism.

So resolved, Helene retraced her steps to the point at which the path diverged, the return to the manor house on her right, the steep path into the village descending to her left. Shifting her gaze toward her new destination, however, Helene saw the first disheartening blot on what had otherwise been a pleasant diversion. Set deep in the woods, well beyond the path's convergence, lay the charred remains of a small building. Helene recognized it at once as the old gamekeeper's cottage. The stone dwelling had fallen into disuse before her time at Chalcote—probably around the time Randy Rutledge's straits had tightened to the point he could no longer afford a gamekeeper's salary.

In years past, Rutledge had made rather lax efforts to keep the cottage windows boarded against passing gypsies and trysting lovers, with little success on either score. Mischief-makers had finally put an end to the lovely cottage, it seemed. Only the stone walls remained, rising apathetically from a pile of weed-choked rubble. Around the edges where the undergrowth was more accessible, a flock of Cam's plump, placid sheep tugged and chewed at the grass.

One old ewe lifted her chin to bleat inquiringly at Helene as she strolled past, but otherwise, the scene was blanketed in an uncomfortable silence. Helene jerked her gaze away, then lifted her skirts and continued to pick her way down the path toward Saint Michael's. She could not bear to gaze too long at the burned-out cottage, for it struck her as a painful symbol of what remained of her dreams at Chalcote, the walls seemingly intact, but the once sheltering interior charred beyond recognition.

Once inside the peaceful, well-kept churchyard, however, Helene was able to relax. A low stone wall seemed to rise up from the very earth, to cradle the church and the tottering gravestones which liberally dotted the northwest quadrants of the churchyard. As Helene's eyes took in the serenity, however, a bit of color and motion in the distance caught her eye. Across the lawn, a young girl in a dark green cloak was striding rapidly from the bell tower. She picked her way through the distant gravestones, moving rapidly toward the front gate, which opened at the top of the village's High Street.

As she turned to lift the latch, however, the girl cut a sideways glance and spied Helene. A cloud of red-blonde hair, in mild disarray, lifted lightly on the breeze. Her eyes widened, as if with alarm. For a moment, their gazes locked. Helene lifted her hand in greeting, but the girl whirled rapidly about and darted through the gateposts, leaving the iron gate to clatter shut in the clear air.

Fleetingly, Helene assumed that she had been recognized—and just as quickly shunned. But after a second thought, she realized that the girl in green had been far too young to remember the wayward Helene Middleton. Perhaps like Helene herself, the girl merely sought a moment of privacy, to pray, or perhaps to mourn. Nonetheless, the feeling of unease persisted long after the girl had disappeared.

Shrugging off the sensation, Helene strolled along the path which rimmed the inner wall. As if pulled by an unseen force, she moved slowly toward the corner nearest the vine-covered chancel. Randolph Rutledge might be in his grave now, but all the same, Helene would not be fully convinced until she saw it for herself. And she knew just where to look.

And at last, she found it. It was true. Randolph was dead. Helene stared down and inhaled the rich scent of damp, freshly turned earth. The stonecutter had not yet had time to complete a tombstone, so the grave still lay unmarked amidst the rows of Rutledges and Camdens. But it was undoubtedly Randolph's.

Inwardly, she smiled in bemusement. Perhaps someone was still struggling with the proper sort of epithet for the late Earl of Treyhern. Indeed, what would one inscribe on the grave of such a man? *Eat, drink, and be merry . . . ?*

Helene shrugged and moved away. The past was best forgotten. Randolph had not meant to ruin her life. He'd meant only to protect his one remaining asset—his son. God rest his soul, the poor fellow was dead now, and the thought did nothing to gladden Helene's heart. In truth, she felt very little as she stared down at the patch of bare earth. Then her eyes caught sight of the grave adjacent to Randolph's.

CASSANDRA RUTLEDGE, BELOVED WIFE AND MOTHER.

A small but elegant bouquet of fresh flowers lay atop it, all done up in a ribbon of yellow and white. Someone, it would appear, had gone to a great deal of trouble, for the flowers were not autumn varieties, but rather costly hothouse blooms. Helene's gaze drifted to the dates chiseled into the stone, and then back to the gate through which the girl in green had departed. Had she left these flowers?

After careful consideration, Helene decided it was unlikely, for the girl seemed to have appeared from well beyond the Rutledge plot, out of the small door tucked into the side of the church itself, she guessed. Obviously, however, someone fondly remembered the late Mrs. Camden Rutledge.

Undoubtedly, it was Cam himself. Helene swallowed hard and looked away from the flowers. Cassandra

Rutledge had reportedly been a stunning beauty. Cam had probably been devoted to her. Certainly something had left him bitter and hard. But that was not Helene's concern.

Ariane, however, was. How hard it must be for a little girl to grow up without a mother! And the date of Mrs. Rutledge's death—that was troubling, too. No doubt Ariane had lost her mother at a very difficult stage in her development. Desperately hoping she would be able to help the child, Helene mulled it all over as she picked up her skirts to move on.

After strolling around the churchyard for another several yards, Helene paused to admire a climbing rose which had spread up the stone wall and over the top, its few remaining buds now withered from the cold. Suddenly, a gust of cool wind kicked up, billowing Helene's skirts about her ankles, and sending a shower of dry pink petals whirling to the ground. Those which did not cling to her pelisse or catch in the ribbons of her bonnet came to rest on a broken tombstone at her feet.

"Well, a fairer sight I never hoped to see," said a rich, cheerful voice from the shadows of the chancel. "At least, not in my own churchyard."

Helene looked up to see a young man in cleric's garb strolling casually down the path toward her. In his black coat, outlined against the low afternoon sun, the man was not plainly visible, but Helene could not mistake his blond hair, broad shoulders, and distinctly friendly tone. "Good afternoon," he said, drawing up before her, his hand extended. A brilliant smile lit his deep blue eyes. "Allow me the pleasure of an introduction. Thomas Lowe, rector of St. Michael's, humbly at your service."

Helene took his hand. "How kind you are, Mr. Lowe," she answered. "I'm Helene de Severs. I am to be governess to Lady Ariane Rutledge."

Unexpectedly, Thomas Lowe gave her a rather conspiratorial wink. "Oh, come now, Miss de Severs! I already knew that much. You must tell me some exciting secret about yourself instead, so that I might trade it over tea with Mrs. Wimbley at the mercantile. Gossip is a precious commodity indeed!"

"Dear me!" laughed Helene unsteadily as she untied the ribbons of her bonnet and lifted it off to give it a shake. "I hope I do not as yet fall into the category of gossip?"

The rector blushed. "Certainly not," he responded apologetically. "I only mean to say how very pleased we are to have someone new at Chalcote Court." He reached for her bonnet. "Here, ma'am, permit me." With great care, he began to dust the dried petals from the dark brown velvet.

Helene shook off her pelisse, then reclaimed her hat, tying it securely in place. "I thank you, sir. You are exceedingly helpful."

Thomas Lowe gave her his dazzling smile again. "Not at all! Now, Miss de Severs—and by the by, my dear, that's *such* a French name!" His elegant blond brows shot up. "I do hope you are not *Catholic!*"

Helene gave him a tight smile. "Would it matter so very much?"

Thomas Lowe grinned, and opened his arms in an expansive gesture. "Very little, in truth. I merely wished to tease you. But if you are good old C. of E.—?"

"I am," she interjected dryly.

The rector widened his arms further still. "Then let me be the first to invite you to attend St. Michael's, and to make yourself a part of our little community."

"I thank you," she answered. Suddenly, his cleric's clothing stirred her memory. "Do you know, sir, I fancy I saw you yesterday . . . on the footpath near Chalcote?"

The rector's brows drew together as he hesitated. "No, not yesterday, Miss de Severs. Though I often walk that way. We all do. It makes for such a pleasant shortcut to Coln St. Andrews—that's our neighboring village, you see."

"Yes, I knew that," said Helene vaguely. "Yet I certainly saw someone; someone in black . . . ?"

"Did you?" returned Lowe thoughtfully. Suddenly, he brightened. "I daresay it was my curate, Mr. Rhoades. I seem to recollect his mentioning that he needed to pay a call near Coln St. Andrews." Then he shrugged equivocally and gave her his blinding smile again. "But it might have been almost anyone, given this unseasonably fine weather. Indeed, Miss de Severs, I fancy you've brought a hint of spring back to Gloucestershire! Now, what about my invitation?"

Detecting nothing but kindness in his voice, Helene studied the handsome young gentleman. In truth, he was far more youthful—and altogether more vivacious—than any parish priest she'd ever met.

"Yes, of course I would be pleased to attend St. Michael's, Mr. Lowe," she responded brightly. "And you are indeed the very first to ask, for I just arrived yesterday."

"Excellent!" he said, offering his arm. "May I give you a tour of the church and its grounds? We are justifiably proud of it, you know. The tower and chancel are Saxon, whilst the north and south bays are Norman . . ."

And so it was that Helene found herself spending the next half-hour with Thomas Lowe. The rector was delightful, but not inappropriately so, and Helene found his company diverting. Despite his youthful appearance, he was almost fervent in describing his work.

In Helene's experience, all too many Englishmen seemed called to the Church, not by faith, but by economic necessity. She was unaccountably pleased to see that Thomas Lowe did not appear to fall into that category. Certainly he had not allowed the mantle of the

Church to weigh down his natural buoyancy. As they strolled slowly through the cool, musty aisles of the church's interior, here and there sunbeams speared through the jewel-toned glass of St. Michael's Gothic arches.

Mr. Lowe pointed out the extraordinarily fine series of medieval panels in the south bay, explaining every detail of each window's history. His enthusiasm was contagious, and for the first time in over a fortnight, Helene felt herself truly relax.

When the tour was over, Mr. Lowe escorted Helene back through the churchyard to a heavy wooden door set deep into the thick stone wall that separated St. Michael's burial grounds from Chalcote's rear apple orchard. The door squealed vehemently as he heaved, forcing its rusty hinges to swing outward.

"There," said Mr. Lowe, with a little grunt of satisfaction. He gave the door a swift and decidedly secular kick with the toe of his shoe, then pointed through the apple trees to a footpath that lay just beyond. "Now, Miss de Severs, that winding pathway will lead you around the hill and eventually up to the kitchen gardens of the manor house. You shall be able to make your way from there, will you not?"

Helene stared into the orchard, then turned to face him, trying to suppress the twitch of wry humor which pulled at her mouth. Indeed, she knew the old orchard path so well, she could probably have made her way to Chalcote in the dead of a moonless night. But she could hardly confess to the Reverend Mr. Lowe that a goodly part of her wicked youth had been spent clambering up Chalcote's tallest fruit tree to hurl green apples at St. Michael's gravestones.

In silly, adolescent contests that pitted Cam's skillful aim against her sheer determination, the two of them had often climbed the apple trees to issue bold challenges to one another, each of them taking care to choose the most distant—or the most obstructed—gravestone they could espy from their leafy hideaway.

As with most of their games, Helene was the instigator, but Cam was usually the winner. As the years went by, however, she and Cam were more apt to simply fritter away an afternoon hiding amidst the branches, sharing secrets, and wondering if they would ever be missed by the hapless servant who had been assigned the marginal task of lending countenance to their odd situation.

And once, on a glorious summer day in this very orchard, Helene had accidentally slipped as she climbed down from her leafy perch, only to land, shrieking with terror, in Cam's outstretched arms. The force of the impact had sent them both tumbling into the warm orchard grass, where they had landed in a foaming heap of India muslin and white lace.

The memory was indelibly burnt into Helene's consciousness, though the air had been knocked from her chest. Oh, yes. She remembered Cam hovering anxiously above her, his long legs entangled in her skirts, his face pale and sick with fright. Cam, brushing the snarls of hair from her forehead, and desperately pleading with her to say something, to breathe, or to scream, anything . . . until at last, Helene's wind had returned and she had sucked in a ragged, tremulous breath.

Cam's bloodless visage had slowly regained its color then, and ultimately had turned a little red, when he realized just where his hands were. But still a little frightened, and invariably foolish where Cam was concerned, Helene had let herself cling to him, and slowly, almost against his will, Cam's mouth had come down on hers. His arms had trembled, his long, black lashes had dropped shyly closed, and despite their inexperience, they had kissed as if they had been lovers for a lifetime.

Still stretched out along her length, Cam had kissed

her long and hard, cradling the back of her head in a hand which even then was broad and strong from hard work. Helene would never forget how wantonly she had arched up to meet him; how Cam had then stroked his fingertips through the hair at her temple as he slid his warm, full lips away from her mouth to kiss her cheek, and her brow, and finally, the corner of her eye.

All the while, Cam's nostrils had flared with urgency, drawing deep, desperate breaths of air, as if he might suffocate from need. As if he could not get enough of her. And even at that young age, as she'd lain in the grass beneath that apple tree, Helene had known with a certainty that she was in love.

With a foolish desperation, she had responded by drawing Cam's mouth back to hers, and sliding her tongue across his lower lip, just as she had once seen her mother do to Randolph, when the pair of them were both a little drunk, and convinced no one was watching.

To her shock, Cam had groaned as if in pain, and then had driven his tongue into the depths of her mouth to possess her with a wild, heated intimacy. Over and over, he had thrust into her as she foolishly urged him closer and closer, until he lay full on top of her. Helene remembered with exquisite agony the strange warmth that flooded her stomach, then languidly slid lower, until she felt the embarrassing, confusing slickness of her own desire.

Oh, the folly! It had never occurred to Helen to stop, to push him away. Only now did she truly understand the risks she had run, not to mention the sheer torture she had put Cam through by responding so shamelessly. Yes, Helene now realized that she had urged him on by permitting her willful, eager hands to slide instinctively down from his shoulders, to skim his narrow waist, and go beyond, as she searched for—ached for—something she had not truly understood, but had so desperately wanted from him . . .

"Miss de Severs?"

Thomas Lowe's anxious voice came at her as if from a distance. "Miss de Severs? I say, are you perfectly all right?" Suddenly, Helene realized she had been staring blindly through the arched doorway and into Chalcote's orchard. Smoothly, she spun back to face the rector, feeling the heat of embarrassment flood her face.

"Oh, heavens yes," she murmured, waving her hand dismissively. "Perfectly all right. You must forgive me, Mr. Lowe, I was just remembering something . . . important."

Mr. Lowe stared at her dubiously, then pressed the back of his cool fingertips against her heated cheek. "But my dear, you feel absolutely feverish! I daresay you've overexerted yourself with all this tramping about in the countryside. My curate is at work in the vestry. May I send him for my carriage?"

"Oh no! Indeed, I pray you will not," Helene insisted, stepping quickly down onto the path just outside the wall. "Really, I am perfectly well. Merely woolgathering. You see, I have so much on my mind just now . . ."

"Oh, to be sure," responded Mr. Lowe smoothly, seeming to accept her veiled excuses. "Your burdens are many, I am certain, what with our dear Ariane's . . . affliction."

Helene flicked her gaze up at the rector. "Yes, she's very much on my mind, I confess," she said reluctantly. "I am determined to help Ariane, however, and I believe that I can."

Mr. Lowe looked at her sharply, his perfect blond brows going up in apparent surprise. "Do you indeed? You believe, I take it, that the child can be taught to speak? What a blessing, to be sure!"

Reluctantly, Helene shook her head. "It is far too soon to know, but I shall certainly be of no help if I selfishly linger here." Abruptly, she forced a smile and extended her hand upward. "Sir, I thank you. It was a pleasure to meet you."

From his position on the step above, Thomas Lowe bent down to shake her hand, then oddly, he pressed his left hand on top of hers in an exceedingly warm gesture. "Miss de Severs," he said, a bit unsteadily, "might I call on you at Chalcote tomorrow to . . . to inquire after your health?"

Helene pushed up the brim of her hat to better look up at him on the step above. His warm hands, his ardent eyes, and the odd intensity of his expression all conspired to disconcert her, and suddenly, she was not at all sure of what he was asking. "Sir, I cannot think—you see, Lord Treyhern and I have not discussed—that is to say, I have only just arrived."

The rector was insistent. "Lord Treyhern is a good friend. He shan't object. And as Chalcote's rector, I should feel I had shamelessly neglected my parishioners if I failed to confirm that you are truly recovered from your exertions."

Too absorbed in her own confusing emotions to argue any further, Helene murmured her acquiescence, then left the rector standing in the open arch as she made her way between the apple trees. All thought of the handsome young rector quickly faded from her mind as she walked back up the hill to Chalcote Court.

Helene's visit to the church had done more than awaken old dreams. It had made her increasingly anxious for Ariane Rutledge. She very much hoped to see the child again this afternoon, even if only for a few moments. If Helene truly meant to stay at Chalcote, Ariane deserved the whole of her attention. And Helene was eager to give it. Impatiently, she stepped up her pace.

5

If a Man will begin with Certainties, he Shall end in Doubts

Well! So much for being certain, swift and uncompromising in his decisions, thought Cam. He stood before the window of his private sitting room watching as Helene made her way up the hill toward the kitchen garden. His new governess was looking decidedly at home in the country, dressed in her brown velvet pelisse with its pert, matching bonnet, and wading through the tall autumn grass which fringed Chalcote's lawns.

Cam looked down at the cat who was soaking up the last rays of sun in the wide window sill. "What is it about that woman, Boadicea," he mused, "that can make a man open his mouth with every good intention of saying one thing, only to hear the precise opposite come tumbling out?"

Wisely, Boadicea merely yawned, then rolled artfully around to have her belly scratched. Cam, however, was not quite finished. "Did I not go resolutely upstairs this morning to tell her to leave? And she meant to go, too," he murmured softly. "But I suppose I must set aside my preferences if she can help Ariane."

Almost tentatively, Cam lifted his hands to press his

fingertips against the thick pane of glass. It felt bitterly cold to the touch, like the rest of his house.

He had known, of course, the precise moment Helene had left Chalcote. Oh, it was true that he felt almost linked to her by some metaphysical bond. But this particular knowledge of her departure was discerned by no unnatural gift of prescience. He had been staring out the window as she left, as if he were some sort of abandoned lapdog.

In truth, it had begun to seem to Cam as if he had spent entirely too much of his existence watching life through a pane of glass; coolly observing, but never touching. And for the first time in his life he felt a mild resentment that his life should be so.

After his early-morning meeting with Helene, for example, instead of riding out to visit one of his tenant farms as he would normally have done, he'd lingered about the house all morning, and taken a long, leisurely luncheon with Ariane. But all the while, he'd been listening for the swishing of Helene's skirts or the quick tap-tap of her slippers. It made no sense at all. Despite his frustrations, however, he was still waiting near the window when Helene returned.

And so he saw at once what his troublesome younger brother was about. Bentley intercepted Helene near the kitchen garden, stepping into her path and sweeping a low, pretentious bow over her hand, as if she were the damned Duchess of Kent instead of the governess. Had the impudent devil not set out with his bird dog and best gun in tow, Cam would have sworn that the boy had planned the assignation. Perhaps Bentley had been watching Helene from the windows too? The mere thought drove him to distraction, yet Cam could hardly blame the boy. Helene did make a winsome sight, her cheeks flushed with exertion, the wind playing with her hair.

Blister it, the whelp still had hold of her hand! Was he proposing marriage? Telling her fortune? Or just pleading for the name of her glover? Cam snorted in disgust. More likely, Bentley was just trying to get a good glimpse down her bodice. Cam felt his groin tighten uncomfortably just as the dressing room door opened to admit Crane. In fact, he must have groaned aloud, for suddenly, the old man was at his elbow.

"My lord?" said the portly valet in a solicitous tone.

Cam let his fist smack hard against the window frame, startling the cat. "Nothing, Crane. Just . . . clearing my throat."

"Oh," said the elderly man vaguely. "I feared you were suffering some sort of discomfort." Crane set down his boot brush on a nearby table and leaned forward to stare out the window too, as if curious about what had captivated his master's attention.

"Ah—!" he sighed appreciatively. "Lovely, is she not?" He paused for a long moment. "I say, young Bentham appears quite smitten."

"Well, Bentley is often smitten," snapped Cam, shoving his hands into his pockets. "But he'd best watch that one. She may tell him to go to the devil."

Crane merely chuckled. "Oh, and the lad may do just that! But none too soon, I fancy. He may be, as they say, hell-bent. But he's too much like his sire to go with any alacrity. Yes, Mr. Bentley will lead Old Harry a merry chase."

"Aren't we the philosopher today," grumbled Cam, eyeing both Bentley and his bird dog suspiciously.

"Umm," replied the old valet noncommittally, still staring out the window.

Out in the dirt of the kitchen garden, Old Harry's worthy quarry was on bended knee now, doing his level best to get the energetic setter to offer up his paw to Helene. The dog, who was the only player in the farce unaffected by Helene's charms, ignored them both and darted anxiously away to christen a row of what looked like withering carrots. That business finished, the setter then proceeded to scurry about, whuffing at the dirt with his nose. Then he hunkered down to do something far worse.

Bentley, otherwise absorbed, did not notice. Cam jerked his head toward the glass. "Crane," he asked darkly, "does Mrs. Naffles have all the root crops in?"

"Oh, yes, sir," murmured the old man, lifting a gnarled finger to point toward Helene, who was struggling valiantly to help Bentley up from the ground. The young man clutched at his knee in a theatrical gesture of agony. Helene threw back her head and laughed, then hefted him to his feet.

"What do you think, my lord? The dark purple? Or the brownish-gold shades?"

Cam turned to stare down at the man as if he'd sprouted wings. "What the devil are you rambling about, Crane?"

Crane continued to gaze placidly through the glass. "Miss de Severs's gown, my lord. Do you prefer the amethyst? Or that odd shade of dark gold? For my part, I think the amethyst really sets her fine eyes to advantage, but on the other hand, with that mass of black hair—"

"Good God, man!" exploded Cam. "Surely there's room in the garden for another captivated suitor. Go, Crane! Have at it, if you fancy you've a chance."

"Oh, heavens no, my lord," answered the elderly man with a rueful shake of his head. "Not my type at all! No, I suspect there are very few men who could long hold the attention of such a woman. Very few indeed." Slowly, Crane picked up the boot brush and returned to his task. Cam returned his attentions to Bentley and Helene.

After a few minutes had passed, Crane spoke again. "Knew her mother, I did," he murmured from across the room. "What a fine looking woman she was!"

"What—?" snapped Cam, turning away from the window again. The cat darted away.

"I . . . remember . . . her . . . mother," repeated the valet slowly, as if it were Cam and not himself who had grown hard of hearing. "Back when I was valet to your father. And I remember the girl, too, my lord. Don't you?"

"Yes," said Cam softly, his arms folded across his chest now. "Yes, I remember her."

Crane set the brush down again. "Such a pretty, sweet-natured thing, even when she was young. And a proper favorite with the staff, you know. Never haughty, nor above herself in any way."

Cam wanted to remark that it would have taken but a short climb in order for the Middletons to have gotten above themselves, but the mean-spirited words stuck in his mouth.

And then, the full import of what the valet was saying struck him like a brickbat. *First Naffles. Now Crane!* Burn it, who else knew about his relationship with Helene? And just what did they know? Had he been as transparent in his attentions toward her as Bentley? Lord, probably worse.

"I always wondered," said the old man slowly, "if it wouldn't have been better for your father had he simply married Mrs. Middleton," he murmured, almost to himself.

Cam walked to the side table near the window and yanked the stopper from a decanter of cognac. "Marie Middleton was a vulgar tart who ignored her own child," he said simply as he sloshed the amber liquid into a waiting glass.

The elder man looked suddenly pained. "Oh, such harsh words, my lord! The lady possessed a good heart, but she was little more than a child herself."

"A child, do you say—?" Cam gave a bark of laughter, then tossed off half the glass as he walked back to the window. "I fancy not." He planted his booted foot solidly in the middle of the deep window sill.

Suddenly, Crane was back by his side. "Take my word on this, my lord, for I'm an old man who's seen much. A great many women are destined to be naught but children until the day they die. All they can hope for is to find a man—any man—to care for them. But there are others," he said in a softer tone, gazing out the window again, "who are born . . . not precisely old, but possessed of a wisdom far beyond their years. They know just who they are, and exactly what they want, from a very young age."

"I have no idea what you are talking about, Crane," he answered abruptly, turning to let his foot slip away from the window sill.

"Do you not, my lord?" said the old man sadly. "A pity, then."

Without further response, Cam strode to the bell pull and yanked it hard. "Milford," he said when the butler finally answered, "please send word to Miss de Severs. I should like to see her in my study after dinner, if it is not inconvenient."

"Very good, my lord," intoned Milford in his gloomiest voice, then he lingered in the doorway for a long moment. "What shall I do if it is . . . ?"

Cam's head swiveled back toward the open door. "If it is *what?*" he asked irascibly.

"Inconvenient."

Cam felt another rush of irritation. "It damned well won't be," he snapped. Milford's long, gangling figure darted away.

Cam set his brandy down with a sharp clatter, then focused hard on the glass. Good God, what was happening to him? He never drank spirits before dinner, yet there sat his glass, very nearly drained. And he never spoke sharply to his servants, and yet in the space of a quarter-hour, he'd insulted both his valet and his butler. With a jerk, he turned, crossed the room toward the door.

"Crane?" he said over his shoulder, one hand clenching the cold, brass doorknob.

"Yes, my lord?" Blinking, the old man looked up from his work.

Cam dropped his gaze to the polished oak floor. "My sarcasm was inappropriate. I find I am not myself today. I'm very sorry."

"I know, my lord." Crane nodded gently. "I know."

His mood still raw, Cam strode down the long corridor which led from his suite of rooms and past the entrance to his daughter's wing. Abruptly, he halted, paused but a moment, then turned sharply left toward the schoolroom. Two doors beyond, he knocked perfunctorily, then entered. Martha leapt from her chair, her needlework tumbling to the floor.

Ariane stood on tiptoes at the high mullioned window, leaning intently into the well, and staring out across the back lawns of Chalcote. But Cam knew she did not stare in the direction of Helene and Bentley, as he had done. Instead, Ariane looked well beyond, toward the old footpath that ran from the village of Cheston, through Chalcote, and on to Coln St. Andrews. It was the path she had so often taken with her mother.

Inwardly, Cam wondered yet again. Was that simply it? Was his daughter still grieving over—or confused by—the death of her mother? After all this time, Cam still did not know. And plead and coax and scold as he might, Ariane could be persuaded to say nothing.

"Good afternoon, Martha," he said quietly. "How is everything?"

Martha's brows lifted in a neutral expression. "Much as usual, m'lord. Miss Ariane's terrible interested in looking out the window. I dessay 'tis the brightly colored leaves . . . so pretty, the reds and golds are."

Cam wanted to remind the girl that half the leaves were already gone, and that they both knew Ariane spared no thought for what was left. But he saw Martha's inaccuracy for what it was; kindness. And really, what else could one say? Ariane often stared out the window when she wasn't hiding in the closets or attics or cupboards.

"Thank you, Martha," he gently returned. "Why do you not go down to the kitchen and have your tea? I'd like to sit with Ariane for a bit."

Martha bobbed gratefully and left without comment, for this was a routine they often shared. As was his habit, Cam crossed the room to the old oak rocker that sat in one corner. As if just now sensing his presence, Ariane turned to look over one shoulder at him. Cam crooked a finger, motioning her to him. "Come, minx, and bear your poor old papa company, eh?"

With what looked like the ghost of a smile, Ariane turned and came swiftly toward him, crawling into his lap and curling against his chest. Cam slowly rocked her, just as he had done since she was a babe. As he tipped the chair back and forth in that familiar, soothing rhythm, Cam settled one cheek against the soft blonde hair and remembered those sweet, sweet days of—not happiness, exactly—but promise, because Ariane's future had seemed so bright.

She had been more than just a healthy, happy babe. Within six months of her birth, Ariane had begun crawling off her blanket to tug at Cam's trouser hems—and at his heartstrings. Oh, he had not wanted her, it was true. But it had been impossible to resent the beautiful, blue-eyed child. Later, it seemed as if he'd loved her on sight. And Ariane's development had proceeded with alarming speed. At nine months, she could toddle about unaided, and before the year was out, she could form simple sentences.

"A veritable prodigy!" their old family doctor had often proclaimed, cheerfully ruffling Ariane's cornsilk hair. "You must provide this one with the very best, Mr. Rutledge! Fine picture books! Excellent governesses! And grand finishing schools, I do not doubt, for I daresay she'll be something special!" And instead of hiding or crying, Ariane would giggle; her eyes sparkling with mischief as if she and the doctor shared some sort of joke.

"Oh, you may be sure I will, Masters," Cam had laughingly promised. "You may be sure I will." In his heart, however, he'd already known Ariane was something special.

But old Dr. Masters was dead these four years past. And the promises Cam had made to him—and to Ariane—had gone more or less unfulfilled. Oh, he'd bought the picture books and hired the governesses. But what good did it do anyone when Ariane could not avail herself of them?

With a little choking sound, Cam pulled his daughter tighter to his chest and prayed as he rocked her back as forth. It was almost too much to bear.

"Please, please," he inwardly chanted, in rhythm with the squeaking sound of the old rocking chair. *"Please—just this once—let my instincts be right! Please let Helene know what to do."*

Helene pushed back her bonnet just a fraction in order to better view the handsome young man before her. Randolph Bentham Rutledge was already as tall as his brother, almost as handsome, and twice as charming. Moreover, unless one looked beyond his artful smile to the youthful innocence which lingered in his eyes, he looked far older than the seventeen Helene had believed him to be. Indeed, Bentley was startlingly like his namesake in both looks and charm.

If this was the sight Cam's mother had beheld when she first met Randy Rutledge, it was little wonder the poor woman had succumbed to his flattering guile.

Young Bentley, attired in heavy boots and a long, drab duster, stood well over six feet. In the crook of his arm, he balanced an elegantly carved fowling gun, and beneath his broad-brimmed hat, he wore a smile that could have melted the Arctic.

Despite the boy's youth and Helene's hard-won experience, she felt a little unsteady under the onslaught of Rutledge charm. She forced her most governess-like smile. "Pray continue with your hunting before the light entirely fails us, Mr. Rutledge. I can assure you that I am perfectly able to make my way home alone, since it is but another three hundred yards." She nodded her head toward the rear gates of the courtyard.

Bentley Rutledge looked momentarily crushed, but the effervescent smile quickly returned. "You know, I fancy it really is too near dusk for hunting now, ma'am. You are exceedingly good to remind me! Come, let me enjoy your charms but a few moments more—?"

"I think not, Mr. Rutledge," she firmly interjected.

Bentley's full lower lip came out just a fraction. "A game of backgammon in the yellow parlor, perhaps? I vow, it's awfully dull at Chalcote, and I'm exceedingly glad you've come to give us a spot of distraction."

"I've come, Mr. Rutledge," she answered in a slightly scathing tone, "to care for your niece, not to distract handsome young men who've more time than sense."

"Oh—!" he exclaimed in a soft, appreciative voice. "I do like a woman with spit and fire, Miss de Severs. May I call you Helene?" His smile ratcheted up another notch.

"No."

"I am crushed," answered Bentley Rutledge, with no discernible loss of enthusiasm.

"I rather doubt that, Mr. Rutledge," returned Helene dryly. "And now I bid you a good evening. It was an interesting experience making your acquaintance. And to meet your dog. And to help drag you to your feet—"

"Ah, yes! And it takes the very best sort of woman to pull a man up out of the mud, ma'am, or so I have been told."

"Pray do not regard it, Mr. Rutledge. Now, please go away."

"Come now, ma'am—just a game of backgammon? And perhaps just a little glass of sherry?" he wheedled, suddenly sounding like the boy he very nearly was.

Unexpectedly, Helene sensed an undertone of genuine loneliness in his voice, and she was struck with how dissimilar he was from his elder brother. At seventeen, Cam's strength and maturity had helped him bear his unhappiness in stoic silence. But Bentley Rutledge would never be the silent type; he would demand what he wanted of life, and probably get it. Nonetheless, the brothers had shared one thing. Neither of them, she was certain, had had a happy childhood. Her expression must have betrayed her sympathy.

"Oh, splendid, Miss de Severs!" he cried, clapping his hands together in a most appealing gesture. "You've taken pity on me." He offered her his arm and with an exasperated sigh, she slid her hand lightly beneath his elbow.

"One game, Mr. Rutledge," she said through clenched teeth. "But only if you agree to my terms."

"Your wish is my command, Miss de Severs."

"I want you to invite Ariane," explained Helene as they set off toward the rear gate. "I'm eager to spend time with her, but she's still a little frightened of me. I want you to use that charm of yours to coax her into joining us. I somehow imagine you'll have no difficulty."

Bentley nodded. "Fact is, the chit's dashed fond of me, ma'am."

"Why am I not surprised?" asked Helene dryly. "And whilst we play, Mr. Rutledge, you shall explain to me precisely what an Oxford man is doing here at Chalcote in the midst of Michaelmas term. I've not been so long from England that I've forgotten the school calendar."

As they reached the walled courtyard, Bentley had the good grace to blush. "Well, I've just this week been sent down, you see."

"No, Mr. Rutledge, I do not see at all," she crisply responded as they turned into the gate. "That is my point."

Along with a starless night, a hint of a chill had fallen across the Cotswolds. In the shadows of his study, Cam sat, sprawled in Boadicea's deep armchair by the hearth, dutifully scratching the cat, and trying without success to enjoy the fire.

Just then, his clock struck eight. Cam drew out his watch to confirm the hour. "Helene is late," he announced to the cat. Somehow, he was surprised, for despite her reckless ways, Helene had always been a punctual, capable sort of female.

It was, oddly enough, a contrast he had never before considered. Indeed, during their years apart, it seemed that Helene had become a study in contrasts, as mysterious to him now as ice layered over a core of fire. So intriguing. So dangerous. As he stared into the depths of the empty room, Cam tried to remember that with one sidelong look from those dark blue eyes, Helene de Severs had once been able to turn him into a besotted fool.

That appeared to be pretty much what she had done to Bentley, though granted, Bentley had been halfway there when she crossed his path. Cam was no longer a green lad, yet he was beginning to fear that his self-discipline amounted to about as much as his brother's where Helene was concerned. While staring at them through his window, Cam had kept telling himself that it was Helene and Bentley for whom he worried; that Helene was too friendly for her own good, and Bentley so wholly lacking in common sense as to be a danger to them both. But when he looked a little deeper, Cam had to admit that the larger part of what he had felt had been envy.

Upon leaving Ariane's room with his emotions still unsettled, Cam had turned to his work. He had gone downstairs to review his plans for a series of new tenant houses, but upon entering the sanctuary of his study, he'd been further incensed to hear Helene's laughter, mingled with Bentley's, floating from the adjoining yellow parlor. It sounded unnatural, almost out of place.

It was then that he realized that laughter had become far too rare a commodity at Chalcote. Yet at that particular moment, he could find no gratitude in his heart, for he had been irrationally angry that it was his brother, and not himself, enjoying Helene's good cheer.

Cam had yanked open the connecting door, strode through the narrow service pantry, and walked into the parlor to see them, heads bent low over the marquetry card table, which had been opened to reveal what looked to be a boisterous game of backgammon.

To add insult to injury, Bentley had had one arm around Ariane's waist, bouncing her on his knee as he effusively explained just what a "bang-up governess Miss Helene was going to be!" The warm, familial atmosphere had been palpable, and the child—who just this morning had had to be all but dragged from the cupboard—had looked almost contented! And she'd had been watching Helene with decided interest.

Helene had noticed it, too. Soon, she had coaxed the child to her side of the table. Though Ariane had refused the offer of Helene's lap, she had stood by her side, listening attentively as Helene explained the moves of the game. In marked contrast to Ariane's previous teachers, Helene had used words which were simple, but in no way condescending.

Cam had spent a quarter-hour trying to feel a part of it all, while watching Helene issue the *coup de grace* to his laughing brother. Then abruptly, Cam had turned on his heels and walked out of the room. He still did not know why he had left in such haste.

All he knew was that as he had studied Helene's hand moving deftly back and forth across the board as his daughter smiled shyly at her side, Cam had been inescapably drawn toward the scene by some slow, exquisitely tormenting emotion. He had felt . . . something much more intense and compelling than physical desire, when all he wanted to feel was nothing, at least where Helene was concerned.

"Do warlocks have familiars?" From the shadows of the doorway, the throaty, seductive voice severed his concentration.

Much to the cat's displeasure, Cam jerked abruptly from his chair. "I beg your pardon?" he asked, as Helene stepped smoothly into the lamplight.

"It's just that you look so dark and sullen," she said lightly. "Rather intimidating, really, lurking there in the shadows. And since that cat seems determined to follow you everywhere— "

"I would not be at all surprised to learn that Boadicea is possessed of unnatural powers," said Cam dryly. He crossed the room to stand behind his desk. "Unfortunately, I am all too mortal. Won't you be seated?" He motioned toward the chair opposite.

After an exchange of pleasantries, Cam leaned back in his chair to stare across the desk at her. Despite his request to speak with Helene this evening, he was determined to keep his distance. He could hardly afford a repetition of what had occurred in the schoolroom. Oh, he had wanted Helene to stay at Chalcote, he told himself. Because Ariane needed a teacher. But he had not wanted to laugh with such spontaneity, to let down his guard so gratefully, or to confide in her with such ease. And yet, Helene had unwittingly encouraged all those things and worse. She had made him feel a spike of long-suppressed lust. And she had made him yearn for something he dared not give words to.

Perhaps both he and Bentley were just too much like their father. The critical difference was that Cam fought it, while Bentley seemed determined to flaunt it. And Cam's fight was proving much harder with Helene around. Indeed, yesterday afternoon he'd felt unaccountably like a young boy in her presence. His emotions had run rampant, his reason had melted, and he felt as if he could not breathe, as if his bloody collar was too tight.

And last night, wallowing in old memories, had he not stripped off his clothing to pull on his nightshirt, his breeches would have been too damned tight as well. And in the wrong place. It had been a hellish, hot, sleepless night, and he was not about to suffer another. Nonetheless, he had important things to discuss with his new governess, and it was best to get it over with quickly.

"I suppose you are wondering why I asked you here this evening?" he began, glancing across the desk at her.

Tonight, Helene's heavy black hair shimmered like silk in the firelight. *Beauty like the night* . . . Byron's evocative words kept running through his head. Cam let his eyes drift appreciably down to the long column of her neck, and then further, to the low scoop of her bodice, seductively veiled beneath the lace of her fichu. Jerking his attention back to his desk, Cam began to meticulously organize its surface, placing his wax jack, pounce box, and other assorted desk items in a perfectly straight row across the back edge.

Helene seemed to stare at his fingers rather intently, yet her voice was cool, and perfectly even. "Not at all, my lord. I am your employee. I assumed there was something we need to discuss." She lifted her gaze to meet his, her expression one of polite concern and nothing more.

"Just so," he replied, squashing an idiotic wave of disappointment. Shifting his attention to his pile of correspondence, Cam began to shuffle through it. "I did not feel that we had finished our discussion about Ariane," he continued. "I spoke to her at some length just before dinner. I explained that you were not an ordinary sort of governess. And that you were a . . . a friend of mine."

"Did you indeed?" Helene sounded surprised.

"I did," he confirmed, pausing to flawlessly position a sheet of foolscap to one side of his desk, then following suit with each in turn, forming a neat row down the left edge. "And it seemed to help. Also, I thought she looked rather at ease with you this afternoon."

"Yes, I was inordinately relieved," she murmured.

"As am I. Why do we not begin work in the schoolroom tomorrow? I see no need to wait, unless she is resistant."

"Thank you." Helene paused, then drew a deep breath. "But first, my lord, there is something further I would ask—?"

"By all means," he replied, flicking his gaze up at her. Helene's tone had sounded unusually tentative.

"What can you share with me about the circumstances surrounding Ariane's loss of speech?" she asked, her voice gentle. "I have no wish to pry, nor to open wounds, but I was in the churchyard—"

"The churchyard?" he responded sharply. "Pray whatever for?"

Helene watched her employer as he took out his penknife and began to whittle on the first of several quills. "I took a walk," she answered, studying the precise motions of his fingers. Cam had such perfect hands; a little too big and rugged to be those of an artist, but deft and graceful all the same. Yet, his need to control not only himself, but almost everything around him, was made apparent by his every move.

She drew a deep, steadying breath and forced herself to focus on his eyes instead. "I was strolling through the churchyard and noticed your late wife's gravestone. The date—it caught my eye. Given Ariane's age, one cannot help but notice how closely the date corresponded with—"

"Yes," interjected Cam rather sharply, tugging open his top desk drawer. "I know what you are going to say. You are right. Ariane's ability to speak vanished after her mother's death."

"Poor child," Helene mused. "It must have been the shock."

For a moment, Cam stopped straightening his desk and pens and papers. His expression held a deep, weary sadness. "Initially, it seemed so," he softly agreed. "But the more we tried to question her, the less responsive she became. Over time, the shock has seemingly lessened, but the power of speech has not returned."

"Then we are dealing with something a vast deal more complex than grief," said Helene.

Cam nodded. "I agree. Moreover, Ariane and her mother were not particularly close."

"Not close?" Helene was sure she'd misunderstood. "Forgive me, but I cannot imagine . . ."

Cam's broad shoulders seemed to slump a little, but his voice was unwavering. "The sad truth is that my wife was not content with her role in life. In hindsight, I realize that Cassandra was not ready to be a mother. Nor had she much interest in being the wife of a country squire, which is essentially what I am."

Helene felt a sting of outrage. "And yet she married you?"

Cam flashed her a cynical look. "My father-in-law

wanted his family elevated to a title, Helene. Father was heir to his uncle's earldom, and Uncle was old, unwed, and unwell." His mouth pulled into a wry half-smile. "Oh, it was all done subtly enough, but Cassandra's family forced her to have me, just as surely as my father forced me to have her."

"Forced? I do not understand."

"Money, Helene." He laughed bitterly. "Did it not always come down to money? Your mother, my father—they were like willful children unleashed in a sweet shop with no notion of self-discipline."

When she made no response, Cam took up a slender, gilt-trimmed book from the corner of his desk, and thumbed through it. "What was it, Helene, that dear Byron once said? *Let us have wine and women, mirth and laughter; Sermons and soda water the day after?*" Cam snapped shut the book, and gazed blindly into the shadows. "Yet Father never quite made it to the part about sermons and soda water," he quietly added.

Helene felt an aching sense of sadness. "Could not Cassandra have simply refused you?"

Cam made a sarcastic sound and tossed the book back onto his desk. "Her father was a cit who aspired to loftier things—blue-blooded grandchildren and an old name—and he meant to buy the stud services required to obtain them."

Inwardly, Helene choked with mortification. The picture he painted was crude, yet his words rang horribly true. "My lord, the specifics of your marriage are none of my concern, but might I ask one question about your wife's death?" Helene kept her voice as nonconfrontational as possible. "Was there anything about it that might have been . . . too traumatic for Ariane's comprehension? Sometimes, children can be exposed to . . . to things which can cause them to simply shut out the . . ."

Helene let her words slip. Cam was staring at her, a

starkly painful expression on his face. A protracted silence fell across the room. "Do you mean to say, Helene," he finally replied, "that a person can see something which frightens them, and thereby lose the faculty of speech?"

"No, not lose it. But . . . unknowingly suppress it, if you see the difference?"

Cam froze in midmotion. "I suppose it had something to do with the fire," he finally said, dropping the penknife back into the drawer with an awkward clatter.

"I beg your pardon?"

Cam exhaled sharply, as if he had been punched in the stomach. "My wife—Cassandra—she died in a fire. Ariane may have seen it—or seen something worse." He shoved one hand roughly through his hair, his quills and papers at last forgotten.

Helene leaned forward and laid her fingertips lightly upon the desk. "Was it here at Chalcote? Was Ariane hurt in any way? I'm very much afraid I need to know."

After a protracted silence, Cam turned his intense stare back toward her, as if he'd briefly forgotten she was there. "No. No, not here," he said in a voice which was suddenly devoid of emotion. "It happened when Ariane was but three. Late one afternoon, the child was discovered wandering alone along one of the forest paths by one of Chalcote's tenants. He thought he saw smoke in the wood beyond, but he rushed Ariane to safety first. We went back, of course. But by then, the fire was raging. It was too late."

"Too late?"

"Too late save my wife," he said without blinking. "Cassandra died in the fire. At the old gamekeeper's cottage."

"I—yes, I recall it," she replied uneasily.

"We did not know—indeed, still do not know—what happened. How Ariane came to be in the cottage, or if she was ever there at all. It seemed she was trying to find her way home when she was found."

"But that is over a mile away! A child of three could hardly travel so far alone."

Cam's face went strangely blank. "One would think not. However, it was a path she'd often traveled with her mother. Cassandra liked to stroll in the woods with Ariane. It was one of the few things they shared." His tone was edged with bitterness.

A dozen ugly questions whirled through Helene's mind, but she was loath to ask any of them. She had some notion of the cause of Ariane's trauma, and as she had suspected, it was more than a child's grief for the loss of her mother. But why had Cassandra Rutledge been inside the gamekeeper's cottage? How had the fire started? Had the poor child been with her? Or attempting to find her?

But the question she had the least business asking was whether Cam had loved his wife. Was it grief which had wrought such changes in the man she had once loved? Determinedly, Helene forced away the thought. It would be prudent to remember that Cam's anguish was not her concern. Ariane's, however, was. "My lord, another question, if I may. How many physicians have seen Ariane?"

"Three," he bit out, his eyes narrowing in silent warning.

"And their diagnoses?"

"You may have your choice," he sharply responded. "My daughter reacts little better to physicians than they react to her, which is to say, quite irrationally. You would have to see her in one of her wild fits of temper in order to fully appreciate just how unrestrained she can be."

"But she is frightened! Of course she behaves badly."

"That is precisely what I have tried to tell them,"

agreed Cam, looking at her appreciatively. "But to them, she is either willful, simple-minded, or insane. They have not an ounce of compassion among them, and their remedies range from bleeding, beating, and confinement, to outright exorcism. One resourceful fellow proposed to do all four, just for good measure."

Helene was horrified, remembering her blithe lecture about Dr. Pinel. No wonder Cam had winced and changed the subject. At one time or another, such dreadful therapies had been acceptable treatments for a wide range of mental disturbances. None of them, however, was effective.

And in Ariane's case, any of them could have caused grave harm. She drew an unsteady breath. "My lord, you did not—?"

"Bloody well right, I didn't," he interjected, his voice edged with frustration. "I sent the devils packing. Along with their leeches and their restraints and their opiates, too. Their coming here was nothing but a needless distress, each more so than the last. The poor child has suffered one stranger after another, examining, and prodding, and cajoling her."

Suddenly, he looked straight into her eyes, his anger slipping away to reveal a look of overwhelming fatigue. "Helene," he said quietly, "I simply do not know what further to do. This is tearing me up inside. And if I cannot bear it, how must it feel to Ariane?"

As if begging for her help, Cam held out his hands, palms open, on his desktop. Helene had to fight hard against the urge to go to him. Instead, she bit back her words of comfort, inadvertently sounding coldly professional. "To be sure, my lord, it is exceedingly hard for Ariane. But the child will improve. We will use patience, and consistency."

Cam slumped back against his chair, as if she had not responded as he had hoped.

Suddenly, Helene realized that she should go; that remaining in such proximity to Cam was imprudent. She rose from her chair, anxiously smoothing down her skirts just as the clock struck half-past. "It grows late, my lord," she said softly. "I should go now, if you have nothing further?"

6

In which Treyhern tastes the bitters of Love

Cam stared up at her for a long moment, then something which looked like surrender passed across his face. "I . . . no. Please stay, Helene," he answered, his eyes edged with faint desperation. It was the look of a man who did not want to be left alone with his ghosts. "I grow weary discussing my troubles. Sit down and tell me of yourself. We have not discussed your studies, nor how you became a teacher."

Reluctantly, Helene sat back down. "Do you wish to further review my credentials?" she asked uneasily.

Suddenly, the room felt close and uncomfortable. Then, for the briefest of moments, Cam let down his impenetrable resolve, and Helene glimpsed the loneliness etched into the strong, stark lines of his face. But she could afford to give him nothing beyond her skill and training in the care of his daughter.

Slowly, Cam shook his head. "No, I have your credentials and references," he answered very quietly. "I want to know where you have been. What you have done. Tell me . . . tell me what your life has been like, Helene, since we—since you—went away."

Helene was taken aback. A man who had risen as high

as the Earl of Treyhern could scarce have cared where she had been these past many years. Moreover, she really had no wish to remain alone with him. Cam's obvious grief and his dark good looks were far too disturbing a combination to a woman who was trained to give comfort to those in pain.

Her eyes roamed over his face and beyond. Though he and his brother had dined alone tonight, Cam had still dressed for dinner in a coat of rich black superfine, with a waistcoat of pure ivory. Despite his fashionable clothing, however, Cam still managed to look hard, even a little uncivilized. When he dressed in his rough wool and plain linen, Helene found the contrast less startling. But tonight, emphasized by formal attire, the elegant bones of Cam's face took on a hint of wildness.

Helene noticed that his black hair was overlong and that his face was again shadowed by a heavy beard. There was a hollowness beneath his high, hard cheekbones, while the tanned skin of his throat contrasted sharply with the elegantly tied neckcloth.

Whipcord lean, full of constrained energy and sullen moodiness, Cam reminded Helene of a wild, black cat she had once seen at a Bavarian fair; a huge, restless thing, confined in a way that was at odds with his nature, and suffering from the loss of something which was hard to define.

Nonetheless, her employer had asked a reasonable question. Again, Helene smoothed the sweating palms of her hands down her skirt and forced a neutral smile. "Where shall I begin?" she asked, in as conversational a tone as she could muster. "I believe you are aware that I was educated in Switzerland, at a rather prestigious girls' school?"

"Yes, I did eventually learn that much," he interjected, withering Helene's false composure. What a stupid thing to have said. Of course he knew. What she had never known, however, was how he had felt about her being sent away. Had he agreed to it? Had he been relieved by it? Had he missed her at all?

But it hardly mattered now, in their very different worlds. "Of course, it was an enlightening experience," she continued with artificial brightness. "I was surrounded by excellent teachers who were able to provide an outlet for my natural curiosity and energies."

"Indeed?" responded Cam in a tight, neutral voice. "You seemed to have enjoyed it vastly."

"My education enabled me to escape a lifestyle to which I was not suited, my lord," Helene answered, trying to keep the bitterness from her tone. "Moreover, it helped me to realize that I had a purpose in life."

"What sort of purpose might that be, Helene?" he interjected cynically. "To be a governess to other women's children?"

"I think you know it is a vast deal more than that," she returned, deliberately elevating her brows. "I help children who are not well, and it is very gratifying to bring joy to a life which has suffered."

"And what of your life, Helene?" he asked abruptly. "Have you known joy? Or only that gratification you speak of?"

"I have been by no means unhappy, my lord," she answered. "My work sustains me."

"Yes, your work," he echoed hollowly. "I own, it still surprises me."

"Why?" she sharply returned. "It doesn't surprise *me*. I have long understood that I would be required to earn my way in the world."

Cam looked a little contrite. "Yes, but why this sort of career?"

The question made Helene a little angry. "The choices for women are rather limited. I was fortunate in that my headmistress was the sister of a noted physician. He required a . . . a sort of teacher and nurse for a young patient. The position was in Vienna, which suited me, as I did not wish to return to England at the time."

"And after Vienna?" He looked at her intensely, as if he were probing for something as yet unsaid.

Helene lifted her shoulders in a deliberately Gallic shrug. "I moved from position to position, until I acquired something of a reputation amongst doctors who were treating mental diseases—a very different sort of reputation from the one I would undoubtedly have had, had I remained in England," she added caustically.

Uneasily, Cam shifted in his chair, then picked up his stack of correspondence and began to rearrange it yet again. "I suppose I was surprised, Helene," he said softly, "that your mother had the foresight to educate you so well. I would not have believed her—" his words jerked to a halt.

Helene bit back a flash of temper. "You did not believe her *capable* of properly valuing such an education?" she said with deceptive softness. "Is that your meaning?"

Cam paled ever so slightly. "No . . . but such a school is expensive."

Helene's voice was tight with emotion. "How astute of you, my lord. But you'll recall that I was offered little alternative. And so I took care to choose the best school I could find, for it was plain my very future depended upon it. As for the cost—surely you must know that was your father's doing."

Cam looked at her in stunned silence. "My *father?* I'm afraid I don't understand."

"Do you not?" she asked bitterly. "Whatever else she may have been, my lord, my mother was no fool. In her eyes, I was ruined, and there were but two remedies. The first—well, your father simply would not agree to. As for the second, it was plain even to *Maman* that I had to leave England."

"But why, Helene?" Cam softly interjected. "Even had I been an outright cad—which I was not—you can hardly have believed that I would have said anything to cause you harm."

Blinking back an unexpected tear, Helene rose abruptly from her seat and withdrew to the deep window across the room. "You will excuse my saying so, my lord, but Randolph had a tendency toward indiscretion. I daresay he thought it a very fine joke, particularly when in his cups. It was he who most concerned my mother," she answered, her back turned to him.

"Helene, please—"

"Oh, yes," she softly interjected. "Your father made his position clear." Now that she no longer faced him, Helene found it easy to unleash her bitter anger. "His eldest son would wed nothing less than an heiress who could replenish the family coffers. Not some impoverished French chit, whose only claim to good breeding—her father—was so thoughtless as to get his head caught beneath the blade of a guillotine."

"Helene, I'm sorry—"

"And it was your father," Helene continued, ignoring his apology, "who funded my education." Her voice was hard and bitter. "Surely you knew. My mother gave him little choice. That was her price. Though I daresay it tightened his gaming purse a tad."

Silence fell across the room as Cam's chair creaked in the darkness behind her. In the hearth, the coals continued to hiss, while on the opposite wall, the old walnut clock continued to tick off the interminable minutes.

"Good God, Helene. I swear I knew nothing of this!" Cam finally whispered. Helene was taken aback to realize that he stood just behind her.

Lightly, he placed one hand upon her shoulder. "I suppose I assumed . . . that your leaving was just temporary.

I always believed that as soon as you were able, you would come home. To England. I am sorry."

"As am I, my lord." Her outburst over, Helene was stunned by the imprudence of her words. Was it possible Cam spoke the truth? She drew a steadying breath. "I thank you for your sympathy," she added, "but I have little need of it. Things always work out for the best."

She shifted her stance, but he seemed reluctant to move away from her. Finally, the warmth of his hand slid from her shoulder. "Did you know I wrote to you?" he whispered, his voice hesitant. "*Did* you?"

"Wrote to me?" She looked at him over her shoulder, her words softly incredulous.

"God help me, Helene, I knew it was wrong. But every month, for two bloody years, I wrote. Did you receive none of my letters?"

Cam stood beside her now. Helene turned to stare at him, her mind spinning with uncertainties. "I received nothing."

Cam made an odd, choking sound, whether one of disbelief or anger, she did not know. He stretched his arm out and braced it high on the window frame, leaning into it as if for support, his dark hair falling forward to shadow his face. "Twice I stole Father's curricle," he whispered hoarsely. "Once, I made it all the way to Hampstead. But your mother's house was shut up, the knocker was down, and no one knew where she'd gone." He gave a bitter laugh. "Good God, I must have looked an utter fool."

"I heard nothing of any visit," she answered, struggling to steady her voice. "If letters came, my mother quite likely burnt them."

"*If* letters came—?" Suddenly, Cam seized her by the shoulders with his huge, callused hands, and jerked her toward him. "Oh, they came, Helene! They came. How in God's name could she have been so cruel?"

Helene felt weary with sadness. "You could not give my mother what she wanted, Cam," she gently replied, pulling away from the heat of his touch. "You were underage, and you could not give me the protection of your name. And had you somehow managed it, your father made it plain he would sever your allowance, and disinherit you to every extent he could."

"Every extent—?" Cam gave her a violent shake and jerked her closer. "What nonsense, Helene!" He stared down at her, his eyes filled with an anger so volatile that it was rapidly burning into something else.

"I . . . I do not know what you mean," Helene tried to step backward, but Cam held stubbornly to her shoulders.

His hand came up to cup her face, his strong fingers sliding roughly around the curve of her jaw, to jerk her gaze back into his. "My allowance, my inheritance, even this very home, Helene—all were part of Mother's marriage settlement," he rasped. "Father could not touch them, else they'd have gone to his creditors years ago."

His words rang painfully true. Had her dreams—and perhaps even his—been shattered by a selfish man's lies? A dizzying sense of grief, as sickening as the one she'd suffered over a decade past, began to swell in her chest. Good God, she could not give in to that again.

"Our parents are dead," Helene insisted, jerking her head away, "and perhaps we shall never know the truth. Perhaps my mother was indeed misled, but it matters little now."

He moved so quickly, Helene could not help gasping as his fingers dug into her arm, his other hand sliding into the small of her spine to roughly pull her against him. "By God, Helene, it matters to me," he muttered, as his mouth came down to crush hers.

Helene's hands came up to fight, to shove him away, but her willful fingers curled into the fine lawn of his shirt instead. Cam's blazing anger, his protestations of innocence—indeed, his very loss of self-control—sent bittersweet pleasure coursing through her.

Blinded by a need too long denied, she let his heat and anger wash over her, even as his mouth slid over hers. New sorrow fused with old dreams, hot and uncontrollable in the pit of her belly. Cam's lips were certain, his touch demanding, as he dragged her high against his chest. He drove her head back, rasping her skin with his beard.

Unlike the boy she had once loved, this man was neither tender nor tentative. But it seemed she did not care. She could not resist. Did not want to resist. Helene clawed against his chest, drawing him closer. The warm male scent of him filled her nostrils and his tongue filled her mouth. It was as if the empty years had never been. As if a horrible error had been put to rights. Her heart flooded with relief, and surged with passion.

Wordlessly, foolishly, Helene begged him for more. In harmony with her thoughts, Cam's hand left her arm and slid beneath her breast to shape the weight of it in his broad hand. When he moved to pull away the thin fichu which discreetly covered her neckline, she shuddered against him.

Cam understood that he should stop. The tremor which ran through Helene warned him, too late. As if some wall of restraint had exploded, his long repressed desire swelled forth. Desperately, he urged Helene's dress off one shoulder. When she responded, arching against him, relief fanned his need to an open flame.

She still hungered for him. She was still offering.

Yes. And this time, he would take. This time, by God, no one would stop him, either.

His actions were rash—even dangerous. And for once in his life, Cam ignored that fact. Dragging Helene into his arms, he settled himself across the window seat. The fine silk slithered further, baring one full breast. In his memories, Helene's breasts were perfect; high and small, with nipples of pale pink. Now, swelling from the top of her stays, they were much fuller, the nipples dusky rose, and hard with need. Still high and perfect, they were a woman's breasts, begging to be suckled until pleasure and pain became one.

Groaning with desire, Cam touched his tongue to one tight bud and Helene writhed in his arms. "Oh—!" she softly exclaimed into his hair. Helene wanted him, and in that moment, Cam would have walked across the fires of hell to please her. Undoubtedly, she had been alone for far too long. Certainly, he had.

His former resolve forgotten, Cam decided this had to be right. He resolved to take his time. To pleasure her fully. His pulse pounding, Cam skimmed his hand up the silk of her stocking, dragging her hems past her garters, and brushing the satiny skin of her inner thigh. Across his lap, she stirred seductively. *So, so sweet!* God, he would explode if he did not have her soon.

In answer, Helene's fingers speared into his hair, burning the skin of his temples with her eagerness. "Ahh," she breathed, her voice a sigh, as his fingers pushed away the soft cotton of her drawers to slide into the silky wet flesh beyond.

Helene felt herself melting. Reduced to a puddle of warm desire. Rough but gentle fingers slid between her thighs to cup and caress her most private of places. As always, she felt no sense of shame with Cam. Instead, the blood thrummed and pulsed through her body with a sensation of perfect rightness. Wantonly, she opened to him, savoring the slickness of her desire. She understood—indeed, embraced—her body's signal to welcome Cam. She wanted him to know the evidence of her desire, and to revel in it.

That her actions were reckless, she vaguely understood, but mindless need overwhelmed reason. Cam's fingers slid further, probed deeper, until at last, he entered her, then slid the ball of his thumb up through her heat to find the core of her pleasure. Helene bit back a scream at the sensation, but Cam's touch was sure.

Shamelessly, she arched against his hand, wanting, demanding, until he returned his touch to the sweet, secret place, moving against her in earnest until a bone-deep trembling took her, hurtling her over an invisible edge, into a bright light of pleasure so extraordinary that Helene ceased to think, or even to breathe.

As Cam felt Helene's tremors subside, he brushed his lips across her brow, then lifted her smoothly to stride across the room to the door. With one deft motion, he twisted the key which hung in the lock, then returned to lay Helene down across the soft carpet before the glowing hearth.

As he stretched out along her side, Cam was amazed at Helene's size. She was tall, and yet, beside his length, she looked infinitely more fragile. For a moment, Cam was seized with a fear of hurting her. But when he looked into her eyes to see the moistness which shimmered there, when he felt her arms draw him down in invitation, reason vanished.

Helene was no innocent. This time, she had to comprehend. And he had to have her. Abruptly, he reached out to capture her hand and drag it to the thick bulk which strained against the close of his trousers.

"Helene," he breathed, his lips pressing fervent kisses across her face. "I want you. God help me, but I can think of nothing else." He opened his mouth possessively over hers and surged inside again, thrusting into the warmth of her mouth in an urgent, sensual imitation of his intent.

In response, Helene let her hand tighten and slide down the taut length of his erection. Suddenly, she swallowed hard, her eyes flying open. He felt a rush of masculine pride. Ordinarily a humble man, Cam knew he possessed one particularly fine asset. He was relieved to know Helene was impressed.

And in that moment, Cam could no longer think of one single reason why he should not ask Helene to be . . . to be *his*. Devil take it, he was hard put to recollect why he had not already done so. Certainly the wish had been intuitively bedeviling him since her arrival. And now, she was in his arms, her eyes luminescent with passion, her every gesture begging him to take her.

In that moment, all Cam was certain of was that he had suffered too long without her. He whipped off his coat and waistcoat. He yanked loose his shirt hems with a violence. The fact that Helene made him feel as mindlessly avaricious as his father ceased to matter. He was losing control. Drowning. Willingly sliding into the madness Helene always created.

He was aware of nothing but the burning need to have her beneath him. The need to drive himself into her warm, welcoming depths. It was lust, pure and simple. And for once, he meant to slake it. Beside him, Helene moaned softly, sliding one hand beneath his shirt to skim around his waist and slide lower still.

Then he remembered.

Bloody hell—! *Joan!*

Damn. Joan. What a tangle. But he'd have to deal with that later. His hands tore at his neckcloth. His mind—what was left of it—raced. He had to have Helene.

But the blasted linen knotted fast. Suddenly, it felt too tight about his neck, like a hellish noose twined out of guilt and lust. Just then, Helene slid her palms enticingly around the curve of his ribs. His skin shivered at her touch. Sweet heaven! Helene was going to drive him insane. But he was supposed to marry Joan. Yet he wanted Helene. A wife and a . . . a what? *A mistress—?*

Yes. Some men had both. He tried to jerk free the stubborn neckcloth, nearly strangling himself.

A mistress! Christ, was he crazy? Yes. No! He simply had to persuade . . . who? Helene? Himself? Oh, he'd always avoided the chaos that a paramour would bring. But he knew the requirements; the house, the carriage, the gifts.

Perhaps—yes, perhaps it could be finessed. With a desperate moan, Helene eased her eager fingers into the bearer of his trousers. Good God—it *had* to be finessed! With one last burst of frustration, Cam ripped free the cravat and began to jerk open the close of his trousers.

As his fingers freed each button in turn, Helene tentatively touched her tongue to one corner of her perfect, pink mouth. Cam was almost undone by the sweetly erotic gesture. He stifled a groan and moved his fingers faster. Yes, his wedding could be postponed. He would insist on a long engagement. Very long. Perhaps Joan would find someone else. Perhaps the devil would fly away with his aunt.

Cam's fingers caught on the last button and he tried to force it free. Yes, he could make do with Bentley as his heir. With Helene as his mistress—available, but kept at a distance—perhaps his undisciplined lust would not drive him to total ruination.

As Cam pushed away his clothing, his throbbing rod sprang free, rising up from the crumpled fabric between them, and his need knew no bounds. Eagerly, Helene's hand returned to caress him, and with another soft sound of amazement, she drew her slender hand down the swollen length of his bare, burning flesh.

This time, Cam did groan, a deep, guttural sound of compelling need. She slid her hand back up again, and he prayed he would not disgrace himself. *"Ahh, Helene—!"* He rasped out the words, the backs of his fingertips stroking lightly over her cheek. But out of nowhere, some dreadful fear of losing her—some urgent need for reassurance—checked his lust. He couldn't have her once, and then never again. No, not that!

Cam dragged in his breath. "Please, my darling—!" he begged. "You need to know that this is more than lust run mad. I want you, Helene. Not just tonight. Forever. I'll take care of you. Provide for you. Say yes. Please."

Against the pulsing heat of his cock, he felt Helene's hand jerk, then still. He felt a stab of uncertainty.

"Will you, Helene?" he whispered fiercely. "Will you have me? And no other?"

"Ma foi!" she softly breathed, here eyes wide. "You wish—you want—a *belle amie?"*

Cam let his hand slide beneath her chin to gently cup it. "My *lover,* Helene. And I swear, darling, that I will treat you as no man ever has."

Helene squeezed shut her eyes. "Why . . . somehow, Cam, I do not doubt that for a moment," she murmured, her voice increasingly unsteady. The warmth of her fingers was gone.

Oh, God! He was losing her. Again. And this time, he could not bear it. Desperation took hold. "Helene," he said, urgently taking back her hand, "I shall take good care of you. Money is no object. I swear you'll want for nothing. Just name it . . . "

Cam let his words dissolve. Helene had rolled away from him and onto her back. Flickering firelight played across her swollen breasts, where only moments earlier, his ravenous mouth had feasted.

Levering himself onto one elbow, Cam stared down at her, watching her breathe, feeling awkward and uncertain. The sweet promise of passion was gone. Briefly, Helene had wanted him, but now he could hear her mind at work. Despite his near-stupefying lust, Cam knew it for a bad sign.

"Cam, my dear," she said abruptly, yanking upward on the sagging décolletage of her gown. "I've inadvertently led you on." Smoothly, she pulled herself into a seated position and began to adjust her sleeves upward with neat, hard jerks. "I have no interest in becoming your mistress. Indeed, I have not the time for it. It would interfere with my . . . with my duties. *Teaching* duties," she clarified, jiggling her breasts into place inside her bodice.

"Oh, Helene—!" he said softly. "No!"

But she simply stared past him, blinking rapidly as she viciously stabbed dangling hairpins back into place. "In fact, we both seem to have confused my place here altogether," she continued, as coolly as if she had been discussing the probability of rain. "We are employer and employee, Cam."

"Yes, but—"

"And I am paid to teach, not to lie upon my back and give you pleasure, *n'est-ce pas?* I think we had both better get that straight."

In mute shock, Cam watched her spring gracefully from the floor. Helene shoved her feet into the small, kid-skin slippers which had somehow fallen off, then shook the wrinkles from her chemise and gown.

Cam, still stretched out across the rug, let his head drop back with a thud. The ignominy of his position on the floor escaped him. Cam couldn't think straight. He was in over his head. He had completely forgotten that his shirttail was rucked up. That his trousers were undone.

Helene was leaving. *Bloody, bloody hell!* He had ignorantly managed to say or to do the wrong thing; his worst adolescent nightmare had come to life. He lifted his head to plead with her, just in time to see Helene's wrist flick open the lock, and her skirts go whirling out the door.

For the first time in his adult life, Camden Rutledge failed to rise as a lady left the room.

Damn, damn, and damn, he thought, staring up at the plasterwork ceiling. Helene Middleton had done it to him again. She had bewitched him, melted his reason, enticed him into recklessness, then left him, leaving everything—everything but a relentlessly hard cock—lying in a crumpled heap.

Suddenly, Boadicea slid from the shadows, settled on the rug beside his outstretched arm, and began to rumble contentedly. Despite the suddenly overwhelming sense of despair, Cam's shaft twitched with insistence, cruelly tormenting him.

"Oh, God, please just go away," groaned Cam, hitching up the fall of his trousers.

7

What! Must I hold a candle to my shames?

"Talking to your cat?" asked a cheerfully drunken voice from the doorway. "Or are you addressing that pathetic excuse of a cock-stand you're doubtless suffering?" To Cam's utter humiliation, Bentley strolled into the room, a broad, semisober leer on his face, a half-empty glass in his hand.

With a grace that defied his obvious inebriation, Bentley smoothly swooped down to seize something from the carpet, and came back up swinging Helene's lace fichu from his fingertips. Muttering a vile curse under his breath, Cam jerked inelegantly to his feet, feeling as if Bentley had just kicked him in the ballocks. Savagely, he began to stab his shirttail into place as Bentley continued his drunken taunts.

Cam tried to think straight. Obviously, the boy had observed Helene flying out of his study, as if the hounds of hell were on her heels. No one, not even an inebriated lout, could have mistaken the cause of her distress. Damn it, he had not meant to insult her. Nor openly humiliate her. Yet he'd somehow managed both. Good God, could life possibly get worse?

"Tut, tut, Saint Cam!" chortled Bentley, dangling the

lacy garment in Cam's face. "Seems yon fair maiden has spurned your offer! A pity! Why do you not just continue clutching that precious virtue of yours, whilst I follow her upstairs to show her how it's properly done?"

Giving the night he'd had, it was just one damned step too far. Cam took his brother down with one solid blow to the chest. Bentley's brandy glass was hurled back against the marble mantel to rain shards of crystal all about them. They tumbled onto the carpet in a flying knot of knees and elbows, grunting and shoving like rutting bulls.

At some point in the fracas, Cam succeeded in wrapping Helene's fichu around Bentley's neck. He was well on his way to throttling him, but the delicate garment was not up to the task. It tore apart with an ugly ripping sound. Bentley responded by jerking his knee sharply upward in a gesture clearly aimed at destroying what was left of his brother's manhood. But Cam was sober and swift.

Almost effortlessly, he pitched Bentley onto his belly, then with a fistful of his brother's hair, proceeded to pound his face into the rug. But Bentley was feeling no pain. With a stroke of luck and a well-placed yank on Cam's flying shirttail, Bentley wrestled his way back on top. For the most part, they then proceeded to roll around aimlessly, thumping against furniture, terrorizing the cat, and generally thrashing the devil out of one another, but to no good end. Bentley was too drunk to present any serious challenge, and Cam's heart just wasn't in it.

Oh, but he did want to throttle someone. Himself.

After a half-dozen good blows had been landed, and each of them sported a split lip, Cam simply staggered up from the carpet, shook the glass off himself, and went up the stairs to brood. Somehow, it just didn't seem worth the effort to give Bentley the drubbing he so richly deserved. Why the hell bother? Even half-sprung, the boy had immediately discerned what had just occurred. It was insult heaped upon injury.

Helene managed to cling to her composure just long enough to dash up the two flights of stairs to fling open her bedchamber door. She fell back against it, her damp palms pressed against the cold, smooth wood, her breath perilously close to deep, shuddering sobs.

Gingerly, she pressed the back of one hand to her mouth, then lifted her eyes to stare across the dimly lit room, catching her reflection in the gilt pier glass which hung opposite. Her flushed face, her disheveled hair, her nearly bare bosom, still trembling with agitation; yes, all gave evidence of what she had very nearly done. Of what she had almost become.

Rutledge's whore.

She'd once heard those words whispered behind her mother's back. The tears flooded forth then, hot and bitter. They trickled down her nose and over her cheeks, but Helene could only stare at herself in the mirror. Good Lord, she had tried. She had tried to make something of herself; to be something other than what destiny had decreed.

Since her last lapse in judgment so many years ago, Helene had struggled to educate herself, to cultivate a professional reputation, and to suppress, to the extent it was humanly possible, her impulsive nature. And she had succeeded rather admirably until now.

Until she had been foolish enough to return to Chalcote Court. To Camden Rutledge. She had come to work with his child, for pity's sake! A child who desperately needed her, and whom Helene desperately wanted to help. And perhaps—just *perhaps*—she needed Ariane, too.

But now, she had let her years of self-discipline slip. What had she been thinking? Certainly, it was apparent what *he* had been thinking. Cam's vile suggestion was another hurtful reminder of the new disparity in their circumstances.

And yet, it had not always been so. In Randy Rutledge's day, English society had seen their families in much the same light; marginally acceptable, fashionably risqué, and nearly insolvent. Never received in the very best drawing rooms, but rarely given the cut direct by anyone. But now, their paths had diverged; his as a result of fate, when he'd married wealth and inherited a title, and hers by choice, when she had decided to make herself into something other than what her mother had been.

Inwardly, she tried to laugh at how foolishly they had once planned their lives together. And when the worst had happened, her mother had known better than to press Randolph Rutledge for a wedding ring for her daughter. When a man was sly enough to avoid giving his light o' love such a token, why would he trouble himself over her daughter? It had undoubtedly been a happy transaction all around. Randolph's valuable heir was saved from a marital embarrassment, and with her daughter safely tucked away on the Continent, *Maman* had been able to shave yet another five years off her age.

It was no relief at all to realize that Cam still wanted her, not when he thought her fit only to be his mistress. *His mistress!* Her blood ran cold at such a suggestion, though admittedly, it was not the first time a man had made such an overture. When a woman was in service, men quickly leapt to all manner of assumptions. Inexplicably, however, Cam's offer had sounded much more vulgar, and far more rapacious, than any she had previously spurned.

But what had she expected? What had she thought Cam meant when he dragged her across his lap and bared her breasts to his mouth? When he had touched her so intimately, and driven her nearly mad with need?

Had it not been for those ugly words, spoken just as Helene clung to her last vestige of sanity, Cam would be buried deep inside her now. And when he had finished with her, Helene would have been buried with shame.

It had taken a potent mixture of panic and indignation to pull herself up, half-naked, from Cam's floor, with her composure intact. Yes, she looked like her mother, and was cursed with her mother's appetites. But she was not—and would never be—like Marie Middleton.

With the back of one hand, Helene wiped at the dampness of her cheeks and rummaged about for a handkerchief. Tomorrow she would speak to Cam about leaving. She would insist that she be allowed to renege on her agreement and return to Hampstead.

But then she remembered the child. Ariane. Oh, she wanted so much to help her!

And she remembered something else, too. She remembered Cam's hard, cold eyes. She had gained the upper hand on him tonight, but it would not last. Cam had become an unyielding, exacting man. A powerful man. And he desperately wanted his child to get well. What if he simply refused to let her go?

A part of her believed that Cam, for all his hard ways, was still an honorable man. And yet, her body remembered the burning intensity of his touch, the demanding grip of his hands. Did she really think she could ever win a contest of wills against Cam Rutledge?

Suddenly, Helene's thoughts were disturbed by a faint noise. The soft, swishing sound had seemingly come from beneath her bed. Grateful for the lamp which a maid had left burning low, Helene stared into the dimness of the room.

Beneath the bed, something rustled. Abruptly, Helene pulled herself away from the door and walked closer. She heard the noise again, soft, yet unmistakable. "*Mon Dieu!*" she whispered. "Who is there?"

After a long pause, two tiny hands poked out from beneath the hem of her counterpane, and with a minimum of effort, the rest of Ariane Rutledge slid out onto the carpet.

"Oh, *Ariane—!*" Helene sat down on the edge of the bed, a wave of relief passing over her. "Dear child, you frightened me to death!"

As pale and as silent as a ghost, Ariane wavered uncertainly by the bed in her nightclothes. Then, as if she had made up her mind about something, the child dug one hand deep into the pocket of her robe. Like a nervous squirrel, she darted forward, dropped a handkerchief into Helene's lap, and skittered back again. She stood, hands clasped behind her back, starring fixedly at Helene.

Helene remained calm. She had no doubt that any rapid movement on her part would send Ariane Rutledge scrabbling beneath the bed, clambering into a closet, or heaven forfend, leaping out a window. Forcing a smile, Helene lifted the little scrap of linen to wipe her cheeks.

"Thank you, Ariane," she said softly.

Seemingly from nowhere, a draft stirred the hems of Ariane's nightgown. Helene could almost believe that the child was an apparition which might well vanish on her next breath. In a halo of yellow-white floss, Ariane's hair settled around her face, then flowed down her tiny shoulders, almost to her waist. The girl's eyes were wide, and even in the dark, their stark blue color was haunting.

"I daresay I'm a bit homesick, Ariane," Helene gently prevaricated. "Did you guess my secret?"

The child made no response, and so Helene ventured further. "Ariane, you have been watching me, have you not?"

Her face flushing slightly, the little girl flicked her gaze upward, then made a slight, uncertain motion with her head, more a jerk than a nod. Yes, Ariane Rutledge understood virtually everything which was said to her—and everything she overheard, no doubt. Given the girl's propensity for hiding, and the fact that some people undoubtedly treated her as if she were both deaf and dim-witted, heaven only knew what manner of things she might have overheard.

Then, much to Helene's amazement, Ariane took one step, and then another, but stopped a bit short of the bed. Gracefully, her tiny hand came up, two fingers outstretched, to touch her own pale cheek just below the eye, her expression gently inquiring.

The child's question was plain. In acknowledgment, Helene repeated the gesture. "Yes," she said quietly. "I was sad. But now, I feel better. Your visit has made me feel better."

With a ghost of a smile, Ariane Rutledge disappeared, floating silently around the bed, and through the dressing room into the schoolroom.

In the gray light of dawn, Cam awoke to discover a suffocating layer of guilt spread heavily across his chest, a sensation far more weighty than the heap of bedcovers that shut out the chill of the Cotswold morn. Had he been attentive enough to note that the hour was already advanced well beyond his rigid schedule, he would have been further exasperated.

But Cam did not notice, for he had scarcely slept. Moreover, in those rare moments when he had managed to doze, he had quickly regretted it. Erotic dreams of his Circe writhing, naked and insatiable beneath him, had tempted him relentlessly until dawn.

It was precisely what he deserved, too, he acknowledged, crawling naked from his bed and stumbling to the washstand to stare at himself in the mirror. "You, sir, are a pig," he informed the bruised and haggard fellow who glared back at him. "And an idiot. And a libertine."

Yes, that about summed it up. He admitted it, now that his mind was clear of lust. Setting aside all the emotional turmoil which an affair with Helene would undoubtedly have caused him, only an idiotic libertine pig would have attempted to seduce his daughter's governess, especially when Ariane so desperately needed one.

What in God's name had seized hold of his mind? Had he really offered to set Helene up in a love nest? He was ashamed he'd sunk low enough to ask. And heart-sick that she'd refused him. A pity she hadn't smacked his teeth loose while she was at it. Indeed, a good, brisk slap would not come amiss just now.

Well! There was yet another harrowing thought! Lately, he seemed to be developing a rather alarming penchant for pain, and at the moment, he absolutely craved it. Suddenly, an erotic vision of Helene—in a risqué black gown, impatiently flicking a leather crop against her thigh—danced wickedly through his mind. Cam felt his rod stir appreciatively.

Oh, God! He clasped his face in his hands. Was he really that unhinged? Abruptly, he leaned closer to the mirror and raked the hair harshly back off his forehead, studying his face. What did a depraved pervert look like, anyway? Cam snorted aloud. A vast deal like Randolph Rutledge, he rather suspected.

For his part, though, Cam looked much as he always did in the mornings. A heavy black stubble of beard shadowed his tanned skin, and his eyes looked narrow and mean. Today, however, his usual glower was further enhanced by a yellowish bruise and a trickle of dried blood, evidencing Bentley's well-planted facer. Cam straightened up and pensively scratched his bare belly. Good Lord. Perhaps it was a wonder Helene had ever desired him at all.

Turning from the mirror with a sigh, Cam yanked the bell for Crane. He had business to attend. No matter what Helene had once been to him—and no matter what she had or hadn't chosen to be to other men—the woman was now his employee. Helene's passionate nature did not excuse his ungentlemanly behavior. Had he not learned that lesson long ago?

Oh, Cam was angry with Helene. Both angry that she had tempted him, and angry that she had rejected him. But his anger was as irrational as his behavior, and he was man enough to admit it. As if atoning for his sins, Cam doused his head with cold water.

Straightening up from the shock of it, he began to wonder if some arcane rule of physics made it impossible to sustain rational thought when Helene entered the room. It would have come as no surprise to Cam. After all, he'd deliberately set out to maintain his distance, yet within a matter of minutes, he'd dragged Helene across his lap, rucked up her skirts, and fondled her as if she were a tavern whore.

It was almost laughable. The only thing Cam had kept at a distance was his code of honor. Now it was time to make amends, and it would take every inch of his self-control to do it. Nonetheless, he would apologize to Helene, and hope like hell that she did not abandon him—or Ariane. Please, God! Anything but that.

Ariane was already intrigued by her new governess. That had to be a good sign, did it not? Already he had noticed the child peeping out at Helene through draperies, shadows, and potted palms. Moreover, during yesterday's backgammon game, she'd looked almost at ease. Yes, there was hope—if he did not ruin it.

Across the room, the door swung inward on silent hinges. "Good morning, my lord," said Crane. A fresh towel lay neatly across his stout arm and he carried a burnished brass water can.

"Morning," returned Cam with measured reluctance, plopping down to be shaved.

The old valet leaned forward to set down his burden with a grunt. He peered at his master's face. "Nasty bruise, m'lord, if you don't mind my mentioning it."

"I do."

Crane shrugged and tipped the brass can forward to fill a porcelain bowl. "Going to be the devil to shave around that lip," he murmured in a cautionary tone.

"You have my full faith and confidence," grumbled Cam.

Crane merely smiled, and opened up the towel with an artful snap of his wrist. "And does young Mr. Bentham look any worse?" he ventured, flicking open the razor and laying it to one side.

"Aye, a bit," admitted Cam with a snort of satisfaction. As the valet tucked the towel around his neck, Cam's brows drew together. "Lay out my old brown breeches and frieze coat when we're finished, please, Crane," he added.

"Very good, my lord," he murmured, leaning over him to soap up a lather. "Planning to help clear the south fields today, are we?" he added, after a moment had passed.

Cam jerked a little straighter in his chair. "I might do. Why do you ask?"

Crane merely shrugged, his razor poised, high and glinting. "Well, my lord, you have that look," he said, neatly laying the blade to Cam's face and drawing it neatly down.

Cam gave his valet a hard stare until the blade lifted. "Blister it, what look?" he asked. "I don't fancy I have any sort of *look* at all."

The old valet made a sort of *tsk, tsk,* noise. "That rather penitent expression which comes over you, my lord," Crane clarified, taking another expert stroke. "It inevitably signals your intent to engage in the filthiest, most grueling chore to be found. A tad unseemly for a man of your station; nonetheless, today is the day to clear fieldstone for fencing and I know—"

"Damn it all, Crane, just shave!" interjected Cam irritably. "If I wanted to be rigged-out by a bloody fortune teller, I'd go fetch myself a gypsy wench."

By the time Cam strode downstairs to breakfast, he had realized his tardiness, and the knowledge had not enhanced his mood. It was the worst possible day for Bentley to have arisen early. No matter Cam's schedule, it had always been a certainty that he would have dined long before Bentley bestirred himself from bed.

And so it was with a great deal of shock, and no small amount of exasperation, that Cam stepped into the dining room to find his younger brother polishing off a thick slab of ham and what appeared to have been, only moments earlier, a whole loaf of bread.

Of all the horrors of the preceding evening, Cam had decided that Bentley constituted the least of his concerns. Aside from the inevitable taunts, Bentley would keep his mouth shut about Helene, for the boy was that most perplexing of combinations, both a scoundrel and a gentleman. As for Cam, he had been humiliated by his young sibling's mockery, it was true. But he was rapidly reaching the conclusion that humiliation was good for the soul when it was deserved. Moreover, he'd often seen Bentley at his worst, and it was no pretty sight.

Cam therefore resolved to ignore his brother. If the boy continued to plague him, Cam would simply drag him along to haul fieldstone for the remainder of the day. Perhaps they would stay at it for the rest of the week. Cam was not yet certain just how much penance would be required—from either of them.

He gritted his teeth and boldly entered the dining room. Bentley's bruises were indeed apparent. "Hmph,"

Cam grunted, striding toward the head of the long mahogany table. "Up at cock-crow nowadays, are we?"

Lavishly buttering a second chunk of bread, Bentley elevated his eyebrows suggestively. "Ah, perhaps one oughtn't assume I went to sleep, Brother."

"Just bugger off, Bentley," retorted Cam in a silky undertone as he slid into his chair. "Or I'll have that skinny arse of yours planted in the south pastures for the week. And you're sober enough now, I'll warrant, to take a proper drubbing, too."

Bentley merely grinned, then bit voraciously into his bread. It only served to further irritate Cam. His brother's unflagging ability to waste an evening in debauchery, only to arise hale and hearty on the morn, had always aggravated him. The aggravation was especially acute on this particular day, when Cam's stomach roiled at the mere sight of food for no reason whatsoever, while his brother wolfed down breakfast like a half-starved cur.

When Cam continued to glare across the table, Bentley wiped the grin off his face and set down his knife with a sharp chink. "Had to roll out a bit earlier than usual," he finally explained. "I'm to take Aunt Belmont to Cheltenham today."

"To Cheltenham?" asked Cam, motioning to the footman for his toast. "Whatever for?" He stared across the table at Bentley's plate, which was filled near to overflowing. Good God, did the boy suffer no ill effects from alcohol?

"Horses," mumbled Bentley, chewing around another generous mouthful of ham as he forked up his eggs. "Dawson's got a pair of grays he's hoping to foist off, so I thought I'd best go along." He winked at Cam. "Got to protect the ladies, right?"

Just then, a thin shadow fell across the table. Cam looked up to see Helene lingering uncertainly in the doorway.

"Oh," she said, clutching her hands in an awkwardly girlish gesture. "I thought to be the first down."

Cam and Bentley rose from the table at once, but it was Bentley who made her a sweeping, theatrical bow. "Ah, a ray of early morning sunshine!" he cried. "Do brighten our table, Miss de Severs."

Helene wavered in the doorway. "Oh, no indeed! I would not wish to . . . to intrude," she said hesitantly. "I usually breakfast alone."

"Ah, yes, but we are left to suffer the loss, eh, Cam?" answered Bentley, grinning shamelessly at his brother.

In response, Cam grabbed the back of the chair nearest him, and yanked it out with a scrape. "By all means, do sit down, Miss de Severs."

"Yes, by all means," echoed Bentley, reseating himself as Helene reluctantly accepted the chair. Without instruction, a footman came forward with coffee as Bentley grinned down the table at his brother.

After a quarter-hour of casual conversation, all of it prompted and carried by Bentley, the young man pulled the linen serviette from his lap and rose. "Well, this has been exceedingly pleasant, Miss de Severs. I say, I have a capital idea! Why do you not join us for dinner each evening?"

"I—well, I . . ."

Bentley gave her a brilliant smile. "But I think you ought, rather than leave us bachelors alone to wallow in our miserable fraternity." His voice took on a pleading desperation as he pressed the back of one limp hand to his forehead. "Indeed, you should take pity on my youth and vivacity, ma'am! Cam's an insufferably dull dog. I languish in his company."

Already suffering from embarrassment, Helene felt a flush of heat rise to her face and politely waited for Cam to charge into the fray with some diplomatic interdiction. It was not her place to inform young Bentley that his brother had never asked her to dine with the family. Moreover, a tray in her room seemed infinitely preferable to choking down food under Cam's cold scrutiny. Indeed, she very nearly choked on her coffee at Cam's next words.

"An excellent suggestion," he smoothly responded. "We dine at seven, Miss de Severs, if that suits?"

Cam noted the expression of alarm which spread across Helene's face as she watched Bentley seize an apple from the silver epergne, then ramble out of the dining room, casually polishing it on his coat sleeve. Helene looked rather like a mouse left to break her fast with a starved cat, and Cam liked it little better. The thought of dining with Helene now, and for every evening hereafter, was daunting.

Nonetheless, Bentley's offer had not discomfited him, as it had probably been timed to do. Cam had decided he needed to keep an eye on Bentley's interaction with Helene. Initially, Cam had discounted Bentley's threat to seduce Helene. Now, he was not so sure. Last night, beneath Bentley's mocking tone and drunken swagger, there had been something which looked like resentment. But why would his brother be jealous of him? It had to have something to do with Helene, for she was the only woman Cam was . . . was *infatuated* with.

Yes, it would be necessary to watch the two of them. In fact, it was his duty, was it not? No more surreptitious backgammon games, no more garden strolls, for young Hell-Bent. Not if Cam could thwart them. With the merest flick of his gaze, Cam dismissed the footman.

"Calm yourself, Miss de Severs," he said, as she critically observed the servant's departure. Anger sparked in her eyes, but she made no answer.

"Excuse me, then," he said stiffly, jerking out of his chair. "I shall leave you to your breakfast. Afterward, however, I would speak with you." Cam swallowed hard. "I believe I have an apology to make."

Helene coolly lifted her coffee cup. "Very well."

Cam paused, assessing her for a moment. Helene sat stiffly at the table, her spine ramrod straight. The usual warmth of her eyes had turned a cold, slate gray, and her chin was set at a proud angle.

Today she wore the purple gown again, but her polished elegance was missing, and it tore at his heart to think that he might have been the cause. Helene was meant to sparkle with fire and glory, but instead, she looked drawn and pale. Was it his imagination, or did her hand tremble just a little as she held her coffee?

"Miss de Severs," he spoke abruptly, "do you still ride?"

She was taken aback. "A little, yes, but very ill."

"Then perhaps you would consent to ride with me after breakfast. I wish to speak with you privately."

Helene colored furiously. Cam suppressed a wave of anger. After all, he had attempted to seduce his own employee, a woman who, to some extent, was at his mercy. But Helene was not the sort of woman who would consent to being held at any man's mercy for very long. Cam was certain of that.

"Helene, my motives are honorable," he said softly.

Helene dropped her gaze to her plate. "I am engaged to work with Ariane this morning, my lord. Recall, if you will, that that is my job—*if* I am to stay here."

Cam did not need to be reminded. The fear of losing Helene stabbed at him again. "Excellent. Then we will take the curricle, and Ariane shall accompany us. The fresh air will do her good." He paused to think. "Do you know the arched bridge which crosses the Coln to the west?"

Helene brushed at a wisp of hair with the back of her hand. She still looked distressed. "I—yes. I think I remember it."

"Ariane and I go there often. She loves to play near the waterfall. That will give us a moment to speak freely." Eagerly, Cam shoved his chair beneath the table.

"I think not," said Helene fractiously. "I have prepared for our work in the schoolroom, my lord. Moreover, it is far too cold to go hurling about in a curricle this morning."

Too late, Cam realized how right Helene was. Indeed, Ariane would undoubtedly have frozen, and perhaps the two of them with her. Nonetheless, the autumn day held promise. "You are right, of course," he agreed. "We must wait until the afternoon."

Helene set down her coffee rather gracelessly and stared at him. "I am sorry, my lord, but I simply cannot accompany you. I have plans for this afternoon."

"Plans—?" The word came more querulous than he had intended.

Helene lifted her chin steadily. "My afternoons are to be my own, are they not? That was my understanding. In any event, I am expecting the Reverend Mr. Lowe."

"Lowe—?" Cam was seriously nonplused at that. "Do you mean to say *Thomas* Lowe?"

"The very same, unless some odd sort of hoax has been perpetrated upon me," answered Helene in a voice so nonchalant that Cam wanted to jerk her from her chair and kiss her insolent mouth until she was senseless. "That is your rector's name, is it not?"

"I—yes," agreed Cam, biting back his temper again. "But how very odd! Lowe is not normally so diligent in greeting his new parishioners."

"Is he not?" Helene's eyebrows rose delicately, and something warm unfurled in Cam's belly. Damn it, how could a woman so inflame him, with just the merest tilt of an eyebrow?

"Perhaps I should explain that Mr. Lowe and I met yesterday," continued Helene. "He was kind enough to escort me around St. Michael's. I believe he thought me overtired from my travels and now he merely wishes to be kind."

"Yes, of course. *Kind . . ."* mused Cam. He paced the length of the room, then turned just in front of the door to stare at her heatedly. "Very well," he said at last. "I shall come with Ariane to the schoolroom shortly. And I shall see you both in the hall at half past noon. *Tomorrow."*

And without giving her time to refuse, Cam strode quickly from the dining room and down the corridor to the blessed sanctuary of his study.

This new lady—Miss Helene—was different, Ariane thought, as she watched her move about the schoolroom, tidying up from their morning's work. Miss Helene did not make scratching marks on the slate, and then look at her, eyebrows all up high on her forehead, as if she was supposed to do something clever. Instead of making marks, Miss Helene had brought . . . games.

Yes, they were games, Ariane decided. But not quite like Bentley's game, which he called backgammon. That was her favorite game. Not because she could play it. But because she liked to shape the sound in her mouth.

Backgammon. Backgammon. But not just plain *gammon,* which was the word Mama always used to say, every time Papa said *"I love you, Cassandra."* Cassandra—that was her mama's name. It was a name almost as good as backgammon for saying in your head.

But anyway, Miss Helene had brought games. Little circles and blocks and other shapes—she did not know the words or names for them—that fit into holes in a big board. Miss Helene had spread the shapes out across the schoolroom table, and then watched while they raced, she and her papa, to see who could put the circles and blocks in their holes the fastest.

After a while, Papa had patted her on the head and

left her to play alone with Miss Helene. Miss Helene was very, very fast. She did not let Ariane win, but once, when Miss Helene dropped a circle on the floor, it rolled beneath the cupboard, and Ariane did win. Miss Helene laughed and laughed, and clapped her hands. Papa was right. She was a very nice lady.

And then they had painted! Ariane understood painting. She liked to go up to the long gallery and look at the pictures there. *Paintings,* Papa had told her long ago, pointing at them and smiling at her with his eyes.

Sometimes he would go with her, and take her hand, and walk up and down the gallery, telling her the names of each person in the painting. There was Grandpapa Camden, and great aunt somebody-or-other, and a second cousin once removed from . . . something. She couldn't quite remember what he had been removed from. But it didn't matter. Ariane just loved to look at paintings.

Last Easter, Papa had taken her all the way to Salisbury. There, she had seen a man sitting in the close, painting a picture of the church. Papa called it the *cathedral,* which was a word that meant a very tall church. Salisbury was her favorite place in all the world. Well, it was almost the only place she had ever been, but she loved it most anyway.

The man with the painting had smiled at her, and Papa had let her stand and watch for as long as she wanted. That was how she learned about painting.

Anyway, Ariane's painting—and Miss Helene's, too, for that matter—didn't look much like any of the paintings she had seen. But it was fun. And Miss Helene said that they did not have to be great painters to enjoy painting. She said that they should paint what they felt, not what they saw. And then Miss Helene painted a great, red circle with slashing lines through it, like thunderbolts, but colored black.

"This is what I feel like when I am *angry,*" said Miss Helene.

Ariane could see from the colors and shapes just how Miss Helene felt. She wondered who had made her so angry. Ariane thought that she was angry, too, sometimes. But not today. Today she was just . . . well, she did not know the words for what she was. So she had just painted some blue and white and yellow shapes.

Miss Helene said they were *clouds* but they weren't just clouds. The shapes were her mama going up to heaven. Up through the clouds, going even higher than the spire of Salisbury Cathedral. That was where heaven was, Papa had said.

It was all right, Ariane supposed, to play games and paint with Miss Helene. *Wasn't it?* What sort of bad thing might happen? She was not doing anything she was not supposed to do. She was not saying words. She was not telling secrets. She was just . . . *having a spot of fun.* That's what Bentley would call it.

As Ariane scrubbed the back of one hand across her pert nose, Helene rose and tugged on the bell pull. When Martha answered, Helene sent her belowstairs for a jug of hot water. Ariane was covered from elbow to chin in yellow paint. But she was smiling, and tapping one toe rhythmically against her chair leg, as if keeping time to some inner music that only she could hear. And as her toe tapped, her plump fingers flew, unfolding a string of paper dolls which Helene had just cut.

All in all, it had been a very productive morning, Helene decided, as she tidied up the schoolroom. With a sigh, she straightened up from wiping the table and looked down its well-worn surface to stare at her new pupil. How anyone could conclude that Ariane Rutledge was either simple-minded or mad was beyond her.

Initially, the little girl had been uneasy about Cam's

leaving her in the schoolroom, it was true. Ariane was obviously riddled with anxieties. But within half an hour, most of her overt fear had worn away. Soon, the child had thrown herself into their games, her mind grasping the purpose of each one as swiftly as any child Helene had ever worked with.

For today, however, lessons were over. After luncheon, they would go outside to play, thereby giving Helene yet another opportunity to observe Ariane's motor skills—not that she expected to see any problems. Then tomorrow, Helene would attempt to determine if Ariane could identify colors, and perform any simple counting tasks. Obviously, the child could not read or write, but few children her age did so with any degree of proficiency.

If Ariane could learn to speak—and perhaps even if she could not—reading and writing were possible, given a little patience. But such skills were by no means a priority. And as best Helene could conclude, this was where Ariane's previous governesses had failed.

At this point, it was important to assess Ariane's ability to assimilate information and express her emotions. Again, Helene would use art, music, and games, most of which she had created herself. With children, she had discovered, it was far better to learn from observation. Today, for example, Helene had had many of her worst fears put to rest. She had learned that Ariane was willing to follow simple instructions, that she had a quick wit, and a healthy dash of ambition. But more important, she had seen Ariane smile.

As Martha returned to wash Ariane's face and hands, Helene studied the child. Today, she was appropriately dressed, including shoes and stockings, and her cloud of wild blonde hair was pulled back into a neat plait, yet nothing could suppress the blue of her eyes. Again, Helene was struck by how little Ariane resembled her father. Neither did she favor Bentley, nor Catherine, nor any other member of the family whom Helene had ever seen.

Cam's wife had reportedly been an incomparable beauty, and Helene had begun to suspect that Ariane was the very picture of Cassandra Rutledge. She could not help but wonder how Cam felt about that.

8

Behold a Plain, Blunt Man

With a manly grunt and a mighty heave, Cam slid another flat rock atop the object on which he'd chosen to unleash his frustrations, a low stone wall which edged between the sloping field and the road above it. Across the stubbled corn rows behind him, his workers labored with picks, shovels, and the strong of their backs, unearthing more fieldstone. A few yards downhill from Cam, one of his tenant farmers was meticulously laying a similar stretch of wall.

Dragging one shirt sleeve across the perspiration which threatened to trickle over his forehead and into his eyes, Cam turned to stare assessingly down the length of the wall.

It was a good day's effort, he decided. A satisfying, tangible result of hard work, and as good a way as any for a man to spend his frustration. The new wall ran straight and true, and with another three days' labor, it would be finished, and the workers could move on to the next task, or the next field. Casually lifting his hand to motion for the waterboy, Cam let his eyes drift higher, to the wold beyond, counting with satisfaction the sheep which thickly dotted the hillside.

It had been a good spring lambing, followed by a fine summer. The hay had been plentiful, and his flocks were fat for the coming winter. Inhaling a deep draught of fresh air, Cam realized that for the first time in a great many days he felt infused with a sense of peace.

His family did not understand his burning need to be close to the land. In fact, his father had belittled it, despite the fact that in leaner years, Cam's efforts had significantly contributed to the estate's survival. Now, his presence here mattered very little to anyone other than himself. Although smaller than the seat of his Devonshire earldom, Chalcote was his home. Some would say the master had no business here at all toiling in the fields like a common serf. Indeed, his Aunt Belmont, with her disdaining sense of propriety, roundly scolded him for it.

The young waterboy reached him then, panting and stumbling over the last row of turned and hardened earth. "A fresh bucket, m'lord," said the lad a little too cheerfully, righting himself without spilling a drop. As Cam dipped deep into the cool water and threw back his head to drink, he saw from the corner of his eye that the lad had begun to scuffle uneasily in his worn work boots.

"What's amiss, Jasper?" Cam dabbed at his mouth with the back of one hand as he tossed the dipper back into the bucket.

The boy looked up at him, squinting hard against the afternoon sun. "A big traveling coach, m'lord. Old Angus saw it turn off the Cheltenham Road when he brought up the water. 'Twill soon round the bend."

Cam scowled. "Mrs. Belmont on her way home, I daresay."

"Aye," nodded Jasper sympathetically. "Thought y'ought t'know."

As the boy walked away with his bucket, Cam suppressed the urge to accompany him. Cam's mount was staked in a patch of grass below. He could go home. But

Helene was at Chalcote. Probably offering a dish of tea to the sycophantic rector, who was no doubt waxing poetic over her charming wit and lovely blue eyes while Cam stood here sweating in the sun. No, he couldn't bear to watch that.

And yet, in another two minutes, his Aunt Belmont's carriage would come rumbling unavoidably up the hill, right past this very spot. The sense of satisfaction he had enjoyed moments earlier faded as he watched the old coach swing around the bend and grind into its ascent.

But Cam was not so lacking in temerity as to turn tail and run. He would stand his ground and suffer the consequences. Resigned to his fate, he hefted the next stone. There was no doubt Aunt Belmont would recognize him, despite the fact that he stood along the edge of a common field, hatless, coatless, and wearing a sweat-stained leather waistcoat.

And recognize him she did. Given the steep hill, it was no difficult matter to bring the coach to a halt just a few yards beyond his position by the fence. "Whoa up!" cried her coachman amidst the jingle and creak of harnesses. A footman—a new fellow by the look of him—leapt down and flung open the carriage door to receive his mistress's orders before the vehicle had stopped rocking.

After nodding subserviently at the person within, the footman peered over his shoulder at Cam, his expression bewildered. Apparently not recognizing the object of his errand as someone with whom his mistress might ordinarily converse, the hapless young servant had the audacity to turn back again, as if to clarify her instructions.

"Poor bastard," Cam mumbled.

At once, a bony finger protruded from the carriage to jab at the footman's nose. "I *said* to tell that man to come here right this very instant!" bellowed an imperiously feminine voice from the depths of the carriage. "And be quick about it, sirrah! I'm to have my tea at four sharp or you'll be on your way back to that Cornish coal mine from whence you sprang!"

The bewigged and wide-eyed footman turned back to Cam. With one hand inching toward his throat as if to forestall some invisible noose, he started toward the fence. Resigned to the inevitable, Cam threw one miry boot over a low spot in the stone wall, clambered over, strolled toward the carriage, and bravely threw open the door.

Aunt Belmont sat stiffly against the rear squabs while his cousin Joan seemed to cower in the less desirable front seat. He nodded politely to them both. "Good afternoon, Aunt. Joan."

His aunt flicked open her lorgnette with one deft motion, then coldly eyed him up and down. Cam knew it was an affectation solely designed to intimidate, for the old lady had eyes like a hawk. Without the benefit of a salutation, she swooped down upon her prey. "What in heaven's name are you about, Camden Rutledge? You look like someone's serf in that rig-out." The glasses still at hand, she leaned marginally forward, then swiftly recoiled, her noise wrinkled in disgust. "And good Lord, but you stink of—of—"

"Sweat?" supplied Cam thoughtfully.

"Camden!" said his aunt in a cautionary tone. "I grow increasingly alarmed at this propensity you have for manual labor." The old lady jerked her head rather obviously toward Joan. "Indeed, what must *others* think of you? It makes a very ill impression! Very ill indeed!"

"I am sorry if my appearance offends your delicate sensibilities, ma'am."

"Delicate? Ha! And your appearance isn't the half of it! It is your stubbornness. But have we not discussed this time and again?" she asked archly.

"Well, ma'am, you have often discussed it. And I have often listened."

"And yet you persist?"

Cam smiled. "I can only be grateful that you love me in spite of my faults, Aunt. I am a recalcitrant sort, to be sure."

Mrs. Belmont exhaled sharply. "Like the devil who spawned you," she remarked in a low undertone. "That unrepentant wastrel my sister wed! You did not get such ways from our Camden line, to be sure! Honestly! I often despair of your ever making anything of yourself!"

Out of deference to his aunt, Cam forbore to point out that he rather thought he *had* made something of himself. Aside from the title and estates that fate had bestowed upon him, he had all but tripled the output of his lands, and built a vast fortune out of nothing more than a shrewd mind and a hefty marriage portion.

But Mrs. Belmont was already aware of these successes. Still, they paled in comparison to his failures—foremost among them was his refusal to bend to her iron will. Indeed, his equanimity drove her to distraction. But it was his marked delay in announcing his betrothal that had incurred her flaming wrath of late.

Undoubtedly, Aunt Belmont had caught wind of his new governess. Perhaps she had even learned Helene's identity. Cam harbored some faint hope that she had not, but discovery was inevitable, and he would deal with it. Even his haughty aunt dared not issue Cam an ultimatum on any topic.

Smoothly, Mrs. Belmont switched tactics. "I collect that your brother is again fixed at Chalcote." She twitched her skirts irritably. "The rascal had the impudence to offer his assistance in my business at Cheltenham today. I take it he has been sent down from Oxford for good?"

"I fear so, ma'am," admitted Cam, suddenly wondering what had become of his sibling. "Did Bentley not give you his escort today?"

"Oh, upon my word! What need have Joan and I of a fawning puppy?"

"And did you buy your matched grays, ma'am?" asked Cam conversationally, leaning against the door of her carriage.

"Lord, no! Dawson is either an out-and-out cheat or the most unenlightened judge of horseflesh I have ever had the displeasure of dealing with. Well-matched my eye! Both short in the withers and weak in the hindquarters, but otherwise—*hmph!*—they matched not at all." She eyed Cam narrowly. "I fancy Dawson took me for as much of a fool as did young Bentham, but I daresay I've set 'em both to rights."

Cam coughed discreetly into one fist, restraining a choke of laughter. The old woman might be a harridan, but she was far from a fool, a lesson which Bentley must have learned today, probably to his undying regret.

Unexpectedly, Mrs. Belmont assumed a mollifying tone, always a harbinger of danger. "Well, really, Camden, we have seen nothing of you. You shall dine with us tomorrow," she directed, reaching out to give his damp locks a hesitant pat. "Indeed, you may even bring that scamp Bentley, if you wish."

Swiftly, he stripped away his filthy glove, then took her hand and kissed it. "Ma'am, I thank you, but I must decline. Pressing business keeps me at Chalcote just now."

"Does it indeed?" Mrs. Belmont's next words confirmed his suspicions. "By the by, I am given to understand you have a new servant at Chalcote," she said leaning a little farther from the depths of her carriage.

"Not a servant, ma'am," Cam gently corrected. "A special sort of teacher who has come from the Continent to work with Ariane."

"Hmph!" said Mrs. Belmont. "You waste your time in more ways than one, Camden! That child is some sort of changeling."

"Much as it distresses me to risk your good opinion, ma'am," said Cam in a deceptively quiet voice, "I must insist you have a care with your words. Ariane is your niece. And my daughter."

Mrs. Belmont drew herself up again. "Is she?" his aunt asked softly. "I vow, I was never sure of it, given that raffish crowd Cassandra kept."

"Your pardon, ma'am, but I observe that your tact has been exhausted by your journey," said Cam stiffly, placing his hand upon the carriage door as if to shut it. "Otherwise, I am sure you would never say such a thing. Particularly when servants are about. I fear I must bid you good day."

With the reluctance of one who has been trumped, Mrs. Belmont stiffly inclined her head. "My apologies," she said, her expression now carefully veiled. She looked past his shoulder for a moment before returning her sharp, calculating gaze to his. "Of course, you must do your duty by the girl, just as you will do your duty by all of us. Whatever else I may say of you, Camden, you were ever a dutiful son and nephew. I know you will not fail the family in any way."

"No, ma'am," he soberly replied. "I shall not."

As if an unspoken agreement had been reached, his aunt gave a smile of satisfaction, then lifted her hand in a queenly gesture, signaling that their conversation was at an end. "Walk on!" she cried to the coachman. Cam gratefully thumped shut the carriage door.

Helene was pleased to see that, true to Cam's prediction, the November chill had given way to a bright afternoon sun. By two o'clock, the day was almost warm. Despite her rather pointed admonition to Cam, Helene was perfectly content to spend her afternoons with Ariane, and the pair of them were happily engaged in kicking a ball about in the rear gardens when the butler appeared.

"Good afternoon, Milford," said Helene, panting ever so slightly as she pushed a lock of hair away from her forehead.

Milford, his face even paler than normal, clutched his hands neatly behind his back and hesitated. "Mr. Lowe has called for you, ma'am," he said, just as Ariane sent the ball skittering across the grass to Helene.

"Oh, excellent!" said Helene, returning the ball with a swift but misplaced kick, which sent it flying into the topiary garden. "Would you be so obliging as to ask him to join us here?"

Ariane darted into the shrubbery to retrieve the ball. Again, Milford wavered. "Well, ma'am—it is hardly my place to say, but you need to know that the young miss is not fond of visitors. And there are some whom she dislikes a vast deal more than others."

"What are you saying, Milford?"

"Miss Ariane does not like strangers of any sort." He cleared his throat uncomfortably. "But it has always been apparent to me that she particularly does not like men. Indeed, she dislikes some of them excessively, including the rector, I am sorry to say. And there is also his young cousin—"

"Miss Rutledge does not like the rector's cousin?" asked Helene, not entirely sure that she was following Milford.

"The curate, Mr. Rhoades," he reluctantly explained. "Miss Ariane took quite a dislike to him. And then there is that solicitor from London, Mr. Brightsmith—"

"Miss Rutledge dislikes Mr. Brightsmith?" she interjected. In this, Ariane had Helene's sympathy.

"Oh, no ma'am!" Milford shook his head. "Pays him

no heed! It's his clerk, young Mr. Kelly. The child throws a fit when he calls. And there is the magistrate who lives near Coln St. Andrews. She bit him once."

"Bit him?" echoed Helene hollowly. "With her teeth?"

"Oh, indeed! Poor man bent down to chuck her under the chin—as brash, cheerful fellows are wont to do with a pretty child. And she just clamped right down." Milford made a ghastly face. "Drew blood, too."

Helene winced at the image. "Well, we cannot very well send our village parson packing, can we, Milford? But neither can we have him bitten. Fetch Martha to play with Miss Rutledge, and show the rector into the yellow parlor. I shall join him there shortly."

Milford still hesitated. "Well, ma'am, the rector is accompanied by some . . . er, young persons."

"Young persons? Do you mean his children?" Strangely enough, Helene had simply assumed Thomas Lowe was unwed.

"Oh, no, ma'am!" answered the butler, as if it were obvious. "Mr. Lowe is not yet wed. I believe these particular young persons to be his nieces, aged about six and eight years. I collect that they are making an extended visit to the rectory."

A low rustle in the shrub nearest her elbow made Helene very keenly aware that Ariane had not reappeared from the hedge with the ball. "Well, Milford," she said, in a loud voice, "I am excessively fond of Mr. Lowe. And I should like very much to meet these young ladies. Why do you not show them into the conservatory? That way, I shall be able to observe Ariane in the gardens. It will be left to her as to whether or not she chooses to come inside and pay her respects to our guests, or remain outside."

Milford inclined his head stiffly. "Very good, ma'am."

Following his aunt's departure, Cam had returned to his fence with a renewed vigor. It was much later—long after the heat of his wrath had been spent on yet another layer of fieldstone—when Cam realized that, other than a perfunctory greeting, he'd said not a word to his prospective bride, nor she to him. Indeed, the lovely young Joan seemed to shrink ever deeper into the shadows, both literally and figuratively, every time he saw her.

Cam knew that other than his title and wealth, he had little to recommend him, particularly to a girl who was a dozen years younger. He was handsome enough, or so he had been told, but certainly not in the fashionable way, for he was big and dark, not lithe and fair, as was the style. Certainly, he possessed little elegance. His hands were rough and his arms were thickly corded with tendons.

Worse still, he was pensive and studious; some might even say a little dull. Cam's idea of a splendid evening was to settle by the fire with a bottle of wine, a book of verse, and a fine, fat cat—not dance until dawn with a horde of people he cared nothing about. Perhaps Joan was no longer eager to wed him, if ever she had been. But that hopeful thought brought Cam no comfort. Joan, too, would do her duty. His mind still unsettled by thoughts of Helene, Cam realized he was prodigiously tired, and that the afternoon had grown late.

Now, sprawled beneath a spreading oak tree, Cam was in the middle of a comfortable cose with his field hands, puffing some fine tobacco and enjoying the cool jug of cider which was making the rounds. Across the patch of grass, young Jasper leaned eagerly forward and passed the jug along to the man who sat beside him.

"What di'ye have in your pockets today, m'lord?" asked the boy eagerly, tossing a sidelong glance toward his master. "A book or a verse, mayhap?"

Laying aside his smoldering briarwood pipe, Cam smiled and began rummaging through the pockets of his discarded coat. "Perhaps just a small one," he admitted, pulling out a slender volume of verse. Then, to a chorus of encouragement, he leafed through the dog-eared pages, ceremoniously cleared his throat, and solemnly began:

"The curfew tolls the knell of parting day,
The lowing herd wind slowly o'er the lea,
The plowman homeward plods his weary way—"

"Och! Nae sa fast, m'lord!" interrupted Old Angus, waving a gnarled hand in censure. "That 'un sounds tae much like wark! I dinna wish to hear aboot some ploddin' auld plowman when I'm already fair fagged!"

"But I *like* Thomas Gray," protested Jasper. "We ain't listened to that'n in e'er so long!" But after glancing at the tired old Scotsman, the lad shrugged his narrow shoulders. "Oh, I reckon Angus is right, m'lord. 'Tis been a long day. Let's have some more o' that lively Byron, aye?"

With a shake of his head, Cam thumbed through the pages again. He had no wish to read Byron, for it made him think of Helene. Finally, he found what he sought. "Ahem!" he announced, looking up at the crowd with a wink and a grin. "In honor of Old Angus's discerning literary tastes, I give you something which is guaranteed to stir the blood of even the weariest Caledonian!

Scots, wha hae wi' Wallace bled,
Scots, wham Bruce has aften led,
Welcome to your gory bed,
Or to victorie!

Now's the day, and now's the hour;
See the front o' battle lour;
See approach proud Edward's power—
Chains and slaverie!

Wha will be a traitor knave?
Wha can fill a coward's grave?
Wha sae base as be a slave?
Let him turn and flee!"

The rousing poem went on for several stanzas, and as Cam finished, the fellow seated on the ground beside Angus leaned over and punched the old Scot soundly in the shoulder. "Now, take that and hush, ye auld bugger!" he teased in his best Scottish brogue.

"Aye, and I'll be glad of it!" insisted Angus, in mock indignity. "Tis nae aften I ha' a fine English lord gi'me *Bruce's March to Bannockburn*!"

As the crowd roared with laughter and started the jug around once more, Cam stretched out against the tree, and laid aside the verses. Thumping his now-dead pipe soundly across his boot heel, he watched the ashes skitter across the grass and wondered what Helene was doing at this moment.

He snorted aloud and gave the pipe another whack. Pouring tea for the overbearing parson, most likely. And Lowe would fawn and charm his way into her good graces, just as he did with every woman from eight to eighty. Oh, he was a nice enough fellow, if you liked that sort; overly personable and rather too handsome . . .

Would Helene find Lowe handsome? Probably. And as for the rector, any man—of the cloth or otherwise—could not but be enchanted by Helene, had he an ounce of red blood in his veins. And the rector was of an age when men thought seriously of making a match. Indeed, Lowe was always friendly toward Chalcote's governesses. But then, he was friendly toward everyone.

Nonetheless, with a sick feeling of dread, Cam shoved the old pipe deep into his coat pocket and took up his book. It was time to go home. Time to face Helene's lovely, daggerlike eyes, and the ensuing mélange of desire and guilt that burned beneath his breast. Thomas Lowe was, in truth, the least of Cam's problems.

"Why, this is cozy indeed!" announced the rector, waving an expansive hand about the conservatory. He turned his warm countenance upon Helene and strode across the tiled floor, wading through the potted palms and ferns, two pretty, yellow-haired girls at his heels.

"Good afternoon, Mr. Lowe," said Helene, going swiftly toward him.

"My dear Miss de Severs!" he returned, making a neat bow. "I observe that I have been needlessly worried for your health! Indeed, you are in great good looks, ma'am."

Helene murmured her thanks as Lowe brought forth his nieces. "Lucy and Lizzie Fane, my sister's girls," he declared, as Helene motioned them toward chairs.

Just as Milford had predicted, the young ladies were aged six and eight, respectively, and both possessed of riotous blonde hair and impudent grins. They were dressed alike in a shade of blue muslin which perfectly matched their eyes. Indeed, they greatly resembled their uncle, whom Helene did not doubt had his hands full with two such energetic-looking girls.

The uncle in question settled back into his chair and laid one of those hands gracefully across his knee. "And how is Miss Ariane Rutledge today?" asked Lowe. "Shall we see her at all? I own, my nieces would very much like to make her acquaintance, if, of course, you think it perfectly all right?"

Helene paused to carefully consider the rector's question. On the surface, it seemed a wonderful idea. But had Ariane any experience with other children? It was not something she and Cam had discussed. Across the expanse of the rear garden, Helene could see Ariane lingering among the shrubbery, desultorily tossing the ball into the air. She would not, Helene was convinced, come into the conservatory, despite the fact that she had almost certainly been eavesdropping on Helene's conversation with Milford.

After a moment of consideration, Helene decided that having friends was an essential part of growing up, and gave the girls a quick lecture about Ariane's shyness. The girls nodded cheerfully, and Helene escorted them out into the gardens. Ariane looked nervously at Lucy and Lizzie, but she jerked her head in faint acknowledgment when Helene instructed her to share the ball with their guests. Uneasily, Helene returned to the conservatory, determined to keep a close watch.

"In truth, Miss de Severs, how does the child go on?" asked Lowe quietly as she stepped back through the door. "Will it be perfectly all right for the girls to play with her? I would not wish Ariane to suffer any discomfort at our expense."

"I think all will be well," murmured Helene, settling into a chair that held an unobstructed view of the lawn. "Let us see how Ariane does. Perhaps they shall become friends."

Lowe smiled again. "Lucy and Lizzie would be so pleased. I confess, they have been a little bored since coming to the village. And you must know what a challenge bored children can present." The rector spread his hands wide, a helpless look upon his face.

Helene found herself laughing at the charming, perplexed expression. "The girls have come to stay with you for a time, I understand?"

The smile slipped away. "Yes, but through no happy circumstance, I regret to say. My sister is newly widowed. She and the girls are to make their home with me for a time."

Helene easily understood the words which were left

unsaid. The rector's sister had undoubtedly been impoverished by her husband's death. How fortunate she had a brother; one who seemed perfectly willing to take her and her children in. Thomas Lowe rose in Helene's estimation.

Helene smiled. "I hope that your sister has found friends here?"

The rector smiled a little shyly. "Well, as to that, Miss de Severs, I should very much like her to meet you. Would you do us the honor of taking tea with us Sunday? I hope you don't find my invitation forward."

"Not at all," answered Helene, pleasantly surprised. "I should account it a great pleasure. It must be wonderful to have family living with you."

"Oh, indeed! Most of our family is in Norfolk."

"Yes, but you have a cousin here, do you not?"

The rector leaned intimately toward her. "Why, yes! Fancy you should know it. My curate, Mr. Rhoades, is a distant relation." He dropped his voice to a soft, confiding tone. "Poor Basil is an exceedingly fine fellow, Miss de Severs. But rather too bashful, I fear, to do the Lord's work. Time will tell, of course."

"Yes, of course," answered Helene, inwardly wondering if Thomas Lowe had anything more than a passing acquaintance with the term *bashful*.

"And what of yourself, Miss de Severs? That faint French accent is lovely."

Helene tried to return his smile. "Indeed, my parents were Parisian, but following my father's death, my mother and I came to live in England. He died in the aftermath of the Revolution."

"I am so very sorry," he said, his expression one of concern.

Helene waved her hand in obviation. "I never knew my father, Mr. Lowe. I feel very much at home here. Indeed, I had two English stepfathers. "

"Ah!" he answered knowingly. "And where were you

brought up? Who were your stepfathers? I own, I am inordinately curious about you." He smiled again.

Helene had been braced for this question since returning from Bavaria. Moreover, she had vowed to be truthful. If the rector now chose to scorn her background, so be it. "I was raised by my mother's second husband, Captain Henry Middleton, a naval man. We made our home near Hampstead Heath, but he was often at sea, and died when I was a girl."

"Ah!" he said again. "The name's familiar! Died in the line of duty, did he not? A brave fellow, as I recall."

"Yes, I thought him exceedingly brave," agreed Helene. And it was very true. Though Captain Henry had been dead for almost two decades, Helene had never forgotten his kindness in dandling her on his knee, and in bringing her trinkets from around the world.

Her mother had wed him when Helene was but five, just one year after the death of her second husband, an infamous London blood who had cared more for his valet than for his stepdaughter, and who had quickly died in a notorious dawn appointment defending his new bride's honor. Helene shuddered to think what her mother must have done to prompt such a challenge.

Marie had been fortunate to remarry after such a scandal, even if Henry Middleton had been a little rough around the edges. But for all his roughness, Middleton had put a roof over their heads, and had welcomed Helene to share his name. Often, Helene could not help but wonder what their lives would have been like had the captain lived. Perhaps no different. Perhaps her mother would have driven Captain Middleton to the sword-point with her indiscreet flirtations.

"I seem to recall hearing someone mention that your mother was a close acquaintance of his lordship." Lowe's voice jerked Helene coldly into the present. "The previous Lord Treyhern, I should say."

Helene forced a taut smile. "I believe they were rather well acquainted at one time," she answered vaguely, but her heart had begun to hammer.

The rector waved his hand casually. "I was still at university, of course. But for my part, Miss de Severs," Lowe leaned uncomfortably near, "I think you must account your mother most fortunate. His lordship was not, you know, *marriage* material."

"Was he not?" asked Helene stiffly, rising to her feet. "Excuse me. I believe I shall check on Ariane."

"By all means." Lowe pointed toward a nest of rhododendron. "I daresay you shall find them engaged in mild girlish mischief just there. Indeed, I saw them not two minutes ago."

Her face hot, Helene went out the door and through the gardens, only to find Lucy and Lizzie busy poking sticks at an empty bird's nest which they had managed to drag from the branches of the rhododendron. Behind them, her eyes wide with interest, Ariane watched.

Inwardly, Helene wanted to laugh at herself. Ariane was obviously fascinated by her new companions, and in no need of Helene's help. She lifted her chin stiffly, then marched back into the conservatory. "They are perfectly fine," she announced, sweeping back into her seat and forcing herself to smile at the rector.

Immediately, Thomas Lowe leaned forward, and before she knew what he was about, the rector had seized her hand, pressing it ardently between his own. "My dear Miss de Severs, I owe you the deepest of apologies. I meant no offense by my words about the late Lord Treyhern! Indeed, I should not have said them at all! It is simply that—" the rector halted, dropping his long, blond lashes nearly shut, "—you are so easy to talk to, which makes me inclined to share confidences, which I know I ought not do on such short acquaintance, but—but I—"

A rustle in the foliage cut him short. "Oh, there you are, Miss de Severs!" Bentley Rutledge's voice rang through the conservatory with hearty good cheer. Suddenly, his head popped up from the thicket of potted palms which encircled the low wooden benches. His eyes were alight with an unholy glee. "Been looking all over for you, m'dear! We've a backgammon match to set about, if you'll recall."

Bentley's heavy boots rang across the tile floor as he strolled around to the opening in the greenery, then rather ineffectively feigned surprise as he peered into the sitting area. "Why look here! Hang me if it ain't the padre!" Bentley came forward to stick out his hand. "Beg pardon, I'm sure, Lowe! Didn't mean to interrupt."

But the rector was on his feet and looking just a little ill at ease. "Mr. Rutledge! How delightful. I fancy I've not had the pleasure of seeing you in church since . . . oh, since your father's funeral."

Bentley's grin widened. "Ha! Take your point, old fellow, but I've been away at school. One must get properly educated, you know." The young man rubbed his hands together rather too vigorously. "Now, to what do we owe this pleasure, Lowe?" Without invitation, Bentley flung himself down on the chaise beside Helene.

But the rector was having none of it. "No, and regrettably, I must now bid you both a good afternoon," he said briskly, taking up his hat and stick. "Mr. Rhoades and I have some church business to which we must attend, and then I'm expected home."

Smoothly, Helene rose, as did Bentley. "Then I shall see you out, Mr. Lowe," she said graciously.

"No need to go on my account, Lowe," added Bentley generously.

Lowe bowed stiffly. "By no means do I go on your account, Mr. Rutledge. Do keep your seat, Miss de Severs. I shall just collect my nieces and return to St. Michael's by the rear gardens."

"Of course," Helene answered quietly. "Do bring the girls again soon."

"Yes, I thank you. Perhaps the day after tomorrow?" The rector's smile had warmed again.

Helene nodded, then stood, arms crossed over her chest, as Thomas Lowe strolled out into the afternoon sunlight to take his lively nieces in each hand. Ariane, who had darted into the shrubbery again, peered out rather forlornly, observing their departure.

Slowly, Helene rounded on Bentley. "Now precisely what were you about here, Mr. Rutledge?" She tried to keep a straight face. "We have no plans for this afternoon. In fact, I was given to understand that you had gone to Cheltenham for the day."

Bentley's face was red with barely suppressed mirth. "I am now persuaded, Helene, that you really are quite the *femme fatale!*" he chuckled, ignoring her question. "Poor old Lowe was almost on his knees."

Helene fought the urge to smile. "Mr. Rutledge, I am *Miss de Severs*. And I find your terminology mean-spirited. Poor Mr. Lowe was merely—"

"—merely making an ass of himself," finished Bentley on a choke of laughter. "Now, confess it, ma'am. The old boy was looking pathetically besotted. And you were more relieved than you care to admit, I'll wager, when you saw me come thrashing through this jungle." He bent down to stare her straight in the face. "Ah, yes! I see it just there—the light of gratitude in your lovely eyes!"

Helene snagged her bottom lip and bit hard. The impudent puppy was right. Lowe was a pleasant man, but at that particular moment, she had wished the earth to split open and swallow one of them. The rector's questions about her mother's relationship with Randy Rutledge had troubled her.

"There now," Bentley said softly, cupping his palm beneath her elbow. "That smile is infinitely more charming than your governess frown! And since Aunt Belmont had no use for me, her loss shall be your gain. Now, come, take a turn about the room with me," Bentley urged, propelling her through the greenery. "Educate me! For I've a sad lack of learning when it comes to horticulture, and I'll wager you know the names of these hanging vines. And these little potted trees, too, I imagine?"

He bent forward to study a plant, then looked up at her with a sidelong glance as he stroked a soft green leaf between two fingers.

"But you *were* out of line, Mr. Rutledge," she insisted, watching his long fingers which looked so very like his brother's. "Your beguiling ways shan't deter my argument."

The young man's eyes glittered mischievously as he straightened up. "Be wary of our pious priest, ma'am. His intentions may well be no more honorable than mine. Less so, I daresay."

Reluctantly, Helene strolled a little deeper into the conservatory with him. "Mr. Rutledge, you are incorrigible."

Bentley gave a harsh, cynical laugh. "Yes, that is one of the finer sentiments my brother uses to describe me." They were shielded from the garden by a cascade of ferns now. "Tell me, Miss de Severs, do you think me beyond redemption? For I can assure you my saintly sibling does."

"You are young, sir," she returned, softening her tone. "You have many years to make of yourself what you will. It was wrong of me to call you incorrigible, even in teasing. Nor should your brother say you are beyond redemption, for you are neither."

"What if I mean to be, Miss de Severs?" As if unsettled by her kindness, Bentley gave her an insolent wink. "Perhaps I am not as young—nor as inexperienced—as you might think." His voice held more than a hint of masculine arrogance.

Helene stopped in her tracks. "You overstep yourself, Mr. Rutledge," she stated coolly.

"Ah! Am I to be hanged for my impure thoughts, madam?" he asked, one eyebrow cocked inquisitively. "Better a sheep than a lamb, then." Abruptly, Helene found herself yanked against the young man's chest, and her mouth crushed beneath his.

Despite her prodigious experience at evading just such catastrophes, Helene was caught totally unaware, her arms trapped by her sides in Bentley's strong grip. His lips moved sensually against hers in a kiss that was deep, wanton, and shockingly rich with experience. Regrettably, he felt, smelled, and tasted very like his brother, and for the briefest of moments, Helene's senses overwhelmed her brain.

As Bentley's tongue raked over her lips, Helene very nearly forgot herself until she heard a soft moan of pleasure in the back of Bentley's throat, and felt his hand slide farther down into the small of her back to pull her hips into his. Seizing the moment of near freedom, Helene jerked hard, lifting one knee sharply and almost catching the young man square in the testicles.

The result was instantaneous. Bentley pitched forward with a violent convulsion, then shoved her away, his eyes wide and tearing with pain. One hand flew to his mouth, as if he'd bitten his tongue. Just for good measure, Helene caught him across the face with a resounding smack.

"Aathh, Christhh—!" sputtered Bentley, nursing his wounded tongue, one arm lashed tight about his belly. Helene could see that the young man was courageously resisting the impulse to clutch his privates.

Never too faint of heart to add insult to injury, Helene grabbed Bentley by the earlobe and dragged him, groaning and cursing, back through the ferns. Planting one palm firmly against his chest, Helene shoved him backward onto the chaise.

"That was disgracefully done, Mr. Rutledge," she scolded, staring down at his gracelessly sprawled figure. "Now cease cursing and explain to me precisely what it is that you think you are about here."

Bentley lifted his gaze to hers as she dropped resolutely into the chair across from his. The young man's eyes shimmered, and fleetingly, Helene found herself wondering if the tears were entirely pain-induced. Abruptly, he jerked his gaze from hers. "Oh, burn it, Helene!" he grumbled. "I just tried to steal a little kiss."

Gingerly, Bentley fingered the spot on his face where she had hit him. Helene was dismayed to see that her blow had hurt more than she had intended, for his cheek was already shadowed by an old bruise. "Thought you were enjoying it, too," he belatedly grumbled.

Helene stared at the boy, utterly certain she was losing her mind, based on what she was about to say. "Well, I did, Mr. Rutledge," she announced, watching his pained expression shift to one of deep suspicion. "Or, rather, I would have, had I any interest in being kissed by you. But alas, I have none, your inordinate skill notwithstanding."

Bentley slumped dejectedly in his chair. "Don't try to cozen me, Helene," he said softly, his eyes still bright with emotion.

Given the fact that the young man had very nearly had his tongue in her mouth, Helene was hard put to insist upon the formality of surnames. Instead, she sighed a little wearily and made a few quick adjustments to her gown and her hair. Unfortunately, such actions seemed to be necessary with a rather startling frequency when one spent any amount of time in the Rutledge household.

"Bentley," she finally said, stabbing in a hairpin while gazing at him in exasperation, "you are a handsome fellow. And yes, you are prodigious charming. But I am not interested in making love with you, and you insult me by assuming that because I am a servant in this house, you may have your way with me."

The young man looked insulted. "But that's not what I—"

"Hush, Bentley," interjected Helene, pointing a finger at his nose. "Moreover, I cannot believe that you have any interest in me. Indeed, you do not, do you?"

Bentley dropped his chin. "Well, you're damned pretty," he admitted, coloring slightly. "And I know you let Cam kiss you. You cannot deny that."

Inside, Helene froze, but her composure held. "I shall neither admit it nor deny it," she hotly insisted. "What I do with your brother is none of your concern, sir. I should set your ears afire—"

"Oh, have done, Helene!" Bentley lifted up his head, the familiar, charming grin spreading slowly across his face. "That just won't fly! A woman cannot kiss as exquisitely as you do, and then expect a fellow to take a scold from those very same lips!"

"Bentley, your incessant flirting will not work on me." Helene relaxed, and chose a different approach. "Indeed, I think you are too much of a gentleman to save me from the rector's alleged clutches, simply to corner me behind the ferns to sneak a kiss—a kiss which a dozen other women would willingly bestow upon you. Now tell me, just what did you hope to gain?"

He paused for a long moment. "I think not," retorted Bentley, eyeing her warily while gingerly fingering his jaw. "I have need of my teeth, I thank you."

"Tell me!"

The young man scowled at her insistence. "I just don't care for Lowe. Didn't care for the way the fellow was looking at you, his lashes all lowered, grasping at your hand and panting—"

"Commendable," she said dryly, "but Thomas Lowe did not drag me behind the ferns and force his attentions on me."

Bentley reddened furiously. "Sorry," he finally mumbled. "I daresay you mean to tell Cam, don't you?"

Helene settled her hands on her hips and studied the boy for a long moment. "Now, why do I get the impression that you'd like nothing better?"

Elbows resting on his knees, Bentley let his head fall forward into his hands, as if an overriding weariness had seized him. "I really don't give a bloody damn what you tell old Saint Camden. He'll think what he likes, and do what he likes, anyway."

"Your brother loves you, Bentley."

"Ha," he said scornfully. "You cannot begin to comprehend my brother, Helene. You have known him but a few short days. I have been saddled with him all my life. Pompous, pious, self-righteous prig."

Helene was torn by the desire to tell him that not only were his adjectives redundant, they were patently wrong. She wanted to tell Bentley that she had known Camden Rutledge for almost a dozen years, and that even as a boy, Cam had been wracked by worry for his family. The responsibility for them all had been set upon his shoulders, and he had borne it willingly, with a devotion which defied his years.

Gently, Helene reached out to touch him lightly on one knee. "What is it, Bentley? Why are you so angry with your brother? You say I don't know him, but that's not entirely true. A long time ago, when you were very young, I knew him well. My mother was friends with your father, and I often came here as a girl. And it was obvious even then how much he loved you and Catherine."

Bentley looked disinterested in her past. "Really?" he said, sounding unconvinced.

"Yes, really," Helene insisted. "I know he can often seem stubborn and unfeeling, but in truth, he cares for you. More than you know. Can you not talk to him? Can you not talk to me?"

"No," he said defensively. "It is nothing, in any event. Nothing you can help."

"Why do you not try to tell me, and see?"

Bentley vacillated for a moment, clearly fighting some inner struggle. But reticence won. "He just wants to lord his authority over us, that's all. First it was Catherine. Cam ordered her around, until she married against his wishes."

"Against his wishes?"

"Aye, to Squire Wodeway's son. Cam thought she could make a better match, but Cat wanted to move on with her life."

Little Catherine married a Wodeway? That did surprise Helene, for she remembered all of the widowed Squire Wodeway's half-dozen sons with perfect clarity; a rambunctious gang of near-ruffians who possessed few pretensions to good manners, or even domesticity, come to that. Little wonder Cam might harbor misgivings about binding his sister to such a fellow, despite the fact that the family was by no means impecunious, and that their mother had reputedly been a woman of connections and breeding.

Helene was confused. Cam had said that his sister married young, and indeed, Catherine was but a few years older than Bentley, if memory served. "I believe I do not perfectly understand, Bentley. Did they run away? To Scotland perhaps? And what did your father say of the match?"

Bentley shook his head. "No, they were wed at St. Michael's. Father said little—and cared even less. And why should he? But Cam held the purse strings, and Cat had a devil of a time persuading him."

"When were they wed?" asked Helene, ignoring his snide question.

"Don't remember," muttered Bentley. "Some five years past, I daresay."

Helene did some quick computations in her head. "Well, good heavens, Bentley! Catherine could not have been more than seventeen! I understand Cam's concern."

Bentley shrugged, his expression cold. "You need say no more! I should have known you would take his side."

"I am taking no one's side, Bentley," she softly insisted.

"I hate him," spat Bentley, suddenly sounding like the boy he was instead of the man he looked to be. "And I do not care to speak of it further. If you wish to tell Saint Camden I tried to make love to you, Helene, then by all means do so. Indeed, he will be glad for some excuse to have me out on my head, for he has already threatened to do just that."

"Bentley, I hardly think I require your brother to guard my virtue." The young man was almost irrationally angry with his brother, and Helene sensed that something deeply distressing lay behind it. Perhaps Bentley would eventually confide in her. "Come now," she said softly, holding out her hand. "Let's cry friends, shall we?"

A long moment passed between them, until slowly, Bentley reached out and grasped her fingers in his very large hand. "Yes, all right," he said in a surprisingly soft voice. "Friends."

As she clutched Bentley's hand, Helene stared thoughtfully out into the garden. The shadows had lengthened now, and across the lawns, Helene could see Ariane walking toward the door, her ball tucked neatly under one arm. Helene dropped Bentley's hand to wave at her, and suddenly, Ariane looked up, smiling broadly when she saw Helene standing at the window. It was a sweet, wonderful smile, full of hope and promise.

"Do you know, I find it has grown cold in this room, Bentley," said Helene pensively as Ariane pulled open the door. "Why do we not stir up the fire in the parlor, all three of us, then you and I shall have that game of backgammon after all."

9

Oh, Hesperus! Wake the wish and melt the heart!

The night wind soughed and ebbed through the trees surrounding Chalcote. Weary from a day spent in the fields, Cam had collapsed into bed and fallen at once into a black well of oblivion. Now, however, the wind kept teasing him back from that restful sleep and into a dreamlike haze.

But he had not meant to sleep. Had he? No. He remembered now. He'd meant to simply drowse atop his coverlet while he waited for his father's house party to fall silent.

In the muffled darkness, he lay motionless, one hand lightly caressing the red velvet box beneath his pillow. *It was Helene's birthday.* He knew it, just as he knew that Marie Middleton had forgotten it. Why it mattered to Helene was beyond his grasp, but girls were just different. Helene had tried to pretend it didn't matter when the day had ended without so much as a new hair ribbon from her mother. But he had seen the tears. And he had hurt for her.

Cam brushed the box again. Warm red velvet, like Helene's mouth. He felt his belly clench with fear and anticipation. It was wrong, perhaps, to kiss and to touch and to stroke one another as they did. Especially when they were supposed to be just friends. But for the longest time, she had been so much more to him. Save for his brother and sister, Hellie was his whole life.

She wanted more than friendship, too. Helene wanted him in *that* way. And she no longer hid her desire by mischievously teasing and tormenting him. For his part, despite all the trouble she was forever dragging him into, Cam loved no one so well as Helene. Soon, somehow, they would be wed.

Oh, his father was beginning to grumble a bit about his friendship with "Marie's wild chit," as he disdainfully called Helene. And there had been some half-hearted threats of Oxford in the spring. But Cam knew it would all come to naught, for by the year's first quarter day, Papa wouldn't have a feather to fly with. Hunting season had already bled him very nearly dry, what with three new horses in the stables and half of society's scapegraces soaking up Chalcote's wine for days on end.

But perhaps he was little better than his father's friends? Cam eased his fingers around the velvet box, clutched it tight, and thought of things no gentleman ever should. Beneath his nightshirt, his cock sprang to life, hard, pulsing, and needful. He could not resist the urge to slide his hand beneath the coverlet to touch himself. But *that* was no longer enough.

Ahh, Helene! He felt the rush of hot blood beneath his skin and knew a wild, urgent ache pulling at him. He needed Helene so desperately, and for many reasons. Yet no one understood. They thought him too young to know his own mind. But he wasn't. No, despite the fact that he was a little shy—*dull and dour*, he'd once heard his father say—Cam was as sure of his love for Helene as he was sure of his own abilities.

Yes, dull and dour he might be, but this year, the home farm had turned a profit, which was twice the amount of last year's, and Cam knew that the sweat of his brow and his head for numbers had made the difference. Still, his father laughed, scorning him for his refusal to participate in Chalcote's frivolities.

Last night, Randolph had thrust a buxom widow in Cam's direction, with a suggestion so lewd that Cam had been embarrassed for her. She, however, had merely taken umbrage at Cam's disinterest. Randolph had turned his back on them. *"No son of mine,"* he had muttered in a tone loud enough for a half-dozen guests to hear.

Tonight, the dinner party two floors below was growing ever more boisterous. It seemed likely that the rugs had been rolled back for an impromptu dance, for the drunken revelry now rang through the hall. No need for silence then. He would risk it. Noiselessly, Cam slid from his bed and into the corridor.

As expected, no light shone beneath Helene's door. He gave the secret knock, and slipped inside. In a thin shaft of moonlight, he saw Helene toss back her bedcovers and spin to a sitting position on the mattress. Silently, he crossed the room to her, bent one knee to the bed, and settled beside her.

"Happy birthday," he whispered, leaning close, and pressing the small box into her hand.

Helene stared at him for a moment, then flicked open the velvet lid. A sigh of pleasure escaped her as she lifted the ornate chain and stared at the large emerald nestled in its filigree setting. In the dim light, he saw her snag her lower lip and give her head an almost imperceptible shake. "Cam, *mais non!* You cannot give me this," she whispered in her soft, lilting voice. "But oh! How lovely it is."

"It is yours," he replied, absently running a finger down the curve of her jaw. "Mother left it to me, and it is mine to give as I choose." He took the pendant from her hand. "Turn around, Hellie."

His fingers shook as he lifted Helene's thick braid to one side, then fastened the chain around her neck. As she turned toward him, she loosened the tie of her nightdress and stared down at her chest. In the darkness, he could barely see the necklace against her skin. It did not matter. He knew all too well what her skin looked like.

"What do you think, Cam?" she asked with a feminine laugh. "If I wore this with a silk ball gown, how would I look?" In the dark, she looked up at him, her eyes wide, her full mouth half curved into that mischievous grin he both loved and feared.

He swallowed hard, then leaned forward to gently kiss her. "Someday, Hellie, I will give you silk, too. Emerald silk, to match this stone. I want you always to dress in rich, dark colors, for they suit you."

Helene came up onto her knees and flung her arms around his shoulders. "*Merci,* Cam," she whispered, pressing little kisses over his face. "It is the finest gift ever!"

He let his hands slide up her back as his mouth found hers again. He felt Helene's breasts urge against him as they fell back into the tangle of bedding, no longer laughing as had once been their habit. Somewhere along the way, they had stopped giggling beneath the bedcovers, and things had become very, very serious thereafter. He kissed her again, with his lips and his tongue.

Willingly, Helene opened her mouth on a soft, breathless sigh, and took him inside. The kiss went on and on, blissfully sweet in its intensity. They were well past the point of any awkwardness, if ever there had been any between them. Cam really couldn't recall any. He remembered only that he wanted her; had wanted her forever, it seemed. He pulled himself on top of her, dragging her nightgown up between her legs with the weight of his knee.

"Helene," he finally managed to say, barely lifting his mouth from hers, "perhaps we ought to stop."

"Non, non!" she softly cried, arching against him as she dragged her fingers down through his hair. "Please, Cam! I love you. I will love you till I die. It is the very same for you, *n'est-ce pas?"*

"Ah, Helene, you know it is," he answered, his lips moving lightly across her forehead. "And someday I will have a right to . . . to be with you like this. But not yet. Not now."

" 'Tis nonsense," she whispered, her breathing already fast and shallow. Impatiently, Helene jerked upward on his nightshirt. "I shall wait for you forever if I must, but why do we wait? And for what? Who knows or cares what we do?"

And suddenly, Cam decided that he agreed with her. Indeed, in his heart, he suspected that he'd wanted her to react just so. Perhaps he had come to Helene's bedchamber not only to comfort her, but to make love to her—just as he'd wanted to do since the first time he'd seen her. For a long time, he'd been ashamed of his desire for Helene. But now he understood it, and it no longer felt wrong.

In the pale light, he imagined that her eyes twinkled mischievously. And in the next moment, she slid her hand beneath his nightshirt, wrapping her long, capable fingers around his swollen shaft, and Cam could not suppress a moan of sweet pain.

"Can I touch you, Cam?" she asked, her voice unusually thick. "Can I please you with my . . . well, you know—as that woman pleases her lover in your papa's book of naughty drawings?" Playfully, she came up off the mattress and nipped at his ear with her sharp, white teeth.

Cam felt his face suffuse with color. He knew exactly which book—and which drawing—she meant. And it *was* naughty. And rather more excitement than he could bear at the moment. A little awkwardly, he jerked to his knees and dragged off his nightshirt. Though they had seen each other in various states of dishabille many times over the years, he heard Helene gasp at his naked, blatantly aroused state. Suddenly, all playfulness vanished. Cam let his hand skim over the soft skin of her knee to catch at the hem of her gown.

"Take this off, Helene," he heard himself rasp, almost choking on the words, and the urgency which propelled them. He let his fingers slide beneath the white linen and into the familiar warmth between her legs, caressing her until her breathing grew faster still.

Cam was well aware what they were about to do. Of what they had come so close to doing a half-dozen times over the last year. But Hellie was seventeen now, an age by which many girls were wed. And at eighteen, Cam knew his own mind. He would gladly wed her at once if necessary. He almost hoped it would be necessary, for it would simplify a great many things.

"Take it off, Hellie," he repeated, and Helene snaked up her nightclothes to reveal her sweetly flared hips, and breasts that looked like small, perfect peaches in the moonlight. Although he had touched them on more than one occasion, this was overwhelmingly different. Helene's nipples were hard and dark against her skin, her belly white and smooth, her coltish legs sleek with muscle.

Cam let his eyes drift up and down her length, still intimately caressing her, his heart strangely filled with a serene sense of joy that exceeded even his unslaked lust. It was time, and he was glad. He was tired of resisting. He loved her. Truly, deeply loved her.

The knock, when it came, was abrupt.

They had not a moment in which to hide themselves, nor to conceal what they were doing. Marie Middleton sailed into the room in a cloud of sour wine and stale perfume, a beribboned package clutched loosely in her left hand. She was roaring drunk.

But not nearly drunk enough. After one quick glance, Helene's mother dropped the gift and bolted across the room, her strong backhand catching Cam squarely across the face.

Yet, the knocking on the door continued, even as Cam rolled sickly toward one side of the bed, attempting to cover their nakedness. The knock became louder, farther away, yet more insistent. It hammered at his consciousness. *What the devil . . . ? Why keep pounding on the door? It was too late. Too late.*

But as Cam sank deeper into the sick and certain sensation of impending doom, the vision of Marie Middleton and his aching flood of memories began to fade into daylight.

The pounding came again. "Lord Treyhern?"

Cam rolled over and cursed into his pillow.

"My lord?" said Crane softly. "Please get up! I believe you've overslept again."

By the following afternoon, Helene had gained a proper perspective on her encounter with Bentley, and on her visit from Mr. Lowe as well. She had little to fear from either quarter, she had decided, and perhaps some measure of friendship to be gained.

The rector had sent a kind note after breakfast, confirming his intent to call again the following day. Attached to it had been a little book on the history of the famous wool churches of the Cotswolds.

Helene had hardly seen Cam that afternoon. Despite her fortitude in dealing with Bentley, by dinner time, Helene's courage had failed. Dealing with Cam himself was another thing altogether. Surrendering to apprehension, Helene had sent word that she found herself beset by a headache and unable to join the Rutledges for dinner.

At the time, it had seemed the wisest course of action, and her head indeed had been pounding. Even now, it continued to plague her, but there was no avoiding the indomitable Earl of Treyhern this afternoon. Against her better judgment, Helene directed Martha to dress Ariane in her warmest carriage dress. Then she took the girl down to the hall to meet her father at precisely half past noon, feeling as if she went to her own doom instead.

As she'd expected, Cam was entirely serious about their drive. His curricle and a pair of feisty black geldings already awaited their arrival at the foot of the steps. During the half-hour's journey, she and Cam forced a desultory but amiable conversation for Ariane's benefit, and soon they arrived at a particularly scenic spot on the edge of Chalcote's estate.

As children, she and Cam had often slipped away to this bend in the River Coln, to fritter away an afternoon. For a distance of several yards, the shallow river deepened and slowed, and as Helene stared down at the glistening water, she could not help but wonder if Cam remembered. Some maudlin part of her wanted to believe that he did, and that perhaps those memories were as sweet to him as they were to her.

After they had climbed from the curricle, Cam walked up the hill to spread a heavy blanket beneath a gnarled apple tree. Ariane danced off to play by the water's edge, and the awkward conversation which Helene and Cam had thus far maintained came to an abrupt halt as they settled onto the blanket.

Cam stretched his rangy length across one edge, then leaned back onto his elbows to let his eyes drift across the river below. "Well, Helene," he said, casually crossing his long, booted legs at the ankles. "Here we are."

"Indeed." Helene managed to keep her voice cool. "Here we are."

Across the narrow expanse of grass, Ariane was engrossed in flinging leaves into the whirling current, and she was quite obviously happy.

"Well, here we are," Cam repeated, a little less enthusiastically as Helene carefully smoothed her skirts.

"So you have said, my lord," she murmured.

Abruptly, Cam jerked fully upright, took off his hat, and sent it sailing onto the far corner of the blanket. "Oh, very well then, Helene! You do not mean to make this easy for me, do you?" he said harshly, raking his hair back away from his face. He turned to look at her, his lips drawn into a tight, narrow line. Then, unexpectedly, his expression shifted, softening a little. He looked swiftly away to stare down at the water.

"And indeed, you should not," Cam finally muttered, as if addressing himself rather than her. "No, you should not. I . . . I am sorry, Helene. I treated you abominably two evenings ago, and God knows I regret it. I give you my word as a gentleman that it shan't happen again."

Helene stared across the length of the blanket at Cam. The afternoon sun cast his chiseled face into a near silhouette, his profile sinfully handsome. A sudden breeze stirred the softness of his hair, teasing at his stubborn cowlick. In the brilliant light of day, Cam's dark locks glinted with the occasional strand of purest silver, that time—or perhaps worry—had left him. She resisted a strong impulse to lift her hand to touch it.

Instead, Helene willed herself to relax. In the bare branches overhead, a pair of wrens scolded and skittered, fluffing their feathers against the breeze. In the distance, the subtle sound of water murmured. All around them, the sharp autumn air was lightly laced with the fragrance of fallen apples, now fermenting amid the meadow grass. Across the river, a trio of cows lowed at one another as they trod a deep path along the river's bend toward an old stone byre in the distance.

On the whole, it was a landscape just as idyllic, and just as quintessentially English, as a hundred other such scenes she had enjoyed with Cam in their misspent youth. Helene was a little taken aback by the rush of emotion such a picture evoked—a picture that she had once attempted to forget. Yes, she had often forced herself to view her memories of rural Gloucestershire through the jaded eye of a Continental. She had told herself that pastoral serenity was nothing short of dull. What she could not have, she had attempted to disdain.

But what choice had she had? She had been but seventeen, alone with the memories of a place—and yes, of a love—which had been taken from her. One did what one must. She had been young, yes, but the pain had been all too real.

And yet, the beauty of the scene—indeed, the beauty of the man beside her—still called out to Helene's every instinct. How often had her soul ached for the serenity of this place, and for the quiet, steady companionship of this man? With measured reluctance, Helene tore her gaze from his face. She stared down across the green swath of grass which bordered the river, and reminded herself of how Cam had wounded her with his reprehensible offer.

The cows had disappeared around the bend now. In the late afternoon sun, Ariane continued her happy games, pitching her bits of flotsam into the lazy current. To all outward appearances, the three of them might easily have been a family, enjoying one last burst of sunshine before autumn's end. The sadness that had gnawed at Helene for the last several days grew ever sharper at that thought.

Helene shifted away from Cam. "Your apology is accepted," she finally forced herself to say. "And I give you mine. Let us speak no more of it."

Seated on the blanket beside her, Cam drew one leg toward his chest, then leaned pensively forward to rest his forearm atop his knee. With his face relaxed into gentler lines, he looked unexpectedly boyish again. Not quite seventeen, perhaps. But for an instant, Cam looked very like the young man she had once loved.

He turned to study her, his eyes drifted over her face for what seemed like an eternity. "Together, we make a dangerous pair, Helene," he finally said, as if reading her thoughts. "I daresay we always have, but we were simply too foolish to recognize that danger."

She turned to stare at him. "What on earth do you mean?"

Cam shrugged his shoulders, and the motion became an uneasy stretch, as if his coat were uncomfortably tight. "I think you know," he said softly, his jaw set at a grim angle. "I'm speaking of us, Helene. We can hardly afford to ignore the effect we have on one another. How mad and irresponsible I still become when I look at you. How wildly passionate you are."

"Oh, for pity's sake, Cam!" Helene narrowed her eyes.

Cam ignored her. "Do you never think about our parents, Helene? How reckless, how volatile, they were?" He exhaled sharply. "Blood runs true, Helene. Perhaps we have been fortunate to escape their fate."

His measured warning and its implicit censure stung Helene. "What drivel," she snapped. Perhaps a wiser woman would have been frightened by the dark emotion in his face, but seized by the very recklessness she had just disowned, Helene's sharp tongue overcame her. "Is that what you truly believe? Indeed, is it the fear of what you might become that so torments you? *Mon Dieu*, Camden! Anyone can see how unhappy you are."

Cam caught her gaze, his eyes hard and glittering. "Have a care, Helene," he answered in a dangerous voice. "I would have peace between us, yes. But Ariane is your only charge. I have no need of your help."

"No small blessing, that," she retorted, lifting her gaze steadily to challenge his. "For I find that your obsessions are exceeded only by your arrogance." Helene sat rigidly, her weight borne back on her arms, her hands flat upon the blanket.

Slowly, the blaze of anger died in Cam's eyes, only to be replaced by what looked like weary resignation. Helene felt a stab of sudden disappointment. Dear heavens! Had she wanted to quarrel with him? Perhaps she had. When they were young, she had sought every opportunity to challenge him, and to goad him beyond restraint. Helene felt a flush of shame.

But Cam had dropped his gaze. "You speak of my obsessions," he said quietly, reaching out with one fingertip to stroke her wrist, "but perhaps you *are* my obsession, Helene. I am, after all, my father's son."

His simple, unexpected caress made her skin quiver with pleasure. Angered by her response, she jerked her hand away. "This conversation is nonsense," she said flatly. "You are no more your father than I am my mother."

"I wish that were true, Helene," he said, his voice as soft as silk. "But with you, I'd soon make my father look like a saint."

Helene forced herself to look away again. Had he been his father—or any other man, come to that—she would have considered such a comment little more than flirtatious repartee. But Cam's words had the ring of a confession. She fought the urge to reach out to him, to quicken to his touch again, and to tell him that he was right; that she *was* reckless and he *was* mad. And that neither circumstance mattered, for she wanted him, and always had.

But she could not touch him. She dared not prove him right. "We are neither of us like our parents, Cam," she softly insisted, perhaps as much to herself as to him. "If I cannot believe that of myself, if I cannot have faith that I am my own person, then I am nothing."

"Admirable words, Helene, but can you not see that you have this way about you . . . ?"

"What *way*—?" she returned.

Cam leaned incrementally closer, and ever so briefly, she ceased to breathe. "Ah, Helene—! You can make a man's blood run wild." He paused to run one hand down his face, then dropped it to the blanket again. "Good God, I do not know what came over me that night. It seems I forgot my daughter's needs—and thought only of my own."

"Cam," she said impatiently, "is it not natural for a man to feel desire? Desire which may test even the most—"

He interrupted as if he had not heard. "Ariane needs you as her governess, while I—" he interjected a bitter laugh, "—have absolutely no business with you as my mistress."

The words stung. But Cam's apology, as well as his confusion, seemed perfectly sincere. Yet inexplicably, she was hurt by his explanation. How foolish. What had she wanted him to say? Abruptly, Helene jerked her pelisse tighter to her chest. "You have apologized, my lord. Let us drop the matter."

He obviously noted her return to formality. "I—yes, of course." His gaze held hers, wary and uncertain. "But there is just one more thing which I must ask. Something of utmost importance."

Helene stared. "By all means," she replied coolly.

Cam swallowed uncomfortably. "Just this, Helene. Please keep your distance from Bentley. I am warning you. It is for the best."

"Warning me—?" she echoed. Helene forced herself to stare down at the riverbank, her eyes never leaving Ariane as the child continued in her play. Anger, followed fast by a cold panic, spread through her chest. Her heart began to pound.

Had Bentley said something? Had a servant seen her in his embrace? It was a governess's worst nightmare, and one's innocence in such circumstances accounted for little. She drew a sharp breath and set her shoulders rigidly. "What, precisely, are you saying?"

Cam exhaled on a hiss. "My brother is young, Helene, despite the fact that he looks to be five-and-twenty. Moreover, he is exceedingly foolish. A woman like you is far too much temptation for such a . . . a . . ."

"For such a what, Cam?" she bit out, suddenly angry again. Damn it, she had done nothing wrong! "Do you imagine your brother to be some sort of innocent? Indeed, I can scarce imagine him a neophyte to the ways of iniquity and vice. Nonetheless, you may rest assured that I shall resist all temptation to initiate him."

"Helene," he growled impatiently, his hand lashing out to capture her wrist. "You willfully choose to misunderstand me. I know my brother. I just give you fair warning; keep your distance."

Abruptly, Helene jerked to her feet. "I begin to understand you, Cam," she said, staring coldly down at him. "But no matter what you may think me, I have no interest in being seduced by a mere boy. Nor by anyone else."

Cam bristled. "I think I learnt that lesson well enough two nights past, Helene," he said grimly. "And I did not suggest you have designs on my brother. But Bentley is rather less principled."

Helene laughed bitterly. "I fancy I know how to handle randy young bucks," she retorted, her voice brittle. "I learnt it in hard school, for I had little choice."

"Then I am glad to hear it," he rasped, moving swiftly to his feet to lace one hand tightly about her arm. He pulled her closer to him. "And I hope I may conclude, then, that you can manage to keep the good rector from swooning at your feet?"

"The *rector—?*" Helene yanked her arm from his grip.

Cam still leaned into her. "I know damned well Lowe means to call on you again," he said darkly. "I think the fool is besotted. And he sent you a gift this morning. I saw the footman bring it."

Helene sucked in her breath sharply. "*Ma foi,* Camden!" One hand balled into a tight fist. "My choice of friends is not your concern. Not unless it affects my work. And it does not, does it?"

Cam glowered. "No."

"And it shan't," she sharply retorted. "You are Lowe's benefactor, for pity's sake! He merely wishes me to befriend his sister. And I rather think your energies would be better spent in improving your relationship with your brother."

Cam looked as dark as a thunderhead. "On *my* relationship with Bentley?"

"Dear heavens, Cam!" Helene touched her fingertips to her temples, her headache pounding now. "Can you not see that the boy needs your help? Why do you think he behaves so wickedly?"

"Perhaps because he *is* wicked. God knows he got it honestly. Now sit down, Helene. Ariane is watching." He tugged roughly on her arm and, to her own surprise, Helene sat obediently back down on the blanket.

Cam was right, of course. It wouldn't do for Ariane to see them quarreling. But if she were honest, she would admit that she felt far more vibrant, far more alive, when she and Cam sparred.

"Please, Cam," she finally said. "What your father was has nothing to do with who you and Bentley are. Yet you assume the worst of him. Must you assume the worst of me as well?" She extended one hand to touch him plaintively, then feeling the tension and strength in his arm, sharply drew it back.

10

In which Lord Treyhern throws Caution to the wind

As the heat of her fingers slid away from his forearm, Cam ceased to hear Helene's words, despite the fact that her eyes kept flashing and her lips kept moving. He wanted to explain to Helene that she had misunderstood; that he knew precisely what his young rakehell of a brother wanted from her, because he wanted it, too.

A part of him wished to lash out at her, to tell her that it was she for whom he worried. Helene's good intentions might not protect her from Bentley's clever seduction. Yet, to his utter exasperation, Helene was still raving, talking on and on about brotherly love, and virtue, and understanding.

Inexplicably, he wanted to grab her, and kiss her mouth until she shut up. He wanted to lace his fingers around the long, pale column of her neck, force up her chin with the strength of his thumbs, and silence her in another way altogether. With his hard mouth, and with his . . . *oh, good God, what was wrong with him?*

He had brought Helene here with every intention of apologizing. Yet in the course of fifteen minutes, they had proceeded to quarrel again—not once, but two or three times. He'd literally lost count. And now, watching her luscious mouth and flashing eyes, and feeling his own breath grow shallow, the only clear intention he seemed to be furthering was not in his head, but between his legs.

Dear heaven, the awful truth was that Cam could not bear the thought of his brother—nor of any other man—touching Helene. And now, despite his anger and concern, Cam throbbed with an urgent need to push her down into the rough grass, shove up her skirts, and rut with her in broad daylight like an animal.

He dropped his head with shame and forced himself to look away from her. Had the past taught him nothing? Had his encounter with Helene two nights past taught him nothing?

No, came the answer. *Absolutely nothing.*

"Does it ever occur to you, Cam, that perhaps you are a little too rigid?"

Rigid? That one word finally broke through his stream of lust and self-loathing. Cam's head jerked up, and he stared at her, momentarily unable to ascertain her meaning. But the woman was still arguing on his brother's behalf. Suddenly, he wanted to snort with disgust. God forbid she learn just how *rigid* he was.

Uneasily, Cam adjusted his coat as Helene droned on in her firm, cool, governess voice. "Indeed, one cannot always be in control of every given situation, Cam. One must often make—"

"Helene!" He interrupted her sharply, his voice sounding hoarse and oddly foreign.

One slender finger elegantly raised, she paused and looked directly at him. "Yes?"

"Could you—would you—be good enough to just . . . hush for a moment?"

Helene frowned as Cam struggled to recapture some thread of their conversation and to ignore the throbbing discomfort between his legs. "But Cam," she protested, "I am just trying to point out to you the simple fact that

Bentley has never known a mother's love. And I rather doubt your father was of any benefit in that regard."

Cam stirred to indignation at that. "What are you saying, Helene? I have always taken care of Bentley, and of Catherine, too. My brother knows that I love him. That I would lay down my life for his, were it necessary."

Helene flashed him a look of aggravation. "All Bentley *knows* is that you want what you think is best for him."

"It would appear, then, that you have spent far more time in Bentley's company than I realized," he said coolly, his discomfort shifting to aggravation. "Indeed, you seem to have formed an opinion of his character inside and out."

Helene's chin came up but she made no comment.

Cam puffed out his cheeks in exasperation, then exhaled slowly. "Very well, Helene. What would you have me do? Are you suggesting that I permit Bentley to run roughshod over the countryside, making love to whomever he chooses? Doing naught with his life?"

"No, I just think—"

"And gaming away his allowance?" interjected Cam. "Good God, Helene! He is not yet eighteen."

Helene folded her arms over her chest. "What I am suggesting, Cam, is that you show Bentley that you love him. Does anyone ever listen to him? Can you not give him the benefit of your ear rather than the razor's edge of your tongue? Eventually you must admit that you simply cannot control Bentley, and everything around you."

"Yes, so you have said," he answered, in a clipped tone.

"Control and love are not the same, my lord," she answered.

"I collect that you mean to lecture me, Helene," he said, glowering at her. "But little matter how lacking in sense you think me, recollect that I am not your student."

An angry silence followed, until suddenly, Cam

leaned toward her and covered her hand with his, holding it fast to the blanket. "Oh, for pity's sake, Helene, let us not quarrel! We must work together, you and I, for Ariane's benefit."

Helene suppressed a shiver of awareness as the warmth of Cam's grip spread across her hand, to run up her arm, and become an insidious, traitorous heat. Reluctantly, she slid her fingers from beneath his. "I— yes, you are right."

They fell silent again. Cam's eyes still held an odd expression, but when he finally spoke, his voice was considerably softer. "I brought you here to ask your forgiveness, Helene. And I've tried. Now, I should like to talk about Ariane. How do things go on between you?" There was no animosity in his voice or expression now.

"It goes well, I think," she answered, grateful for his effort at conciliation. She forced away her frustrations over Bentley, and spent the next quarter-hour explaining her initial assessment of Ariane. Cam raised several important points, and did not hesitate to question the things he did not understand. Clearly, he was determined to give his child every opportunity. Finally, Helene laid out her plan for using drawing, painting, and music as a means of emotional expression. And soon, she hoped to initiate rudimentary lessons in counting and lettering.

At last, he seemed satisfied. "I must admit," he said slowly, "that Ariane seems to have taken to you quite easily."

Helene forced a weak smile. "She was a bit ill-at-ease after you left yesterday, but Ariane is a bright, delightful child."

"Then you are the first governess to have said so," he answered grimly.

"Oh, do not lose hope, my lord! Perhaps Ariane cannot be taught by conventional means. Not yet. But I begin to feel more confident of her aptitude. By the time I am gone, I have every hope that she will have learned at least some sort of communication skills."

"By the time you are gone, Helene?" he echoed, his brows snapping together. "But Ariane shall require a governess until she leaves the schoolroom."

Helene shook her head. "Oh, I thought you understood . . ." she weakly began. "It is true that Ariane will need a teacher for some time. But not the sort I am. If Ariane improves, you'll have no need to pay my exorbitant salary. A regular governess will suffice."

"How long?" he asked, in a voice that was oddly constrained. "How long will I—will she—need you?"

Perplexed, Helene studied him for a moment. "It is hard to know. A year? Perhaps two? I have never stayed longer in any position."

Cam shook his head as if to argue with her. "I cannot pretend to understand you, Helene . . . all this moving about. Do you not wish to settle? Do you not wish for a life of your own?"

Helene regarded him sardonically. "A governess does not *settle,* Cam. And she has no life. Not of the type which you mean." She failed to suppress a soft sigh. "I find this hard to explain. Let us speak of something else. Let us talk of happier times."

"Happier times," he repeated, holding her gaze for a long moment. "Do you know, I think that my happiest times were spent with you, Helene. And yet, to confess that one derived such pleasure from indolence and mischief can hardly be admirable."

Helene laughed unsteadily. Cam's quiet confession shook her far more than she wanted him to know. "But we were so young, Cam. And life at any age is to be savored. A little indolence and mischief can be a good thing."

"They are luxuries I can ill afford." His tone was quietly certain.

"You are not your father, Cam," she repeated, softening her voice. "I believe we have ridden over this ground before."

"I pray you are right, Helene, for my father was a profligate care-for-nobody." He smiled at her grimly. "But you always knew that, did you not? Even at a tender age—in the midst of those happy times of which you so nonchalantly speak—you were wise in the ways of the world. I thought it horribly improper that one so young could know so much. Yet I envied you all the same," he said softly.

Slowly, it was as if the last remnants of tension between them melted quietly away, leaving the space beneath the tree charged with a warm intimacy, a feeling that transcended sensual awareness. Her gaze caught his, and the sounds of the birds and the water faded away. It felt as if that ethereal, abiding friendship which she and Cam had once shared had been resurrected, at least in this timeless moment.

She felt inexplicably unconstrained, as if she were a rash young girl again. "Did I corrupt you, Cam?" she softly teased, her own face growing warm. "I confess, I often meant to do so. I was very bad, was I not? And you! You were so perfect, so implacable. So exceedingly tempting. In fact, I almost had your innocence, and you mine. And you are right about one thing—we did not understand the risk."

Cam blushed furiously, then burst into sudden laughter. "Oh, God," he said on a choked moan. His head fell forward against his knee, even as his hand came out to cover hers where it lay on the blanket. "Do you know, Helene, that my father never let me forget that incident? For a time, I collect, it even gave him hope. Until then, I had been something of a disappointment. Indeed, it seemed I never pleased either of my parents."

"What do you mean, Cam?"

He lifted up his head to stare at her, his clear, dark

eyes filled with an enigmatic mix of hurt and humor. "You undoubtedly heard the rumors at Chalcote, Helene," he answered, his mouth quirking up at one corner. "It seems I simply looked too much like a Rutledge to suit my mother, and possessed too much Camden restraint to suit my father."

"But your mother loved you dearly, Cam. Everyone said so."

"Did she?" He shook his head almost imperceptibly, as if mystified by his own question. "I am no longer certain. I think Mother *needed* me."

"Of course she did," said Helene gently. "You were her child."

"I was her hope," said Cam flatly. "She was overcome with fear for the future of her children, and for her home. You can have no notion of what such a woman is like."

Helene laughed without bitterness. "Oh, Cam, how wrong you are! My mother was the very same, after a fashion."

"Your mother?" Cam shot her a warm, but nonetheless skeptical, smile. "Marie Middleton was bold as brass."

"Ah, such was the impression she sought to give! But in truth, *Maman* was always desperately searching for her next husband, her next lover. Could you not see that, Cam? Could you not see that she flitted from man to man out of insecurity?"

Clearly pondering her words, Cam plucked a long blade of grass and absently stuck it between his teeth. "Do you think so?"

"Oh, Cam!" Helene gave a brittle laugh. "A silver hair, the tiniest wrinkle . . . anything could cast her into gloom because, like your mother, she was insecure. As a girl, I swore I would not be like her."

"And so you chose a profession."

"Just so," she answered firmly. "And when my looks fade, I shall be none the worse for it. Indeed, I daresay I shall be better off."

Cam chuckled softly, stretched back onto one elbow, and chewed on his blade of grass. "Your sort of looks will never fade, Helene," he mused with utter candor. "Nor your determination. Do you know, it has so often seemed to me that you need no one. You are strong. A pity my mother was not."

Helene wanted to tell him that she was not strong, she was weak. And growing weaker with every passing day spent near him. But that simply would not do. "Your mother did love you, Cam," she answered instead. "I am sure she must have done."

He nodded slowly. "Perhaps. But even as a child, I was destined to be savior of this family. Not a day passed but what she did not point out to me the bitter fruit of my father's ways. It was a lesson I must learn, I was told. We were always perched upon the brink of ruin, she said. And I was her only hope; I would someday be responsible, not only for her welfare, but for Catherine's and Bentley's as well."

"That was a rather cruel thing to do to a young boy."

"I cannot think she meant to be cruel," answered Cam thoughtfully. "Indeed, I was the center of her life. And I learnt her lessons well. She made certain of it."

"Yes," said Helene softly, careful not to sound accusatory. "But I am not perfectly sure, Cam, that that was healthy."

"Perhaps it had to be done, Helene," he said simply. "Someone had to take care of Bentley and Catherine. You know what Father was like."

Helene shifted her legs uncomfortably, keeping them carefully tucked beneath her hems, reluctant to disturb the harmony between them. And yet, she would never agree that what Mrs. Rutledge had done to her eldest son was just, or even necessary. Therefore, it was best to change the subject.

"That reminds me, Cam," she said in a smooth, light tone. "Did I understand aright from Bentley that Catherine married one of Squire Wodeway's sons? I was rather taken aback. Is it true?"

"True enough," he answered, shooting her a teasing, sideways grin, the solemnity of the moment broken. "She married on her eighteenth birthday. To Wodeway's second. I daresay you remember him rather well, do you not?"

Helene laughed, her face flooding with warmth. "Oh, lud! Not William? That rather impudent rascal with the thatch of bright red hair?"

"Oh, aye, the very same. And a big rascal, too, I'll thank you to remember."

"I remember Will well enough," Helene admitted cautiously. "And I recall, too, that you bloodied his nose once in the middle of the village green."

"Defending your honor, ma'am, if you will recollect."

Warm memories washed over Cam as he watched Helene blush a deep, beautiful shade of pink. "Were you?" she said, with a demure innocence he knew damned well was feigned. "I do not perfectly remember. What had I done?"

"Oh ho, Helene!" He grinned again. "You shake the hand of blame easily enough, do you not? Yes, the trouble was—as usual—all your fault."

"What?" She blinked naively.

"Insufferable hoyden! You picked a nasty quarrel with young Freddie Wodeway, then pushed him into some horse dung in the stable alley."

Helene laughed. "I don't think I believe you."

"You may well believe me! You did it, right enough. And then, in order to escape the consequences of your action"—Cam squinted his eyes as if in thought—

"which, if memory serves, involved some overripe fruit and a rather good aim—you were compelled to scramble up a tree in the village square, thereby exposing your, ah, undergarments to all and sundry below."

Helene looked appropriately horrified. "And what was William's role in all this?"

"Ah, well!" Cam grinned shamelessly. "As to that, old Will simply had the bad judgment to look up your skirts, so that he might describe in lurid detail just what he saw—the rows of lace, that sort of thing—and all in an overloud voice. Of course," Cam added, his grin broadening, "I was compelled to plant him a facer for such ungentlemanly conduct."

She laughed again, a rich, musical sound, and Cam shook his head in amazement. "I often think, Helene, that it is a wonder I survived our friendship with nothing broken save my foolish young heart." Deliberately, Cam kept his words and expression light.

Slowly, the smile slipped from Helene's face and she studied him with an unreadable expression. "You were ever the gentleman, my lord," she murmured. "And I was a troublesome girl. Hardly worthy of such a champion."

Suddenly, she rose to her feet in one smooth, graceful motion. Cam could sense that this time, there would be no stopping her. She was leaving. His half-hour of basking in the paradise of Helene's company was over.

"You must excuse me now," she murmured, pulling close her black velvet pelisse. "I . . . I think I should go down to Ariane."

With a sudden, hot ache in his chest, Cam watched Helene turn away from him to stroll down the gentle slope toward his daughter. She moved with a fine, fluid elegance; the skirts of her deep burgundy carriage dress swaying gracefully from side to side, brushing the stubbled grass as she picked her way down the path toward the water. It was like watching a blood-red sunset in winter, and knowing full well that with the falling darkness, the cold would come.

Overhead, the bare branches clattered nakedly in the breeze. On a sharp exhalation, Cam took up his hastily discarded hat and slapped it back on his head. Had he allowed matters—as well as his feelings—to go beyond what was prudent?

He had owed her an apology for hurting her, but not for making love to her, since they'd both been willing enough. Yet in making his amends, had he allowed himself to be drawn toward an inappropriate level of intimacy? It seemed beyond his ability to treat Helene as nothing more than his employee. Perhaps it was time he accepted the fact that Helene would always be more than that to him; that he would never be able to gird himself against the choking rush of need and tenderness and chaos that her very name evoked.

And now, Helene had spoken of leaving Chalcote. Her casual remark had left him reeling. But why should it have? What had he believed would happen? Had he imagined that Helene would stay forever? That after educating Ariane, Helene would simply hang about, educating the children that he and Joan were expected to bear? His blood ran cold at that thought.

No. It was impossible. And the thought of Helene's leaving was inconceivable. Almost as inconceivable as the idea that he might wed Joan. The whole damned mess suddenly seemed preposterous. And yet, he was all but engaged to the girl. There was an understanding. Joan's father was dead. It was his duty to care for her. There really was no turning back.

Was there?

Good God, there had to be.

His future loomed up before him, a nebulous, stifling haze. Had it been but a few days past that he had seen so clearly the path he was to take through life? Now, in increments so minute that Cam had failed to notice, that straight and narrow path was bending, dipping down into a wide, uncertain route, and leading into a turn he could no longer see beyond. Indeed, he was no longer sure that the course he traveled was even his to choose.

Such uncertainty should have made him uneasy. And it did. But for the first time in a very long while, Cam felt an odd stirring of . . . intrigue. He felt suddenly curious about life, and about the potential it might hold. And with Helene he felt something else, too. Not just confusion, not just exasperation, but a great deal more than lust. Something which felt vaguely akin to exhilaration.

Damn it, *he felt alive*. Perhaps dangerously so.

Cam stared blindly down the hill toward the scene unfolding on the riverbank. He barely noticed that Ariane was now determinedly tugging at what looked to be a long piece of vine which hung from an ancient oak by the water's edge. The old tree had grown at an odd angle, leaning precariously forward, as if it might topple into the current at a moment's notice.

As Ariane tried to pull the vine away from its bark, Helene drew up beside her, and laid a hand lightly on the girl's narrow shoulder. Rather than pulling away from the caress, Ariane smiled up at Helene, and Cam's hot ache melted into an old and nameless longing that lay deep and heavy in the pit of his belly.

From his position on the hill, Cam could not hear Helene's words, but as Ariane held one end of the vine, he absently watched while Helene began to pluck away the tendrils of red-brown creeper which lashed it to the tree trunk. Carried on the light breeze, Helene's musical laughter drew him from the depths of his introspection, and too late, Cam realized what Ariane had discovered.

They were untangling Helene's old rope swing!

It had to be! But surely it would have long since rotted

away? Nonetheless, he remembered that long ago summer's day when Helene had persuaded him to pilfer a brand new length of rope from the stable. A small enough sin, as moral transgressions went. But by the time Helene had finished with him, Cam had been left to guiltily toss and turn in his bed for a fortnight.

Helene had conceived of the scheme on a scorching August afternoon in the midst of one of his father's infamous week-long house parties. For her part in the conspiracy, Helene had stolen a sturdy piece of hickory planking from Mrs. Naffles' kindling box. And with the help of an old wood chisel—purloined, of course, from one of the estate shops—they had fashioned the makeshift rope swing and hiked off toward the riverbank.

Tasked with hanging the swing, Cam had carefully knotted the rope every two feet, then shinnied up and out the thickest branch to secure it. Then Helene had deftly tied the strip of notched wood at the bottom to brace their feet on. After testing the rope's soundness by repeatedly swinging high out over the water, they had accounted the swing a grand success.

By then, however, they were hot and weary from their efforts. When Helene slipped into the bushes for a moment of privacy, Cam had thought nothing of it . . . until she darted back out again moments later, stripped to her chemise.

At the staid old age of sixteen, Cam had been aghast at—and entranced by—the sight of her. In defiance of all propriety, Helene had seized the rope and sailed over the water again. But this time, she'd simply dropped from the height of its arc, and into the middle of the Coln.

Cam could still hear her shriek of glee, and see her trim ankles flailing beneath her chemise as she broke through the glistening surface, then disappeared into the depths. At that point in the river, the remnants of an old dam farther downstream slowed the current so that the water ran languid and cool. After a quarter-hour of wheedling, Helene finally goaded Cam into joining her. And it had been beyond wonderful.

Helene had been a rough-and-tumble sort of girl, and together they had cavorted like fish, only to emerge with the inevitably immodest consequences. The water had rendered Helene's shift all but transparent. The thin cotton clung to her every turn, revealing her rosy, puckered nipples, and the dainty curves of her incipient breasts and hips. Cam, who at the sight of her was suddenly beset by his own physical problems, had faired a little better with his long shirttails and drawers.

Helene had simply laughed, and made a sport of their appearance. But to Cam, it had been a serious matter indeed. In his awkward, adolescent way, he had suddenly longed to seize Helene. To push her down into the fragrant grass of the riverbank, to kiss her laughing mouth, and to do much, much more.

Cam had suffered from no lack of enlightenment with regard to the specifics of the sex act. His experience on the farm—never mind his exposure to his father's ribald habits—had ensured a rather comprehensive education. And so despite his youth, Cam had known exactly what it was that he had wished to do to Helene. And the iniquity of his desire had shamed him to the very depths of his soul. It had not seemed decent, somehow, to want to do such things to your best friend.

He and Helene were no longer best friends, but it seemed that little else had changed. Even now—watching her stretch high above her head to yank free the rope, gazing at the swell of her breasts, reveling in the sound of her laughter—Cam could feel that old hunger surge forth.

He watched the graceful turn of her face as she smiled down at his daughter, and his pulse began to race. The blood in his veins seemed to thicken and slow to a heavy throb. The fading afternoon light caught their hair, warming Helene's dark tresses and shimmering over Ariane's blonde braids, like the lovely contrast of sunlight and moonlight. Together, they reminded him of an artist's rendition of—

Damnation!

As he watched Helene draw back the rope, he realized just what she was about. "No!" he shouted aloud. "No, Helene! Don't even *think* about it—!" Paternalistic arrogance exploded, obliterating his lust. And then, Cam was hurtling down the hill before his brain could assimilate what his feet were doing.

Damn and blast! Helene was *not* going to swing out over the river on that bloody rope! Had he not always known she was mad? Good God, she would kill herself. Or Ariane. Possibly even himself before it was over with, if he knew Helene.

In a matter of seconds, he reached them. Shock registered on Helene's face as he jerked the rope from her grasp. Her foot slipped abruptly off the wooden slat as her mouth went slack with amazement.

"Good Lord, Helene!" he fairly shouted. "Have you no sense? That rope has surely rotted by now."

An indulgent smile played at one corner of Helene's mouth. She stepped back, delicately pointing one finger at the wood. "If you'll but look more closely, my lord, you'll see that both the wood and the rope are somewhat newer than you or I might imagine."

Shaking with a fear-born rage, he ignored her. "But it is not safe, Helene! Must you always be so reckless? Next, you will have Ariane swinging on the bloody thing! I'll not have either of you on it, do you hear?"

"Indeed, my lord." She humbly lowered her gaze. "We'll do as you say."

"Because I said so, that's why n—" Abruptly, he halted in mid-tirade.

Suddenly, Cam realized that he had expected Helene to argue, or to cajole him into some sort of mischief. But the woman who stood before him acted every inch the obedient governess. Perversely, her subservience made Cam suspicious. He let the rope drop from his hands to spin freely through the air. "I apologize for shouting, Miss de Severs. I'm relieved it was not necessary."

"Your concern is reassuring, sir," she responded, her tone almost laughably demure.

She still came as a shock to him, this new Helene. The hoyden he'd once known would have boxed his ears and shoved him into the river by now. But the new Helene was still speaking in her soothing governess voice. "However, if you will but inspect the rope and test the strength of the wood—as I was just in the process of doing—you will see it is in rather good condition. I fancy someone has replaced it since we . . . er, since you would last have had occasion to use it."

Cam saw what she was up to. "I do not give a damn, Helene, if it is a newly forged chain strung up just this morning by my very own blacksmith. It is unsafe for Ariane. And it is unsafe for you."

The sudden rustling of Ariane's skirts in the grass snared Cam's attention. Standing beside Helene, his daughter crossed her arms and fashioned her lips into an uncharacteristically sulky pout which she immediately focused on her father with every intended effect.

Good Lord, what a telling expression! Despite Ariane's silence and Helene's outward obedience, Cam felt beset on all sides by cunning females. But honest to a fault, Cam forced himself to consider Helene's arguments. At once, a shadowy fate loomed up before him.

Something unpleasant—and wholly reckless—was going to happen. Like a change in the weather, or the hum before a lightning strike, Cam could sense it. Ariane's lip came out another fraction. Helene's toe began to tap.

Impatiently, Cam reached out and retrieved the rope, sliding his glove down its length. "Well, perhaps . . . yes, it is relatively new, I'll grant you that much."

Ariane's pout began to recede.

"Indeed," added Helene. "And the wood looks strong enough—"

"Strong enough?" protested Cam, watching the rope slide back and forth through his hands. "Strong enough for what?" The idea of a lynching came suddenly to his mind, only to be quickly replaced by an enhanced—and far more erotic—version of his Helene-in-black-leather fantasy.

Bloody hell! He snapped his head up, dropping the rope as if it were a snake. "Strong enough for what?" he repeated, as Ariane caught the spinning slat of wood in her hand.

"Well . . . strong enough to swing on," admitted Helene.

"Helene—!" Cam set his hands on his hips. "You are going to drive me mad. One of you could be hurt. Even drowned. That rope might snap, and that would be the end of you."

"With all due respect, my lord," said Helene soothingly, "the water is neither deep enough nor swift enough for a drowning. Unpleasantly cold, yes. One would hardly wish to swim in it, unless the weather was absolutely sultry. But could one drown? I fancy not."

Cam could have sworn—absolutely sworn—that Helene de Severs winked at him. But her face remained as serene as an angel's. He forced himself to ignore it. "Ariane cannot swim," he stated bluntly.

"Can she not?" asked Helene archly.

"No."

"Then one of us must teach her when the weather warms." Helene patted Ariane's shoulder and smiled tightly. "However, I swim exceedingly well. And I seem to recall the same of you. So in the unlikely event she should fall, one of us must simply fish her out."

The feeling of doom drew nearer, but with it came a little rush of excitement. "Yes, well . . . what if it scares her to swing so far over the water?"

Helene gave her careless Gallic shrug. "*Mais oui,* it will scare her! Is that not the very idea of the thing?"

Ariane had begun to bounce up and down on her toes. She seemed perfectly willing—almost eager—to be drowned. Fighting back temptation, Cam shook his head. "She could catch a chill if she gets wet. Or she might get rope burns."

Helene shrugged again. Cam was beginning to find the gesture annoying. "Well, for my part," she remarked with a mischievous grin, "I should prefer to die of something other than boredom."

"Dead is dead, Miss de Severs." But God help him, he was beginning to see her logic. Damn it, when Helene was around, the imprudent began to sound strangely rational.

"Ah—! But to experience true *joie de vivre* ere one's death, Lord Treyhern!" Suddenly, Helene laughed, and whirled about in a circle, snapping her fingers in the air like a gypsy dancer. "That is the secret, *n'est-ce pas?* Come!" She clapped her hands high above her head. "Be spontaneous! Be reckless!" Impudence danced in her dark blue eyes.

Damn her, she dared him. She always did.

Obviously, the new Helene could not long repress the exuberance of the old. Yet her enthusiasm was contagious, and in the face of such a challenge, Cam felt his resolve slip.

Lord, to be sixteen again! What would it feel like? To be blindingly happy and free, just for a few fleeting seconds? To swing across that glistening stretch of water with no earthly ties? It seemed so foolish. It seemed so—*fun.*

Ariane must have sensed his surrender. The lip retracted, and her face lit up like a Vauxhall lantern.

"Oh, very well!" he groused, stripping off his driving gloves and slapping them into Helene's open palm. "Give me the bloody rope."

After yanking hard on the swing, then testing it with his full weight, Cam dragged it up the embankment, then turned to face the water. *What in God's name was he about?* he wondered, staring down at the sight below. He must look an utter fool, standing atop this bank, and clutching a rope swing in one hand. But the shimmering water beckoned, while on the riverbank beneath him, Helene and Ariane gazed expectantly upward, their faces alight with anticipation.

Well? What choice had he?

In the face of Helene's argument, he had begun to feel like a caviling spoilsport, while she, as usual, had begun to sound like the voice of reason. And temptation. Now that he had succumbed to their pleas, however, it would be the height of irresponsibility to permit anyone to use the bloody contraption without his having tested it himself. Indeed, if it could bear the burden of his hulking fifteen stone, he had to admit that it could safely carry either of them, or both.

His hat and gloves already dispensed with, Cam toyed with the idea of yanking off his topboots, on the off chance that the rope might snap and drop him into the depths of the Coln. Deciding he could better grip the slat while shod, however, he left them on. Planting his left foot solidly on the left half of the wood, Cam shoved off hard with his right.

And then he was soaring, and soaring . . . into a rush of cool, clean infinity.

The green sward of the embankment, the spread of the oak, and finally the sun-dappled water, rushed toward him, then shimmered beneath his feet as he swung out,

out, and up into the height of the pendulum. All of nature flew past, borne on the autumn air which whistled past his ears. As the swing pulled tight into the apex of its arc, the rope groaned and the tree rattled, its near-skeletal branches clattering like dry bones.

And then, for one infinitesimal moment, Cam stopped—suspended in time and space—as the rope yanked taut against the branch.

Surging in on a wave of exhilaration, old instincts flooded back. Cam grinned, then pitched his weight deftly to one side, sending the swing into a wild twirl. As he turned, he caught a whirling glimpse of Ariane on the shore, hands pressed to her pink cheeks, mouth open wide with silent laughter. And then, the decent began in earnest.

Cam skimmed back across the water, the wind flying through his hair, tugging at his coattails, and playing havoc with what had once been a neatly tied cravat. Helene, Ariane, and the steep green climb of the embankment rushed up to meet him, and Cam threw up his hands, leapt gracefully from the swing, and—missed his step.

Tumbling awkwardly onto his back on the leaf-strewn riverbank, Cam finally managed to right himself, sitting up with a laugh just as Ariane launched herself into his arms, taking him back down again. Helene was smiling, too, as she came down to kneel in the grass beside him. Gracefully, she bent forward to pick a leaf from his hair, and Cam caught her gaze.

"Well done," she said softly.

Her eyes were laughing, yes. But they were veiled and introspective, too. Very definitely introspective. But it had been enough, this sweet, timeless moment of lighthearted intimacy. It was more than enough. Helene's smile, and Ariane's silent mirth, made it all worthwhile. And damn propriety to hell—it *had* been fun!

They spent another hour in their merry diversions by the river, swinging on the rope and cavorting in the grass. And when at last it was time to roll up their blanket and return to Chalcote, an inner peace had settled over Helene. Cam was happy, too. She could see it. And despite the harsh words which had passed between them earlier in the day, she took great pleasure in his joy.

It felt as if they had turned a corner in their strained relationship. Perhaps a few old ghosts had been laid to rest. Perhaps she and Cam could be friends again. The thought warmed her, even as she longed for more.

Once upon a time, Helene had been a dreamer. And now, she foolishly found herself wanting her dreams back. Oh, she might devote her remaining years to the care of other people's children—and do infinite good in the process. But they would never take the place of the children she'd once dreamt of having with Camden Rutledge.

Briefly, she reconsidered Cam's offer to make her his mistress. But it was a very brief consideration indeed. She wanted him, yes. But not on the terms he had offered. And not at the expense of her reputation and career.

11

A bitter homecoming, and a grievous truth

Over the next fortnight, Ariane thought a great deal about what she had seen by the river. Not just the swinging part, though it had been fun flying through the air with Papa's tight, strong arms wrapped all around her. What she thought about most, though, was her papa. About how he had looked with Miss Helene.

Some people thought her papa was too stern. *Obstinate,* she'd heard Grandpapa say. *A dull dog,* Uncle Bentley called him. But Ariane did not think he seemed very dull when Miss Helene was around. And obstinate—well, Ariane was not sure what that meant, but Grandpapa had made it sound bad. So she was pretty sure he wasn't really that, either.

Anyway, Papa looked altogether different nowadays. His face changed all the time. Sometimes he looked cross. Sometimes happy. Sometimes fretful. But always, he looked at Miss Helene.

Usually, Ariane got all Papa's attention. But somehow, she did not mind sharing just a bit. Every day, Ariane went to the schoolroom with Miss Helene. Most days, her papa came, too. At least for a while.

Sometimes, he just stuck his head in the door when

lessons were over, to ask them to walk in the gardens or to go for a drive or to join him for tea. Sometimes the yellow-haired girls came with the rector. But then Papa would just go into his study and shut the door. Ariane knew what he was doing. He was hiding. Ariane did not hide anymore. Well, not much.

In the schoolroom, they were doing something called *counting*. Ariane wasn't exactly sure what counting was. But it seemed to involve little piles of beans and buttons. Two beans and two buttons together was called *four*. It certainly did not seem very hard. But Ariane had not yet decided if she would play the game called counting. It might be best not to. It would just lead to questions as it always did. And Ariane knew answers were supposed to follow questions. That was why she just pretended not to understand.

Oh, it was all very hard! Sometimes, *she* wanted to ask some questions for a change. Sometimes she got tired of being quiet and pretending to be stupid. These days, there seemed to be a lot of things she would like to know. She would like to know if Papa was going to marry Miss Helene. She had heard Crane tell Mrs. Naffles that that was what ought to have happened a long time ago "if people hadn't meddled in things they'd not understood."

Well, Ariane didn't understand much either. But if Papa did marry, would Ariane have a new mama? Because you had to do what your mother said. Didn't you? If a new mother told you something different from your first mother, what were you supposed to do? Talk? Or not talk? Ariane was so confused. And soon, it mightn't matter. Because it was getting harder and harder to keep all these questions from bursting right out of her mouth.

After their adventure by the river, Helene found that the days at Chalcote passed almost lazily, one into another, until one morning, Cam asked Helene and

Ariane to ride with him on an errand to the cottage of one of his more distant tenants. It was a fair, sunny day, and Mrs. Naffles had stuffed a basket full of food for the farmer's wife, who had just given birth to twins. The errand, therefore, was a happy one, and the trip back and forth was pleasant.

During their return, the miles sped past. Ariane held Helene's hand as Cam laughed, joked, and at one point, even whistled an Irish jig. When they pulled into the long sweep of the drive, however, Helene noticed an unfamiliar groom in the distance. He was leading a sturdy cob and a prancing, long-legged chestnut toward the stables.

His mood obviously still light, Cam seemed not to notice the servant. Instead, he leapt down and took Ariane by the waist, lifting her from the curricle and spinning her gaily about before lowering her tiny feet to the graveled drive. Helene also climbed down, then lifted her chin to untie the ribbons of her bonnet.

As she did so, a dash of dark color hovering near the entryway caught her eye. Helene looked around to see that a stranger, a young woman, stood just inside Chalcote's Great Hall. Upon seeing Cam, the woman's face lit with pleasure, and Helene suffered a prick of foolish jealousy.

At once, the woman stepped down from the threshold, moving toward them with quick, bouncing strides. Dressed in an old-fashioned riding habit of gray serge trimmed in black, the young woman wore a rather shabby black hat perched crookedly atop an unruly arrangement of glossy brown curls. A warm smile seemed to spread across the whole of her face.

"Ariane!" she cried, and the little girl flew to her, throwing both arms about the lady.

"Old Will thrown you out again, minx?" asked Cam, leaning over Ariane to kiss the young woman soundly on one cheek. He then turned on one heel to face Helene.

"Miss de Severs," he said, "allow me to introduce to you my sister, Lady Catherine Wodeway—"

"—Just Cat," the woman interjected, tearing away from Ariane to extend her hand to Helene. "How do you do, Miss de Severs? It is such a pleasure to meet you."

The jealously receded at once. Catherine's smile was bright, her voice sincere. There was no element of haughtiness or pretense in her handsome, open countenance.

"I am well, I thank you," Helene replied. "And the pleasure is mine." She felt a moment of awkwardness as the long, cool fingers slipped from her own. But Cam's sister gave no sign of recognition, and no hint of disdain.

Helene breathed a sigh of relief. Perhaps it was not surprising that Cam's sister did not recognize her. Helene certainly would never have recognized Catherine, for she'd been quite young at the time of Helene's exile. But in truth, Lady Catherine Wodeway looked very like her siblings, with Cam's high, strong brow and Bentley's full, good-natured smile.

Catherine was fast approaching three-and-twenty, if memory served, and possessed a fresh-faced, traditional sort of beauty. Animated and energetic, she was a long-legged woman, fashioned very much in what Helene thought of as the English country style. One could find them from Sussex to Scotland, these candid, capable women who, with little deference to fashion or vanity, spent their afternoons riding, hunting, or occasionally, even farming. Undoubtedly, the lively chestnut had belonged to Catherine, and Helene did not doubt her more than a match for the horse.

"Have you ridden all the way from Aldhampton, love?" her brother asked, reaching out in a paternal gesture to brush a bit of hay from her sleeve.

Catherine wrinkled her nose. "Yes, and the long way 'round! I had the misfortune to trip over Aunt Belmont in Cheltenham yesterday. She bade me wait upon her for luncheon this afternoon, and of course, I could scarce refuse."

"A wise choice," murmured Cam dryly. "You have, I hope, brought your groom?"

"Rest easy, Saint Cam!" she flashed a saucy grin, and bowed to him in mock decorum. "I think I know what is due my lofty station. Lady Catherine Wodeway! Exalted personage! Pray pardon me whilst I scrape this morning's pig manure from my boots so that your servants may better lick—"

"Don't patronize me, miss!" scolded Cam, flinging one arm loosely about her shoulders. "It's already near dark!"

Lady Catherine merely smiled, and in amiable silence, the four of them strolled across the drive and entered the hall together. It all seemed harmless enough until Cam paused just inside the threshold. "Do you know, I rather doubt the two of you will remember one another," he said, turning to face them. "Cat, Miss de Severs is an old friend to us. Does she not look familiar?"

Catherine looked Helene over quizzically. "Oh, my!" she exclaimed, clapping one hand to her cheek. A half-dozen emotions sketched rapidly across her face, ending with what looked like relief. "*Helene!* Helene Middleton! Oh, I am right, am I not? And how lovely you've become! As pretty as your mama! How glad I am that you've finally come back."

Helene felt her face flush at Catherine's perplexing outburst. "Why, how kind you are," she managed to murmur.

As they crossed the Great Hall, Catherine appeared to forget her niece and brother entirely, and looped her arm around Helene's. "Do you know, Miss de Severs, I was exceedingly fond of your mama. But I have not seen her since I was . . . oh, what? Aged nine or ten, I daresay."

"Mrs. Middleton has passed away, Cat," Cam murmured softly from behind them.

At that, his sister's face fell. "Oh, how sorry I am to hear it," said Catherine kindly. "She always seemed so full of life. As a child, I thought her the most beautiful thing I had ever seen."

"You are most gracious, Lady Catherine, to remember *Maman* so warmly."

Catherine laid her hand lightly upon Helene's shoulder for a moment. "Why, do you know, Miss de Severs, I used to hope we might become sisters. Indeed, I often laid awake at night, wishing that I could have such a pretty creature as my mama." She gave a soft, self-deprecating laugh, and tossed her hand lightly. "Childish fantasies, I know. Still, I hardly remembered my own mother, so I suppose it was only natural?"

"Yes, perfectly natural," answered Helene smoothly, hiding her amazement. Catherine seemed wholly accepting of both her and her notorious mother. Indeed, she had wanted *Maman* as her own? This was a light in which Helene had never viewed her mother.

"Cat," said Cam in a gently warning tone, "perhaps we should not rehash old memories?"

His sister looked affronted. "Why should we not? Mrs. Middleton was a part of Papa's life for rather a long time. And you must admit, Cam, that Papa was a little more—oh, I don't know—more *settled* when she was here."

"Not a day in Father's life passed by in which the word *settled* might be accurately applied to him," answered Cam sardonically. "Shall we go into the parlor, ladies? Milford will bring us a spot of tea or a glass of cider if you will have it."

Helene stepped away from the trio. "Thank you, but I should see Ariane upstairs now."

"Oh, pish!" said Catherine, turning around to look at Cam and Ariane. "You have obviously been at their mercy all day, Miss de Severs. I can tell you that this pair will make a slave of you, should you be fool enough to permit it. Martha—see, there she is now—Martha will take Ariane up. You must have some tea. You must rest."

As Martha swept down the stairs to take up her charge, Cam clasped his hands behind his back and gave a mocking little bow to Helene. A sly smile seemed to lurk in his eyes. "There you have it, Miss de Severs! Her Royal Highness, Queen Catherine, has spoken."

Helene glanced back and forth between them uncertainly. "But I should not wish—"

"Perhaps not!" he smoothly interjected. "Nonetheless, you must. Now, resign yourself to tea, before my Lady Presumption shouts *'off with your head!'*, or orders you to scrape her miry boots. I vow, I hardly know which would be the worse."

A boyish grin flashed across his face as he jumped neatly aside to avoid his sister's flashing elbow. "And Cat!" he cried, turning to face her as if recollecting something important. "I have a task for you."

"Of what sort?" she asked warily.

"A simple matter, really. Milford has warned me, in the sternest, most butlerly terms, that the parlor draperies offend his sensibilities. I've left out the fabric samples the draper sent. Choose what you like."

With a groan of laughter, Catherine patted her brother lightly on the cheek. "I think not, Cam! That's a task best left to Joan. Or better yet, Milford may choose it himself. Lud, I can assure you I have no eye for fripperies."

"Don't be foolish, Cat." Cam looked suddenly ill at ease. "It is just fabric. No more than a half-dozen scraps. Anyone can choose between—"

"Lord Treyhern?" Milford's rather haunting voice echoed through the vast hall behind them and Cam spun smoothly about. In the rectangle of afternoon sunlight that spilt through the still open door, the black-garbed, bloodless butler seemed literally to flutter in the wind which blew in from the front lawns.

"Yes, what is it, Milford?"

"It's Mr. Kelly, my lord. He's just come up from London not five minutes past. I've put him in your study. Mr. Brightsmith has sent some things for your signature. And there is a messenger from Devon, too. I think you'd best make haste."

Catherine turned her back on Milford and her brother. "Well, that's that! Come along, Miss de Severs," she said, taking Helene's arm. "We may as well leave Cam to his business. You shall have tea with me instead. You must tell me about your work with Ariane. And *I* shall tell *you* all the village gossip!"

As Helene murmured her reluctant acquiescence, Catherine turned back to peck her brother's cheek, then whirled about in her worn gray habit to stride toward the parlor. Then abruptly, she halted, and spun back again.

"Oh, Cam? I also came, you know, to discuss the dinner party . . . ?"

"Dinner?" His hands still clasped behind his back, Cam paused, his brow furrowed.

Catherine tapped her toe impatiently. "Oh, Cam! You have not forgotten my birthday? You promised to give my dinner party here at Chalcote this year."

"Ah!" said Cam, obviously mystified. "Indeed! Did you tell Mrs. Naffles?"

"Of course!"

"Then all will be in readiness, I am sure," he answered vaguely.

"But have you sent the cards?" retorted Catherine.

"Cards?" Cam cast an uneasy glance at Milford.

"A fortnight past, my lord," answered the butler.

An expression of relief passed over Cam's face. "There, you see! I have taken care of it."

This sister looked unconvinced. "Well, to whom did you send them?"

Cam hesitated. "Why, to whomever was on your list.

Aunt Belmont, I collect. And, er . . . Joan, of course. The rector and his sister . . ."

"And . . . ?" Catherine's tone was impatient.

"The curate," whispered Milford audibly.

"Ah!" said Cam. "And that curate . . . the quiet fellow. What the devil's his name?"

"Rhoades," intoned the butler. "The Reverend Mr. Rhoades."

"Exactly so! Rhoades. A small group, in keeping with our mourning."

Silently mouthing the names, Catherine began to count on her long fingers. "Well, with Bentley and Will, that shall give us but nine. Oh, Cam! We shall have an odd number at the table." Her pale brow furrowed in thought. "Well, indeed! What a muttonhead I am, Miss de Severs! You must come as well, and not just to make up our number."

Helene demurred politely. "But Lady Catherine—"

"Just Catherine. Or Cat."

Helene smiled. "Catherine, then. You are exceedingly kind, but I fancy—"

"Well, I fancy you shall come," Catherine cut her off. "And it is my birthday. Oh, do say you will," she wheedled, suddenly sounding very much like her younger brother. "Why, I would have put you on my list from the very first, but I did not know you'd arrived!"

As Cam departed with Milford, Helene followed Catherine into the parlor. With the casual grace of one who has lived in a home all of her life—and still accounts it so—Catherine yanked the bell-pull and sent for tea. Apparently, the matter of the birthday dinner was settled as far as Cam's sister was concerned.

Despite the sunny weather, the old stone walls of Chalcote were slow to warm, and Milford had ordered a fire to be laid. The women settled into chairs on either side of the hearth. Catherine pulled off her shabby hat and tossed it onto an adjacent table.

It was obvious that Cam's sister was curious about her, and Helene got the distinct impression that Catherine was the sort of woman who bluntly spoke her mind. As if reading Helene's thoughts, Catherine drew a deep breath. "Well!" she said. "Now you must tell me what you have done with yourself, Helene, since last we saw one another. I collect that you went away to school?" She smiled expectantly.

"Yes, I was three years in Switzerland," replied Helene. She prayed that Catherine knew nothing of her removal from Chalcote. "And afterward, I went to Vienna to teach."

Unexpectedly, Catherine gave her a wry smile. "It must have been lovely to . . . to get away from Chalcote," said Cam's sister pensively. "I have almost no education at all. The schooling of females—nor of males either, come to that—was not a priority for Papa."

Helene was not surprised to hear it. "But you had a governess, did you not?"

Yet as soon as she spoke the words, Helene knew the answer to that tactless question. To the best of her recollection, she had never seen a governess at Chalcote. And no tutor for Cam, other than the local rector, who hadn't darkened the door with any frequency. There had been no one but an ill-tempered nurse, and she had had her hands full chasing after Bentley, who'd been but a toddler.

"No." Catherine shook her head. "No, Papa did not believe in educating women. I was sent to my Aunt Belmont's sometimes, to study with my cousin Joan. But she's four years my junior."

Helene felt a fleeting sense of guilt. Had her mother's bargain with Randolph Rutledge cheated his own children out of a proper education? On a rational level, she knew the answer. Her tuition might have caused Randolph's vintner and haberdasher some inconvenience. But his children would have probably suffered regardless. "Catherine, I am sorry," said Helene quietly.

Catherine blithely tossed her hand. "Oh, it was no great loss, for I can assure you I never harbored any academic inclinations." She smiled, and the act lit up her face, emphasizing her wholesome, fresh-faced beauty, and reminding Helene yet again of Bentley.

"Look!" said Catherine, suddenly darting out of her chair and crossing the room to take up a little pile of cloth. "These must be the draper's samples. I suppose I must choose something." Snagging her lip between her teeth, Catherine settled back into her chair and spread the fabric across the table between them.

It was time to change the subject. For all her sunny demeanor, Catherine was clearly hurt by the recollection of her father's selfishness, and it did not take a student of human nature to discern it.

Collegially, Helene leaned forward to run her finger across one of the swatches. "They are all quite lovely, Catherine. Which will you choose?"

Catherine's wide brown eyes darted uncertainly from one swatch to the next. "Well, it matters little enough," she said dryly, "for Joan will be sure to renounce my taste by making another choice altogether!" She gave a little laugh, devoid of any bitterness. "And do you know, Helene, I daresay she'd be the wiser for it! But tell me, which do you fancy?"

Joan would choose? It was the second such comment Catherine had made. Deliberately stalling for time, Helene took the fabric samples into her lap and spread them one by one across her skirts. What did Joan Belmont have to do with Chalcote? A heavy, cold sensation pressed down upon Helene's heart as she wracked her brain.

She was vaguely aware of the existence of Cam's cousin. Joan was the young daughter of his maternal aunt. Indeed, the family lived nearby. With a hand that trembled slightly, Helene picked up the sample nearest her left knee, a heavy ivory damask overlaid with wide bands of yellow, alternated with red pinstripes.

"Why I . . . I think there is no doubt," Helene finally said, her voice less than steady. "It ought be this one. That is to say, if he means to keep this carpet. If he does, then nothing else shall perfectly match, I'm afraid."

"Oh, just so, ma'am!" intoned a deep, melancholy voice just behind her.

Helene gave a little squeak of surprise, and jerked about in her chair. The remaining samples went slithering onto the rug just as Milford loomed up beside her. How the man had silently slipped through a closed door with a heavy tea tray was beyond her comprehension.

"Put the tray here, Milford," said Catherine quickly, her nerves obviously unaffected. She patted the low table between them.

Smoothly, the butler set down the tray, then knelt beside Helene's chair to gather up the fabric samples, handing them up to her one by one.

"Forgive my impertinence, ma'am," he said, handing up the last swatch, "but your taste is faultless. Indeed, I endeavored to explain to his lordship that the red pinstripe was required with these Turkish carpets . . . but alas, he could not understand."

"Am I to believe he bothered to voice an opinion?" asked Catherine laughingly as she leaned forward to pour. "Pray do not tell me, Milford, that he chose that dreadful shade of orange!" She cast her eyes toward a particularly hideous piece nearest her elbow.

Gloomily, the butler shook his head. "No, my lady. I fear that Lord Treyhern's view was not quite that strongly held. His lordship spread them out, took one glance, then muttered something about being needed in the stables."

Helene, however, barely took in the friendly banter between the butler and Catherine, for she was still trying to make sense of Catherine's remarks about Joan Belmont. As Milford departed, she could not suppress her curiosity. "I am afraid I have not the pleasure of your young cousin's acquaintance, Catherine. Is Miss Belmont often at Chalcote?"

Catherine passed a teacup across the table to Helene. "Not as often as her mother might wish, to be sure!" She flashed her mischievous grin. "But there—! I daresay I am meddling where I have no business."

"Meddling?"

Cam's sister scowled, and dropped her hands into her lap in a rather frustrated gesture. "Oh, I am being unfair, I confess it! But I have just come from my aunt's, and have had quite enough of her subtle hints. If and when my brother chooses to announce his betrothal, it will be all of his own doing, and none of mine, to be sure."

As Helene's hands clutched her tea, she felt her fingers go numb, then cold. Abruptly, she set the saucer down with an awkward clatter. "Do I take it, then, that your brother has formed an . . . an attachment?"

Her high brow creased thoughtfully, Cam's sister shook her head. "No, I fancy there is little attachment on my brother's part, but . . . there is a very strong expectation. A match between Cam and a Belmont cousin was my late mother's wish, one her sister has fervently resurrected." Delicately, Catherine selected a cucumber sandwich from the silver tray. "And I must say," she mused, absently studying the morsel, "Cam has thus far seemed amenable to the scheme."

"Oh?" asked Helene weakly. "Then Miss Belmont must be all that one could wish for in a wife."

Catherine nodded vaguely and swallowed a nibble of her sandwich. "Oh, I suppose. She's pretty, of course, and very well brought up. Her late father was descended from noble blood on both sides, a circumstance of which my aunt is ever fond of reminding us. And I daresay my brother does need a wife, for he has no heir save Bentley, who has no interest in estate matters. Moreover, Aunt Belmont is forever warning Cam not to repeat the mistake of what she so haughtily calls *'marrying beneath his station'!*"

"Beneath his . . . station?"

"Oh, indeed," said Cam's sister. "Joan was still in the schoolroom, you see, when Cam found it—well, *necessary* to marry the first time. Cassandra's family was in trade, but exceedingly rich. At the time, Aunt Belmont's nose was only slightly out of joint over the match, for Cam wasn't much of a catch then." Catherine shrugged equivocally. "We were all drowning in the River Tick, you understand. There was no guarantee of a title, and Papa was always embarrassing us with one scandal or another."

"But now things are different."

"Ah, indeed they are!" Catherine set down her cup with a clatter and leaned across the table. "Now that Cam is both rich and ennobled, Aunt Belmont has discovered an enthusiasm for the match. Suddenly, it is *her dear sister's dying wish,* and all that rot. She cautions us that our family can ill afford another scandal—or another ignoble marriage."

"And your brother believes her to be sincere?"

"Lord, no!" Catherine giggled, then dropped her voice to a conspiratorial whisper. "But out of a strong sense of duty, Cam does listen. And his first marriage—well, it was not a good match. Though for all Aunt's dire warnings, the *mésalliance* had nothing to do with the fact that Cassandra's father was in trade."

Helene tried to keep her voice from quaking. "But I collect that your cousin is still quite young."

"Joan is exactly Bentley's age, and out of the schoolroom these last six months or better. She is to make her debut in town this season. *If* Cam has not announced the betrothal. My aunt made that much plain today."

"Oh," was Helene's only response.

Pensively, Cam's sister sipped at her tea, letting her eyes settle on a portrait over the mantel. "I find it all rather ironic, to be perfectly honest."

"Indeed?" answered Helene numbly. "In what way?"

"Over the past year, anxiety over Papa's deportment kept Aunt Belmont from pressing too hard for the match. But now that he has turned up his toes, our year of mourning precludes a wedding. My brother could get away with announcing the betrothal in few months, I suppose . . . but he cannot marry until we put off our black." She let her eyes drift from the mantel to the fire. "Yes, Joan is pretty enough, I vow," she mused. "But I wonder Cam does not welcome the delay."

"You do not know his feelings in this regard?"

Catherine shook her head, and seemed to think nothing of Helene's curiosity. "My brother keeps his own counsel, Helene. He always has done. But then, the two of you have long been acquainted, so I expect you knew that."

"Yes," said Helene softly, blindly staring over Catherine's shoulder and through the window. An inexplicable well of bitterness almost choked her. "Yes, he is a very private man."

"Forgive me, Helene. You must be bored to tears by our family gossip."

"No, not . . . not at all."

"It is just that Cam and I—well, we have always been so close. With our mother gone, and Bentley so much younger . . . at times, it has been just the two of us. Or so it seemed. He has always taken care of me. And I him, as best I could. We are inordinately attached, I suppose."

"I envy you that, Catherine," Helene softly replied. "I

was an only child, and so often I longed for a sister or a brother."

Catherine nodded. "Indeed. That is one thing in favor of Cam wedding Joan. I am gravely concerned about Ariane, and another child would be a comfort to her, I do not doubt."

Helene wanted to suggest that that might depend upon the stepmother, but she bit back the words. It was none of her concern. Miss Belmont would undoubtedly make the perfect wife for a man of Cam's stature.

Helene fought a second wave of despair. Surely Miss Belmont would love and protect Ariane as if she were her own? The little girl would be both her cousin and stepdaughter. "Yes," Helene agreed at last. "Moreover, I am sure Ariane would benefit from a stepmother. I daresay she feels the loss of her own mother very deeply."

"Oh? I suppose I had not considered that point," said Catherine vaguely. "Of course, a child would long for her mother, though in truth, the two of them were not as close as one would have hoped."

"Yes, so Lord Treyhern has said."

Catherine's brows shot up. "Did he indeed?"

"We discussed it, yes," Helene murmured, anxious to dispel the impression of any inappropriate familiarity. "You must understand, Catherine, that I am here to help the child. It is rather obvious that Ariane's trauma and loss of speech relates in some way to her mother. I believe he felt it necessary that I understand their relationship."

"Oh, Helene, please do not mistake my meaning! My surprise was not intended to imply otherwise. It is just that Cam, well, even when matters with Cassandra were . . . not smooth, he refused to denounce her in any way. To hear him admit her shortcomings, even in veiled terms, is unusual."

Helene felt the knot of sadness in her chest tighten further still. "I take it, then, that his lordship was deeply in love with his wife."

In the process of sipping her tea, Catherine very nearly sputtered aloud, her long, capable fingers flying to her lips. "Lord, no!" she exclaimed, once she had finished coughing. "It was an arranged marriage in every sense of the word. Indeed, I daresay Cassandra liked it even less than he did. She was miserable, and she made the rest of us so. The first year of having Cassandra and her coterie under Chalcote's roof was utter hell."

"You are speaking of the time prior to your marriage?"

"Yes, I married rather young, did I not? Will and I were good friends. He was so often here, why, it just seemed natural to make a match of it. And living under the same roof as both Papa and my sister-in-law was akin to living in a gunpowder magazine. Something was forever exploding." Catherine smiled grimly. "As you can see, I am occasionally a bit impolitic. Suffice it to say that Cassandra and I did not see eye to eye. And I found that most of her raffish friends were not so very different from Papa's, when all was said and done."

"Oh? In what way?"

"Oh, they were forever here, dancing, drinking, shooting—and a good deal more, to be sure." Catherine gave a little shrug, then bent to fill her cup again. "Cassandra despised the country. And though Cam often traveled to town on business, he made no secret of his abhorrence for it. Yet Cassandra longed for the admiration of her friends, and so she simply invited them to Chalcote. It was like a queen holding court."

"And your brother did not object?"

"Not in the beginning, no," Catherine slowly replied. "I collect he thought it a fair compromise to Cassandra. But for her part, I think she would have liked it a little better had Cam become angry. She once complained to me that Cam was not jealous of her. In truth, I think his emotional restraint angered her. Is that not perverse?"

"Yes, but she was young. And perhaps insecure . . . ?"

Catherine pursed her lips and nodded. "You are rather perceptive, Helene. Yes, that's just how she was. Cassandra required constant reassurance. Indeed, I think that her background—not precisely to the manor born, and all that drivel—left her constantly ill at ease."

"And her friends were happy to provide the reassurance she needed, I am sure."

Catherine looked suddenly uncomfortable. "Yes," she said slowly, "until Cam put a stop to their coming." She paused for a long moment, her gaze flicking up from the table, as if to gauge Helene's reaction. "Cassandra became rather too blatant in some of her behavior. One night, they had a horrible row, and then . . . well, I never asked my brother about it. But the house parties ceased."

"Altogether?"

"Indeed," Catherine rolled her expressive eyes, "and if it had been hell here before, it was ten times that when Cassandra was deprived of her admirers. She became exceedingly bored, and alternately, feverish with energy. She would roam through the house at night, and through the woods by day. But soon, she announced that she was *enceinte*, and for a time, she seemed more settled."

"But by then you had left Chalcote, I take it?"

"Yes," she said. "Cam had finally agreed that Will and I might wed, and Papa did not care."

"I . . . I hope you are very happy," said Helene uncertainly, no longer comfortable with discussing Cam's past.

"Perfectly content," answered Catherine. "Nowadays, it is not my happiness, but my brother's, which most concerns me."

"I . . . I do not know what you mean."

Cam's sister studied Helene's face for a long moment before she answered. "You knew my father well, did you not?"

Helene nodded.

"It will not shock you, then, to know that Cam had little choice but to marry Cassandra. Her father offered a generous dowry, and Cam saw it as his duty to settle Papa's debts and restore our family name to respectability. Of course, I am inordinately grateful. But in truth, Helene, I should have preferred to see my brother happy. I still would."

"And will not Miss Belmont be capable of assuring his happiness?" asked Helene softly, hoping that her hurt and bitterness did not show.

Catherine shook her head uncertainly. "Who can say? From childhood, Cam's life has been one of responsibility. His first marriage was much the same, but I had rather hoped that his second would be made for love. That is what would make him truly happy, do not you think? And as fond as we all are of Joan, I cannot think he loves her."

Suddenly, a sharp knock sounded on the door, and Cam strode into the room to stand before them, his hat clutched rather tightly in his hands. "I beg your pardon, Catherine, Miss de Severs." He spoke rapidly, his words spilling forth. "I fear I have come to take my leave of you. I must go down to Devonshire in all haste."

"To Devon?" Catherine bounced out of her chair. "So suddenly?"

Cam gave a stiff, curt nod, and Helene could plainly see the lines of concern which were deeply etched into his face. All traces of his earlier contentment had vanished. "Yes, Cat," he answered. "It is very sudden. Illness—a severe fever—has swept through Treyhern Castle. It has struck down half my staff and tenants, and already two have died."

"Dear Lord," whispered Catherine, moving unsteadily away from her chair. "What bad news!"

"Aye, bad news indeed." Cam looked grim, his fingers

curling tighter into the fabric of his hat. He looked shaken and tired. "And it gets worse. Hastings, Uncle's old steward, took ill three days ago and is not expected to throw it off. I must go to him straightaway. Crane is putting up my gear now. By all accounts, matters are in a mess."

"He's to put up mine as well," came a voice from the darkened corridor. Bentley paused just long enough to stick his head into the parlor. "I mean to go with you. I think I ought."

Surprise flickered in Cam's eyes as he tossed a glance over his shoulder. "I'd be grateful," he returned. But it was too late. After muttering something about preparing the horses, Bentley had thundered on down the hall toward the rear door which gave on to the stable path.

"What can I do to help, Cam?" asked Catherine. "And when will you return?"

Cam nodded his head. "I do need your help, my dear. I shall be gone at least a fortnight, so I'm afraid I must ask you to attend to matters at Chalcote. Can Will do without you for a bit?"

Lightly, his sister laughed. "It's hunting season, Cam! I'll never be missed."

"Good. Can you ride over twice a week to see to things here? Call upon the tenants, forward any paperwork to Brightsmith, see that the fencing continues on schedule—that sort of thing? You are as capable in farm matters as any man I know. Leave the household to Mrs. Naffles, and otherwise, just send word to Brightsmith if there is anything you cannot handle. And you may as well stay here tonight. Send your footman back to Aldhampton with a message."

"Yes, of course," said Catherine, darting forward to kiss her brother's cheek. "Far better to task me with your sheep than with your draperies." She smiled mischievously. "And on that score, I have been cast into the shade anyway. Milford declares that Miss de Severs's taste is *comme il faut*. So I think it must be she who is tasked with that chore whilst you're away. I think I shall have her redecorate this room."

Strangely enough, the idea appealed to Cam. The room was a little shabby. And Helene seemed to have an unerring grasp of color and beauty. "A fine idea, Miss de Severs," he answered, nodding in her direction.

But suddenly, it dawned on him that he really did not wish to leave Helene and Ariane behind. The afternoon they had shared by the river had marked some sort of turning point, and the following days had left him feeling . . . very different. Helene had always had a way of goading him, challenging him, and now, of forcing him to look at things he would prefer not to see. Yet inexplicably, the last few weeks had been like a balm to his wounds.

There. He had admitted it. He desperately wanted to continue visiting the schoolroom, and hearing Helene's laughter at his dinner table. He wanted to listen to her opinions. Even, perhaps, to her scolds.

Cam, who was unaccustomed to the luxury of speaking so intimately with anyone, had begun to feel strangely unburdened. With Helene, it had always seemed that one could say anything, do anything. It was, perhaps, a fatal illusion, but Helene made him feel as if he could be free, if ever so briefly, of earthly constraints, much as he had felt while flying through the air on that silly rope. And so, for one impetuous moment, Cam toyed with the idea of taking both Helene and Ariane to Devonshire.

Quickly, he set it aside. It would be the height of irresponsibility, for the fever which raged in Devon was quite clearly contagious. Indeed, he was almost afraid to take Bentley, but to refuse would insult the boy unpardonably.

But if he could not have Helene and his daughter with

him, he would at least have the luxury of giving them a proper good-bye. "Miss de Severs," he said abruptly, turning to face her, "may I see you shortly in the schoolroom? I must make my good-bye to Ariane, and then I should like to review your plans for her whilst I'm away."

Smoothly, Helene rose from her seat, her perfect ivory face an emotionless mask, her gaze fixed somewhere in the distance behind him. "Yes, of course, my lord," she said.

Even considering Catherine's presence, Cam thought her voice rather too cool. Intently, he studied her for a long moment, then nodded curtly and turned away. She did not look happy. He vowed to find out why.

His attention torn between the tragedy in Devon and the distant expression on Helene's face, Cam strode through the Great Hall en route to the schoolroom. As he turned the corner, however, he drew up short when he saw Thomas Lowe being admitted by Milford. He felt instantly on guard, like a pack hound with his hackles up. But that simply would not do. The man was his rector, for pity's sake. Still, he was heartily sick of Lowe dogging Helene's heels like a besotted puppy.

"Ah, good afternoon, Treyhern!" proclaimed Lowe, his voice overly cheerful as he dropped his hat into Milford's fingers. The rector came forward, his hand outstretched in greeting, leaving Cam no choice but to reciprocate.

"One might even say good evening, Lowe," replied Cam dryly, grasping the priest's smooth, almost delicate, hand. "It is very nearly half past five."

Lowe was in no way discouraged. "Ah, I take your point, my lord! I shall be brief, for I was just coming from old Clapham's—" Here, the rector dropped his gaze and shook his head mournfully, "—'tis his heart, don't you know. But anyway, by such happenstance, I was passing along your back gate, and thought to step around for a word with Miss de Severs."

"Miss de Severs?" echoed Cam flatly.

Thomas Lowe beamed beatifically. "Indeed! About our plans together."

"Your plans together?" The voice, flatter still, dropped a note.

"Yes, for tomorrow!" answered the handsome young man, still smiling. "We've arranged that the children might have another romp together in the afternoon. Lucy and Lizzy so much enjoy dear Ariane's company."

"How nice," answered Cam, his tone more brusque than he had intended. "Now, if you will excuse me, I must be off to Devon."

Lowe looked taken aback. "At this hour?"

Curtly, Cam nodded and motioned Lowe toward a seat. "A fever has seized hold of my estate and many of my staff are ill." He spun on his boot-heel and headed for the broad oak staircase.

"Then we must keep them in our prayers," murmured Lowe. "Godspeed, my lord."

The rector's gentle words trailed after Cam as he bounded up the stairs, feeling shockingly mean-spirited, and intensely un-Christian. It was a most unpleasant, but nonetheless deeply rooted feeling, and he was a little bit ashamed. From the landing above, he watched as Thomas Lowe settled himself into a chair to await Helene. *Damn!*

With grave reluctance, Helene paused at the schoolroom, her hand raised to knock upon the door, but it already stood ajar. Just inside, Helene could see Cam, already wearing his traveling coat, and looking like a long-legged giant in comparison to the desk chair in which he reclined.

Nestled snugly in her father's lap, with a rag doll dangling from one hand, Ariane was carefully watching his face. Cam's voice was low and gentle. "And so you must be a good girl, sweeting," he said, lightly touching the tip of her nose with his finger. "Two weeks shall pass quickly, I promise. Do all that Miss de Severs asks of you. And remember always that Papa loves you."

His gaze focused somewhere in the distance, Cam kissed the top of the child's head, and Ariane slid obediently from his lap and onto her feet. As she started away, Cam seized her hand and pulled her back to plant a loud kiss on the little girl's open palm.

"Do *everything* that she asks, Ariane, please?" Cam stared down into her limpid blue eyes this time. "*Everything,*" he emphasized, his voice suddenly husky. "I need for you to try very hard this time. Will you do this for me, sweet?"

As if she did not understand, Ariane smiled vaguely, then danced away, still dangling the doll in one hand. As the little girl turned into her bedchamber, Helene let her hand drop, knocking sharply on the doorframe.

"Come in." Cam came swiftly to his feet.

"You wished to speak with me?" asked Helene, keeping her voice smooth as she pushed open the door. She felt as if she had intruded upon an intensely personal scene. To her dismay, she found anger harder to sustain in the face of a father who so clearly loved his child. But if she did not feel anger, she would have to feel grief. And that she could not bear. Not again.

Cam watched Helene step uncertainly into the schoolroom. And indeed, uncertainty was the only emotion he could detect in her restrained demeanor. It felt as if a cold wall of formality had been suddenly flung up between them, where earlier there had existed a sense of quiet intimacy.

Today she again wore her deep burgundy carriage dress, the fabric warming in the candlelight as she came gracefully toward the desk. Rising from his chair, Cam let his eyes roam over her face, trying to gauge her mood. It was useless. Unlike Helene the young girl, Helene the woman could dissemble her emotions as well as any lady of the *ton*.

And yet, he could sense the distancing between them. Cam narrowed his eyes, his gaze hesitating for a moment on her sinfully full lips. Undoubtedly, Helene had seen that dratted rector in the hall below. Yet he did not think Thomas Lowe was the cause of her withdrawal.

Perhaps his sister had simply worn her out? Helene was vivacious, yes. But Catherine's boundless energy had drained the life's blood from lesser mortals. Perhaps his sister had even inadvertently hurt Helene's feelings by something she had said or done. Good heavens—look what she'd almost blurted out about Joan! Cat could be blunt to a fault.

Slowly, he exhaled, stroking his thumb and forefinger pensively over a day's growth of dark, rough stubble. Lord, it had been a long, exhausting day. He did not want to set out for Devon in the dark, and he most assuredly did not want to leave Helene's side.

What he wanted to do was to recapture the feeling—Cam told himself it was friendship—that he knew they'd both begun to feel. Was it possible?

In a foolish attempt to find out, Cam deliberately lifted his hand and tipped her chin up on one finger. "Must I admonish you to be a good girl, too, Hellie?" he asked teasingly, fighting the urge to let his hand slip around to caress the back of her neck and pull her mouth to his.

His efforts fell awkwardly short of the mark. Helene's glacial expression froze both his hand and his lips. Her delicate nostrils flared almost imperceptibly as she withdrew a pace, then stood, utterly still. "You may count on me to do my best for Ariane," she responded evenly, her emotionless tone belied by the cold glitter of her eyes.

Cam dropped his chin and studied Helene through his

eyelashes, a feeling of bone-deep dread stealing slowly over him. Something was very wrong here. Something most precious was slipping from his grasp, leaving Cam with nothing but a desperate sense of urgency.

And then suddenly, amidst all of his fatigue, and all of his worry, an aching, awful reality cut into his heart like a knife. *He was still in love with Helene.*

Deeply. Hopelessly. Eternally, it would seem. The knowledge came, sharp and certain, slicing down upon him with the swiftness of an executioner's sword. Cam felt a shudder pass through him as the nebulous thought took the shape of his worst nightmare. And his only hope.

Please God, he silently whispered. *No, no, no! Not Helene.*

Lust he could manage, though he wanted her badly. And enjoying her companionship, Cam had ruefully discovered, was still an exquisite pleasure. But he could not possibly survive being in love with Helene again. Assuming he had ever stopped loving her. Oh Lord. He hadn't, had he? No, not really.

And yet, then as now, Helene was every dangerous thing he could imagine in a woman: too reckless, too vibrant, and just too bloody beautiful for his own good. Cam felt his well-ordered existence spinning wildly out of control, and off into the netherworld of uncertainty.

That was what most disturbed him. He had no sense of control where Helene was concerned. She was the last woman on earth he would have chosen to love. And yet, Cam was beginning to acknowledge the painful and perplexing lesson that a decade of solitude had taught him: a man did not always get to choose. Without Helene, he simply was not whole. It was a plain truth which he knew, but could not fully understand.

Dear heaven, he needed time! Time to sort this dreadful mess into some semblance of order. Somewhere in the distance, a door thumped shut. A servant strode down the corridor jingling a set of keys. The bell at St. Michael's tolled half past the hour. Cam barely heard these things, so lost was he in his own need and fear and hope.

Yet Helene seemed oblivious to his confusion. Impassively, she gazed at him, flipping open a leather ledger that sat upon the desk. The flashing white pages brought him back into the present. "What may I tell you about our lesson plans before you go, my lord?"

The spell severed, Cam abruptly strode toward the door, pushing it shut. "Helene," he said urgently, spinning about to face her, "I believe . . . that is to say, my dear, I think we must talk."

And there, the words seemed to utterly fail him. Blindly, he stared at Helene. Her gaze neither warmed nor altered. Uncertainly, Cam stepped closer, one hand going to his temple. "Look here, Helene—are you quite all right? You seem . . . rather different."

"I am perfectly well, my lord," she answered, brushing by him to stand behind the desk. The scent of her hair teased at his nostrils as she passed.

Cam set one hand at his hip, ran the other through his already disheveled hair, and let his eyes narrow appraisingly. "See here, Helene—this feels suspiciously like a cut. Not an hour past, we were the best of friends again. And now . . . now . . . "

"Do you know, Cam," she said hesitantly, "I am not at all sure that we ought to be friends." Her voice was soft, with nothing but a hint of bittersweet emotion in it. "I am your employee now."

From his position beside Helene's desk, Cam circled around toward her. "My *employee?*" he echoed hollowly. He stared down into her face. Helene's expression was still smooth and impassive, but in her wide-set, expressive eyes . . . oh, yes. He saw it. In the bottomless depths of those dark blue pools, there was deep, inimitable grief.

Lord, that was something he had not expected to see.

And something he was ill-prepared to deal with. He scrubbed a hand slowly down his face, but nothing altered. Helene was not angry, though he could have dealt with that, Cam suddenly realized. Yes, it was one thing to be shot down by eyes that flashed, cold and brittle, but quite another to see those same lovely orbs flat with an inscrutable despondency.

Suddenly, Cam could no longer bear the thought of being torn from her just now. Nor could he bear her pain and distance. There was too much unresolved between them, and in his own mind. Cam reached out one hand to her, and Helene turned her face away. Still, something more powerful than logic drew his eyes to her mouth, his body to hers. She hurt. He wanted to take her in his arms and comfort her.

But it was suddenly obvious that Helene wanted no comfort from him. She resisted wordlessly as Cam roughly gathered her into his embrace, bent on a course of action he could no longer deny. Knowing full well that he would regret his behavior, Cam ignored Helene's struggle and bent his head to take her mouth with his. Dimly, he reasoned that he could kiss away not just the sadness, but this strange, new coldness as well.

Cam had ached for another taste of Helene from the moment she had strode out of his study that long-ago night, leaving him alone and desperate on the floor. He admitted it now, as his lips raked roughly over hers. Ah, so soft, so sweet, she was. How well he remembered.

In his arms, Helene still clawed at his shirtfront, twisting one fist in his cravat in protest. But beneath his mouth, she had opened easily to him, giving him access to her warm, wet recesses in what felt like a bittersweet caress.

Helene's kiss was everything he had remembered, and more; the taste made even sweeter by her reluctance. Yet she made no move to slip away as Cam slid his hand into the fine, loose hair at her nape and pulled her head back to better plunder her with his mouth.

Beneath him, Helene moaned and rose up to press herself urgently against him, the motion dragging down the fabric of her gown to hint at the swell of full breasts beneath. Her right hand slid from his shirtfront to skim over his hip bone and down into the small of his back, drawing his hips into hers. She kissed him back with a heated, almost heartbreaking, urgency.

The knowledge that she still desired him rushed into Cam's loins like molten fire. He took her deeply, possessively, with a boldness that laid claim to her in the most intimate way a man could claim a woman as his own. All thought of comforting her fled his mind as Cam felt his erection strain rock-hard against his breeches.

He was doomed. He might as well accept it. Vaguely, he could focus on nothing but the fact that he must get Helene out of the schoolroom. Into his bedchamber. Out of her clothes. And make her his.

The fact that he was on his way to a crisis escaped him. Cam swept a hand down her spine and over the perfect curves of her hips, drawing her up against him even as he deepened this kiss to something so carnal he feared he might come before he could ease himself inside her.

And he was going to ease himself inside her this time, he thought, as he slid a fistful of heavy velvet up her hip. Nothing on this earth could sway him—

The knock at the door dashed over Helene like ice-water.

She drew taut, but Cam's arm swept stubbornly upward, stilling her motions again. Desperately, she jerked backward, and this time her panic must have registered, for Cam ripped his mouth from hers, allowing her to catch a fleeting glimpse of Crane, his valet, discreetly backing out of the schoolroom.

Cam saw him, too, sharply sucking in his breath.

"Damn it, Crane! What now?" he roared, setting Helene roughly away from him.

The elderly man froze at the sound of Cam's voice. With a careful little cough, Crane turned back again, the doorknob still clutched in his hand. "Your trunks, my lord. And the medicine and food? All have been loaded into your coach. Young Mr. Rutledge awaits us below, at your convenience." And then, the impassive valet pulled shut the door without another word.

Cam turned to face Helene, his face a mixture of dismay, anger, and thwarted lust. She should have pushed him away, slapped him hard across his insolent mouth, when he pulled her against him and kissed her again, this time hard and swift. But to her utter shame, she did not even try.

"Forget about Crane," Cam said into her hair, his voice as rough as gravel, his arms binding her to his chest. "I swear he is the soul of discretion."

Helene opened her mouth to speak, but Cam simply kissed her again, taking away her breath, then placing his finger over her lips. "I must go, Helene. I shall return, God willing, in two weeks' time. And then, you may rail at me with impunity. But we will sort this muddle out. I promise you."

Helene shook her head, and felt a tear of humiliation threaten to spill from her eye. "There is nothing to sort out, Cam. My position is unchanged. I shan't be your mistress, no matter how much I may desire you."

Cam regarded her in silence for a long moment. "Dear heaven, I begin to believe I've made a near shambles of things, Helene," he finally answered. "Indeed, I would to God I did not have to leave you just now. But I must."

Rather insolently, he kissed her for the third time, then strode toward the hallway, his heavy riding boots ringing on the schoolroom floor. He jerked to a halt when he reached the door. "In two weeks, Helene," he said, rounding on her again, the hems of his greatcoat swirling about his boots. "If matters in Devon cannot be resolved, I shall leave Bentley there, and I shall return to Chalcote. I swear it."

And then he, too, was gone, leaving Helene burning with shame and anger, two fingers pressed hard against her swollen lips.

12

Miss de Severs discovers the Storm and the Strife

Hard and relentless, a wicked rain rolled in late that night, racing across the Bristol Channel and up the Severn, drenching England from Peterborough to Penzance. Caught in the center of the unseasonable storm, the Cotswolds took the brunt of Mother Nature's caprice, with lowland streams bursting from their banks shortly after midnight.

Unable to sleep, Helene pulled back the heavy damask draperies of her bedchamber window just as the clock on the upper landing struck three. She peered into the black night, knowing beyond a doubt that Cam's southwesterly route had taken him into the teeth of the storm. Fretfully, she balled her hand into a fist and rubbed at the glass, to no avail. The night was as heavy and as black as the mood which had haunted her all evening. In the window, there was nothing to see, save the watery reflection of her own stark face.

Behind her, the stump of a candle she had lit upon arising sputtered and died a natural death, steeping the room in a darkness thick with the smell of melting wax. But soon, even that faint scent was gone. No light, no sound, nor any movement stirred the oppressive silence of Chalcote. Helene felt utterly swallowed up by the dearth of sensations. Never had she felt so alone, so bereft. And never had she felt so ashamed.

With the storm's next gasp, Helene pressed her fingertips to the cold glass, just to have something else to feel. She tried not to worry about Cam's whereabouts. She had no business concerning herself with him at all. But surely, he'd had the foresight to put up at an inn somewhere along the way to Devonshire? On horseback, despite their sweeping greatcoats, both he and Bentley would be soaked to the skin.

Moreover, there was the coachman, the footman, and old Crane to consider. Their carriage, laden with Mrs. Naffles's herbs, elixirs, and foodstuffs, might well be mired to the axles by now. Helene let her hand slip slowly from the damp glass, turning back toward her empty bed, angry with herself. She had permitted Cam Rutledge to rob her of yet another night's sleep, much as he had robbed her of her heart, her pride—and yes, her very soul, it so often seemed.

Dejected, she let her arms drop to her sides. The only sound now was the occasional torrent of rain as it shifted and whirled, changing directions to whip and spatter wildly against her window. And then, Helene heard it . . .

A soft, keening, almost inaudible wail. But her ears attuned to it instinctively, as they always did. The sound of a child in distress had always brought her senses to full alert. Was there any sound more heartrending than the unmistakable cry of a child who was afraid of the dark? Or a child caught in the throes of a nightmare . . . ?

Whipping her dressing gown around her nightgown, Helene dashed into the passageway, through the schoolroom, and to the door which connected with Ariane's. There was no mistaking the soft whimpering as Helene pushed open the door and crossed to Ariane's bed. Had it not been for her aimless thrashing, the girl would have been lost in the tangle of bedsheets.

Clearly, she had suffered the effects of an upsetting evening, and had been tossing and turning for quite some time. And was it any wonder? First, her father's unexpected departure, and now this violent storm. Suddenly, the girl's hand fisted in the covers as she writhed toward Helene.

"No," Ariane whimpered softly, one foot flying out to kick repeatedly against the wall. "No, no! Don't leave me!" She gave another keening wail, her words caught on a sob. "No, I shan't tell . . . I shan't! I shan't," she whispered pitifully. "Don't leave me!"

The little girl's words were fraught with pain. And, Helene finally realized, they were absolutely, unerringly flawless in pronunciation. One hand pressed to her mouth in shock, Helene dropped to a crouch beside the small bed, uncertain what she ought to do. Almost in unison, the other two doors leading into Ariane's room flew open. In one, Martha stood, holding a sputtering candle aloft. And from the main hallway, Catherine entered wearing an old flannel nightgown which might once have fit, but was now far too snug.

As Ariane tossed uneasily on the bed, Catherine sized up the situation. "A nightmare, is it?" she whispered, leaning anxiously over the bed.

"Very sorry, Lady Catherine," murmured Martha groggily. "I just this moment heard the poor wee thing! A thumping up against the wall something ter'ble, she was." The maid drew near, lifting her candlestick higher to dispel the shadows from the bed.

Almost at once, Ariane woke, blinking owlishly against the light. She sat up, surveyed the three anxious faces peering over her bed, then with a heart-wrenching gasp, bolted into Helene's arms, very nearly sending them both toppling backward. From behind, Catherine caught Helene with a steadying arm.

"There, there," murmured Helene, lifting the child up from the bed and carrying her to a nearby chair. "You've just had a nightmare. Yes, just a bad dream," she repeated, settling Ariane in her lap as she patted the child rhythmically on the back. "It is all perfectly fine, Ariane. Perfectly fine. Just a storm. A little rain and racket, but nothing to fret over."

Helene continued to murmur, and without another sound, the child nestled closer. Indeed, it seemed almost as if she had never fully awakened. Helene looked at Martha, and with a tilt of her head, she bade the maid to hand her a blanket from the bed, then swathed it about the child's slender form. Across the room, Catherine busied herself by straightening the tousled bedcovers, while the maid lit another brace of candles to better illuminate the room.

"Martha," said Catherine after several quiet moments had passed. "Would you be good enough to go down to the kitchen and heat some milk? I fancy that is just what is needed here."

As the girl dashed off to do as she was bid, Catherine snapped the last of the wrinkles from Ariane's coverlet, then turned to face Helene, her expression one of grave concern.

"Catherine," Helene whispered over Ariane's head, "I rather think the child's asleep. Perhaps the milk is unnecessary?"

Cam's sister studied her rather too closely. "Oh, the milk is for us, Helene," she answered in a soft, knowing voice. "I daresay you've slept no better than have I tonight, else you'd not be awake now."

If Catherine was envious that her niece had hurled herself into Helene's embrace, she gave no indication. Instead, she smoothly flung back the sheets as Helene rose from her chair to lay the child upon the neatly remade bed. Gently, Catherine drew the heavy covers up.

Tucking a thumb in her mouth, Ariane rolled onto one side and snuggled deep into the mattress, her cornsilk tresses fanning across the pillow. The two women stood, quietly looking at the child for a time.

Helene was still unable to fully assimilate what had occurred just before Catherine and Martha had entered Ariane's room. But one thing was clear. Ariane *had* spoken! It was a blessing beyond Helene's prayers, and yet, she hesitated to tell anyone—even Catherine.

Why? Helene was not certain, but it was almost as if she were keeping a confidence, a secret Ariane held close to her heart. For reasons Helene did not fully understand, it seemed exceedingly wrong to announce to the world that a child once thought mute was capable of speech, without knowing the reason for her long-held silence.

Many unanswered questions still lingered. Was Ariane able to speak only when subconscious? Helene did not doubt that such a thing was possible. Or had Ariane deliberately hidden her abilities? And if so, why?

"There is no resemblance at all, is there?" Catherine's innocent comment brought Helene dimly back into the present.

"Mille pardon . . . ?" Helene answered absently. Then, her head snapped up to look at Cam's sister, but Catherine was strolling toward the schoolroom.

Abruptly, Helene followed her through the door. Catherine settled herself into a chair at the big worktable, and began to scratch her thumbnail absently over some ragged initials, carved deep into the ancient surface by some long-dead Camden ancestor. Helene could sense that something troubled her.

"Let us have our milk in here, shall we?" Catherine murmured, as Helene took the chair opposite.

But almost at once, Catherine leapt up again, and began to drift aimlessly through the vast room. "Such old memories," she whispered, picking over a disorderly collection of sea shells. Helene made no answer, and Catherine turned away from the shells and crossed the room to straighten a picture that needed no attention, and then skimmed her long, capable fingers over a shelf of worn textbooks.

Unexpectedly, she wheeled to face Helene at the worktable. "Forgive me. I ought not to have said that," she stated, her expression inscrutable.

Helene looked up at her in confusion. "Old memories, Catherine?" She laughed lightly. "Oh, I rather fear we all have those."

Catherine cut her off with a shake of her head. "That is not what I meant," she said urgently, returning to the table. Abruptly, she leaned forward, splaying her hands across the rough tabletop. "Please—I beg you, Helene. *Never* repeat my words to Cam. I would never wish to hurt him."

"You refer to your comment about Ariane?" asked Helene.

Mutely, Cam's sister nodded and sank back into her chair.

"Of course I shan't," said Helene softly, bending across the table to lay one hand over Catherine's. She gave it a reassuring squeeze. "And what does it signify, Catherine? You are right; the child does not look like her father. But your brother has eyes, and to be sure, he has noticed it long before now. Ariane just simply resembles her mother, that is all."

"No," said Cam's sister grimly. "She does not. The hair, perhaps . . . but even that is not quite the same. I love her, Helene, but often Ariane seems like some sort of a . . . a fairy creature."

"A fairy creature?" repeated Helene. "My dear, what are you trying to say?" But at that very moment, Martha returned from the kitchens and there was no more talk of Ariane.

Pensively, Helene sipped at her milk, considering Catherine's words. It was almost as if something worried Cam's sister. As if there were something she was rather desperate to discuss, and uncertain as to whom she might trust.

But Helene was more than a little reluctant to encourage Catherine in her musings. However warm her feelings toward Cam's sister might be, Helene was mindful of her precarious position in the Rutledge household. Her earlier conversation with Catherine had shown her that all too plainly, and even now, it took all her fortitude to hide her pain. Cam was to wed his young cousin. Helene was but a governess. She had no business speculating about family matters, not even with Catherine.

Indeed, Helene strongly suspected that nothing short of desperation would have driven Catherine to couch such an issue, even in the veiled terms she had used. No, it was all too clear that Catherine loved her niece unequivocally, and would have gone to great lengths to protect her.

They finished their milk in silence. "Well!" said Catherine, setting down her mug and looking across the table for a long, uncertain moment, "I'm for bed, Helene, unless there's something further I might do?"

It was clear that the moment of shared intimacy was at an end, and despite her curiosity, Helene knew it was best. "No," she replied. "Ariane is asleep now. And I thank you, Catherine. I am so glad you decided to remain at Chalcote the night. I believe it helps Ariane to know that you are here. Certainly it is of help to me."

In the dragging hours before dawn, Cam found himself battling his own demons, thrashing irritably beneath sheets that felt both damp and cold. The lamentable condition of his bed linen was partly his fault, as were the dreams that tormented his rest. The evening had seemed interminable, even before the drenching rain blew in.

At first, he had resolved to push forward, come hell or high water. But in the end, the water had won. Cam had found himself pounding on the door of The Swan at well past two in the morning, weary, wet, and bone-cold. Upon securing the innkeeper's last room—a tiny cubbyhole of a place with one lumpy mattress—he'd collapsed into bed, still chilled from the rain, and with every intention of falling instantly into unconsciousness.

But true sleep had eluded him. It had been a mistake, he now realized, to set out for Devon with a storm brewing, both on the horizon and in his heart. With every passing mile, Cam had grown ever more certain that it had been a grievous error to leave Helene's side, particularly with her mood so brittle, and matters so unsettled between them.

Doubt and fear, and the almost overwhelming need to be with her had tortured Cam for the whole of the journey, and he still did not know what he ought to do. Why? He *never* suffered from indecision. But in the schoolroom, he had experienced what amounted to an epiphany, and the ensuing realization that marriage to Joan would be an unutterable mistake continued to plague him.

Yet as he had ridden, Cam had been mindful of the fact that there were others to consider. He'd felt as if the mantle of family duty might well weigh him down into the mire beneath his horse's hooves. Then the spatter of rain had turned into an outright downpour, and the carriage had to be left behind just north of Bath.

Nonetheless, Cam had been determined to go on to Devon in all haste, primarily because he was determined to return home in just the same manner. And so he had pressed onward, leaving Crane and his staff snugly ensconced by a wayside hearth. But Bentley, in some foolish attempt to match his manhood against Cam's, had insisted upon accompanying him. Together, they had made it only as far as Wells before surrendering to the inevitable.

As if to remind him of his brother's presence, a sonorous snore rattled the canopy overhead. With a sour expression, Cam looked across the narrow width of the mattress at his charming bedfellow, and gave the boy a good, solid jab in the ribs, for no better reason than the maddening fact that Bentley could sleep the sleep of the innocent, while he could not. In his current mood, Cam would rather have slept with the horses, but even the stables were full.

Bentley made another resonant sound—more of a choking wheeze this time, like Old Angus's plough horse on a steep climb. Suddenly, the terrifying image of his brother dying of pneumonia flashed before Cam's eyes. He should never have dragged the boy off on such an ill-planned journey!

But on his next breath, Bentley pitched his right arm over Cam's chest, rolled amorously into him, and sighed sweetly into his ear. In disgust, Cam shoved the arm away. But Bentley, imperturbable in his slumber, merely smacked his mouth twice, patted Cam affectionately on the chest, then burrowed beneath the covers.

Cam rolled over and tried to ignore him, intent on focusing on those same things which had so troubled him during last night's travels. For the first eight miles of their ill-fated journey, Cam had deliberately chosen to ride in the carriage with Crane, where the two of them had proceeded to talk at some length, and in something less than total ease.

Cam knew little about Helene's life in the time they had been apart, but for some reason he could ill explain, her past was rapidly ceasing to matter. Nonetheless, he was greatly concerned about her future. He simply could not allow her name to be sullied by his lack of deportment. And although he trusted his old retainer implicitly, he knew, too, that some explanation was owed Crane regarding the compromising situation in which he and Helene had been discovered.

The big traveling coach had lumbered south, with Crane quietly watching him. And after Cam had managed to stammer his obviously fabricated account of the pesky gnat which had flown into Miss de Severs's eye, the valet had maintained his impassive expression, save for the grin which threatened one corner of his mouth.

"Oh, yes," Crane had gently agreed, as Cam fumbled nervously for his pipe. "An eye injury is indeed a vexing thing, and would, of course, require a great deal of ministration."

But as Cam carefully occupied himself with the minutiae of cleaning out the bowl, the old man had begun to ask questions.

His lordship had been required to get very close indeed, had he not, in order to properly assist Miss de Severs with the invasive insect—? In fact, Crane had subtly added, to the uninformed observer, it appeared almost as if his lordship *might* have been kissing his governess—!

"Well, I bloody well was not!" Cam had snapped, shuffling nervously through the pockets of his greatcoat in search of his tobacco.

"Oh indeed, not!" agreed the valet, rather too smoothly. "Miss de Severs is every inch a lady. She would never go about kissing a man to whom she was not utterly devoted."

"Quite right," Cam had added, then forgetting his pipe altogether, he squinted at his servant for a long moment. "What the devil do you mean by that, Crane?" he finally blurted out. "Do you mean to imply that she—that a woman—would not wish to kiss me? That is to say, if my . . . my intentions were honorable? And if I were free to do so, and all that rot?"

Crane had merely shrugged, his gaze fixed out the window. "Oh, I daresay you should ask Miss de Severs that question, my lord," came his soft answer.

Cam had blushed furiously at that. "It was just a rhetorical question, Crane," he insisted. What the devil was he thinking of, anyway? He already talked to his cat. Now, here he was, all but applying to his valet for advice to the lovelorn. It was pathetic.

Long moments had passed before the servant spoke again. "I am exceedingly fond of the young lady myself. Always have been, since she was a sprite of a girl. So charming, and such vivacity, I always thought." The old man paused to clear his throat. "You're rather fond of her, too, are you not, my lord?"

Cam had scowled at the man. "What has that to say to anything, Crane?"

The valet's brows had gently lifted. "Well, indeed, my lord! I am just making conversation. 'Twas you, I collect, who tied your mount to this coach and climbed in to 'blow a cloud and have a chat,' as you so carefully put it."

"Yes," admitted Cam tersely, shoving the unlit pipe and pouch back into his coat. "You are quite right. And yes, I am very fond of Miss de Severs. She is a fine . . . teacher. And as you say, a very fine lady, too."

Crane stared at him rather pointedly for a long time. "Is aught amiss, my lord?" he finally asked. "You seem not yourself of late."

Cam studied the toes of his riding boots. "Nothing, Crane. It's just that Bentley has my temper in a lather these days."

"Oh—?" answered Crane, the feathery white brows shooting up again. "It is young Mr. Bentham, then, who has you in such a foul mood? I thought—but perhaps I am mistaken—that it was Miss de Severs."

In that moment, it had seemed very obvious to Cam that Crane had put far too little starch into his cuffs, and so he set about carefully neatening them. As he did so, he began to think, and to speak, very slowly. "I cannot be sure just what you are implying here, Crane. But as I believe you know, I am expected to announce my betrothal once my mourning is ended. I am expected to wed Miss Belmont, who is a lovely girl. I would be loath to hurt her in any way."

"Forgive me, sir, for saying so," Crane had gently answered, "but Miss Belmont is not yet your wife. Nor has your betrothal been announced. And while it's certainly none of my concern, one wonders if you have even discussed marriage settlements, or any other particulars, with your Aunt Belmont? Indeed, one could almost question if this is a matter of imagined duty, or of genuine affection."

"I have known Joan since she was a babe. Of course I feel affection for her."

Crane frowned. "Well, my lord, let me put it this way: have you offered Miss Belmont your hand? And has she accepted?"

"Are you asking if I have formally proposed? I have not; it is understood."

"Oh? By whom?" Crane's eyes narrowed. "You are not, after all, marrying Mrs. Belmont. Might it be that young Joan desires a love match? After all, we no longer live in the Dark Ages."

"What exactly are you saying, Crane?" Cam asked sharply.

"Just this, my lord. Whilst a man's word is his honor, and to be maintained above all things, one should be unerringly certain that one knows just what one is honoring."

At that remark, Cam had thumped on the carriage roof, climbed out of the door, and hauled himself onto his horse. And from that moment until this, he had not known one moment's peace. Now, in the murky light of dawn, Bentley grunted, snuggled up against Cam's back, and eased his hand beneath the covers to seductively stroke his brother's hip.

As is so often the case, the days following the storm brought bright, clear skies to the Cotswolds. Helene's mood, however, remained cloudy. Much to her consolation, Catherine called at Chalcote with great frequency. On her second visit, Catherine shared a letter from Cam stating that matters were improving in Devonshire, and that he still meant to return within a fortnight.

Helene's life was a little brightened by the fact that Thomas Lowe called every other afternoon, and although she found both his nieces to be a bit rambunctious, it was clear that the girls had served one good purpose: they had drawn Ariane—a little forcibly, perhaps—from her shell. On one occasion, when the girls were playing hide-and-seek in the shrubbery, Helene was almost sure that she had heard Ariane giggling quietly to herself.

For Helene's part, the time passed slowly during Cam's absence, for she found herself obsessed by two very dissimilar concerns. Why would Ariane not speak, when she so obviously could? And what had Cam meant by his last words to her as he left for Devonshire?

As to the first concern, Ariane was doing exceedingly well in the schoolroom, and Helene was increasingly convinced that there was very little wrong with the child. Indeed, she had begun to toy with the idea of simply explaining to the child that she was aware of her ability to speak. Only Helene's ignorance of the reason behind Ariane's silence kept her from doing just that, for she was unwilling to risk any further trauma to the girl.

But when it came to Cam, the power of speech was of no help at all, for Helene had no notion what he had meant by his words to her. *I shall return . . . and we shall sort this muddle out*. That was what he had said. And yet, when Helene had insistently repeated that she would not be his mistress, Cam had made no reply. In fact, he had continued to kiss her. And she had continued to allow it, when what she should have done was slap his face.

It had cut her to the quick to realize that while Cam had been enticing her into his bed, he had been betrothed to Joan Belmont in an arrangement of long standing. Good heavens, how close they had come to making love on the floor of Cam's study! What had she imagined? That he would wed her?

Now, in light of his betrothal, righteous indignation kept Helene awake at night. How dare Cam have asked her to be a kept woman? Perhaps one could argue that Helene's wanton behavior had all but granted him permission to suggest such a thing, but to realize he'd done so while awaiting his wedding day seemed so much worse.

That kind of behavior was wholly unlike the man she had believed Camden Rutledge to be. And she really had thought she knew him. Though Bentley could poke fun at his brother's moral rigidity all he wished, life would eventually teach him—just as it had taught Helene—to value a man who could, by sheer force of will, place duty and honor above all else.

Even in adolescence, Cam's unassailable character had been a large part of what had drawn Helene to him. To her, his strength and constancy had been a beacon amidst a sea of neglect and vice. When Cam gave his word, his word would be kept. It was an honorable trait, and yet, it made the current situation all the more distressing.

As a very young girl, it was true that she had teased and tempted him, but what she had truly craved had been his attention, and eventually, his love. But not his downfall. Oh, no, never that. And she still wanted his love. She still did! And how it hurt her to wonder if he was not who she had believed him to be. Her heart cried out that he had not altered. Yet Helene was afraid to listen.

The autumn sun was warm on Helene's dark cloak, but absorbed in her thoughts, she was only dimly aware of the girlish laughter ringing in the air around her.

"Miss de Severs?"

She looked up from her seat on the garden bench to see that Thomas Lowe had returned from taking his turn at blind man's buff.

"You promised to show me the keyhole garden, did you not?" he said brightly, offering his arm. "The girls can play on their own for a while, I daresay."

With a forced smile, Helene agreed. Together, they strolled through Chalcote's rear lawn and into the tunnel of vines and greenery which led into the circular garden. Outside the circle, the girls darted around and around its perimeter in some strange variation of ring-around-the-rosy, squealing and laughing, bits of skirts and petticoats flashing through the shrubbery as they ran.

"Ashes, ashes!" shrieked Lucy. "They all fall down!"

Through the thinning walls of greenery, Helene watched the children tumble happily into the grass, Ariane included. Thomas Lowe commented warmly on Ariane's participation, but soon, Helene slipped back into her private thoughts. As they strolled around the circle, Helene paused to snap off a wayward stem that protruded from the carefully sculpted shrubbery.

Suddenly, she found the warmth of Lowe's hand pressing lightly against her upper arm. "I want to thank you again, Miss de Severs, for coming to tea again yesterday," the rector said, gently turning her to face him. "You cannot know what it meant to my sister. And," he hesitantly added, "to me."

Helene forced a wan smile, trying to ignore the heat of his hand. Privately, she suspected that her second

Sunday afternoon visit to the rectory had brought the rector's sister no more pleasure than had her first. Indeed, she hardly knew why Mr. Lowe insisted on inviting her.

Helene had been introduced to Mrs. Fane following her first attendance at St. Michael's, and her reception could only have been described as cool. This past Sunday, as the parishioners had lingered in the churchyard, the rector had enthusiastically issued yet another invitation to afternoon tea. His sister, however, had been stiff, formal, and rather less than enthusiastic.

Things had gone little better that afternoon at the rectory. Mrs. Fane had busied herself pouring and serving and scurrying back and forth to the kitchens, despite the fact that a housemaid stood ready to assist. When Mrs. Fane did make conversation, she glowingly referred to her brother as "dear Thomas," and seized every opportunity to emphasize just how fulfilled and godly his existence was.

Oh, dear Thomas is utterly devoted to the Church, Miss— er, Miss de Severs. Indeed, God comes first in his life, just as He ought! Oh, Thomas does so love my apple tart. He says no one's recipe is as good as mine. Of course, Thomas takes the very best care of me, too! And of Lucy and Lizzie.

"And we have two aging aunts at home in Norfolk. Dear Thomas is so good to them! Why, one can plainly see that my brother is a man who understands his family duty. And a good thing, it is, too, for no man was ever possessed of more family obligation than our dear Thomas . . ."

Helene was hardly a fool. She had taken Mrs. Fane's simpering prattle for the subtle warning it was meant to be. But the insecure widow had been determined to beat a dead horse, or in the case at hand, beat her brother's potential interest in matrimony to death.

Helene had barely resisted the urge to clasp the poor woman's hand and say, "Why, rest assured, ma'am, that I am far too frivolous to fall in love with a decent, good-natured rector! Indeed, I favor men who are cold and withdrawn, preferably those who are far above my station, and who would never deign to make an honest woman of me!"

But of course, she had not. Instead, Helene had been as amiable as was humanly possible, and she had told Mrs. Fane in the warmest of tones what lovely, lovely daughters she had. She had paid a dozen small compliments, murmured endless platitudes, praised the apple tart to the high heavens, and then had flown back to Chalcote Court to hide in her room, her face pressed into her bed pillow yet again.

"Miss de Severs?" She was pulled back into the present by Thomas Lowe's searching gaze. "You did enjoy our tea, did you not? I realize that my sister seems a little distant. She still grieves for the loss of her husband, I think. But I harbor such hope that you will come to like her."

Not knowing quite how to respond, Helene sank down onto a little stone bench in the rear of the garden. Lowe sat down beside her and took her hand in his. "Please say that I may count on you, Helene," he said softly. "My sister needs your friendship, just as her daughters need Ariane's. And more important, perhaps, I need your friendship, too."

Beyond the perimeter of garden, the girls still frolicked, their cheerful shrieks rending the crisp autumn air, but inside the circle of greenery, all fell quiet. Helene stared down at their clasped hands, not at all sure what the rector was trying to say.

Abruptly, Lowe leapt from the bench. "Oh, I have no right to ask such things of you," he said flatly, pacing away from her. "I daresay you think me a presumptuous sort of fellow!"

Confused, Helene looked up at him. "Why, I do not fancy you are anything of the sort."

"Do you not?" he answered eagerly, pacing swiftly back to his seat on the bench. "I am so very grateful, Miss de Severs. I could not bear to undermine our growing friendship." Almost wearily, he dragged a hand down his face.

Intently, Helene leaned forward. "Are you perfectly all right, Mr. Lowe?" In truth, the rector looked haggard, as if he were deeply troubled by something.

"Thomas," he said softly, holding her gaze. "Would you find it terribly difficult to call me by my given name when we are not in company, Helene? Sometimes the title of *rector* begins to lay a little heavily upon one's shoulders. Sometimes one wishes to be just . . . *Thomas*."

"Of course," agreed Helene gently. "But if we are indeed to be friends, Thomas, then I daresay you ought to tell me what is wrong. That is, you know, one of the first rules of friendship. And you look as if you passed a rather sleepless night." She smiled ruefully. "I believe I know the signs."

"How astute you are, Helene," he said, giving her a grateful look. "And so very solicitous. In my profession, a man quickly comes to appreciate that. A rector is often called upon to extend sympathy, whilst the converse is rarely true. And you are right; I was up very late last night with . . . with a troubled parishioner."

"Oh? Nothing that could not be resolved, I hope?"

Thomas Lowe rolled his shoulders back, stretching his black frock coat taut across an expanse of shoulders which did not look as if they belonged on a rector. He sighed deeply. "In truth, Helene, I was with my curate, my young cousin, Basil."

"Yes, I have seen him at church. There is some family resemblance between you, I fancy."

"Yes, a little," he agreed sadly. "And I know I may rely upon your confidence when I say that it is so often difficult for the young to find God's true path. I know the devil and his temptations surround us, Helene. But wickedness is often difficult to recognize when one is inexperienced in the ways of the world."

It was the most overtly zealous comment Helene had ever heard Thomas Lowe utter, and it suddenly struck her as being rather too serious, and more than a little out of character. But how foolish! The man was, after all, a rector.

She gave a nervous laugh. "You speak as if you are a moldering relic, Thomas, when you are actually quite young. In truth, I think you are the youngest priest of my acquaintance. Not," she lamely added, "that I have known a great many."

Thomas Lowe uttered a harsh, sharp laugh. "I am no longer young, my dear."

Helene did not know how to respond to that remark. "And what of your young cousin? Do you fear he has lost his way with God?"

"Oh, no," replied Thomas less stridently. "I fancy it hasn't come to that. But Basil is sorely tempted at times. And being young, he cannot understand that we all have our places in life. Our *stations,* if you will. You understand, Helene, do you not?"

"I think that I do."

"Yes," he mused, "we all have our positions in life. And to dream of anything more brings us nothing but pain. Basil has the makings of a fine curate, but he is a landless and impoverished one, for all that. He must accept God's path for him, and understand that other routes are not his to take. He must be ever mindful of his place in society."

Helene was no longer certain that she understood what Thomas was trying to say. Or perhaps she understood all too well. Perhaps the good rector was speaking of more than just his curate's temptations. Indeed, his remarks seemed like veiled warnings; more subtle and compassionate than his sister's, but were they admonitions nonetheless?

Suddenly, Lowe spoke again, but his gaze was distant. "Might I ask, Helene . . . have you ever been in love?"

13

In which Lady Catherine hosts a Tragedy of Errors

It was a shockingly inappropriate question, but inexplicably, Helene did not hesitate to answer it. "Yes, once," she answered hollowly. "A very long time ago."

Thomas turned to face her, his eyes suddenly sharp and assessing. "And did it end tragically?" He touched her lightly on the cheek. "Why—I'm sorry. I fancy that it did."

She laughed a bit unsteadily, and looked intently down at her hands. "I suppose I thought it very tragic at the time. But it was for the best, Thomas. Most things are, you know."

Slowly, the rector nodded and looked away again. "Perhaps you know what I mean, then, Helene, when I speak of the disappointments and temptations of youth. And why I fret so over my cousin."

"Perhaps," she softly agreed.

Just then, Thomas smiled, and changed the subject. "Well, let us speak no more of Basil's mourning over a long lost love! What of Miss Ariane? How do you like your work here?"

Helene smiled brightly, relieved to let the topic go. Thomas's insightful comments had a way of making one decidedly uncomfortable. "Oh, quite well. She is a bright child, and we are making fine progress in the schoolroom."

"I hope that someday she will be able to communicate," said Thomas gently.

Lightly, Helene laughed. "Oh, Ariane communicates, Thomas! She smiles, she frowns, and she can pout until her papa is wrapped around her finger. Although she cannot yet use words to tell us things, I am confident she soon will. Until then, there are many ways of communicating. We must simply listen."

Solemnly, Thomas nodded. "Very true!"

Helene looked through the greenery to where the girls were playing. "Already we have begun work on a rudimentary alphabet, and Ariane grasps it perfectly well—when she wishes to, that is!"

"It would be wonderful," proclaimed Thomas, "simply wonderful if the child can be normal. She deserves to have a happy life. I have always wished that for her. I have always prayed for her."

Once again, Helene was touched by his concern. It seemed that the rector loved children. But Ariane, to Helene's regret, could not fully overcome her fear of men. Just two days earlier, she had fled into Milford's pantry when a pair of strapping, blond-haired glaziers had arrived at Chalcote to repair the windows for the coming winter.

The two men had been friendly enough, and yet, when one of them turned a jovial smile upon Ariane, she paled, and for the first time in a sen'night, she'd scurried away to hide. Now, after several visits from Lucy and Lizzie, Ariane no longer hid from Thomas, but she still kept her distance.

Returning her attention to her guest, Helene turned to Thomas and laid her hand lightly upon his arm. He still gave every appearance of a man with a heavy burden.

"You are still thinking of Basil, are you not? I can see that you are worried about him."

Suddenly, Lowe threw back his head and laughed. "Ah, how well you know me, Helene! I daresay Treyhern is getting his money's worth, for your ability to understand the human mind is a powerful thing!"

"I hope that is a compliment," she murmured.

"It is indeed," Thomas answered, smiling down at her as he rose from the bench. "Now, take one more turn around the lawn with me, and then I must collect my wild imps and be gone."

Helene was a little disappointed. She did not welcome being left alone with her thoughts of Cam. "Can you not stay for tea?"

Slowly, the rector shook his head. "No, no! I dare not risk your butler's censure! I have taken tea here four times this week. Moreover—" Thomas paused to point down the long sweep of drive, "unless I miss my guess, here is Lady Catherine, come to bear you company. No one sits a horse quite as elegantly as she! So I shall bid you a good afternoon, and come again in a day or so."

As Thomas drifted down the garden path with his nieces in tow, Helene strolled toward the house, with Ariane clinging to her hand, hanging close to her skirts. Just outside the conservatory door, Helene stooped down to look the girl in the eye. "Ariane," she calmly began, "will you do something for me? Something important?"

The child nodded, ever so slightly. "Good," said Helene. "I should like you to try to be friends with Mr. Lowe. He is exceedingly fond of you. Please do not worry so about strangers, Ariane. You must remember that you are safe when either your papa or I are near. You understand that, do you not?"

The nod was less certain this time, but in the distance, Helene could see Catherine's groom leading two horses toward the stables. "Come along then," she said cheerfully. "Your aunt has come to tea. We must go in and tidy ourselves."

On the tenth day following Cam's departure, Helene accompanied Catherine on a walk down to Cheston-on-the-Water. It was but a short distance down the hill and past the church, and made even shorter by Catherine's graceful strides. Though the weather was cold, Helene was grateful for the chance to escape Chalcote and her oppressive thoughts of Cam. Together, they strolled through each shop, with Catherine chattering to everyone they met.

Catherine purchased a fine riding crop for her husband and a length of ribbon for Ariane, while Helene stopped only to post a letter to Nanny. On their return to Chalcote Court, Cam's sister suggested they take the route through the churchyard and around to the back gardens of the house.

As they strolled uphill to the ancient gate set deep into the low stone wall, Helene was reminded of an earlier visit, and of the pretty girl she had seen darting surreptitiously through the gravestones.

"Let's go 'round this corner," said Catherine, pointing toward the church. "I want to see if they've set Father's gravestone."

"Yes, of course," answered Helene, lifting up her skirts and setting off after Catherine. "Though it wasn't done last time I visited."

"You visited the family graves?" asked Cam's sister, stepping lightly over an old tree stump.

"Yes," admitted Helene, a little embarrassed. She tried to change the subject. "And that puts me in mind of something odd, Catherine. Indeed, I'd almost forgotten it. I saw the most extraordinary woman here that day, but she all but ran away from me. Young, fair, and very beautiful—"

"Where?" interrupted Catherine sharply. She jerked to a halt, the hem of her heavy walking dress swaying over the frosty grass.

Helene stared at her for a moment, then raised a finger toward the rear of the church. "Why, just there. She appeared, I think, from behind the corner, crossed over these graves, then darted out the gate—the same one through which we just came. She wore green, I seem to remember . . . and had red-blonde hair."

At her mention of the girl's hair, Catherine gave a sharp laugh and set off again. "Red-blonde? How fanciful I am! For a moment, it sounded as though you might have been describing Cassandra. So often one might find her wandering through the churchyard, but doubtless it was just someone from the village."

"Well," began Helene reluctantly, "the girl I saw was flesh and blood. But she was no one from the village whom I've ever met. And quite well-dressed, too."

"A girl, was it then?" Catherine began to retie the ribbons of her bonnet as they walked.

"A young woman," clarified Helene.

They reached Randolph's grave. Catherine knelt, and with quick, neat sweeps of the back of her gloved hand, began to wipe the dead leaves from the base of the new stone. "Then we may take comfort in the knowledge that it was not Cassandra come back to haunt us," she said quietly, looking up at Helene with a bitter smile.

Curiosity got the better of Helene's discretion. "You'll forgive my impertinence, I hope, when I say that from all you have told me, Mrs. Rutledge did not seem the type to linger in the churchyard."

"Ah, but on that count, my dear, you would be quite wrong," retorted Catherine, bouncing up to briskly dust the leaf mold from her gloves. "Cassandra wandered everywhere, day and night. She would drift through the woods and gardens, too. And if Cam expressed any concern at all, or offered to escort her, she would complain that he smothered her, and that Chalcote choked the very life from her."

"But there is no place on earth more beautiful than Chalcote!"

"She was a restless spirit, poor Cassandra. Particularly so, once all her admirers had been exiled. And she despised my brother for it, Helene. In truth, I think she hated him."

"But they had a child together," said Helene, confused. "How could she fail to feel respect, if not admiration, for a man who was such an exemplary father?"

For a long moment, Cam's sister did not answer. Instead, she needlessly adjusted her bonnet again, turned her back to Helene, and walked toward Cassandra Rutledge's grave, her movements strained and abrupt. Tension grew thick in the air as Helene stood, frozen to the ground beside Randolph's gravestone.

From over her shoulder, Catherine spoke. "It would seem, Helene, that you have failed to guess our ugly little secret," she said softly. Then suddenly, she spun about on one heel, her eyes flashing black fire, the similarity to her brothers startlingly obvious.

Mutely, Helene shook her head.

"Then I believe I shall tell you," answered Catherine in a low, throaty voice. "From all that I have seen, I daresay you've every right to know."

"No," whispered Helene, shaking her head again. "Your family matters are not for my ears. I am just the governess."

Catherine gave a sharp laugh. "Oh, do not delude yourself, Helene! You have never been *just the governess.* Not since the day you returned here." Cam's sister's eyes narrowed as she leaned incrementally closer. "And I shall tell you—and Cam be damned if he doesn't like it. Ariane is not my brother's child."

For a moment, it was as if Helene felt the earth sway beneath her feet, and she reached out to place a steadying hand upon Randolph's tombstone. "Not Cam's? But then . . . whose? How . . . how can you be sure?"

As if regretting the bluntness of her words, Catherine drew nearer and laid one hand upon the sleeve of Helene's heavy cloak. "Cam can be sure, Helene. It simply is not possible that Ariane is his flesh." The bitter, knowing smile flashed again. "And as to whose she might be, I daresay even Cassandra mayn't have known. Amongst her many admirers, there was more than one gentleman—and I use the term loosely—who looked a likely candidate. It's even remotely possible that she's my father's child, but I doubt even Cassandra was that desperate. Ariane was very small, too, which makes it harder still to speculate."

Slowly, Helene could feel the blood returning to her head. But the dreadful truth remained. *Ariane was not Cam's child!* The thought was almost as appalling as it was tragic. And yet, it had to be considered, when one studied Ariane's features and coloring. Moreover, this was not the first time Catherine had alluded to such a thing.

She lifted her chin and looked Cam's sister straight into the eyes. "Who else is aware of this, Catherine? It is hardly a secret which should be casually tossed about."

"I knew you would see it so, else I would never have told you," answered Cam's sister a little defensively. "And as to who knows, only I do. Doubtless, others suspect. And Cam will perhaps inform Bentley when he is a little more responsible."

"Then why do you choose to tell *me?*" asked Helene, truly confused now.

"Do you truly not know, Helene?" she asked. When Helene made no answer, Catherine merely shrugged, then clutched tight the close of her cloak, tilting her head back to stare up into the bleak, gray sky.

She looked suddenly very weary, almost delicate, the bones of her face fine and sharp in the weak afternoon light as she studied the bare branches that swayed and clattered overhead. About their feet, dead leaves skittered and whirled in the wintry wind.

With her brother's black eyes and somber countenance, the heavy black wool of her cloak billowing over the winter-dead grass, Catherine looked like a pagan Celt calling forth the long, cold months until spring.

"You asked," she finally said, still staring into the branches, "about Cassandra's respecting a man for being a good father. But can you now see what a hell her life must have been?"

"I fear I do not understand you, Catherine."

Catherine dropped her gaze to stare pointedly at Helene. "Just think of it, Helene. She bore her husband a bastard, probably out of spite. And yet he does nothing? He shows no jealousy. He does not punish her. He does not rail at her. He merely takes the child as his own, and gives it every drop of love he possesses—love, I might add, which he never felt for his wife. And which she disdained to try to earn."

"What are you saying, Catherine?"

"Is that not a just punishment, Helene? To be forced to face that, each and every day of your life? To know that you have done your husband the ultimate injustice? And that he has risen above it? I daresay I might have considered ending my life, too."

"Catherine!" whispered Helene. "You must never say such a thing! I am sure she did not. It was an accident. An accident! Cam—Lord Treyhern—told me so."

"You may believe what you wish, Helene," answered Catherine in an ice-cold voice. "But a silver candelabra does not often get carried into a vacant cottage and tossed into a rubbish pile by accident."

Helene could not suppress a gasp of horror. "But

Ariane was there! Cassandra, she . . . she took her child along! No woman could be mad enough to do such a thing!"

Ever so slowly, Catherine turned her gaze upon Cassandra Rutledge's gravestone and paused. For a long, agonizing moment, she said nothing. "I find I have grown cold, Helene," she finally whispered. "I believe I should like to return to Chalcote now, if you do not mind."

It was a gray and bitter afternoon, precisely two weeks after his departure, when Lord Treyhern and his heir returned from Devon. The portent of winter had made for a miserable journey north, and as he turned into the long sweep of driveway, Cam's only thought was of Helene and Ariane.

Indeed, he had thought of little else for the last twenty miles. All throughout the long journey home, with the crisis at Treyhern Castle finally behind him, the day had grown ever colder. But in truth, he felt as if he had been chilled to the marrow since leaving Helene, and he had the most fanciful notion that he could be warm again only when he reached her.

Nonetheless, there was one thing which had at last come clear to him. He simply could not marry Joan Belmont. Soon—tomorrow morning, in fact—he would wait upon his aunt and make the necessary explanations. She would be outraged, of course, but Cam hardly cared. His Aunt Belmont's rage was no scarce commodity.

It was his fair cousin for whom he worried, perhaps needlessly. Crane, the meddling old devil, was probably right. Joan was young, and the young deserved an opportunity to find love. Indeed, who knew better than he the utter misery of a marriage of convenience? These long weeks away from Helene had reminded him that despite all the pain his youthful passions had caused him, he would not have traded away those sweet memories for anything on God's earth.

His love affair with Helene, it so often seemed, had been the only love he had ever known. And he must find a way to re-create it, no matter how much disorder it brought into his life. It had taken Cam the better half of his two weeks away to accept the rather disconcerting realization that, in truth, matters were much as he had always feared; that he was incapable of living—really *living*—without Helene.

But he had realized something else too. The world would keep spinning upon its axis, even if he admitted his love. Lightning would not rend him in half. Chalcote would not collapse stone by stone. And the rest of his life could still be kept in some semblance of order.

Perhaps more importantly, Cam had given up trying to fight his emotions, or to understand them, or even to justify them to anyone else. In that much, at least, the miserable trip to Devon had been worth every bloody day of discomfort and loneliness.

Upon arriving at Chalcote's wide front steps, Cam slid gratefully from his saddle and bolted for the hall, leaving the horses to Bentley. It was decided. Tomorrow morning, he would ride to the Belmont estate and break the news to his aunt, as gently but as firmly as he could. There was, in truth, little she could do. Nonetheless, he owed her this one small courtesy, and until he had done it, common civility required that he say nothing of the matter to anyone. Not even to Helene.

Wondering if morning would ever come, Cam stepped into the shadows of the empty hall, his eyes slowly adjusting to the light.

"Ah! Good afternoon, Treyhern!" boomed an all-too-familiar voice, and Cam looked up to see Thomas Lowe rise from his chair near the twisting stairway. The very same chair, in fact, that the rector had occupied just prior to Cam's departure for Devon.

It gave one the rather disconcerting impression that Lowe had been encamped in Chalcote's hall for the past two weeks. Perhaps the presumptuous ass meant to move in. Cam looked about, half expecting to see a portmanteau on the floor beside the chair.

"Afternoon, Lowe," he finally answered, stripping away his riding gloves. "You've come to pay us yet another call?"

The rector leapt to his feet. "Indeed I have! Helene—Miss de Severs, that is—and Ariane have expressed an interest in going to Fairford today, to view the misericords at Saint Mary the Virgin. I thought I would take them this afternoon in my carriage." He paused for a short moment. "You have, I hope, no objection, Treyhern?"

"Objection—?" muttered Cam. Damned right he had an objection. He should have known better than to leave Gloucestershire. Helene's social life had obviously jumped forward by leaps and bounds. Absently, Cam slapped his gloves onto a side table.

"Any objection to my paying a personal call on a member of your staff, my lord?" clarified Lowe.

Cam hurled his hat on top of the gloves and stared at the rector rather too pointedly. "Is that what you are about here, sir? A *personal* call? Not a *parish* call?"

Thomas Lowe's face flushed with color. "Yes, Treyhern. I think it has rather quickly come to that. In fact," the rector dropped to a soft, uncertain undertone, "I daresay this will seem rather too sudden, but I must admit, I'm quite taken with Miss de Severs."

"Are you indeed?" Cam's tone was deliberately arch. "And do you fancy your affections are returned?"

The rector looked suddenly solemn. "Yes, my lord, I rather believe that they are," Lowe answered in that tone he often used to convey sad tidings. "Indeed, I would very much like your permission to court her."

Cam felt his gut clench into knots. "My permission?" He managed to choke out the words with a semblance of civility. "I hardly think you need it, Thomas. She is, after all, a woman grown."

A look which might have been bitterness flashed across the rector's face, but just as quickly vanished. "I am hardly a fool, my lord. I hold the living of Saint Michael's by your good grace, and Helene—Miss de Severs—is your servant."

"She is *not* my servant," retorted Cam, barely hiding his anger. "She is Ariane's teacher. And I account her a . . . a good friend as well."

"Indeed," replied Thomas Lowe ambiguously.

Cam ran his hands through his already disordered hair. "Look here, Thomas. Have you any idea what you are getting into?" He paused to jab one finger at the man's chest. "You're the damned rector! And Helene is . . . is—"

"—a very worthy woman, Treyhern," finished Lowe, in a voice that held just a hint of a threat. "I daresay I know what you are thinking. Whilst it's true that Miss de Severs's background is quite dissimilar to mine, she is a good woman in every respect. I am not overly concerned about her, er, lack of connections."

Cam felt as if someone had punched the air from his lungs. Lowe seemed perfectly sincere. And there wasn't a damned thing he could do about it.

Abruptly, Cam picked up his hat. "Then I wish you joy of your courtship, Thomas," he managed to say as he grabbed up his hat and gloves. "Perhaps the lady shall choose to accept your suit. Now, if you will excuse me, I have matters which require my immediate attention. I bid you safe travel to Fairford."

Lowe gave a half-bow. "Until tonight, then."

"Tonight—?" Already on the third step, Cam turned back to face the rector.

"Tonight," Lowe repeated, his mouth curling into a slightly sarcastic smile. "You invited me, my lord, to Lady Catherine's birthday dinner. May I hope that I have done nothing to make myself *persona non grata?"*

Slowly, Cam shook his head. Cat's bloody birthday dinner! Damn and blast! It had completely slipped his mind.

But Lowe was still staring at up him with a look of mild unease. "Do not be absurd, Thomas," Cam finally managed to answer. "I had simply forgotten. You are as welcome as ever in my home."

As the rector returned to his chair, Cam trudged up the next flight of steps, his disappointment now painfully acute. His hell-for-leather ride home had been for naught. He was not to be rewarded by even one moment alone with Helene.

Worse, he would have no opportunity to discover what there was between Helene and Lowe. Not that Cam had any clue as to how a gentleman went about asking such a thing. And there was, apparently, *something* between them. Lowe seemed very sure of himself.

Cam's feet flew faster and faster up the stairs. How in God's name had it happened so quickly? Or had anything happened at all? He reminded himself that Helene was often almost inappropriately friendly; open and congenial with everyone, be they servants, villagers, or her equals. Lowe had simply misinterpreted her warmth. Had he not?

Cam hurtled around the last turn, resisting the urge to rip the newel post with his bare hands and send it hurtling down into the hall below. Bloody hell! He had to get hold of himself. Two minutes under the same roof as Helene and his emotions were running wild. And now, she was off for a drive with the rector, and taking his daughter along, leaving Cam unable to reassure himself that they were well—and that perhaps they had both missed him just a little.

He reached his bedchamber, thrust open the door and strode toward the front windows. Boadicea bounded off his bed with a throaty trill of welcome, apparently the only one he was going to get. In the driveway below, his traveling coach was being moved to make room for Thomas Lowe's curricle, which was coming back around from the stables. The rather ironic bit of symbolism did not escape Cam, and it did nothing to improve his mood.

A quarter-hour before their appointed departure, Helene descended from the schoolroom wing only to discover that Thomas had arrived well ahead of schedule. Helene's heavy traveling cloak was draped over one arm, and with the other hand, she led Ariane down the twisting staircase. Smiling pleasantly, Lowe leapt from his chair and came quickly forward to assist.

"One moment, Thomas," she murmured absently, as he reached for her cloak. "His lordship is expected home later this afternoon." She rummaged through the pocket of the cloak, then tugged out a carefully folded note. "I must leave him a personal message to let him know where Ariane and I have gone."

"Allow me," said Thomas warmly, taking both the paper and the cloak from her. "You are most thoughtful, Miss de Severs, but Treyhern returned a quarter-hour ago. I took the liberty of mentioning our plans."

Helene was a little nonplussed at that. She supposed she had secretly hoped that Cam would seek her out upon his return. Or at least make inquiries as to his daughter's progress during the past two weeks. Her dismay must have been mortifyingly apparent.

Thomas cleared this throat tentatively. "There was, I

collect, a matter of some urgency that required Treyhern's attention. He said he would see us at dinner tonight."

"Tonight? Yes, of course."

The rector looked about as if searching for something, then carelessly shoving the note into his pocket, he took up the cloak again, and spread it neatly across Helene's shoulders. Smartly, he offered his arm. "Shall we away to Fairford, ladies?" he asked heartily, casting a reassuring smile in Ariane's direction. "One of my horses came up with a loose nail, but Treyhern's groom has kindly mended it, and my carriage has come back around to await us."

"By all means," answered Helene, tugging anxiously at the ties of her bonnet.

"Then what a fortunate fellow I am!" the rector announced as they set off. "Spending the afternoon with what must surely be the two prettiest ladies in all of Gloucestershire!"

Never taking his eyes from the carriage below, Cam absently bent down to scoop up Boadicea, who had leapt from the bed to twine about his feet. At least someone had awaited his homecoming. The cat clambered up his coat to settle loosely over his shoulder, purring contentedly. But Cam felt far from content. Behind him, he heard Crane directing the footmen to haul the trunks into his dressing room, but he did not turn around.

"Good God!" he muttered as soon as Crane had left. "What could she possibly see in him?"

"Thrum, thrum," said the cat, kneading his shoulder with her claws. She went too deep, digging one claw through his coat, and the resulting prick of pain was as acute as his disappointment.

He would have no opportunity to tell Helene all the things he wanted to say—not that Cam knew how to say them. He felt so awkward. So angry. So thwarted and so damnably inexperienced.

"Aye, I daresay you're right to dig at me," he told Boadicea. "Even Bentley would have managed better, I have no doubt. And tonight, there'll be the devil to pay."

Yes, tonight of all nights, he would to be required to stare at his aunt and Joan across his own dinner table! He would be compelled to play the part of the congenial host to Lowe, his obsequious sister, and that quiet curate, Basil what's-his-name. And now, he would have to watch his brother resume his fawning over Helene, with the rector in close competition.

Throughout the ride home, Bentley had turned time and again to the topic of Helene, his fascination apparent. Although the arrogant puppy had refrained from any overtly improper remarks, his comments had made plain his intent to remain friends with her. And Cam had been forced to admit to himself that he had no good reason to refuse him.

He still didn't know why his brother had accompanied him to Devon, but he was damned grateful. Bentley had been a huge help. Still, the tension between them had continued unabated. And at last, he'd decided what it was. It felt suspiciously like old-fashioned masculine jealousy.

But over Helene? That made no sense, for Bentley had been fractious long before her arrival. And it occurred to Cam that he was being insanely, unreasonably jealous of Helene. He knew it, and yet he felt powerless to stop himself.

For the first time in his life, Cam found himself wishing that he had a little more experience with the female mind. Even Bentley had probably bedded more women; certainly, he had tried to seduce more. The thought should have been galling, but it wasn't. Cam had never in the whole of his life seduced anyone. And why?

Because Cam had never truly wanted anyone other than Helene.

There. It was out. The truth again. He must have jerked convulsively, for Boadicea made a noise of feline annoyance, then leapt from his shoulder, sinking in another claw as she went. But Cam scarcely noticed.

Below, he watched the rector hand Ariane up into his carriage. Helene stood to one side, smiling at the two of them. In response, Cam reached toward the side table, poured a healthy measure of brandy into a glass, and tossed back half.

Helene came reluctantly down to dinner in her best gown of dark blue silk trimmed with black braid. Catherine had enthusiastically chosen it from Helene's wardrobe, though the dress was, perhaps, a bit too ostentatious for her position. Nonetheless, Cam's sister had insisted, and had brought her own lady's maid from Aldhampton to dress their hair.

It had not helped. Apprehension and grief sat in the pit of Helene's stomach like a stone. She had not seen Cam since that dreadful day when he'd kissed her goodbye and set off to Devon. And she had no wish to see him—especially not with Joan Belmont on his arm.

But what choice did she have, save feigning a headache, or making some other transparent excuse? And she could hardly be so rude to Cam's sister, whom she liked so much.

And so Helene dredged up her courage, and slipped quietly down the stairs to enter the yellow parlor shortly after the arrival of Catherine's husband, and just in time for a glass of wine before dinner. William Wodeway was a large, blustery blond-haired fellow who greeted Helene warmly, but showed no sign of recognition. Nor did Catherine remind him of their past acquaintance, Helene noted with interest.

Cam stood across the room, talking quietly with Thomas Lowe's sister, and looking stunningly handsome in his formal attire. Roughly, Helene jerked her gaze away, returning her attention to Catherine's husband. Almost at once, Wodeway engaged the slender, fair-haired gentleman to their right in a rather one-sided discussion of the hunting season.

Helene listened dispassionately, contributing little, as Catherine's husband explained that the bird hunting this year had been sadly lacking. Worse, even, than the cubbing season that had come before. And no one, Helene learned, knew how to properly cross-breed a foxhound nowadays. *Confirmation all wrong, ears too long . . .*

On and on Wodeway rambled, while the young man—the rector's cousin, Mr. Rhoades, whom Helene had met at church—murmured his polite agreement to every lament. From across the room, Helene caught Thomas's eye. The gleam of humor which flickered there was all too apparent. Immediately, he crossed the room to stand beside her.

"Have you no interest in the merits of Wodeway's hounds, Miss de Severs?" he whispered, flashing her a teasing smile. "Basil, I fear, must suffer in his usual silence—but with poor Will, silence will suffice." He raised his glass to gesture toward Mrs. Fane. "However, I daresay you ought to join my sister across the room."

Helene turned her gaze toward the corner she had been deliberately avoiding. "I fancy," continued Thomas, "that my sister is impressing Treyhern with her knowledge of crops and livestock. The late Mr. Fane having been a gentleman farmer, she has a fondness for agriculture."

From her seated position, Mrs. Fane looked up at Cam, who was bent politely over her chair, an empty wineglass clutched loosely in the palm of his hand. But at that precise moment, whatever interest Cam may have felt for the rector's sister must have lapsed. As if sensing Helene's presence in the room, he lifted his gaze to stare just over the top of Mrs. Fane's head, to catch and hold Helene's gaze with a startling intensity.

At once, Thomas laid his hand lightly upon Helene's arm. "Look!" he exclaimed, turning Helene toward the door. "There is Mrs. Belmont and her daughter! They normally attend church in Coln St. Andrews, so I daresay you've not yet been introduced?"

Weakly, Helene confessed she'd not had the pleasure, and before she was aware of it, Thomas was propelling her toward them. Just then, Will Wodeway stepped to one side, and Helene caught an unobstructed view of the young woman who stood so rigidly at Mrs. Belmont's elbow.

The young woman from the churchyard!

There was no doubt at all. Again, she wore pale green, the perfect foil for her cloud of red-blonde hair. As Mrs. Belmont chattered on like a queen holding court, her daughter suddenly lifted a pair of rather shy blue eyes and glanced about the room as if searching for someone. Almost at once, her gaze caught on Helene, and a burst of color lit her cheeks.

Suddenly, Thomas was urging Helene forward from the crowd and introducing her. Mrs. Belmont snapped open a silver lorgnette, and peered at her with a few cool words of acknowledgment, while Joan seemed to almost shrink into the background. The girl's eyes had widened with what looked like true fear, and as Helene took her hand, a look of almost pleading desperation sketched across her face.

Her meaning could not have been more plain. Joan Belmont was afraid that Helene had recognized her, and might mention having seen her in the churchyard. Indeed, had she not gone to great lengths in order to avoid Helene that day?

Despite her own loss, Helene could not find it in her heart to be cruel. "I have long desired to make your acquaintance, Miss Belmont," Helene answered in a clear, carrying voice. "I regret that we could not have met sooner." And then, she forced herself to smile at the girl—at Cam's wife-to-be.

Suddenly, a knot of sorrow caught in her throat, robbing her of speech, but she need not have worried. Mrs. Belmont had turned her attentions to Thomas Lowe, and a look of weak relief had spread across Joan's face.

Helene chose that moment to slip away from the group, and move toward the table on which Milford had placed several bottles and glasses. Bentley stood there, his eyes as black as thunderclouds, refilling his glass as he looked over the swelling crowd. His jaw was rigid, his feet set wide apart, and as his eyes lit on the women near the door, there was no misinterpreting the darkening glower on the young man's face. He set down the wine bottle with an unsteady clatter. Something was dreadfully wrong.

Helene drew up beside him, and touched him lightly upon the arm. Bentley's head jerked around, and he stared down into her eyes as if she were a stranger.

As his gaze took in the unfolding scene, Cam lifted his glass, and with an abrupt motion, tossed back the contents. From one corner of his eye, he could not help but see Helene as she laid her hand on his brother's arm, then stared up into Bentley's face with an expression of such sweet concern it tied Cam's stomach in a knot.

Worse, in her eagerness to reach Bentley, Helene had failed to note that the besotted rector was on her heels like a trusty hound. Already he had escaped the Belmonts, and was crossing the room to return to her side. But Helene was urging Bentley away from the crowd and toward an empty corner.

It was more than Cam cared to watch. He would have given half his fortune to have had this evening alone with her. So much had been left unsaid. Though in truth, Cam hardly knew what he should say. But if he could just have been alone with Helene, the right words would have come. Only with Helene had he ever been able to be himself. And so often, words had simply been unnecessary.

Cam watched as Lowe interjected himself into Helene's rather intense conversation with Bentley. He let his cold gaze drift down Lowe's length. Indeed, it had shocked him to learn this afternoon from Milford just how frequently Lowe had called at Chalcote during Cam's absence.

His only consolation, and a weak one at that, was that it had been Thomas, and not Bentley, to whose charms Helene had apparently succumbed. He used the term *succumbed,* because surely Lowe would not have baldly suggested a courtship without encouragement from Helene. Would he?

Lowe was laughing cheerfully now, and thumping Bentley on the back. The rector had strategically placed himself between Helene and Bentley in what seemed a very proprietary way. Something akin to hatred burned in Cam's belly at the thought of Thomas Lowe enjoying Helene's companionship. Had he perhaps enjoyed something more? If so, that would explain a great deal. Thomas was a rector, yes, but he was a man. And a man had only to brush his lips over Helene's, and all judgment was lost.

Cam crossed the room and refilled his own glass. Yes, Thomas Lowe was a fine sort of fellow, he thought, slopping a healthy measure out of the bottle. The rector was handsome and polished, with an easy sort of charm that Cam could never hope to possess. Socially, it would not be the most prudent of matches, since Cam supposed Helene would bring little to the marriage save her cottage in Hampstead, and her mother's reputation, which sooner or later would come out.

Nonetheless, Thomas's position within the Church hierarchy was solid. His living was unassailably linked to Chalcote, and despite the rector's fears, Cam could never bring himself to remove the man out of spite. A marriage with Helene might impede Thomas's advancement, but it would hardly ruin him. And from it, he would have much to gain. His life would never be devoid of light. Or fire.

Cam returned his gaze to Helene and asked himself honestly if he could blame her for being flattered by Lowe's attentions. What further had she to look forward to if her life continued as it was? Years of working for low wages, in the homes of strangers who would never truly care for her? People who might not appreciate her skill and warmth and honesty?

Helene must once have wanted a normal life, a family of her own. Indeed, she was still young enough to have one, if only she could settle down with more success than her mother had. Was Thomas Lowe the first man on earth who'd been willing to overlook her less than circumspect upbringing?

Suddenly, Cam felt a rush of heated shame. He, of all people, had no right to look askance at Lowe's offer. Despite the conclusions he'd recently reached, what had Cam offered her? Almost nothing. No—worse. An insult!

Instead of courting her gently as Lowe had apparently been doing, he'd torn at her clothing and pawed at her body like an overeager schoolboy, then gratuitously offered to make her his mistress. *His mistress!* It was a wonder she hadn't left on the first mail coach. That was most certainly what he had deserved.

But perhaps he deserved something worse, he considered, watching Helene move through the room with her fluid grace. Perhaps he deserved to watch Thomas Lowe walk down the aisle of St. Michael's with Helene clinging to his arm. The thought of having to sit across the aisle from Helene every Sunday for the rest of his life seemed more like hell on earth than a religious experience. It would be more than Cam could bear.

He watched as Helene drew Bentley toward a pair of armchairs, the dark blue silk of her gown clinging to her curves in a way that was graceful yet alluring. Somehow, she had gotten rid of the rector. He wondered what she was thinking. What she had thought of when she had first looked across the room and caught his eye? Had she missed him at all? He could not guess.

Yes, Helene would undoubtedly lead the rector a merry dance, but in the end, they might make a match of it. Nevertheless, as Milford arrived to announce dinner, Cam realized that, by God, he did not have to make it easy on Thomas. With an abrupt toss of his hand, he sent the butler away, then pushed through the crowd toward Catherine.

Just as Milford appeared in the doorway to call them in to dinner, Helene saw Cam approach his sister and speak a few low words into her ear. Appearing a little nonplussed, Catherine nodded, then began pairing the group for seating. To her surprise, Helen found herself being taken in to dinner by Mr. Rhoades, the quiet curate, and seated next to Catherine's husband. She had seen Catherine's seating chart, and Cam had clearly asked her to alter it at the last minute. Why?

Helene was to have a great deal of time in which to consider it, for dinner was interminable. Despite Helene's best efforts, the curate answered her questions only in stuttered monotones, while Will Wodeway's banter was limited to crops, the weather, and the already much-belabored topic of hounds and hunting.

Several courses and a vast deal of wine passed through the room as Catherine's health was toasted a half-dozen times. By the time the meal had ended, and the ladies had risen to remove to the parlor, all the gentlemen save the curate were more than a trifle deep. Bentley's habits came as no surprise, but Helene had been a little taken aback watching Cam and the rector match the brawny Will glass for glass.

The gentlemen did not linger long over their port, and what followed should have been a typical evening of rural entertainment. Miss Belmont was asked to demonstrate her skills at the pianoforte, and began to play quite prettily, if a little timorously. After sending the curate to turn Joan's pages, Catherine began to solicit players for a game of whist. A sullen Bentley resisted her challenge, but Catherine's husband, along with Thomas Lowe and his sister, were soon persuaded to make a foursome. Helene joined Bentley on the long leather sofa and again attempted to engage the young man in conversation.

His back turned toward the fire, Cam stood unsociably alone at the end of the room, his arms crossed casually over his chest, one heel propped behind him on the brass fender. As the card players settled into their chairs, Cam let his foot slip slowly from the rail and turned toward his aunt. Despite the distance, his quiet words carried.

"It would appear, ma'am, that all of my guests are otherwise engaged," Cam said, in a voice that was remarkably steady given the quantity of alcohol he had consumed. "Would you be so obliging as to step through to my study, so that we might speak in privacy?"

With a rather smug smile, Mrs. Belmont rose, and the two of them disappeared through the service pantry. At once, Joan's playing faltered rather badly. Bentley sat down his empty glass with a force that snapped off the stem. In the distant corner, the card players seemed not to have noticed the sudden tension in the air. The curate diligently flipped another page. Joan picked up her melody and went on.

"One may well guess what that is all about," hissed Bentley, jerking his head toward Cam's study. He picked up the broken stem and began to toy with it rather carelessly.

"For my part, I do not care to guess," insisted Helene, abruptly plucking the glass from his fingers and laying it down beside the broken bowl. "And it's none of our concern."

Bentley's dark eyes narrowed, and he looked surprisingly sober. "Is it not?" he asked, his voice a raw undertone. "Is your heart indeed made of stone, Helene?"

As she stared across the length of the sofa at Bentley, the final chords of Joan's sonata ground to a halt. Helene was dimly aware that the girl got up from the pianoforte and left the room in some haste. In the distant corner, Catherine squealed and took another trick as the card table roared with laughter. Mr. Rhoades walked quickly toward the fire. The ticking of the mantel clock grew louder and louder. Unable to bear the tension any longer, Helene turned to face Cam's brother.

"Very well, then, Bentley," she heard herself say, to her unending shame. "Just what do you imagine *that* is all about?"

"My beloved brother is finalizing his wedding plans," he answered, choking out the words. "And he cares not one whit for Joan's feelings. *She cannot possibly love him!* Indeed, I am persuaded that she does not. I have known her all my life. She would have told me if she cared for Cam! I tell you, Helene, I won't stand for this! And neither will Joan!"

But in truth, the young man sounded as though he sought to convince himself, and not Helene. Was this the source of Bentley's bitterness? Was Cam about to wed the girl his younger brother loved? Suddenly, it seemed to

Helene that she was far too near the hearth. The atmosphere inside the parlor seemed close, almost airless.

Could Bentley's words be true? Was she to be compelled to live under the same roof with Cam and his new wife, at least until her obligation to Ariane was ended? To watch Cam and his bride begin their life together? To even, perhaps, watch Joan Belmont grow round with the child of the man Helene loved more than life itself? It would be too much to bear. Her head swam uncertainly.

Abruptly, Helene jerked from her seat. "I beg you will excuse me, Bentley," she managed to murmur. "I find I am in need of a little air."

Before Bentley could offer to accompany her, Helene bolted from the room and down the darkened corridor to the ladies' retiring room. As she darted through the door, however, she was taken aback by Miss Belmont, who leapt from the vanity table in a rush of muslin, the corner of something white slithering down between the folds of her skirts.

"Oh—! Miss de Severs!" Joan's fingers flew to her mouth. "You quite startled me."

Despite her own distress, Helene could not but notice that Joan's hand shook pathetically. It was obvious the young woman had been crying. However, before Helene could reply, Joan had pushed past her, and through the door. It seemed she believed her fate was sealed, and was none too happy about it.

Torn between sympathy for the fleeing young woman, and pity for herself, Helene studied her too-pale face in the mirror and surrendered, sinking into the seat Joan had just vacated. Slowly, she bent forward, lowering her forehead onto her arm, which rested across the vanity, and forced herself to draw in deep draughts of air. The retiring room was blessedly cold, and the blood slowly returned to her head.

Bentley, it seemed, had been right in his guess. Clearly,

poor Joan agreed. And given both their rather distressed reactions to Cam's meeting with Mrs. Belmont, there was little doubt in Helene's mind as to just what had brought Joan to St. Michael's churchyard that fine autumn day. It was but a short walk through the church's rear gate and into the orchards of Chalcote Court. Once inside the estate, there were a hundred romantic trysting places. And who would know that better than Helene?

A bitter, self-deprecating smile pulled at her mouth as a warm tear slid down her nose. Shamed by her lack of control, Helene jerked up her head to dash away the tear, and it was only then that she saw the scrap of white paper beneath the vanity. Without thinking, she snatched it up, and immediately the words caught her eye.

My dearest Joan—
It must be tomorrow. I beg you. We dare not delay. All will be in readiness at the appointed time & place. Your mother must simply forgive us. My eternal love— B.R.

The paper was tattered, the masculine writing splashed untidily across the page as if the author had scrawled his note in great haste. The implication was all too damning, and Helene had no doubt as to whom the writer was. Bentley intended to elope with Joan Belmont—probably to Scotland, since neither was of age.

Good God! He meant to deliberately snatch his brother's bride from beneath Cam's nose, and perhaps forever damn both himself and Joan to society's censure, and to her mother's endless fury.

Cam would surely kill him. Still clutched in Helene's hand, the letter trembled like a leaf. She recoiled at the thought of what she must do. If she approached Bentley, he would simply deny it all. Helene skimmed the note again. *It must be tomorrow night.* Thank God she had some time in which to think.

Perhaps she could reason with Bentley tomorrow when he was fully sober. Perhaps she could persuade him to confide in her. If she could not—well, there remained but one choice. She would give the note to Cam. Would it wound him to discover how cruelly his brother and his cousin had plotted against him? No matter what had occurred between them, Helene suddenly realized that she had no wish to see Cam suffer. Life had dealt with him harshly enough.

Yes, approaching Cam must be her last resort. And in truth, Helene had more than a little sympathy for star-crossed lovers. Cam's unleashed wrath was a horrible thing to behold, and Bentley would no doubt take the brunt of it, for he was hardly in his brother's good graces. Yes, Helene would throw Bentley to the wolves only if no other alternative was left to her. As much as she loved Cam—and she did, all too much—she would not stand idly by while Bentley ruined his life, and that of an innocent, impressionable young girl.

So resolved, Helene slid one hand down her dress and muttered a sudden oath. The blue silk gown was one of the few she possessed with no pocket slits at all, and because they were dining at Chalcote, she had rejected its matching reticule as unnecessary. Carefully, Helene folded the note and concealed it in the palm of her hand, unnerved to hear the clock strike eleven. She had been gone from the parlor far too long. Anxiously, her eyes darted about the retiring room for a secure nook, to no avail.

And then Helene remembered. Earlier in the evening, she had seen Mrs. Fane and Catherine go into the study to fetch a volume of poetry from Cam's bookshelves, apparently to settle some debate that had arisen over dinner. The book now lay forgotten upon a side table.

Drawing in a deep, steadying breath, Helene pushed open the door and reentered the corridor. A gust of frigid air assailed her. In the Great Hall beyond, she could hear footmen beginning to stir, followed by the unmistakable sound of someone's carriage being brought around from the stables. *Thank God.* This horrible, interminable evening would soon be over.

Ariane leaned across the second floor railing to peer down into the milling servants in the Great Hall below. Watching the different colors of livery was like watching fish dart about in a pond. Footmen ran to and fro. On the cobblestones outside the door, she could see Aunt Belmont's carriage coming 'round from the coach house. By the arched entranceway, Milford was handing Larkin a heap of coats and cloaks.

Good! It was over.

She had thought and thought, very carefully. And for a very long time. She was certain, almost certain, that he was near. The memories were no longer clear. The words had slipped away, hushed by a thousand whispers in her mind. But in her sleep sometimes, she could remember them. Until the very moment when she awoke. Alone. In the darkness. Waiting for Helene, who knew her secret—or part of it, anyway.

Helene wanted her to talk. But what had Mama said? *Don't tell.* But Mama had not known Helene. If she had, surely she would have understood? Yes, she would have. Helene was not like the others. Quietly, Ariane crouched down behind the railing to watch the guests as they departed.

14

In which Mrs. Belmont sets her Cauldron a'boil

The violent sound of ripping paper tore through the silence of the earl's study. With an agility which belied her age, Agnes Belmont leapt to her feet and stalked toward the hearth, pitching what was left of Cam's quickly penned document onto the blazing fire.

She whirled to face her nephew. "You, Camden Rutledge—" she clearly enunciated, one bony, quivering finger pointing toward the greedy flames, "—may burn in hell in just such a way, if you think to renege on your betrothal to my daughter."

Since his aunt had seen fit to leap from her chair, Cam rose respectfully from his own. He stood immutably, hands clasped behind his back, at his wide oak desk. "I am offering," he quietly repeated, "to sponsor Joan for a season in town—two or three, if she cannot find a husband who suits her. And I have offered a dowry which is three times that left her by your late husband. As the head of this family, I can do no less."

"What you will *do,* young man," insisted Mrs. Belmont, the finger still trembling, "is stand up to your obligations and take that girl to the marriage bed, or suffer the consequences."

Cam bowed his head. "I am sorry to have distressed you, ma'am. But as I have already stated, I find I cannot in all fairness marry Joan when my heart is not engaged. I realize that we have discussed, on more than one occasion, the convenience of my wedding her, but I know too well that the heart is sometimes not so wise, and that convenience can often become just another word for endless misery."

"Misery?" sneered Mrs. Belmont. "I vow, what would you know of *misery?"*

"Enough to know I would not wish it on anyone, and certainly not on someone who has been as dear to me as my cousin."

"Very pretty words, my boy! But you are a besotted dreamer." Her gaze narrowed knowingly. "You see through the eyes of a fool."

Somberly, Cam shook his head. "No, ma'am. At long last, I see things as they are. Indeed, have you troubled yourself to ask what Joan wants? She can no longer even look me in the eyes! What was once an avuncular affection has been replaced by stark dread. In truth, I cannot but wonder if her affections are not directed elsewhere."

With two long strides, Mrs. Belmont crossed the carpet to face her nephew. For the briefest of moments, the woman looked as if she might strike him. "Just what are you implying, Camden? My daughter is as pure as the driven snow, and I have made perfectly sure of it! She has not escaped my protection, not for one moment!"

Cam threw up his hands. "Escape?" he whispered hoarsely. "Pray consider your choice of words, madam! She is a young woman, not a prisoner!"

Mrs. Belmont's eyes narrowed further still. "You would do well, my lord, to tend to your home fires, and leave me to mine. Would you have me permit Joan to run fast and free, like that wastrel brother of yours? Is that your notion of a proper upbringing?" His aunt swept an expansive arm through the room. "Thank God my sister is dead and cannot see what you have wrought here."

Cam stalked away from the desk, shoving his chair beneath it with a violence. "What I have wrought here, madam, is a profitable estate—an estate dragged from the brink of ruin by the sweat of my brow. And I have seen to the upbringing of my brother and sister as best I was able. I do not deign to discuss it further with you. Now, I have given you my offer. Your pitching it into the fire in no way obviates my wish to take care of Joan."

"You must marry her! You do not know what you are doing!"

Cam could not suppress a grim smile. "You are closer to the truth than I care to admit. But I shall sort out my life soon enough."

Mrs. Belmont sneered knowingly. "Do not imagine, my boy, that I cannot guess what's afoot here. You mean to set up that French tart as your mistress. But Joan is no fool. She knows that men must have their diversions."

Cam suppressed the urge to throttle the woman. Her callousness made him want to retch. "Joan deserves something a little better than a faithless husband," he softly concluded. "And my governess is a *lady*."

Mrs. Belmont rested the tip of one gloved finger upon the corner of Cam's desk. "What Helene Middleton is, sirrah, is the daughter of a demimondaine!"

Her use of Helene's former name did not escape his notice. Cam stood in mute anger, gripping the back of his chair with both hands.

His aunt laughed. "Oh, Camden, my boy! Are you such a fool as all that? It took so very little effort to reveal her scandalous past! Flitting about the Continent with whomever could afford her so-called wages! Ha! One has but to look at her to see her mother's resemblance and depravity."

With long, angry strides, Cam stalked toward the door and yanked it open. Despite his almost blinding anger, through the passageway he could see his guests crowded around Catherine. His sister was seated at the pianoforte, leading the group in a lively song.

When Cam spoke, his voice was cold with rage. "You'll tell Joan what I have said, madam. *And you'll tell her tonight,* lest her health collapse. Or something worse happens." Cam stared blindly into the depths of the parlor. "This conversation is at an end."

He stared down at his knuckles, which had gone white against the brass of the doorknob. He was frightened by the depth of his anger, terrified by his desire to lash out and strike his aunt. Cam squeezed shut his eyes. The thought petrified him. He was losing control. Losing his grip. Again and again. It kept happening.

Mrs. Belmont walked toward him and laid her fine-boned hand over his, and his eyes flew open wide. "At an end?" she asked softly, staring at the guests who crowded his parlor. "No, I rather doubt it, Camden. Not unless you are willing to have your light o'love humiliated. A few choice words said in a carrying tone, and I shall be the focus of everyone's attention."

It felt as if the doorknob might come off in his hand. *The bitch had him.* Already, Will had stopped singing, and had turned to look over his shoulder.

Cam pushed the door shut. Mrs. Belmont smiled. "Yes," she said sweetly, "it would be difficult to have all of them learn the truth about your so-called governess. How terribly sordid! The Earl of Treyhern's only child, surrendered into the care of a high-flying courtesan!"

"Miss de Severs is nothing of the sort," Cam returned, forcing a calm tone. Good God! He had expected his aunt to react badly, but this was beyond the pale.

"Ha!" shouted Mrs. Belmont derisively. "Do you think for one moment that I do not know perfectly well the history of what went on between you two? I had the whole story from your worthless sire."

"My father knew nothing," muttered Cam.

Mrs. Belmont smiled serenely. "Oh, he knew it! And he told it! And then he slapped his knee with hilarity over your escape! And now, you mean to throw yourself at the feet of a woman who could be had for a pittance? A woman whom you, and a dozen others, have already had? It merely proves what everyone has long suspected—that you are every inch the fool your father was."

Cam ignored his aunt's lies. And as for the truth, well—there was no point in denying his feelings for Helene. He did not believe that his aunt's description of her past was wholly accurate. But he had almost ceased to care.

"You know nothing of Miss de Severs's character, madam," he said darkly. "You'd be well advised to hold your tongue."

"She is naught but a whore's daughter!" Mrs. Belmont stamped her foot upon the carpet. "She is not and never has been any better than she should be."

"It is over, madam," he said calmly, his fear swallowed up in rage. Whatever storm his aunt conjured up, he and Helene would ride it out together.

"No! I am your blood! You'll do as I ask or suffer the consequences."

Cam could see the woman's grasp on reality slipping away. Had it meant that much to see her child wed to wealth and a title? It was time to be brutal.

"You are right," he said softly. "I love Helene. Whatever that may make me—and you may hurl your insults at me as you will—Miss de Severs is a lady. And I love Joan, too, but not in the way that a man should love the woman he means to marry. I have told you what I will do for her. It must suffice." Abruptly, he laid his hand back upon the knob and yanked open the door.

"Camden." His aunt's voice sounded deep and

ragged, as if it arose from the torments of hell. "Please! I beg you! I am your only maternal aunt. Our family has been weakened—almost destroyed—by immoral excess. The salvation of it is left to us!"

Blindly, Cam turned to her. "I find I have grown weary, madam, of being cast in the savior's role. The family must flounder on without one. But I shall do all that I can for you and for Joan. I shall take her under my wing—even into my home, should she wish it. Catherine will take her to town and bring her out. But I cannot wed her. My heart is otherwise engaged. I am sorry."

"No!" his aunt whispered hoarsely. "You cannot—why, you would not *dare* to marry that woman—!"

Cam merely pulled the door open wider still.

"She is a whore!" hissed his aunt. "Camden, I made inquiries! There can be no doubt! You may have been her first, but you shan't be her last! She imagines you to be a fool like your father! She will take what she can get, and drag you into dissolution. Why else would she return after all these years? Have you asked yourself that?"

Cam strode away from his study, leaving his aunt alone in the doorway. There was just enough truth in her accusations to trouble him. But not about Helene. About himself.

It was himself, always himself, that Cam was left to doubt. There was no question that Helene disordered his mind. All self-discipline and every good intention flew out the window the minute she entered the room. And it would never change.

Behind him, his aunt said nothing. Thank God. Through weary eyes, he watched Helene reenter the parlor, seize a book from the side table, and then hasten toward his brother, who was still sprawled upon the sofa, his perpetually sullen glower even darker than usual.

For once, Helene's expression was telling. She looked

serious, almost distraught, as she settled onto the sofa and leaned toward Bentley. So absorbed was he in studying the intense look which passed between the pair, Cam barely noticed that his guests were now wandering away from the pianoforte and beginning to make their goodbyes to his sister.

Just then, Helene shifted on the sofa, turning toward Bentley so that he could no longer see her face. Illogically, Cam felt another stab of rejection, as if he had once again been shut out of Helene's life—what should have been *their* life—had fate not played them false.

His aunt's angry words echoed in Cam's head. *Did* he mean to marry Helene? Yes, he did. If she would have him.

And unless she were truly in love with the rector, a possibility his aunt would have surely belittled, then only one of two things were true. Either her love for him had endured, just as his had. Or she was as disingenuous and worldly as his aunt claimed, and had merely returned to see if he were as big a fool as the boy she had left behind.

Cam no longer believed the latter, but again, he simply did not care. His aunt had given words not only to his fears, but to his future. He would have Helene, and damn the cost.

Just then, the rector trotted across the carpet to make a low, graceful bow over Helene's hand. Her laughter, a little brittle, seemed to carry through the room. Something, he finally realized, was exceedingly wrong.

Suddenly, Cam found his view of the sofa briefly obscured by Mrs. Fane, who was coming toward him, obviously intent upon saying goodnight. He feigned civility, taking her hand, and thanking her for the pleasure of her company. And yet, the whole of his attention was focused upon Helene.

Helene. She had laid her hand upon Bentley's coat

sleeve. It looked as if she were asking him something. Why was she so attentive toward Bentley tonight? How would she react to Cam's proposal of marriage? Would she laugh in his face? If she refused him—perhaps out of feminine pride or some misplaced wish for independence—he would press the issue as far as he dared. Indeed, this time, he would make certain that his was an offer no sane woman could refuse.

Catherine's laughter dragged him back into the present, and Cam looked up to see that Helene had vanished. Larkin was passing out coats and cloaks.

Thank God. It was over. He could shut himself up in his study and allow himself the rare luxury of getting blind drunk. Mindful of his guests, Cam rushed forward to help Joan with her cloak. The Belmonts could not possibly be gone from his house soon enough.

It was long after midnight when Helene realized that in her haste to leave the parlor she had left Joan's mysterious note tucked inside the little book. But precisely which book? In her distress, Helene had failed to note so much as the title, or even the color of the leather binding. Good heavens! What had she been thinking?

Shoving her feet back into her satin evening slippers, Helene hastened through the upper hall and down the stairs. Once the book was reshelved by the parlormaid tomorrow, she might never find it again. But sooner or later, someone would. And by then, the letter's reappearance might prove a grave embarrassment to Bentley, and ruin young Joan. And undoubtedly, it would hurt Cam. Perhaps she should want that, but deep in her heart, she simply could not.

The fire had burned to little more than a heap of ash by the time Helene cracked open the parlor door. The room was vacant, she was relieved to see. By the dim glow of the coals, she could see the slender volume perched on the table where she had left it. Darting inside, Helene reached the table, scooped up the book, and dropped it into the pocket of her dressing gown. She turned to go.

"Looking for Saint Camden, m'dear?" drawled a sullen voice from the gloom. Helene whirled about to see Bentley's lanky figure wedged across the window seat, his face half-concealed in shadows. Nonetheless, the indolent depravity in his tone should have warned her of what the dying firelight could not reveal.

Cam's brother sat, his back rigid against the window embrasure, one foot planted high in the center of the opposite wall. Low in his lap, the young man cradled a nearly empty goblet. His cravat and waistcoat were loose, his dark hair had fallen forward to deepen the shadows of his face, and he looked frighteningly like a younger version of his father.

"Bentley, take yourself off to bed," Helene ordered in her sternest tone. "You are drunk."

With a grace that defied her accusation, Bentley spun smoothly about to a sitting position, then strode across the room toward her, leaving his brandy behind. He drew to a halt, far too near for comfort. "I asked," he repeated softly, sliding one finger beneath her chin, "have you come looking for Saint Cam? For if you have, my dear, it shan't do you a damned bit of good."

"For God's sake, Bentley," Helene hissed. "Not only are you now roaring drunk, you are offensive." She spun about and strode toward the door. But Bentley was faster. He reached the door on her heels and thrust a long, powerful arm over her shoulder to hold it shut. Helene's heart leapt into her throat.

Bentley leaned into her then, urging Helene's body against the door. The wood was cold against her breasts. She could hear his breathing in her ear, smell the spirits on his breath. He laughed, low and wicked, against her temple.

"Do you think I cannot see the way he looks at you, Helene, when he fancies no one watches? Why, twice during dinner, I saw the old boy slip his hand under the table to ease himself a bit. I'm persuaded you've thawed him out."

"You are excessively vulgar," she hissed. "Let me go this minute."

He merely chuckled again. "You drive him to distraction, m'dear. Fancy that! My sainted brother with an incurable cock-stand." Strategically, Helene shifted her weight but his other arm came up to brace against the door, trapping her face first against the hard oak.

"Let me go, Bentley," she insisted. "I want no part of your quarrel with Cam."

A little frightened now, Helene knew better than to show her fear. Bentley was trying to use his overt masculinity to intimidate her, that was all. The boy was confused; angry at his brother, and unhappy with his lot in life. Bentley probably meant her no harm, but if she overreacted and created a disturbance, *harm* would not begin to describe what would befall her. Any governess was in jeopardy of such overtures, but Helene, particularly in this house, was at grave risk.

"Ahh, Helene," he whispered against the back of her head, his voice anguished. "You are so bloody beautiful. I can see why he burns for you. But Cam will never wed you. You do know that, do you not?"

"For heaven's sake, Bentley. You are crushing me," she whispered, in as composed a voice as she could muster. "Step back and let me breathe."

Bentley seemed not to have heard her. "Oh, yes. He wants you, sweet Helene. But his noble lordship will do his duty, no matter who must suffer. He'll marry Joan, and devil take anyone who doesn't like it."

"It does not concern me, Bentley," Helene lied softly. "You are hurting me. Let me go."

"Cam is hurting you, Helene. Do you think I cannot see that? He's hurting both of us. But perhaps we could bring one another some small measure of comfort?"

Seductively, the young man let his hand slide over her collarbone and upper arm, as if he might urge the fabric of her dressing gown off one shoulder. But it would not give, and Bentley was forced to shift his hand up and around her throat. Almost absently, the young man began to tug at the ribbons even as his other arm held her hands at bay.

Helene was growing frightened. Bentley had her pinned hard against the door and was swiftly—and rather adroitly—having his way with her nightclothes. Though he was by no means as large as his brother, he doubtless outweighed her by three stone. If he were serious, she could not possibly fight him off. With a sick feeling, Helene recalled how very much like his father he looked.

No! She simply refused to believe that Bentley was that much like his father. And for his sake, she could not let him behave dishonorably. "For God's sake, Bentley, let me go," she hissed, all too aware of the slight bulge Bentley was now urging firmly against her buttocks.

Bentley might be drunk and grieving over Joan, but the boy's male urges seemed not to have noticed. *Good God—was that not just like a man?* To slake his lust and disappointment with whomever was at hand? A woman was not so inconstant. She, of all women, should know.

Bentley, it seemed, cared not one whit for her sentiments. With heated fingers, he slipped loose another ribbon, then ran his tongue deftly down the curve of her ear. "Ah, come, Helene," he breathed against the damp trail of his tongue. "Revenge can be so sweet. I shan't do anything you don't want. And I'm not without experience, you know."

"I do *not* want you to touch me like this, Bentley," she

said, her voice choking on a sob. She tried without success to throw an elbow backward into his ribs. "I thought you were a gentleman. Damn you! I thought you were my *friend—!*"

That did it.

Bentley's grip relaxed, then spasmed against her skin. His hands slid down to span her waist as she felt a bone-deep shudder run through him. At once, he collapsed against her, his brow dropping to rest on the top of her head.

"Oh, God." He rasped the words into her hair. "Helene. Oh, *Helene—!* What am I doing? Christ, I am sorry. *So damned sorry . . .*"

With Bentley's embrace now slackened, Helene managed to turn around in his arms and face him. In the dimly lit room, she could barely make out the tears which pooled in his eyes. Their gazes met, and his eyes searched hers with a pained expression, as if asking for forgiveness.

She slid her hands up between them and pushed firmly against his chest. At once, he stepped back a pace. "Oh, Bentley!" she whispered. "Do you love her so very much?"

Mutely, the young man nodded, his eyes still shimmering in the firelight. "I . . . yes, I'm sure of it. I have loved Joan all my life. I realize that now. Now that it's too late."

Spontaneously, Helene gave his shoulders a gentle shake. "Bentley, I am so sorry. But there can be no good end to this. You cannot behave rashly, which I know is just what you are considering. Too many people will be hurt. You must be strong. Joan will be your sister and—"

"No!" he growled, cutting her off. "That I cannot bear!"

Helene leaned closer and held his painful gaze. Gently, she brushed one thumb across his cheek to wipe away the last trace of his tears. "But you can, Bentley," she gently whispered. "One has no notion of just what the heart can bear until you are faced with—"

Her words were cut short as the door that connected to the study came hurtling inward. Abruptly, Helene jerked her hand from Bentley's cheek.

Cam stood framed in the open doorway, a candelabrum held aloft in one hand. Backlit by the flickering glow from his study, the man looked like Satan stepping from the gates of hell. If Bentley had looked dissolute, then Cam looked . . . malevolent.

Helene watched Cam's eyes take in the scene before him. Mute shock, then obvious rage, swept over the harsh lines of his face. "What the devil is going on in here?" he whispered, his voice slicing through the silence like a knife.

"I . . . I forgot my book," stammered Helene, trying to will her voice to be steady as she pushed Bentley away from her. Cam trod slowly into the room, his footsteps sounding impossibly loud on the thickly carpeted floor.

"A *book* . . . ?" he echoed, his eyes flat and black in the candlelight as he came inexorably toward them.

"I . . . yes. A b-book," Helene stammered, acutely aware of her disordered nightclothes. "I was reading a book earlier, and I came downstairs to retrieve it. I am afraid I disturbed Bentley. He . . . he was still awake."

Cam drew to a halt before them, the candelabrum still held high. His eyes slid down Helene, taking in her hair, her nightgown, her robe. The look he turned on his brother was grim and emotionless. His words, however, were not.

"This time," Cam whispered lethally, "you go too far. Get out. Get out of this room. Get out of my house. Before I fucking kill you."

"Now just you see here, Cam!" said Bentley, lifting an unsteady hand. "This is not what you think! I was . . . was just . . . Helene was trying to—"

"Get out. *And God damn you.*" Cam's voice was chilling.

As she clawed her disheveled clothing closer, Helene felt a trembling begin deep in the pit of her belly. Against the skin of her throat, her own fingers felt like ice. "Go, Bentley," she whispered uncertainly, laying her free hand on his shoulder. "I'm fine. Go to up bed now. We'll sort this out tomorrow."

Bentley exhaled sharply as if he meant to argue, and then quickly thought better of it. Abruptly, he spun on one heel and crossed toward the door that led into the hall.

15

Though this be madness, there's method in't

Cam did not bother to observe his brother's withdrawal. Bentley's inebriation was no longer of concern to him. He, too, had imbibed more than was wise, but he was beyond that, as well. Instead, he stared down at Helene's shoulder, still half-bared.

Good Lord—did they take him for a fool? But even the worst sort of fool—the besotted sort, the sort he was—could see what must have been about to happen here. *Here.* In his own home. His own blood. With the woman he needed above all things.

But surely, Helene would not . . .

Yet she had been caressing Bentley's face. His aunt's words of warning came back to torment him. Words which he would have sworn were half exaggerations, half outright lies. No, damn it—*mostly* lies. Still, wild, irrational thoughts began to scatter and whirl through his mind like dried leaves in a windstorm. His hand shook as he watched the light of the candles play across her flawless ivory skin. *So beautiful, so tempting*. Always.

In confusion, he clutched the metal awkwardly, and a drop of wax spilled onto his wrist. The molten weight of it reminded him yet again that Helene's blood, too, ran hot and tempestuous. That it could burn a man, and burn him badly. Yet she had spurned him. And for what? For a milksop like Lowe, who had nonetheless found the courage to do what Cam had not?

Surely she did not want Bentley, who had the body of a man, the morals of a libertine, and the restraint of a child? Surely she had no need for the mindless devotion of another young suitor? Someone she could precipitously lead down the path to emotional ruin, as she had very nearly done with him? And perhaps could still do, did she but know the truth of it.

The horrible truth stuck in his throat like a shard of glass. Yes, Helene had just that kind of influence over him. Briefly, he closed his eyes and shook his head. But the vision of Helene remained, still clutching her disheveled nightclothes to her throat. Rage boiled up again, cutting through the pain. Helene could not possibly have been a willing participant to this farce. But why had she not screamed?

Slowly, inexorably, Cam watched his hand reach out to draw the fabric away from her collarbone. His fingers seemed to belong to a different man now. Surprisingly, Helene just stared at him as he jerked back her robe, her lovely eyes now wide and dark. Utterly uncomprehending. Cam let his eyes rake over her, enjoying the way she swallowed in response to the heat of his stare.

"Cam, this was not what it seemed," she whispered hollowly.

"Did he mean to force you, Helene?" The cold, distant voice was not his own, yet he willed her to say *yes*.

When she did not speak, Cam fisted his hand in the fabric of her wrapper and jerked her close. "Damn it, tell me the truth!" He bit out the words. "Do not protect him!"

She licked her lips uncertainly, obviously measuring her response. "Not force," she finally answered, jerking her gaze from his. "And whatever it was, it is my concern. Now let me go."

Her concern?

Oh, no. It was a great deal more than that.

Somewhere, in the depths of his mind, Cam took in the mocking symbolism of her attire. White, white lawn. The fabric of purity. The color of innocence. In his wanton dreams of their heated matings, Helene came to him sheathed in jewel-toned silks of red and green and gold; seductive fabrics that slid sinuously up her thighs as she mounted him, then impaled herself onto his shaft.

In those dreams, Helene was forever compelling him toward a blind precipice; pushing him beyond what he understood, and over an emotional edge he found terrifying. But now, he seemed to hold her in his thrall. Deep in the pools of her eyes, he could see some foreign emotion flickering. She licked her lips again, the tip of her tongue darting out to lightly touch one corner of her mouth.

In response, Cam slid the robe from her opposite shoulder, and watched it puddle onto the rug, feeling strangely detached as he did so. One plump breast swelled forth, the pouting nipple almost revealed by the open ribbons of her gown. Quite deliberately, he reached out and twined one ribbon about his index finger, then jerked it down to fully expose her to his gaze.

Roughly, he drew the length of his callused hand over her nipple, watching as Helene's eyes dropped shut. Strangely, he had expected—no, had *wanted*—to be slapped senseless for his effrontery. But Helene was doing nothing. Her delicate nostrils flared wide. Was she afraid? Or was it something else?

Ummm . . . The low, hungry growl came from deep in his own throat.

Suddenly, something inside him snapped. Good God, he was no better than his brother. He jerked his hand away. It hovered, for one brief moment, at the beautiful turn of her jaw. No! He would not do it. Still clutching the candlestick, he bent carelessly to the rug and snatched up her wrapper.

"Go to your room, Helene," he rasped, shoving it at her. "Please. Just get out. Before I simply take what Bentley apparently wanted."

And then, Helene was gone.

The door gaped open in her wake, revealing nothing but darkness beyond. Muttering one last guttural oath, Cam slammed down the candelabrum with a violence that sent one of the flickering candles rolling across the sideboard. As the drowning wick sputtered its last, Cam snatched up another bottle of brandy from the table, pitching its cork into the hearth.

By three in the morning, it had become all too apparent to Cam that liquor would subdue neither his lust nor his self-loathing. His aunt's ugly words kept echoing in his head, tormenting him. Yet the vision of Helene all but caught in his brother's embrace was torture beyond even that.

By the time the mantel clock struck half past, Cam made up his mind. Nothing had changed. She was going to be his, one way or another. And by God, he meant to have answers from her! Helene was going to explain her intentions toward . . . toward whom? Himself? His brother? Lowe? He hardly knew.

Jerking from his chair, Cam strode down the hall and up the two flights of stairs. Dimly aware of what he meant to do, Cam turned into the corridor, and within three strides, reached Helene's room and wrenched open the door. Surprisingly, no force was necessary. The door swung inward on silent hinges, and shut just as quietly.

Cam padded across the carpet in his stocking feet and stared down at the bed. Despite a fire that had burned to a heap of flickering coals, Helene lay uncovered in the coolness of the room, her bed linen in tortured disarray. Her long, dark tresses fanned loosely across the pillow, making Cam shudder with need. His angry questions receded into lust.

Ah, God—! How long had it been since he had run his hands through Helene's thick hair? Too long. Too bloody long. And the infernal woman was more seductive in sleep than by the light of day. He placed his tumbler of brandy upon her night table and dropped into a crouch bedside the bed, careful not to wake her.

Cam let his gaze slide over her. Helene lay partially upon her back, her arms open, her breasts high and nearly bared by the ribbons she had not bothered to refasten. In her flowing white nightgown, she looked like a painting of an angel—a dark, bewitching angel—descending from the heavens into the midst of some cloud-filled medieval altarpiece. But dear God, her swollen eyes. The evidence of her crying still stained their corners.

The throat of her nightgown looked damp, as if tears had flowed unchecked. Anger flashed anew as Cam thought of his brother's vile fingers touching her, exposing her flesh to his view. *Damn him!* How dare he?

The fact that it was more likely his unchecked anger, and not Bentley's lustful hands, that had caused her to cry escaped him in that moment. Helene's right knee was pulled high and bent inward, rucking up the thin white lawn of her gown to mid-thigh. Greedily, Cam let his eyes trail up her leg.

In the hearth, a coal snapped and flared to life, bathing Helene's exposed flesh in a peach-gold light. She murmured restlessly, and rolled a little farther toward him, the neckline of her gown dragging lower still, to coyly unveil the tip of one full breast. It was an elegantly indecent pose.

Cam's fingers yearned to skim up her inner leg, to drag the fabric higher. Uncertainly, he reached forward, then yanked his hand back as if stung. *No!* He would not seduce her while she slept, only to have her wake, tousled and aching, yet uncertain whose touch had inflamed her. When he aroused Helene—and took her, swift and hard—she would know that it was he who did so. He was tired of the wanting and wanting, the ceaseless yearning for something he could not have.

Only a few short weeks ago, Helene had writhed in his arms with an uninhibited passion few women possessed. Somehow, he would unleash that emotion again. Yes, he would please himself, and he would please her. And this time, when he was done, he would leave her so sated, Helene would never again think of another.

It mattered not one whit that he had been so long apart from her that he could not know her preferences, what made her sigh with pleasure, how she liked to be taken. He knew the things that did matter: the taste of her skin, the sound of her need, the scent of her arousal. His own sensory hell.

Yes, he would have her. He would convince her. His hands shook with the lust and the shame of it. Still on his knees, Cam dipped his fingers into his glass, still half-filled with brandy. Touching his fingertips to her nipple, he watched it swell and harden as he laved it with the golden moisture. In her sleep, Helene answered by turning into his touch, her mouth parting, a soft sigh escaping her lips.

Smoothly, he rose and pulled the gown lower, fully exposing her to his view. Dipping into the sweet liquid again, he massaged the fluid into her other nipple, watching as it crested with need. Then bracing his hands on either side of her shoulders, he bent down to suckle, licking away the moisture, rasping her delicate skin with his beard, then drawing her deep into the warmth of his mouth.

To his shock, Helene rolled fully onto her back, and her warm hands came up to cradle his head. Beyond his line of sight, he could hear her foot begin to slide restlessly down the covers and back up again, like a cat seeking the pleasure of a stroke. *"Ahh . . . mmm, Cam, mon amant,"* she murmured drowsily.

He was stunned by her words. And then, she jerked awake, bolting up in bed.

Cam jerked upright. With a soft cry, Helene scrambled backward, pulling into a near crouch against the headboard, dragging her nightclothes together to hide her nakedness. In the firelight's glow, her eyes were wide and angry.

"Take off your clothes, Helene," he said, trying to suppress the tremor in his voice. "I swear, I just can't take it any longer." In the dark, he heard her gasp as he stripped off his already loosened neckcloth and let it slither onto the floor.

"Non!" she said softly, extending her hand, palm out, as if she might hope to hold him off. "No! Who do you think you are? Get out!"

"Oh, Helene," he whispered, his voice raw. "I have grown so weary of this game we play. You were meant for me. Now take off your clothes."

He wanted to watch, he realized, his fingers abruptly ripping loose his shirttail. He wanted to see Helene, shaking with uncertainty, as she stripped just for him. *Power.* Yes, he wanted power over Helene Middleton. The power to make her tremble beneath him. And the power to make her beg.

It was not his way, he knew. That such a desire was wrong—possibly even demented—he knew that, too. But somehow, he just did not care. It was as if something within him had finally snapped under the pressure of wanting her. A lifetime of aching. Years of furiously spending himself inside other women, only to rise apathetically from a cold, unfamiliar bed, appeased yet unsatisfied, time and again.

It was time to make Helene ache as he did. This time, it would be he who dragged *her* into *his* scheme; an intrigue infinitely more dangerous than anything the young and reckless Helene had ever devised. He would take her with his fingers, his tongue, and with his shaft, until she had been driven mad with pleasure.

"I cannot believe you would dare to come into my room," she whispered. "I've had quite enough of your insults."

"Not so very long ago, you did not find my touch insulting," he answered bitterly. "Tell me, Helene, have I grown too old and obdurate to take to your bed? Have you come to prefer a more lighthearted sort of lover?"

Angrily, she shook her head. "What I find insulting is a man who offers *carte blanche* while betrothed to another!" Helene came to her knees, the white nightgown pooling eerily about her on the bed. Unlike her words, she seemed small and delicate in the firelight. "As to what sort of lover I prefer, it is none of your business. What you saw was not what it seemed."

"Was it not?" he asked hollowly, running one hand down to bare her shoulder.

"No! Bentley is . . . is . . ." She shook her head, and slapped away his hand. "He is distraught, and not thinking clearly. He is disturbed by the news of your marriage."

"Oh, is that what he told you?" returned Cam, his voice soft with disdain. "When I remarry, it might indeed prove inconvenient to him. But his worry is precipitous. I have spoken to my aunt. I shan't wed to please her, nor to please anyone but myself. I'm bloody tired of martyring myself for this damned family."

Helene was clearly struggling to understand his words. "But we saw . . . Bentley thought . . ."

Cam threw back his head and laughed richly. "Oh, indeed! Was he *thinking*, my dear? With his cock, perhaps. As I daresay I am now."

"You disgust me, Cam," she hissed.

"I think you lie," he said softly, brushing the back of his hand across her nipple and watching it grow taut with need.

Ruthlessly, she yanked up the neck of her gown. "Get out now, before you do something that cannot be undone. You are as pathetically drunk as your brother."

He gave a half smile. "I would to God I were, Helene," he answered calmly, lightly fingering her nipple through the thin lawn of her gown. She was on her knees, pressed against the headboard. "I want you, and I'm damned tired of waiting, of being tempted beyond reason by you."

She blanched at that, and struck him hard across the forearm. "I do not . . . I *have not* tempted you! Get your hands off me. I have no notion what you mean."

"Do you not?" Cam yanked off his shirt, pitched it onto the floor, then crawled across her bed toward her. Her shoulders already pressed against the wood, Helene tried to scrabble farther away.

"Come now, Helene!" he said mockingly. "Don't be shy. You were never so before." Abruptly, he came to his knees, seizing her and dragging her hard against his chest, opening his mouth over hers, and surging inside.

Fleetingly, she fought him like a wildcat, clawing at his naked shoulders, raking her nails down his back, but Cam did not care. The pain was an exquisite torment, and he kissed her and kissed her until slowly, almost imperceptibly, she leaned away from the headboard and into his embrace.

Triumphant, his mouth left hers then, to open over the turn of her jaw, the curve of her delicate throat, skimming lower still, until he found her breast and drew it lovingly back inside his mouth. Helene whimpered then, and slid her fingers up through his hair. *"Ahh . . . ohh,"* she said softly.

"Oh, Helene," he rasped, pushing her down into the pillows. With his mouth still plundering her, Helene shivered in his embrace. Deftly, Cam shifted to one side, and after bathing his fingers in the brandy again, began massaging her nipple with his fingers, around and around, until she arched away from the pillows, moaning, her hands tangled in the sheet beneath her hips.

He looked up at her then, and saw her eyes, wide and limpid, fixed on his fingers as they worked her. "You want me, do you not?" It was a proclamation of victory, not a question.

"Yes—no—damn you," she breathed, her head tipping backward, her voice choking with need as he drew her nipple between his teeth to torment her. He could feel her anger surging, shifting, and sliding into mindless hunger.

Then, unable to deny himself the pleasure of watching Helene's face, Cam's mouth left her breast as a soft sob tore through her. "Hush, Helene," he whispered, letting his hand slide down to curve over the roundness of her belly. "Just let me love you. As I was meant to." The hand slid lower, to caress the juncture of her thighs through the fabric of her nightgown.

Cam felt utterly depraved, aroused beyond anything he had ever felt before as he watched helpless need play out in her expression, in her breathing, and ultimately, in her trembling. She was blushing hotly, refusing to hold his gaze as he touched her, and Cam found himself obsessed by her thoughts. He was so close. So close to having her.

Would Helene stop him? *Could he stop?* He thought not, on both counts. Cam felt like a man possessed. In the grate, coals sheared off onto the hearth and the fire licked higher. She moaned and urged her flesh against his hand.

They had been too long apart. The night moved too quickly. His pulse raced. His rod throbbed. Light and shadow flickered over them. And still Cam kept touching her, smoothing his hands over her body, suckling her. Worshiping her with his lust. Trying to keep his heart intact. Trying to hold back some small part of himself, while taking what he so desperately needed.

But it would not work. On her next breath, Cam knew it. He dipped his head to nip at her throat again, enthralled at her response to his touch. Like an eager mare, her flesh shivered time and again, as his teeth bit into her skin, then moved from neck to breast to belly and back.

And suddenly, he forced himself to stop. Cam sat back on his heels, the wool of his trousers pulled tight over the muscles of his thighs and the thick ridge of his erection. Beneath him, Helene's breath came quick and shallow. With her nightgown open and her hair in disarray, she panted for him wantonly. It was a gratifying vision of feminine arousal.

It pleased him. Oh, yes. Forcing his respiration to steady, he let his gaze rake over her and saw her face suffuse with color again. With ineffective modesty, she absently tugged at her gown, lowering her lashes into black, feathery fans across her cheeks. The damp linen clung to her crested breasts, a seductive vision indeed.

"Good God, you really are lovely, Helene," he said. "Such exquisite beauty. Such wild, irrepressible desire."

Her eyes flew open, then flared with anger. He could almost hear something inside her snap. "Is that what you think of me, Cam?" she whispered. The sharp pain in her voice knifed at him. *"After all, I am just like my mother—?* Can you not take pleasure from a woman while knowing that she cares for you? That she desires only you?"

To silence the words that he could not bear to believe, Cam pinned her arms high against the headboard and took her mouth again, more roughly this time. Holding her with one powerful arm, he jerked upward on the hem of her gown. He forced his fingers into the damp heat between her thighs, only to find that it was himself, and not Helene, whom he shocked.

Already, she dripped with need. The sweet, agonizing scent of her desire filled his nostrils, almost driving him beyond restraint. He wanted to surrender his own control, and pound his flesh into hers. To simply give himself over to Helene. But he could not.

Slowly, slowly he eased two fingers inside. She was tight, so very tight, as she rode down on his hand. The pressure of her sheath drew him in. A sensual metaphor, perhaps, for the whole of his relationship with Helene.

He kissed her, and against his mouth, she whimpered once more. Cam pulled his hand and mouth away, bringing his dew-slick fingers to his lips. His eyes held hers knowingly. Helene made a fleeting, uncertain gesture with her hand, then jerked her gaze from his. Cam caught her hand, drawing it to his erection, already thick and throbbing. "Just take me, Helene," he whispered. "No more talking."

This time, it was Helene who stared unflinchingly into his eyes. "Do you wish me to act the wanton for you, Cam? Do you want to simply *rut* with me—slaking our need without intimacy or honesty?"

When he made her no answer, Helene jerked violently against him, freeing her hands once more. "Is that all you want? All you can accept?" she demanded, her dark eyes damp and glittering.

Her pain and outrage was his undoing. "I do not know," he confessed into the darkness. "I know only that I need you, Helene. And to have you, I think I would pay you, marry you, or sell my soul to the devil himself."

"Deal with the devil on his terms, Cam," she responded. "Here are mine. You may keep your money, your soul, and your wedding ring!" Grasping the hem of her nightgown, Helene jerked it up until it slid over her thighs, her belly, her breasts, then higher still. Until she knelt naked before him. Until Cam could not breathe. Or think.

She came at him, tearing at the close of his trousers, clawing at him, dragging away fabric, and pushing down the linen of his drawers until his cock sprang free to jut up between them. Helene fell against him then, her tongue sliding down the curve of his jaw, leaving a trail of fire, raking lightly at the same harsh stubble that had rasped her tender breasts.

"You fear the truth, I think," she whispered against his heated flesh. "But if I am wicked, Cam, at least I am honest. Yes, I want you. Yes, I will whore for you. I even have some idea how it's done, you'll recall."

So saying, Helene closed one hand around his shaft and went fully down onto her knees.

Cam gasped, lashing out blindly behind him to seize the bedpost as she took him into her mouth, awkwardly at first. And then slowly, she became greedy, drawing his manhood deeper into her warmth. Down, down into a decadence beyond anything he had ever known. Long, curling black tresses fanned sensually across her back, brushing over the cleft between her buttocks and tickling at the pink heels of her feet.

"Ah, Helene—!" He gasped her name softly, straining not to cry out in the darkness as her hand slid between his legs to fondle him completely. Helene touched him tentatively, then more expertly, caressing the root of his shaft with her fingers, and then her mouth, pleasuring him until he thought he would die. When his hips jerked uncontrollably against her, Helene roughly shoved him down into the soft tangle of sheets at the foot of her bed, but still she did not stop, driving him rapidly over the edge of a bright, white light that sped toward him even as he rushed into it.

He wanted, he wanted . . . ah, ah, how he wanted . . . His hands clutched at the linen of her bed sheets, fisting and clawing and grasping, as his head strained back against the mattress, and *oh, dear God, he was so close . . . so close . . . so close to losing himself.* Spilling himself into her warmth. Losing his mind. *Losing . . . control.*

Suddenly, Helene felt Cam buck beneath her. Roughly, inexplicably, she found herself tumbled onto her back, pinned against the mattress by the brute strength of his arms and the searing heat of his eyes.

"Oh, no, Helene," he whispered seductively, a mocking smile curving his lips. "Not so fast."

There would be, she suddenly understood, no delaying the inevitable. Yet she struggled in his grasp, and with a soft groan, he nudged at her thighs with his knee. "Open for me, sweeting."

Dumbly, Helene shook her head and raked her eyes down Cam's length. She had never been so utterly terrified, nor so desperately enthralled. But perversely, she was terrified of *herself;* enthralled by *him*. By his stark, naked, unbridled beauty. Any trace of his usual restraint and refined civility had been long since burnt away.

Cam's trousers rode off his hips now, his manhood rose between them, still pulsing and slick from her mouth. The dim firelight shone over work-honed shoulders as big as her thighs. The raw power of his nudity was nearly overwhelming. Again, she shook her head.

"This has gone too far, Helene," he softly insisted, reaching out to fondle her. "You cannot give me just a taste. Let me inside, my sweet. You'll find I'm not wholly without skill."

In the dim light, she trembled, knowing she could not long resist him. Cam was determined to shut out her love, along with the depth of his own emotions. But she wanted him anyway.

And apparently, and she was willing to give herself to

him on his limited terms. As she let his weight bear down on her, the silken hardness of his shaft brushed between her thighs, searing her flesh.

Ah, yes! She did want him. She prayed he did not know how much.

Boldly, she stared him up and down in the firelight. He was magnificent, this man she burned for! Hard and taut, with every inch of him layered in muscle and corded with tendons. His masculine beauty, the sheer glory of his body, was her undoing.

"Open your legs, Helene," he softly commanded. "And then tell me that you want—*desperately want*—me inside."

The wicked words skimmed over her like warm silk, arousing her in a way she did not understand. Helene exhaled deeply, focusing on the rapid rise and fall of Cam's heaving chest. Unlike the boy she had loved, he was lightly matted with soft, dark hair. It ran over his rigid nipples and beyond the flat of his belly, then trickled further, to form the coarse thatch that surrounded his sex, now heavy and jutting.

She was driven by a hunger to touch it again, to feel its throbbing weight and velvet surface. Almost involuntarily, she jerked one hand free of his grasp and reached out for him.

"Oh, no," growled Cam, swiftly recapturing her fingers. "Naughty puss! I can see I must have my way with you."

His hands left hers, and to her utter shame, Cam skimmed one hand lightly down her belly to the juncture of her thighs. With his thumb, he spread open the folds of her skin, and lowered his mouth to kiss her there. His tongue slid into her warmth, drowning her in sin and sensation.

A hot yearning coursed through her, pooled in her belly, then tugged at her center. It was too much, *too much* . . . Helene tried to push him away.

"No," he ordered, then his teeth nipped at the tender skin of her inner thigh. "I want you to burn for me now—as I have burned for you all these godforsaken years, Helene. I want you to ache and writhe and drown in it."

And beneath the sensual onslaught, Helene felt herself slip deeper into the abyss. Firmly, his fingertips slid inside, touching her with a jolt of pleasure as he urged her apart to taste her more intimately. Helene cried out in shock, then strained hard against him as Cam's tongue touched her very core.

She shook, then thrashed, as Cam continued touching her. Any shred of control she might have possessed was gone. This went far, far beyond their adolescent desires. Oh, Cam was treacherous. And he would have his way, because she would concede it. Willingly.

Helene no longer thought to guard herself against him, to be insulted or hurt. She stared down at herself. Cam had one hand on her knee, urging her legs wider, the other hand stroking her breast as his tongue slid sinuously into her most secret recesses, robbing her of all modesty, all restraint, and any pride she might ever have possessed. She wanted the edge just ahead; that sharp, shimmering blade of sensation that tantalized somewhere just beyond her reach.

And Cam could take her there. Helene had only to surrender to him, and . . . and she felt the edge draw nearer. Yes. So sweet, so very close. Her hips bucked again. Something inside her began to give way.

And abruptly, Cam stopped. She bit back a cry of frustration. In the darkness, she heard the spark and hiss of the dying fire. "Tell me, Helene," he rasped, his fingers digging into her thigh. "Tell me that you are mine!"

Helene felt herself shudder with an ache so deep she thought she would die. Against the pillow, she thrashed her head. "Please . . ." she whispered. "Don't stop. *Finish it*. Cam, please—!"

Roughly, he jerked her thighs wider still and slid up her length. "Mine, Helene," he growled against her temple. "You belong to me! And by God, I mean to throttle the next man who so much as looks at you, do you hear me?"

She tried to nod, but failed.

Cam's teeth raked across her throat and down to her breast. *"Ah, Helene—!"* he said, his voice dropping to an unsteady whisper. "My sweet Helene—what am I saying? I must be mad with jealousy. Insane with desire. I love you too much. Too much."

Helene listened to the words, all too aware of the weight and heat of his shaft at her entrance. If she gave herself to him now, there would be no turning back from Cam.

But had there ever been?

No. Never.

And so she wrapped her arms about Cam's waist, lifted her knees, and pulled him into her. Cam let his weight fall forward, bracing his hands near her shoulders. She felt him probe her, spread her, and then slowly begin to fill her. *So very, very good.* Better, even, than his mouth.

Eagerly, Helene tipped her hips up to take him, aching with a strange, soul-deep emptiness. Cam's eyes dropped shut, and in the gloom she could barely see the long, dark lashes that fanned across his cheeks. A bitter smile of satisfaction curved at his mouth as he thrust fully into her, then pushed swiftly, deeply inside.

And suddenly froze.

Helene's eyes opened wide at the burst of pain, more acute than she had imagined. She jerked against Cam, suppressing a cry. The fluid, sinuous heat was gone, and in its place was a sharp, brief agony.

16

In which Adversity discovers Virtue

Cam had never deflowered a virgin. Even his bride had never conceded him that one small honor. But when Helene jerked beneath him, and he felt his flesh tear through hers, he was horribly and unerringly certain that he had done precisely that.

And yet, it was incomprehensible. But in truth, the whole of his behavior, since setting foot inside Helene's bedchamber, was incomprehensible. Time slowed. Then stopped. He froze in mid-stroke and stared down at her, the woman he thought he knew.

The color had drained from her face. Cam could hear the pounding of his heart, the roar of his own blood. The utter horror of his assumption, the awesome significance of what Helene had just surrendered—all of it momentarily dimmed in comparison to her.

Helene blinked, then swallowed, breaking the spell. "Finish it, Cam," she said again, her voice strangely calm.

Wracked with shame and lust, Cam dropped his forehead to lightly touch hers. "*Finish* it?" he whispered, breathing deeply, trying to force the lump from his chest. "Dear God, Helene. What have I started—?"

Beneath him, Helene shifted, rocking her hips

upward, taking him incrementally deeper in a sweet intimation of her wishes. Despite the heated press of tears behind his eyes, Cam found that below the waist, his flesh was too weak to refuse her. His baser instincts still ruled. Buried deep inside Helene's feminine warmth, his rod hardened unrepentantly.

"Mmmm . . ." she breathed. As if she had willed it, Cam began to move inside her again, knowing that he had no right.

But pace for pace, Helene matched him, rising up to meet his thrusts as he glided over her. Bracing his weight on his hands, Cam lifted himself high, and gazed down at Helene as he filled her with long, gentle strokes. Her hands came up to caress his waist, then slid smoothly around to the small of his back. Lower still, she skimmed over the taut muscles of his buttocks, under the tangle of his breeches and drawers, urging him fully against her.

Her eyes fell shut as he stroked her. Her breath came short and fast. She parted her lips, and Cam could see the pink of her tongue—the same tongue which had so erotically tortured him—pressed high against her upper teeth.

"I love you, Hellie." He breathed the old words into the darkness, feeling Helene quicken beneath him. Her legs came around his waist and her fingers pressed into the muscles of his thrusting hips. After that—and seemingly into infinity—there was nothing but the glide of flesh over flesh, raw gasps of pleasure, unrestrained groans. His or hers? Cam did not know.

The sounds of passion filled the night. He loved her. So much, he loved her. He always had, even when she drove him mad with frustration or wild with jealousy. Helene would be the death of him. He'd always known it, and yet he'd always loved her. He lowered his head, placed his lips to her ear, and told her so again.

Helene's climax came upon her fast, and he held her close, never flagging in his pace as she thrust hard against him. Softly, she cried out, clinging to him so sweetly that Cam felt the tears of love and guilt spring unbidden to his eyes as she crested, and called out his name from far, far away. So near, so powerful . . . the pleasure rolled through his belly, then rose up to pull him under its rich, churning depths.

Long moments later, Cam dragged himself from atop her and rolled to one side of Helene's bed and lay limply across her sheets. Now sated, he should have been drowsy, but he was far from it. His mind began to taunt him. *Helene.* Dear heaven, for all her elegant sophistication, her feminine wiles—she had yet been a virgin?

But there was no mistaking what he had done. What she had been. All these years. Wasted years, they suddenly seemed. The significance did not escape him. And now, he had taken something precious from her. And in the ugliest, most brutish of ways, too. Deeply ashamed, he shifted to one side to stare at Helene.

She lay perfectly still, her eyes shut. Slowly, he drew one hand down his face, but the reality did not change. Helene was still there. Beside him, he felt her tremble.

"Are you sorry?" She spoke without opening her eyes.

"My God, Helene," he whispered, evading her question. "What have we—what have *I* done?" Cam levered up higher, and looked down at her. Had he harbored any doubt at all, the damning evidence was smeared faintly across her thigh.

"What have we done?" she echoed softly. "Only what we set out to do, long ago."

"Helene," his voice was pleading. "Why did you not tell me?"

"Would you have believed me?" Her voice was husky with passion, but her eyes were narrow and knowing.

"I—yes," he answered, hoping he spoke the truth. "Of course. Why did you not tell me?"

She rolled into him then, and suddenly he could see

the unshed tears pooling in those cool, blue eyes. "Do you know, Cam, I think I did," she softly protested. "I told you everything, a very long time ago. *I love you. I shall love you until I die. I will wait for you. There will be no one else for me but you.* Did you remember none of that?"

Cam could only stare at her, and Helene continued. "No. Of course you do not," she answered dully, her head falling back onto her pillow. "You have gone on with your life. If I did not . . . choose the same path, that was my decision."

"Oh, Helene!" he softly cried, rolling into her, and dragging her fine-boned body against him. "Just tell me. Do you—can you—still feel love for me?"

"Do not speak to me of love, Cam," she said quietly. "It is not necessary. Not all virgins are innocent. We both know that."

Cam rolled onto his back and dragged one arm over his face. "Damn it," he whispered hollowly. "I am going to pay for this mistake in the worst sort of way, am I not? And rightly so."

When she did not respond, he continued. "I came to believe, Helene, that you willingly abandoned me. That you surrendered our dreams in favor of something or someone else. I convinced myself you must have done so, else you would have returned to me. We've wasted too much time. And now, I have ruined you. We cannot delay our marriage."

"Ruined me?" Helene gave a short, bitter laugh as she stared into the canopy above. "Women of my uncertain background do not get *ruined*, Cam. Nor do they get a wedding ring in recompense for their naiveté. I thought your father explained that long ago."

"My father can rot in hell," he answered, pulling her still closer into his embrace. "We shall be married, and it will be soon. And not because of what we have done."

"Then why?" she asked suspiciously. "Only yesterday, your attentions were fixed elsewhere."

"My attentions have been fixed on nothing but you since the moment you arrived and made my marriage to anyone else impossible," he insisted, lightly touching his mouth to hers again. "And I rode like a fiend all the way home from Devon to tell you so. Because no matter how far away you go, no matter what you do, I have never stopped loving you." He kissed her again, and drew her closer still.

"Oh, Cam—! I think I shall never fully understand you," she insisted, but she snuggled into his embrace. He was winning her, perhaps. But he was almost afraid to hope.

Cam sighed into her hair. "Look here, Helene. I deeply regret some of my assumptions. But I'll not lie and say I regret the outcome. I know we have much to sort out. I tried to say as much."

Helene stared up at him, unblinking. Cam's mouth curved a little bitterly. "Yes, Helene. A part of you is justifiably angry. Can you trust me to make it right? Can you set aside your wrath, just for tonight? We are both so wounded, so emotionally raw. For just a few hours, can we pretend that we are lovers, alone in the world, with no trouble between us? As it used to be?"

Helene did not know what to do. And so for once, she simply did as she wished. She tucked herself into the crook of Cam's shoulder, inhaled his warm, familiar scent, and listened as the comforting sound of his breathing deepened into sleep.

Oh, she knew that Cam had wronged her. But with his words, not his actions. The physical act of lovemaking had been as much her fault as his. Helene knew a dozen ways to discourage an amorous suitor, and had used none of them tonight.

Instead, she had remained in her bed, half enthralled, half indignant, and in truth, only a little frightened. As always, she relished an argument with Cam. She almost enjoyed undermining his resolve, and driving him to distraction. Theirs had always been a volatile, passionate relationship. In that, at least, nothing had changed.

For a long while, she lay perfectly still, listening to the sounds of the night.

"Helene—?" she heard Cam murmur into his pillow. He sounded half asleep.

"Yes?" She slid closer to his face.

"Your mouth," he whispered, the words slow and thick with sleep. "Your mouth is so sinfully beautiful. The way you touch me . . . it's extraordinary. So innocently . . . *wicked.*"

There was no misunderstanding what he referred to, and Helene grew warm at the thought of how wantonly she had behaved. *Like a whore*. Only whores usually did that, *Maman* had said. But she had wanted desperately to torment Cam, and Helene was reminded yet again that life with her mother had exposed her to things that a respectable woman would know nothing about.

She recalled with deep humiliation the time she and Cam had discovered Randolph's collection of lewd drawings, left open in the drawing room after a night of revelry. At the age of fourteen, Helene had rarely paused to remember that there were some things young ladies did not discuss, and so she had boldly asked her mother about one drawing in particular.

In her usual halfhearted way, *Maman* had scolded her for meddling, then laughingly explained that what Helene had seen was something gentlemen liked—but ladies *never* did. "Unless," *Maman* quickly added, "they had done something very bad, such as dreadfully overspend their allowance."

Helene had taken the explanation to heart, and repeated it to Cam verbatim. For a time, they had found it wildly humorous, and terribly naughty. But that was before things had changed. Before things had become serious between them.

Suddenly, Helene was seized with a restlessness she could not define. "Cam?"

Beside her, Cam exhaled sonorously, but said nothing. Helene nudged him with her elbow. *"Cam—!"*

Half on his belly, Cam lifted his head from the pillow and stared blearily at her through a shock of black hair. *"What?"*

Helene felt her face flush with heat again, but she needed to know. "Did you like my mouth . . . that is to say . . . did you think what I did was—" And then, words simply failed her.

With a deep, manly groan, Cam rolled onto his back and covered his face with the pillow. "Good God, Helene!" he muttered from beneath the heap of feathers. "There's nothing you won't dare to say or do. It's embarrassing."

Helene had recovered her resolve. "Answer my question."

In the dying firelight, she watched Cam drag the pillow from his face and look up at her with eyes that were seductively heavy from sleep. Somehow, he managed a wink. "Let me just say, Helene, that if you will marry me, you may feel free to overspend your allowance at will."

At her stunned expression, Cam threw back his head and almost laughed aloud, then reached out with one strong arm to drag her nearer to his side. "Just go to sleep, Helene. Just hush up. I have waited a lifetime to drift off with you in my arms."

Helene was not certain just how long she drowsed in Cam's embrace, stroking her hand down his chest and drifting on the edge of slumber. An hour perhaps had passed when the pitiful sound awakened her well before dawn. She came fully awake and slid from the bed to scrabble among the clothing which lay scattered across the floor.

The plaintive cry sounded again, louder and more fearful now. Helene had no time in which to think about the risk that she had run in drifting off to sleep in Cam's arms, no time at all in which to chastise herself for behaving so foolishly. Ariane's voice was unmistakable, carrying faintly but certainly through the schoolroom.

In the darkness, she found her wrapper and jerked it on. Cam still slept in the center of her bed, his breathing deep and steady. With neither a lamp nor a candle, Helene hastened into the passageway and through the schoolroom to Ariane's bedchamber. As she pushed open the door, she remembered that Martha was away. Her mother had fallen ill in the village. Tonight, there was no one save Helene to hear Ariane's cries.

As Helene felt her way across Ariane's bedchamber, the little girl began sobbing; deep, almost silent sounds of unmistakable terror.

"Ariane," Helene spoke in the most reassuring voice she could muster as she approached the bed. "All is well, sweet. 'Twas a nightmare, nothing more."

She settled onto the bed just as Ariane flew into her arms. The child clung to Helene with a frightened desperation. In the dark, Helene could see nothing, but she sensed that Ariane was now fully awake. As Helene murmured soft words of comfort, the girl's wracking sobs slowly eased, until at last Helene was able to scrabble about on the night table for a light. The candle flared in the darkness, illuminating the haunted expression on Ariane's face.

Helene leaned across the bed, and tipped up Ariane's chin with her finger to stare into the girl's limpid eyes. "Poor dear!" she whispered softly. "Poor, poor child! I do wish you would tell me what it is which so frightens you."

Ariane's eyes dropped to the linen sheet, now knotted tightly in her fist.

This time, Helene persisted. "You *can* tell me, Ariane. I know that you can."

Mutely, the child shook her head, signaling her refusal, an action which, in and of itself, was an accomplishment.

Determinedly, Helene pushed. "You have guessed, Ariane, have you not, that I know your secret? Yes, I do. I know you can speak. I have heard you. Just once or twice—but enough to know what a smart girl you are."

The child's eyes widened with alarm, and Helene laid a gentle hand across her knee. "Do not worry, my dear. I shall keep your secret. But I do wish you would confide in me. I know only that you are afraid."

Ariane dropped her chin, and shook her head again; small, stubborn jerks which confirmed that the girl would not yield. Lightly, Helene patted her leg. "Very well. You need say nothing until you wish to. Now, do you feel that you can sleep?"

She watched as Ariane scrubbed a fist under one eye. "Then I shall go, my sweet. But if you feel frightened again, you must cry out, or come through the schoolroom and knock hard upon my dressing room door." Helene bent to kiss the child goodnight. "I will light your lamp on my way out. If I turn it down low, it shall likely burn until dawn."

After lighting the lamp and pulling the door shut, Helene stepped into the pitch-black schoolroom and straight into Cam's embrace. She suppressed a gasp as his arms came around her, firm and powerful. His mouth sought hers in the dark, and kissed her, hard, quick, but nonetheless unyielding.

His lips brushed against her ear. "What was that all about?" he breathed, his voice all but silent. "Is she ill? Is she frightened?"

Helene drew away from him, and led him back through the passageway into her bedchamber, then pushed the door firmly closed. "A nightmare, but she is fine now," she whispered, feeling Cam's tension ebb. "Did you hear everything?"

"Yes. Is it true?" he asked anxiously. In the darkness, she could feel his eyes searching her face.

"About my having heard her speak? Yes, it is true."

"When?" His voice held unwavering concern; so much concern that one would never have guessed he knew the child was not his.

"The night you left for Devon," she quickly answered. "Ariane had a terrible nightmare. And twice last week, I heard her whispering to herself in the garden when she thought herself alone."

"She is well—?" he asked eagerly.

Helene shook her head. "I cannot say. But I began to think there's nothing too terribly wrong. She is frightened and confused, yes. But her mind is in no way disordered, of that I am sure. I think we must be patient."

Slowly, Cam nodded, then obviously deep in thought, knelt by the hearth to poke up the fire. The coals sprang weakly to life, illuminating his utter nakedness, and leaving Helene with the breathtaking impression of a majestic, untamed savage.

His dark hair was now a bit too long, not having been cut since well before his journey, and as he turned from the hearth to look at her, it brushed enticingly over his face like heavy black silk. He rose with the smooth, controlled grace of an athlete, the warm light limning his strong legs and perfectly muscled buttocks.

Helene drank in his image as Cam came toward her with absolute confidence. He was a quiet man; a man far more certain of his body and its abilities than with hollow words or pointless conversation. He had the hands of a farmer and the soul of a poet. And yet, he did not know himself. Or if he ever had, the twists and turns of fate had wrung that knowledge out of him.

But perhaps all was not lost? Holding her gaze predatorily, he caught Helene about the waist, leaned into her with his male hardness, and slid one hand up into her hair, stilling her for a kiss. A kiss which was long, deep, and just as confident as the rest of his movements.

After a lengthy moment, he set her away from him and shot her a quizzical smile. "This has been a most eventful evening," he said softly. He crossed to the bed, drew back the covers and tilted his head to indicate that she should get in.

"Actually, it's almost morning." She hesitated. "I think you'd best go, Cam."

Still holding the covers, he nodded. "Aye, soon," he said quietly. "After we've settled a few things. Now get in. 'Tis too cold to stand about in your robe."

He would not be swayed. She knew it, and surrendered. He crawled beneath the sheets beside her, and his weight settling onto the bed gave her a fleeting sense of security and contentment. Was this how it would feel to share a bed with the man you loved, night after night? Helene did not know, and had no wish to dwell overlong on the subject.

Cam pulled her into his embrace and dragged her deep beneath the heavy covers. "Thank you," he said, kissing her lightly on the nose. "Thank you for caring for my child. Thank you for sharing so much with me this night."

When Helene made no answer, Cam slid his big hand around her face and turned it into his. "Look, Helene, I'm a simple man with simple words. My temper's quick, and my ways are rough, but I want to know if you'll wed me despite it all. I think, you know, that you ought."

She pulled her face away, and shook her head. "Cam, it is not . . . necessary."

"*Ah—!*" he said knowingly. "*Not necessary*. Necessary to whom, do you think? To you? To me? Or to the child you might be carrying? Certainly, I can answer for at least two of us."

"Answer for yourself, Cam. There is no child."

Cam smiled grimly. "You cannot know that, my dear. But let me concede the point, and speak only for myself. You are as necessary to me as air and water. It has always been so. You are my most exquisite pleasure. And my most exquisite torment."

"What nonsense." Helene tugged aimlessly at the coverlet. "You have existed perfectly well without me for years. Perhaps I can be forgiven for assuming you've not been alone in your bed."

Cam sighed wearily. "Helene, I have been a widower for a long time now. And in that time, I have had women, yes. But bloody few. They brought me relief, but little comfort. For God's sake, Helene, I am a man. What more can I say?"

"That is not my point, Cam," she answered quietly. "I have no wish to hear a recitation of the beds you've warmed." She shook her head. "I fear it may be too late for us, Cam. Perhaps it always was."

"You do not understand." His voice was husky now. "I waited for you, Helene. I may have looked like a green boy when you left me, but I knew my own mind. It may have been imprudent to love you so, but I did. And I waited."

"Why do you keep tormenting me, Cam? I do not want to hear it. I cannot bear to believe it." She pressed her fingertips into her temples as if to will the memories away.

"Believe it, Helene," he said, almost bitterly. "I regret having spoken in anger to you tonight. My words were worse than vile. But I have always loved you. I wrote to you for two long years. Until there could be no doubt that your education was finished. After my fateful trip to Hampstead, Father laughed at me, told me to get on with life."

"As perhaps you should have done."

Cam shook his head. "No, I struggled and I waited two more years, trying to make something of myself, fighting to keep Chalcote from ruin. Waiting for you to come home. Wondering if you hated me. And in the end, I did what I had to do. What I should never have done. I let reason crush my dreams."

"You married to save your family," she said quietly.

"Aye, I did what I thought was the right thing. And I went to my bride's bed a twenty-three-year-old virgin. Imagine my shock to discover that I was the only one there."

Helene was stunned by his words, but she knew he spoke the truth. "And yet, you were ever faithful to her, were you not?" she whispered.

In the bed beside her, she felt Cam nod tersely. "I stood up at St. Michael's and pledged Cassandra my faith, my honor—and all my worldly possessions, for what little they were worth at the time. And yes, I kept my vow."

"Yes, you would, wouldn't you?" Cam would have kept his word, no matter the cost. But now, he had apparently broken his agreement with Mrs. Belmont.

Helene suddenly saw what such an action must have cost him. Why had he done it? For her? For them? Helene could not think clearly. Nonetheless, she was sure of one thing. Joan would be relieved, though Cam could not possibly know it. Just as he had had no way of knowing the hell his first marriage would eventually become.

Hesitantly, she spoke. "And yet, your wife was not so faithful, was she?"

She felt him relax, almost collapse inside. "Christ, Helene! Is there anything you do not see? Or must I thank my sister again?"

"Oh, you mustn't blame Catherine," Helene gently responded. "I know you, Cam, all too well. I can also see that Ariane is, in every respect that matters, your daughter."

Cam rolled over to sit on the edge of the mattress, and dropped his head into his hands. "I would have no secrets between us, Helene," he finally whispered. "I am glad you know. But Ariane is an innocent, and no more accountable for the sins of her parents than you and I were responsible for the sins of ours."

Helene came up onto her knees behind him, encircled him with her arms, and rested her head upon his broad expanse of shoulders.

After a long moment, Cam spoke again. "I *knew*, Helene. I knew—and Cassandra knew—that the child she carried was not mine. I had not gone to my wife's bed in months. And yet, I said nothing. In hindsight, I think I considered it my punishment for wedding a woman whom I did not—*could not* love."

"Oh, Cam!" she said sadly. "Why do you imagine you should be punished?"

Cam gave a soft, bitter laugh. "Unlike Cassandra, I went to the marriage bed a virgin. But I took with me a heart that was as shattered as her maidenhead. And I wonder, Helene—whose sin was the greater?"

Wearily, Helene settled back into the bed. "You committed no sin, Cam. Marriages can be made without love. But they cannot be maintained without fidelity."

Abruptly, Cam rose and strode across the room to the window, pulling back the draperies to stare out into the night. For many moments he stood there in silence. "Dawn will be upon us in another hour, Helene," he finally said. "I must go soon, or run the risk of compromising your virtue even further." Slowly, he turned to face her. "I would have this business of our marriage settled now."

"No!" Helene raised an unsteady hand and pushed

her heavy, untidy hair over one shoulder. "I won't be bullied, Cam! Things have changed."

"Precisely what things, Helene? What do you mean?"

"I have made a life for myself, Cam, just as you have done. Forgive me if I am in no haste to throw it all away."

"You do not trust me to take care of you?" Pain flared in his eyes.

"I must trust *me* to take care of me, Cam. As I have always done." Uncertainly, she paused. "Tell me this, Cam: when you came to my bed tonight, did you have any faith at all in my honor? Or my virtue?"

From his position silhouetted in the window, she heard Cam mutter a vile oath. "You wish me to suffer, then? I know I deserve it."

"Not *suffer,* Cam!" She raised her hands in exasperation. "It merely seems to me a rather sudden change in your intentions."

Suddenly, he crossed the room toward her. "No," he whispered hoarsely, laying his finger to her lips. "Not sudden, Helene." Cam stood over her, staring into the depths of her eyes. "A slow and certain acceptance that I cannot live without you. Good God, it has torn me apart."

In compromise, Helene drew back the bedcovers and Cam dropped down beside her. "I tried, I suppose, to come to terms with my increasing desperation," he continued, scrubbing a hand wearily down his face. "I tried to discover an honorable way to extricate Joan and myself from a miserable future. Did I not tell you when I left that when I returned from Devon, we would sort this out?"

He held up a hand when Helene began to interrupt. "But then," he continued stubbornly, "this afternoon, I had scarce set foot inside my own house when the damned rector appears to regale me with stories of your mutual admiration, and to vow his undying affection for you. Words which I now know held far more hope than truth."

Helene made a little choking sound, but Cam kept talking.

"And as if that were not enough, I see you caressing my rogue of a brother. And yes, I *do* think he was forcing his attentions on you, and I *do* suspect that you are protecting him, and I *do* believe that I may still have to throttle him. But my point is, damn it, that I lost my temper. In a most reprehensible way."

"The rector?" choked Helene, ignoring everything else Cam had said. "Do you mean to say poor Thomas? Is this some sort of joke?" She dragged herself into a sitting position.

"*Poor Thomas,* my arse," said Cam, following her up. "I had it from the fellow himself."

Helene shook her head. "I think you misunderstood."

Raking his hair back off his forehead with one hand, Cam stared at her. "No, I didn't," he answered darkly. "Lowe quite boldly asked my permission to court you. And I was . . . well, dash it all, I was just incensed. The very thought that whilst I was alone and miserable in Devon, the two of you had been—" Cam's eyes closed tightly as words failed him.

Helene dropped back against her pillow. "Thomas Lowe is a pleasant man, and I enjoy his company. But he does not care for me in that way, nor I him."

"Then perhaps God is using him to torment me," muttered Cam grimly. "I cannot bear to imagine, let alone watch, another man touching you."

Suddenly, Helene's gaze flicked up at him uneasily. Instantly, he sensed his words had gone amiss. "You did misunderstand what you saw tonight, Cam," she said softly.

"In part," he agreed dryly. "But know this, Helene. I shan't have you—or any other female under my care—dishonored by my brother. Those should have been the first words from my lips. I am ashamed that they were not."

Helene made a clucking sound. "Oh, Bentley was more distressed than anything else. He was a little forward, yes. But he was mostly just drunk and depressed."

Cam could sense that there was a great deal more to the story than Helene was willing to share. She did not fully trust his temper, and not without reason. "Very well, Helene," he answered gently. "Protect Bentley if you must, but forgive me for questioning the depth of his despair. My brother loves himself too well to suffer overmuch."

"You mistake him, Cam. I think he loves Joan Belmont." Helene's deep, blue gaze flicked up at him, as if gauging his reaction.

"Does he indeed?" The very idea stunned Cam. He stared at Helene, who looked quite serious. Could it be so? Was this the thing that had so upset his brother of late? Could it be that Bentley did not resent the possibility of being supplanted as heir so much as he hated the thought of Joan wedding another? It was true that Bentley and Joan had been devoted to one another as children. "So Bentley has formed a *tendre* for our cousin, has he?"

"Is that so surprising?"

Cam paused to think. "Well . . . yes. It is true that he followed Joan about quite faithfully when they were young, and often expressed his intent to wed her. Of course, when I was seven, I similarly declared myself to Mrs. Naffles, and gave her a nosegay to seal the bargain. Of course, she graciously cried off when I came of age."

Beside him, he heard a laugh escape Helene's lips, and turned to smile at her. "Darling, if Bentley is indeed serious about Joan—if he has truly considered it, and wishes to seek her hand—I should not dream of discouraging him."

"You would give him your blessing, then?" asked Helene eagerly, rolling up onto one elbow beside him.

"How could I refuse, Helene? *If* he loves her, and means to commit himself to her happiness? I daresay my aunt shall be less easily persuaded, but given his unfailing charm, Bentley will have his way with her in the end, I am confident."

Helene seemed to sigh with relief. "Will you tell him tomorrow, Cam? At breakfast? Please? You must promise me."

Cam gathered her snugly to his side. "Are you so eager to be rid of your companion, then?" he teased, bending his head to kiss her hair. "Yes, love, I'll speak with Bentley at breakfast. But a word of caution, Helene! I do not understand why you harbor such hope for this match, but recollect that my brother is as far from a saint as a young man can possibly be—"

"What are you saying, Cam? Do you fear that Joan will not return his affection? If so, let me assure you that she finds him—well, that any young woman would find him charming," she managed to finish.

Cam peered down at her. "I just find it all quite odd."

Helene's brows shot up. "In what way?"

Thoughtfully, Cam rubbed his heavy stubble with the back of one hand. "Well, since Bentley turned twelve and discovered what his cock was for—your pardon, m'dear—his attentions have hardly been confined to Joan Belmont. Indeed, he had paid her no heed at all, so far as I have noticed. I daresay it's just a case of dog in the manger. When he discovers that I shan't be proposing, his interest in Joan will wane."

Beside him, Helene shifted uncomfortably, but said nothing. Her brow, however, was creased in thought.

"Enough of Bentley, my dear." Cam grinned, then rolled toward her with the familiarity of an old lover, dragging her beneath him and down into the bed with one smooth motion. "If you'll not wed me, at least love me once more before you cast me aside."

"No!" she protested weakly.

But his teeth were already nibbling playfully at the tender skin of her throat, and moving lower. She hummed with pleasure when he found her breast, teasing it through the fabric of her robe. And then he felt Helene surrender to his lovemaking.

He took her again, slowly and gently, as the dark horizon began to soften with the promise of dawn. She moved beneath him with a deliberate, graceful rhythm, and Cam felt foolishly young. And foolishly like crying. For the briefest of moments, he felt certain that Helene loved him as he loved her. And as he spilled himself inside her, he felt like the most fortunate man on earth.

17

In which Miss de Severs suffers some Consequences

Inside the schoolroom, all was silence, save for the occasional *clack-clack* of Ariane's chalk as she slowly tried to scratch numbers on her slate. Helene sat at the narrow table, her head bent to her task. "Ariane?" Helene turned the slate about and tapped her finger on one of the problems. "There is one small error here. Can you see it?"

With a puzzled expression, the little girl looked up, then dropped her gaze to the numbers. Helene reached forward to a pile of buttons which lay upon the table, and lined up seven in a row. "Here," she said calmly. "Let's try to imagine it." She pushed four away from the other three and suppressed a sigh. Progress was slowed by Ariane's refusal to speak, but at least the child no longer pretended not to hear.

Slowly, a smile spread across the little girl's face, and she leaned forward to scratch out the six and make it a seven. Just then, a knock sounded at the door and Milford stepped inside.

"Your pardon, ma'am, but his lordship would like a word in his study?"

Her stomach flip-flopping anxiously, Helene nodded and passed Ariane her next set of sums. "Finish these, my dear," she said, dusting the chalk from her fingers. "I shall return shortly."

Helene made her way down to the study, neatening her hair as she went. On the landing, she paused, forcing her breathing to calm just as the longcase clock below struck ten. She stared down at her hands, disconcerted to see how violently they shook.

She had not seen Cam since his departure from her room shortly before dawn. Strangely enough, she had no wish to see him now. And yet, she longed to do so.

Such emotional inconstancy was unlike her. Helene had never doubted herself. Now, she felt nothing but doubt. Good God, what had happened?

Camden Rutledge had turned her world upside down, that was what had happened. Just as she had known he would, if ever she let him touch her again. Helene sighed, and continued down the stairs. The beautiful boy she had loved too well had grown into a handsome man, who still possessed just a hint of his youthful innocence, and all of his unyielding arrogance. A lethal combination indeed.

Last night had been a raging storm of emotions: anger, lust, bitterness, and passion. This morning she felt emotionally spent, profoundly confused, and fearful of what the next few moments might bring. Cam had sworn that he loved her—*that he had always loved her*—words she had waited a lifetime to hear.

Would he now somehow undo them? In the light of day, would he regret his uncharacteristically rash behavior? Helene knew that just such a thing was possible. In some people. But not in Camden Rutledge, she did not think. Pressing her lips tightly together, she knocked lightly, laid her hand upon the cold doorknob, and entered.

"You wished to see me?" Helene kept her voice composed.

Cam stood with his back to the window, his hands clutched loosely behind him. Stretched out along the cushioned window seat, the ginger tabby preened herself in a shaft of morning sun. A low fire burned in the grate, with a coffee service laid out on the table before it. The room was a scene of utter domestic harmony.

Cam met her with a solemn gaze, saying nothing for a long moment. Then slowly, his eyes began to crinkle at the corners, and he smiled. "They do say, Helene, that absence makes the heart grow fonder," he said softly. "Given the empty hours I've spent since dawn, I daresay it must be true."

Relief surged through her. Helene came farther into the room, willing the blush from her cheeks. "How poetic you are this morning," she lightly remarked.

Cam glanced back at the drowsy cat. "Oh! Do you hear that, Boadicea? The lady is a lover of verse. Can we charm her, do you think?"

Slowly, he strolled toward Helene, dropping his arms to his side. In his right hand, he held a small book, one finger wedged inside to mark his place. With gentle laughter still in his eyes, he flipped it open and began. "Now, let me see . . . Ah!"

She walked in beauty with me last night
Beneath silk bedhangings, and my starry eyes—
And all that best of love and light
Met in our loins when at last we—

Before she could stop herself, Helene exploded into laughter, futilely pressing her fingers to her mouth. "Oh, I do not think, sir," she managed to wheeze, "that Lord Byron ever wrote anything *quite* like that!"

Tossing the book down, Cam grinned and moved forward as if to embrace her. "Perhaps not. But then, he had not the pleasure of—" Abruptly, he stopped, his expression contrite. "Ah, Helene, I forget myself, do I not? Now is hardly the time, nor the place."

"No," Helene answered, feeling a little disappointed.

After offering her coffee, Cam motioned Helene toward one of two chairs set before the fire and settled down opposite. His face took on a serious cast.

"Last night, you begged a favor of me, my dear," he gently began. "And I have faithfully carried out your task. This morning—once I persuaded Bentley that I did not intend to kill him for his conduct last night—I sat him down and attempted to speak with him regarding his affections for Joan."

"Did you?" Helene was surprised. It seemed Cam had taken her very seriously.

"As I promised I would," he said softly, lowering his eyes to his coffee. "But Bentley seemed grievously bedeviled by a hangover this morning—I dare to hope that his intemperance is catching up with him at last—and he took the news of my nonexistent betrothal with a remarkable degree of equanimity."

"And *then*—?" Helene leaned intently forward in her chair.

Cam shrugged. "And then . . . *nothing*. Although I went on to assure Bentley that if he did truly hold Joan in some serious affection, I would press Aunt Belmont to accept his suit. But it seems Bentley is unwilling to take me into his confidence."

Remembering Bentley's tears of last night, Helene felt her mouth drop open. "He asked nothing? He confessed—*er*—confided nothing?"

Cam shook his head and smiled indulgently. "Indeed, he put me very much in mind of Boadicea in her kittenhood. When the minx would finally succeed in catching her tail, she would just look about uncertainly, as if wondering what ought to be done with it."

"Well!" remarked Helene, unable to hide her surprise. "I hardly know what to say."

Cam leaned forward, propped his elbows onto his

knees, and clasped his hands loosely. "Helene, my dear, Bentley had not the look of a man who was truly in love. And I fancy I can be considered something of an authority."

"Oh." Helene picked uncertainly at the folds of her skirt. "And what else did you . . . *explain* to Bentley?"

Cam gave a sad half-smile, and looked away into the fire. "It seems I am not at liberty to tell Bentley anything that would be of the remotest interest to him. Indeed, Helene, my hands are tied. I believe you bound them rather tightly last night. I await your leave to make any further announcements."

Helene felt her cheeks flame, and glanced up to see Cam staring at her. "Yes," she managed to say. Desperately, she changed the subject. "And what were Bentley's plans for today, did he say?"

Abruptly, Cam leaned back into his chair, and scrubbed a hand down his face. "He announced his intention of skulking off to Catherine's for a day or two—said he meant to go shooting with Will. He put up a change of clothing and his razor, and left not half an hour past."

Helene felt a moment of grave concern. It must have shown in her face.

Cam gave a resigned sigh. "Helene, I expect you'd best confess everything. I know you too well, my dear."

Uncertainly, Helene bit her lip. What should she do? Had Bentley really gone to visit the Wodeways? Had Joan come to her senses? Or had word of Cam's discussion with Mrs. Belmont reached them, ending their impulsive flight? The scrap of paper in her pocket seemed to be burning a hole right through her petticoats.

Ruthlessly, Helene shoved her hand into the folds of her skirts and handed it to Cam. "Bentley gave this to Joan last night. She dropped it in the ladies' retiring room."

Deftly, Cam flicked open the note, his eyes darting across it. His head snapped up again, and he held her gaze intently. "Is this what you were attempting to discuss with Bentley last night? Is this what you feared would anger me?"

Mutely, Helene nodded.

Cam paused for a long moment. "Perhaps it would have," he said quietly, "had I any feelings for Joan. As matters stand, however, I daresay it is just as well. Set your mind at ease, Helene. Bentley departed in his oldest coat, and carrying nothing but his shooting gear. He'll not be rushing to the altar with Joan now. *If* he goes at all."

"You think he will not?"

Cam shrugged. "Now that he is sober, and no longer imagines himself to have been shoved aside, Bentley may find both his heartache and his devotion somewhat diminished."

"Let us hope that you are right," murmured Helene. "After all, I want only his happiness."

He cast her an inscrutable look. "As I want only yours, Helene."

Abruptly, Cam rose from his chair and strode to the fireplace, taking up the poker, and jabbing rather ruthlessly at the fire. She was reminded yet again of how beautiful and untamed he had been last night.

After a moment, he braced one hand high on the mantel and spoke into the fire. "I must go to London tomorrow. It will be but a short trip, four days at most."

When she made him no reply, he turned to face her, the rod balanced loosely across his palm. "You spoke of happiness, Helene," he softly explained. "Whilst I'm away, I would ask that you carefully consider just what would make you happy. And if it is in my power, you shall have it. I will not pressure you further. I have no right."

Helene nodded but made no reply. The meeting was at an end, she sensed, and Cam had nothing more to say.

Abruptly, he put down the poker and went to her chair, taking her hand in his and drawing it fleetingly to his lips. Resisting the urge to fly into his arms, Helene rose and murmured a hasty good-bye.

She rushed out and up the stairs, her mind and heart in turmoil. His question echoed in her head and in her heart. What *would* make her happy?

Camden. That was the answer. It never changed.

She paused for a moment on the landing. Did Cam still want her? Yes, it would seem so, though he had kept his distance until the last moment. Somehow, she was not as relieved by his reticence as she should have been. Somehow, the things that had led her to refuse him last night—her work, her life, and yes, her indignation over Cam's assumptions—all seemed to pale in the light of morning. Today, she could think more rationally.

She had reached the schoolroom, but could not will herself to enter. For a long moment, she lingered, staring through the long, mullioned windows at the end of the empty corridor. Through them, she could see Chalcote's formal gardens, which stretched into orchards, then rolled into fields, now lying fallow for winter. And along with that sweetly familiar view, the memories of her girlhood rolled out before her as well, reminding Helene yet again that while she could not excuse Cam's behavior, she could somewhat understand it.

But she was no longer the reckless girl she'd once been. During the years they had been apart, Helene had changed, at least outwardly. Yet somehow, Cam always brought out the worst in her.

Or was it, perhaps, the best? She still wanted to challenge him, to shock him. And while that particular shortcoming had shown itself all to clearly in bed last night, it seemed not to have troubled Cam at all.

As to Cam's lovemaking, Helene was convinced that no one save herself would have recognized the man who had bedded her so ruthlessly, and yet so gently, last night. With his legendary restraint in tatters, all of Cam's raw sensuality had been unleashed. And it had been beautiful, not frightening, to behold.

Yes, outwardly, they were polar opposites. In reality, they were soul mates.

It was, perhaps, as simple as that.

Without another word from Cam, Helene saw the day of his departure dawn, warm and unseasonably sunny. Traveling without a carriage or servants, Cam set out for London at mid-morning. Almost as if she had timed it thus, Catherine arrived shortly before luncheon, her brother's dust barely settled.

Helene was freshening up in her bedchamber when she saw Cam's sister turning into the drive. Mounted on her huge, heavily lathered bay, Catherine had apparently come without her usual groom. Hastily, she slid from the saddle and vaulted up the steps.

Wondering what could have brought Cam's sister in such haste, Helene quickly splashed water over her face, slid a quick hand over her hair, and left her bedchamber. Then she remembered. *Bentley had gone to the Wodeways.* Hadn't he? Or had he run away with Joan after all? Helene suppressed a sick wave of fear, and rushed downstairs, only to find Cam's sister chatting casually with Milford.

But Helene was not fooled. Catherine's restless energy thrummed through the room. Upon seeing Helene descend, Catherine hastened to the foot of the stairs, still clutching her gloves and crop.

"Oh, Helene, how glad I am that you are home! Will and Bentley have left me bored to tears, and so I have abandoned them, and come to join you for luncheon."

She made a dramatic gesture with her empty hand. "Will you feed me?"

"Yes, of course," Helene answered, a little mystified. "And Bentley—do you mean to say that he is at Aldhampton?"

Catherine looked at her strangely. "Indeed, he's to go shooting with Will today. Where else might he be?"

Muttering a vague response, Helene turned to Milford and asked that the noon meal be brought to them in the yellow parlor. Catherine preceded her into the room, shoved the door closed, then leaned back to press her palms against the wood, as if the door might pop open of its own accord.

"Oh, Helene!" she whispered conspiratorially. "I came as soon as I heard. Is it *true—?*" An unholy light seemed to flicker in her eyes.

Busy pulling out a chair for Catherine, Helene jerked her head up quickly. "Is what true?"

Catherine came away from the door and rushed toward the small dining table, almost tripping over her habit. Bracing her arms on the polished surface, she leaned intently forward, and words began to spill from her mouth. "Is it true that Cam has broken with Joan—? Is it? Bentley says it is! And my parlormaid, Betty—she's a sister to Larkin the footman—they had it from Mrs. Naffles that there was a terrible row between Cam and Aunt Belmont."

Helene was still shaking her head as Catherine continued speaking.

"But it must have been right here, Helene!" she insisted. "At my birthday dinner! I saw them go into the study. And Cam—*hoo!*" Catherine paused to roll her eyes heavenward. "He was in a rare wicked mood all night, was he not?"

You don't know the half of it, thought Helene wryly.

"Anyway, what do you think has happened?"

Catherine leaned away from the table. "Come, Helene! Out with it."

Helene made a pretense of moving a vase of flowers from the table to the window. "Perhaps you should speak with your brother, Catherine—"

"Well, I cannot very well do that now, can I?" retorted Catherine, coming around the table to follow her, "when he has gone off to town, and left me here to perish of curiosity? Now, I *know* you know, Helene, so you may as well tell it, or I shall wheedle you to death." Catherine turned a sweetly stubborn smile upon Helene.

One hand set on her hip, Helene studied the younger woman. While it was true that Catherine resembled Cam when she was angry, at her most persuasive moments, she and Bentley might have been twins. Which meant, of course, that she was irresistible.

"Oh, very well then!" exclaimed Helene, dropping down into a chair by the table. "Though I ought to be discharged for gossiping about the family."

"Oh, twaddle!" announced Catherine, with another dismissive toss of her hand. She sank into the opposite chair. "We *are* the family, you goose. Now, out with it!"

Helene stared down at the table. "As I understand it, Lord Treyhern came to realize that he and Miss Belmont were not well suited. I collect that he discussed it with Mrs. Belmont after dinner, and she agreed."

"*Agreed?* Ha!" shouted Catherine. "I rather doubt that!"

Helene's brows shot up. "That is all I know, Catherine."

Across the table, Catherine's face broke into a shameless grin. "Somehow, I rather doubt that, too. But keep your secrets, my dear, if it pleases you!"

Suddenly, a knock sounded on the door, and Milford stepped in. "Pardon me, Lady Catherine, Miss de Severs, but Mr. Lowe has just arrived—"

From behind him, Thomas Lowe slipped around and into the room, freezing in his tracks at the sight of Catherine.

"—on a matter of some urgency, he says," finished the butler haughtily, cutting his eyes toward the visitor.

Helene looked about uncertainly. What on earth did Thomas mean by barging in? "Well, do come in, Mr. Lowe," she managed to utter, rather needlessly, since he had already done just that. "Milford, please lay a third for luncheon."

"Very good, ma'am," intoned Milford, pulling shut the door.

Still in his greatcoat, Thomas laid his hat on the table and shifted his eyes back and forth between the ladies. "I cannot stay to dine," he finally blurted out. "Forgive me for intruding. But a matter of some importance has arisen, and I—" he paused uncertainly, and glanced at Catherine.

With the merest crook of one brow, Cam's sister rose gracefully from her chair as if to leave.

"No," said Helene firmly. "You will sit down, Catherine. This is your home, not mine. Moreover, there is nothing the rector and I might discuss to which you ought not be privy, I'm sure." She smiled calmly at Thomas.

"Oh, no indeed! Indeed not," he readily agreed.

If Thomas was disappointed in Helene's position, his expression did not reveal it. Instead, he sank into a chair at the table and ran a hand through his thick blond hair. "In truth, I daresay it is news more appropriate for your ears, Lady Catherine," he said grimly. "I fear I bring very bad news. Very bad indeed! Despite all my efforts, the worst has finally happened." The rector's voice dropped to a haunted whisper. "Treyhern will be rid of me now, without a doubt." He shook his head mournfully and said no more.

"What—?" chimed Catherine and Helene in unison.

"It's B–Basil," stuttered Thomas, lifting his bleak gaze from his lap. "He's gone. His bed has not been slept in. His gig has disappeared. And I am sure"—with every syllable, he pounded his fist on the table—*"that he has taken her to Gretna Green!"*

"Who—?" answered the ladies at once.

His next two blows rattled the epergne, sending an orange bouncing across the table. "Miss Belmont!" shouted the rector, ignoring the flying fruit. For an instant, his expression shifted from one of mere anxiety to a flash of heated anger. "My cousin—my *curate*—has run off with his lordship's intended wife! Oh, yes, I knew of Treyhern's secret betrothal! I had it from Mrs. Belmont herself! And now—oh, dear! This, on top of all else, and I am done for. Well and truly done for!"

"Basil Rhoades has eloped with Joan?" Catherine sounded precariously close to giggling, but Thomas seemed not to notice. "Come now! You cannot possibly be serious!"

"Oh, perfectly serious," moaned Thomas. "And that's not the half of it!"

"Well, do go on!" urged Catherine, clearly relishing the conversation. Helene looked back and forth between them, feeling like an unwilling actor in bad farce.

Brows arched high, Thomas's eyes opened wider still. "Why—they have been secretly meeting," he whispered hoarsely. "Lovers' trysts! Right in the vestry, no less!"

"Trysts?" hissed Catherine, obviously fascinated. "Behind those red velvet curtains?"

Suddenly, the signature on Joan Belmont's note danced before Helene's eyes. *B.R.—Basil Rhoades!* At once, Helene understood just why Joan had rushed through the churchyard that day, and why she had been so desperate to keep that fact from her mother. It had nothing to do with Bentley! Innocent young Joan had been cavorting with St. Michael's curate!

Helene could not help but wonder who else suspected. Chalcote was the quintessential English hamlet, which meant that half the villagers and all of the servants undoubtedly knew of the illicit liaison.

Thomas nodded mechanically, then drew another deep breath. "And what's worse, she is—or he claims that she is with—" Abruptly, the rector broke off and swallowed hard.

Helene bit her lip in silence, dreading to hear the inevitable. Catherine, apparently, suffered no such qualms. *"Not with child—?"* she breathed.

Eyes squeezed shut again, the rector nodded. "And now I find that Lord Treyhern has gone off to London, and I have no notion what I ought to do. Should I ride after him? Should I ride after *them?* Should I call upon Mrs. Belmont and confess my suspicions?"

After a long pause, Catherine leaned forward, and with a gracious, lady-of-the-manor gesture, patted him lightly on the arm. "Don't think another thing of it, Thomas," she said sweetly. "This is all for the best, to be sure. In truth, my brother and Joan had recently decided that they did not suit at all! She and Basil shall make a lovely couple, and Cam will wish them very happy, you may be confident."

Thomas Lowe looked suddenly on guard. "What's this? Do you mean to say there was to be no betrothal after all?"

"Just so," agreed Catherine with a punctilious nod. "You have nothing at all to worry about. In fact, I have long suspected that my brother's affections are fixed elsewhere, though I cannot be sure if the lady he fancies returns the sentiment." Across the table, Cam's sister lifted her knowing gaze to boldly catch Helene's. Her eyes held a smile, and a hint of a challenge, too.

Thomas's face, however, fell. "But what of Mrs. Belmont? *That* must still be reckoned with, and there shall be no escaping one such as she." He cast an uneasy glance over one shoulder, as if the lady herself might pounce from the china closet.

Catherine patted him again. "You would do well to leave all this unpleasantness to me, Thomas! Do I not always act in my brother's stead when he is away? And I daresay I know just what ought to be done with my aunt, so you may set your mind at ease. Now, do go home and comfort your sister. I can only guess that poor Mrs. Fane must be terribly overset."

Looking quite unconvinced, Thomas rose, and with an uneasy glance back and forth between the ladies, took up his hat. "Then I must thank you, Lady Catherine. You are all kindness, I am sure." He made an abrupt, uncertain bow, and headed toward the door.

Helene was on her feet before the door thumped shut. "Catherine!" she hissed, rounding on Cam's sister. "I do not like this one bit. What do you mean—*you know just what ought to be done with your aunt?*"

"But I do know!" Cam's sister said sweetly. "The old crone ought to be drowned in a cask of cheap whisky. Alas, I've not the heart for it."

Helene stalked around the table toward Catherine's chair. "Then just what do you mean to do, pray tell?"

Catherine shrugged and made a dismissive motion with her hands. "Why, I shall do just as Cam would have done. I shall do nothing! If Joan has finally taken hold of her life with both hands, then who are we to meddle? She's hardly a fool, Helene. And Basil's a quiet, good fellow, whilst Aunt Belmont, on the other hand, is a bloody tyrant."

"But where shall they go? How will they live?"

Cam's sister rose from her chair and went to the window. Finally, she cut a sharp look over her shoulder toward Helene. "Have you truly lost all faith in the power of young love, Helene?" Her tone was a little bitter. "Joan and Basil will make do. There is always a way, if one does not give up one's dream."

"Do you think so?" asked Helene unsteadily, no longer certain of what or whom they were discussing. She began to feel exceedingly ill-at-ease.

"I do." Catherine turned quickly from the window. "Joan shall come into her money in another few years, and until then, I know I speak for Cam in saying that he will assist them if need be. Do not be concerned for them, Helene. Worry for yourself, instead."

Helene looked up in surprise, her fingertips pressed to her chest. "*Myself—?*" she asked, growing increasingly uncomfortable. "In what regard, Catherine? I vow, I wish you would speak plainly."

"Oh, Helene, do you think me such a fool that I cannot see what has been going on in this house these last few weeks?"

Helene felt her face suffuse with heat. "Why, I . . . I really cannot think what you mean."

"My brother is, and always has been, utterly in love with you. He has never forgotten you. Never gotten over you. Why ever do you imagine he hired you in the first place?"

Cam's sister seemed to know a great deal. Helene fought back a wave of panic. "How foolish you are, Catherine," she argued, feeling her breath quicken anxiously. "I can assure you that Lord Treyhern had no notion who I was."

"There's yet another thing I rather doubt, Helene," Catherine dryly responded. "*Helene*—it is not a common sort of name at all, is it? And *de Severs*—so decidedly French. That, combined with your age, and your Swiss education . . . I daresay it took no great leap of imagination to suspect. Or to hope, perhaps in the back of his mind."

Helene bristled a little at that. "Do you think so? Well, I can assure you that I had no idea of—"

"Pax, Helene!" interjected Catherine, flinging up her palm as she paced across the carpet. "I am sure you did not. But I knew, from the first moment I saw Cam look at you, that he was seriously affected by your presence. And slowly, it all came back to me. Oh, yes, Helene. *I remembered*. So how could my brother not? He loved you more than life itself."

She paused again by the window, and let her fingers slide up and down one of the heavy damask panels that she had urged Helene into choosing. During Cam's long stay in Devonshire, Catherine had written to him, suggesting that all of the downstairs rooms be refurbished, and that Helene be given the task. Suddenly, another piece of the puzzle clicked into place. Like a lowly pawn sliding over a chess-board to displace the queen, Helene had been deliberately positioned by Catherine to supplant her cousin.

"Alas, poor Joan suffers much in comparison to you," Catherine said softly, dropping the drapery and spinning about with a devilish smile on her face. "I know my brother, and I am well aware of the perverse way in which his mind works."

"Certainly you seem just as willful," remarked Helene dryly.

Catherine ignored her pique. "And what's more, Helene, I have a long memory. When they sent you away, I was what—aged nine? Ten? But I was much older than that before my brother stopped mourning your loss. After a while, it is not something an impressionable young lady fails to notice."

"But . . . but I do not understand. That very first day . . . why, you told me quite plainly that Cam and Joan were to marry—"

Catherine cut in with a sharp bark of laughter. "Indeed I did! I decided the sooner that little secret came out, the sooner it could be dispensed with. It was something you needed to know, Helene. And I am not sorry I told you."

Helene cut a sly, sidelong glance toward Cam's sister. "Just as you took it upon yourself to tell me about Ariane?"

"Yes," she said emphatically. "And make no mistake, Helene, about Cam's love for Ariane. Nor mine. If her parentage was an uncertainty that you were unable to accept, then again, it was—"

"—something I needed to know?"

"Something we all needed to know."

Just then, all conversation came to a halt as the door opened again to admit a maid who began to lay the table for luncheon. From the corridor, Larkin came forward, bearing a tray laden with dishes. Helene was almost relieved to see them.

Once again, Cam's sister had managed to disconcert her with those black, all-seeing eyes, and her smooth, deceptively glib demeanor. Had Helene once imagined her to be nothing more than a good-natured English gentlewoman? How astoundingly wrong she had been. Again.

Belatedly, Helene had discovered that no one and nothing at Chalcote was as simple as she'd first assumed.

18

In which Treyhern completes a long-awaited Mission

In stark contrast to his beloved country home, Cam usually found autumn in London oppressive, because the incessant haze of coal smoke draped over the city like a woolly, mustard-colored blanket. On this particular afternoon, however, his spirits were unassailable, and the bleak sky went almost unnoticed. Nonetheless, it was midafternoon before he was able to venture forth on the second of the three important tasks that had brought him to Town.

He had come in too much haste to open his house in Mortimer Street, and after stepping down into the lobby of his hotel, he sent 'round for his horse. Across the room, a smiling chambermaid paused to look him over, cocking a hip invitingly. Appreciatively, Cam returned the smile, but shifted his gaze back to the window.

Within a few short moments, the ostler had brought forth his mount. And within the hour, Cam found himself riding beyond Cheapside, past the bank, and along the storefronts stuffed cheek-by-jowl with the sundry financial institutions which crowded the City of London. Today, however, they escaped his notice.

At last, he reached the familiar environs of upper

Threadneedle Street, and the offices of Brightsmith, Howard and Kelly. The young Mr. Kelly scraped and groveled, then ushered him into the senior solicitor's office.

After another ritual exchange of pleasantries, Mr. Brightsmith rose to cross the room and, with a little grunt, hefted down Cam's mother's small but ornately carved chest, banded in brass, and embellished with the Camden coat of arms. Reverently, he placed it on the desk.

"In accordance with your letter," the old solicitor said, in the somber tones of one surrendering up his firstborn, "the jewels were brought up from the vault this morning." With his gnarled fingers, Brightsmith lifted the lid. "As you see, the set is intact, save for the necklace, which was not here when the jewels were conveyed into our safekeeping."

"I know where that is," answered Cam impatiently, his hand hovering over the chest. He let his eyes search the contents, inhaling sharply when he found what he sought. "What I have come for," he whispered, "is this."

Reverently, Cam lifted his treasure high into the meager stream of sunlight that trickled through Brightsmith's window. It was sufficient. Together, they watched in awe as a half-dozen emeralds sprang brilliantly to life. Delicately, Cam turned the wide, gold band this way and that, studying the sparkling winks of fire.

"Your great-grandmother's ring—?" muttered Brightsmith, still staring at the gemstones, his curiosity obviously piqued. "You mean to take only that, my lord?"

"Just the ring for now," Cam absently responded, his heart awash in memories. Forcing himself into the present, he shifted his gaze back to the elderly man's face. "Will you wish me happy, Mr. Brightsmith? As it happens, I have some hope of remarrying soon."

"Indeed?" returned Brightsmith.

"Yes." Cam closed the chest and rose. "Now, if you will excuse me, I have a length of green silk to fetch in Bond Street."

In Gloucestershire, the afternoon had turned cloudy, and a chilly wind sailed down from the north and over the wolds, sending the villagers of Cheston-on-the-Water scurrying for their shawls and hearths. In the house on the hill above St. Michael's, however, Helene spared no thought for the weather. She paced the floor of her bedchamber, restlessness impelling her forward, even as the wind whipped 'round the corners with its howling emptiness.

Chalcote, too, felt empty. Ariane's studies were finished for the day. Bentley was still traipsing about the hunting fields with his brother-in-law. Catherine had not called since their fateful luncheon the previous day, and Cam was still away in London.

And that was the real source of her discontent, was it not? Chalcote was empty because he was away. Indeed, her very existence felt empty without him. He could not possibly come home soon enough.

Home. The one word carried with it a simple truth. For home had always been Chalcote, where Cam was. As the realization dawned, Helene ceased her pacing to stand squarely in front of her canopied bed. She stared down at it, now empty and neatly made. But she remembered. Ah, how she remembered what he had done to her in that bed, not three days past. It had been her undoing.

A shiver of sensual awareness ran down her spine at the thought of his hands, so strong, so sure. Like so much of Cam, they were an enigma. His were the fine-boned hands of an aristocrat, and yet, she had trembled at the unmistakable power in their touch, reveled in their work-roughened surface, as his hands had skimmed up the flesh of her thigh and beyond.

Remember? No woman could possibly forget.

A flash of heat rushed over her. Dear heavens, such memories would drive her insane. She had best get out of the house. In a trice, Helene had exchanged her slippers for half-boots and tossed her heaviest cloak over her shoulders. If the memories did not drive her mad, unslaked desire might. A long tramp over the hills and along the woods would be just the thing. And with today's bad weather, she would be utterly alone.

Helene had no idea how long she had walked in the cold, nor just how long she had sat propped on the low stone wall across from the burnt-out cottage, remembering the times she and Cam had hidden there during their misspent youth. Her feet were drawn up almost beneath her skirts, braced upon a stone that jutted conveniently from the masonry. But inside her fur-lined gloves, her hands were frozen solid. She realized it only when a deep voice behind spoke her name aloud.

She jumped, and her numb fingers lost their grip, very nearly pitching her forward. "Thomas?" She slid onto her feet in the stubbled grass of the cottage yard.

He approached quickly, his blond hair whipping back from his coat collar in the breeze, and leaned across toward her. "My dear, you must get out of this wind." His brows drew together fretfully. "What could possibly have brought you out on such a day?"

Helene toyed with asking the same of him as the rector hastened through the gate that had long since rotted from its hinges. She really had no wish to see him today. She had come to be alone. But she was indeed frozen to the bone, and when Thomas took her arm, urging her toward a small building below the burnt ruins, she realized she had indeed sat too long in the cold.

The low shed had been dug into the shelter of the sloping land, and the downhill side stood open, but inside, the three thick walls provided ample refuge from the elements. But the shelter was small, and Lowe seemed to take up a great deal of space inside it. Suddenly, Helene found the rector's proximity disconcerting.

But how fanciful. She was allowing Cam's remarks about the rector to vex her, when he had merely misinterpreted one of Thomas's blithe, innocuous compliments. How could a rector wish to court her, of all people? The idea seemed faintly ridiculous.

"Warm yourself, my dear," the rector said, "then I shall see you safely home. Today is no day for a pleasant stroll."

Briskly rubbing her hands, Helene studied him. "And yet you have come out walking, Thomas," she remarked rather sharply. "Are you worried about Basil?"

"My cousin is now beyond my help," he replied ambiguously. "Now, you must tell me why you sat perched atop that ridge, and right on the wall, where the wind blows the coldest." Thomas flashed his charming smile. "I would not wish to see you ill, my dear."

Helene shrugged. "I often walk past here when I feel the need for exercise. But today, I suppose I was thinking of Ariane's troubles. And about her mother, too. They say, you know, that Cassandra Rutledge died here. I vow, I should very much like to know what Ariane saw up here that day." She gave a sardonic laugh. "Perhaps I think those ruins might speak to me, were I patient enough."

"There is little to tell, I daresay," he returned.

"But can you understand, Thomas, that I need to know what happened here?" she explained. "Indeed, I may be unable to help Ariane if I do not know."

At those words, Thomas drew near to her side and laid a staying hand upon her shoulder. His touch felt heavy through her cloak. "Listen to me, Helene! Cassandra Rutledge was an evil woman," he whispered, his words hanging in the cold silence. "She was wicked.

And faithless. And she's best forgotten, for Ariane's sake."

Helene stared at him in surprise. "You knew her? Did you hold the living of Saint Michael's then?"

Dully, Thomas nodded. "Oh, I knew her well enough. Well enough to see what she was."

"How cold you sound, Thomas." Helene looked at him somewhat imploringly. "Did she never attend church? Did she never seem open to . . . to . . ."

"To what, Helene?" he interjected bitterly. "Having her soul saved?" He pitched back his head as if he might laugh aloud, but instead he simply blinked repeatedly.

Finally he spoke again. "Yes, Helene, I had a Christian duty to help Mrs. Rutledge walk life's true path. I tried my best, but she wanted no help. I was naive, just two years out of my divinity studies; young, brash, and woefully ignorant." He dropped his chin and looked Helene squarely in the eyes. "And yes, I failed. Miserably. And in so doing, I left Ariane to suffer the sins of her mother."

"Oh, Thomas, you mustn't blame your—"

Thomas cut her off with an angry flick of his hand. "Perhaps a more experienced man might have succeeded, Helene. But God in His infinite wisdom had seen fit to send me here, and one might argue that I failed them both."

Helene came swiftly to his side then, and leaned intently toward him. "Thomas, I am sure that is not so! No one holds you in any way responsible."

Thomas made no answer. The wind seemed to change direction, whistling with renewed vigor past the open end of the shed. For several moments, neither of them spoke, until at last, Thomas shifted closer, and to Helene's initial relief, changed the subject.

"Do you know, Helene," he said rather wistfully, his eyes drifting over the rough stone walls, "I so often find myself restless and yearning for *something* . . . something

I am not entirely certain I can define. And yet, a brisk walk can set aright a great many of life's ills. We share that habit, do we not, Helene?"

She managed a weak smile. "Why, yes," she murmured. "I suppose we do." He stared down at her openly, his eyes sincere, his smile warm. Gently, he lifted her gloved hand in his.

His every gesture was amiable, but in light of Cam's recent warning, his proximity made Helene ill-at-ease. And when he looked down at her again, from beneath a sweep of long brown lashes, Helene was abruptly convinced that everything Cam had repeated to her had been true. Thomas was flirting with her.

"Helene." His husky voice arrested her motion, his fingers tightened urgently around her hand. "I know my words are precipitous, but I can no longer be silent. I think that you and I share a great deal more than just a love of the outdoors." His tone dropped to a solemn whisper. "Enough, I think, to build upon."

Helene drew her hand from his. "Of course I value your friendship, Thomas," she said uncertainly.

The rector cleared his throat. "Helene, in the past weeks, our friendship has deepened to something exceedingly precious, and I think—indeed, I *pray*—that you are not immune to my affection."

"Oh, Thomas . . . I don't think—"

His gloved hand came up to touch her lightly on the lips. "Shush, Helene! Let me speak before I lose all courage." And then, the words Helene could not bear to hear poured forth. "As a woman, as a teacher of children, and as a Christian, you are everything I could want in a wife."

"But Thomas—!"

Again, he cut off her interjection. "Oh, I realize that I am by no means wealthy, but I can provide you with a few of life's luxuries. I want us to be married, Helene, and soon. I realize you're fond of Treyhern's daughter, but I want you in *my* home, teaching *our* children. Just say yes, and then you need never depend upon strangers again. I shall care for you for the rest of your life."

The sincerity of his words tore at her heart. "Oh, Thomas, how you do honor me!" she answered unsteadily. "I am the most fortunate of women to have your admiration. But I cannot marry you."

Thomas drew abruptly away then, and strode to the mouth of the shed. He stood there, frozen in silence, staring out over the valley below. Helene could see that he breathed deeply, almost raggedly, for a time.

Finally, he spoke. "Do I take it, then, that your affections are otherwise engaged, Helene?" His words were even and emotionless.

Not knowing what to say, Helene followed him to the opening of the shed. Of course, her affections were engaged. They always had been. But was she at liberty to answer Thomas's question?

"At present, I'm devoted to Ariane," she answered quietly. "She must be the focus of my efforts just now, and beyond that, I cannot guess what my future holds. But Thomas, surely you must *know*—" she paused, feeling the heat rise to her face, and swallowed hard, "—you must know that many would consider me unworthy of you. My blood is French, and my father died most violently. And as to my mother—well, she was not admired by all of society."

Abruptly, he spun around from the shed's opening, his hands clutched tightly behind his back. "And so, in short, you simply will not have me, Helene?" he responded. "Is that what these excuses amount to? For you will notice that I did not ask for an accounting of your past, nor of your bloodlines. They mean nothing to me. I love you for who you are."

Feeling a little ashamed, Helene stared down at the toes of her boots. "No, Thomas, you did not ask. And you are correct. I am refusing you, and not without a measure of regret, for you are a most worthy man."

Suddenly, Thomas seemed to go limp, as if the strength had been sapped from him. "Ah, well!" he sighed. "If it is not to be, then I must console myself by preserving our friendship. May we do that, Helene? May we continue on as we have been, as the best of friends?" Much of his disappointment seemed to have been carried away on the sharp north wind.

"Why . . . yes, of course," she managed to answer, relieved by the sudden change in his demeanor. "I hope that we shall always be friends."

"Then, thank God," he answered, his usual smile almost returning. "It would leave me despondent to find that I had ruined our friendship with rash words." He moved to stand beside her, and offered his arm. "Come, Helene. Let me see you safely back to Chalcote. It will be dark before five, given this dreadfully overcast sky."

Forcing a smile, Helene slipped her hand through the crook of Thomas's arm, but just as they reached the cottage gate, he paused to speak again. "By the way, Helene, old Mr. Clapham tells me that tomorrow shall be one of our last warm days." He laughed lightly. "Since his weather predictions are nigh infallible, will you seal your vow of friendship by joining me for a drive in the country? And Ariane too, of course."

Uncertainly, Helene opened her mouth to respond, but she must have hesitated a moment too long. Abruptly, Thomas pulled her to a halt in the middle of the footpath, his expression a little perplexed. "Your silence frightens me, Helene. Surely, I have not given offense?" His tone was edged with concern. "I beg you to assure me that I have not destroyed everything, merely by speaking my heart!"

"By no means," she answered, willing the uncertainty from her voice. "Of course we are still the best of friends,

Thomas. I should be pleased to drive out with you tomorrow."

Ariane sighed into the darkness. Miss Helene had returned from her walk, just as she had promised. But Papa had not come back. Dark had come quickly, and dinner was over. Now Chalcote lay under a warm blanket of silence, drifting off to sleep just as the big house always did.

Normally, this was her favorite time, because it was the time when her papa would come up to tuck her in. Then he would stretch out on the bed beside her, and tell her a story about King Arthur. Or of magical fairy forests and dancing druids. Once he had even told her a silly tale about a singing pig. She had certainly not believed *that* one, but she had laughed anyway—inside her head, of course.

It never seemed to trouble Papa that she did not talk back, nor ask any questions about the stories. But often, she did want to ask questions, very desperately. They tickled at the tip of her tongue, but she did not let them out.

Often, Papa would guess her questions, and simply say them out loud. Somehow, he always knew just what it was that she wanted to ask.

"*Ah ha!*" he would exclaim. "I can see just what you are thinking, Ariane! *How did the brave knight save the Fairy Queen from the fire-breathing dragon's jaws?*" The question would be whispered in a small, breathless voice. It was just the sort of voice Ariane would have used, too.

It was really quite nice to have a papa who understood such things. He had a different tale to tell every night. But tonight he was not home, and she did not know when he would return.

"*Perhaps in two days, ma'am,*" she had overheard Milford explaining to her fretful Aunt Belmont this afternoon. Aunt Belmont's visit to Chalcote had come about rather unexpectedly. After Miss Helene set off for her walk, Ariane had heard her great-aunt's big coach come rumbling up the drive.

She had peered out through the schoolroom window to see a vast, rolling cloud of dust. The coach was moving very fast, just as her aunt had proceeded to do, once the vehicle stopped.

Aunt Belmont had sprung from the carriage door, then hopped quickly up the front steps. She looked like a rabbit escaping its hutch, then bolting for a hedgerow.

That had been the signal. Ariane had hurried to the balcony. With grown-ups, she could always predict when something exciting was about to happen. They moved fast, and spoke loudly. And Mrs. Belmont had indeed been speaking very loudly. Nothing Milford said could stop her.

For reasons Ariane did not understand, Mrs. Belmont was quite put out with Milford. In the hall below, Mrs. Belmont screeched like a bird and hopped about like a rabbit, while poor Milford had grown quieter, and even whiter, than before.

Except for Milford, Ariane had thought it all very funny. Papa had once told Aunt Cat that ladies never moved fast, and never shouted. Somebody, it seemed, had forgotten to tell Aunt Belmont.

At last, Miss Helene had come in through the conservatory. Aunt Belmont had shot her a cold look, jumped back into her coach, and driven away as fast as she'd come.

And now, long after dark, with the events of the day at an end and her papa still not home, Ariane stood at her bedchamber window, staring across the rear gardens and into the pitch-black night. Miss Helene, though, was very near. And so, even with the draperies open, Ariane felt safe.

She could no longer remember just what he looked like up close. But she knew that he was out there. The watcher. Just as he had promised. She had seen him in daylight, and she had seen him at dusk. A hundred times she had seen him, and twice as often she had felt that he was near. Like tonight. Even in the dark. He lurked in the woods and on the paths of Chalcote, hanging about the house like Boadicea prowling around a mouse hole. And Ariane felt like the mouse.

But what did he want? All he had ever done was watch, and from far away, too. Sometimes Ariane would see someone up close—someone who she thought *might* be him. Then she would hide. But eventually, a grown-up would come—Papa, or Uncle Bentley, or Miss Helene—and drag her out and tell her that the person was *safe*. That he was not a *bad man*.

When she had been little, Ariane had feared the watcher greatly. She had imagined he might pounce from beneath her bed, or snatch her up in the gardens, and force her to tell everything—or force her *not* to tell anything. *Ever.*

Now that she was bigger, Ariane was not sure what he wanted. The things that he had once said seemed all tangled up with the things that Mama had said. Like so much of what she used to know, the words and memories had turned into muddle. The memories that had once been clear had become mostly just . . . feelings.

And now, she no longer feared the watcher was under her bed. In fact, maybe she wasn't afraid of him at all. Well, perhaps a little. But lately, after listening to Miss Helene's talking and questioning, Ariane felt more angry than frightened.

And so often now, when Miss Helene would hold her hand and stare into her eyes, Ariane found that she wanted to tell her everything. Sometimes, the words would come bubbling right up from the tight spot in her tummy—as if they might explode from her throat.

But if she let them out, there would be no way to hide

anything. There would be no way to keep her promise, once the words started coming out. And what would happen then?

Helene awoke the following morning with a vague sense of annoyance. It took but a moment to recall the source of her bad humor when she pulled back the curtains to see that the skies were high and clear. Just as Thomas Lowe had promised, a sunny day was dawning over the Cotswolds.

She really had no wish to drive out with Thomas today. Indeed, what she wished to do was stay home and await Cam's homecoming, although it was highly unlikely he would return so soon.

But the problem today was not Cam, but Thomas. Although she had vehemently denied it, his sudden offer of marriage had changed everything between them. The agreeable friendship she had felt for him had suddenly shifted into something far less comfortable. And what was worse, the fault was hers, not his, for in the face of her refusal, Thomas had been all that was gracious and kind.

With a sigh, Helene rang for coffee and began to prepare for the long day ahead. Against her better judgment, she had allowed Thomas to persuade her to forgo Ariane's lessons in honor of their excursion, an outing to the old Saxon town of Cricklade. There, the three of them would picnic near the village ramparts, then visit the old Tudor church. Initially, Helene had been resistant to traveling such a distance with Ariane, but as Thomas had correctly pointed out, it was an excellent educational opportunity.

At the appointed time, Helene took Ariane down. Thomas had apparently arrived, for his curricle stood outside, hitched to a team of four fine blacks, but the rector was nowhere to be seen. A little disconcerted, she left

Ariane to wait while she set off down the hall in search of Thomas.

Along the main corridor, past the parlor and Cam's study, all was shrouded in silence. At the end of the passageway, however, just as she turned right toward the servant's wing, Helene heard a door click lightly open in the shadowed corridor beyond.

Retracing her steps, Helene peered around the corner. The rector was exiting Cam's study.

"Why, Thomas!" she cried, darting back around the corner. "I wondered where you'd—"

"Miss de Severs!" The rector spun about.

"I'm sorry," she answered. "I observe that I have startled you."

In the distance, Helene was vaguely aware of Milford silently stepping out of the yellow parlor. With the merest glance at the rector's back, the butler continued down the hall.

Thomas met Helene with an elegant bow. "Not *startled*, my dear!" he answered smoothly. "I was simply arrested by your beauty! But I did think the corridor quite empty. I believe I must have been woolgathering."

He turned to give her his arm, and continued to chatter brightly. "Yes, my mind was occupied by the book that I had just returned to his lordship's shelf. Do you know, Helene, that Treyhern has a most extensive collection of modern and ancient poetry? And so generous in lending it, too. I do think the measure of a man can be taken in part by what he reads. Do not you agree?"

The rector's soliloquy on literature and character continued until they arrived in the hall to collect Ariane and put on their wraps. And he was still talking about it as they went out and down the steps.

"Oh!" said Helene, hesitating in the drive. "I did not see Milford! I daresay I ought to tell him where we're to go."

"I had a word with him on my way in, my dear," Thomas reassured her. "I told him we were off to Cricklade for the afternoon."

Helene thanked him, and turned to look at the waiting curricle. "I observe that you have ample horseflesh for today's journey," she remarked as Thomas handed her up. "We are certainly stepping out in fine style!"

Beaming with pleasure, Thomas bent down to scoop up Ariane, who was even more sullen in appearance than she had been the day before.

"Indeed," answered the rector, following Ariane up and taking the ribbons. "I find I have grown weary of plodding about with only a pair under the pole. I bought these fine fellows just last week. Are they not well-matched, Miss Ariane?"

Casually, the rector turned around to chuck her on the chin, but Ariane seemed to be having none of it. In fact, she drew a little nearer to Helene, though given the crowded seat, such a maneuver was hardly possible.

Nonetheless, Thomas looked instantly hurt, as he always did when Ariane rebuffed his little advances. Helene sought to draw his attention elsewhere. "Well, I think them very grand indeed, sir," she said, staring down at the fidgety animals. "Fresh, too, so I daresay we shall make prodigious good time down to Cricklade!"

Immediately, Lowe turned his sunny gaze upon her. "So we shall, my dear! Are we off?"

Helene forced herself to smile back, and in short order, they were spinning merrily down the drive, then down the hill and away from the village.

After a late night at a wayside inn, and several hours of arduous travel, Lord Treyhern and his flagging mount arrived home a day early, only to find his much-missed country house as silent as the grave—and seemingly empty, too. It was a crushing disappointment to a man who had thought of nothing but hearth and home during a long, lonely journey.

He had hoped to be greeted at the door by Ariane, if not Helene. At least the blasted rector wasn't sitting by the stairs. That, he supposed, was a small comfort. Wearily, Cam tossed his hat onto the hall table and began stripping off his gloves just as Milford came floating down the stairs.

The butler hastened forward to greet him just as Cam slid out of his greatcoat. "Where the devil is everyone?" asked Cam sourly. "Have I been from home so long that I am to be left standing in my own hall, forgotten by my staff as well as my family?"

"Sorry, my lord," mumbled the butler, taking up his master's coat. "I was in the guest wing counting linen with Mrs. Naffles. As to the family, Mr. Rutledge remains, so far as I know, with your sister at Aldhampton—"

"But what of the ladies?" interjected Cam, immediately regretting his sharp tone. "Where is my daughter and Miss de Severs? Have they not come down for luncheon?"

"No, my lord. They left over half an hour past. I fancy you just missed them as they passed through the village."

Cam felt a sinking sense of disappointment. "I saw no one in Cheston. Where did they go?"

Milford seemed to waver uncertainly. "They departed in Mr. Lowe's curricle, my lord. As to where they went, I fear I cannot say."

Cam's disappointment grew certain and heavy. Once more, there was to be no welcome home from Helene. All of his cherished plans—to immediately pull her into his arms, to whisper his undying love, and to press his proposal of marriage—all these pleasures were to be further postponed. And why?

Because of the bloody rector! Again.

But Helene loved him—*not Lowe.* Cam willed himself to

remember that fact. There was no need to be uneasy. And yet he was. Very uneasy. Why had she not waited for him at home?

Because you were too foolish to send word of your early arrival, came the honest response.

Yes, he'd meant to surprise Helene and Ariane. But now they were gone. And there was little he could do about it, unless he meant to go after them like some barbarian and drag them back home again. What a tempting thought that was. But it would never do.

Abruptly, Cam set his jaw at a grim angle and stalked off across the hall. "I shall be in my study, Milford. I daresay there is much to be done."

The butler inclined his head in acknowledgment. "And your luncheon, my lord?"

Cam spoke over his shoulder. "I find I have no appetite, Milford. I thank you."

Once inside the study, however, the silence was even more oppressive. Because his return had been unexpected, no fire burned in his hearth. In its absence, even his cat had fled for warmer climes—the corner behind Cook's stove, in all likelihood. With a sense of resignation, Cam flung open the draperies and sat down to sort his mail. There, in the center of his desk, lay a folded note bearing Helene's handwriting.

With a strange sense of foreboding, Cam picked it up, noting as he did so that it bore no seal. It was nothing of a personal nature, then. He did not know whether that was good or bad . . .

Anxiously, he flicked it open. The note simply stated that she and Ariane were traveling to Fairford with Thomas Lowe and would return in the late afternoon.

Fairford again? What the devil was of such great interest there? Why, one could pitch a stone from one end of the village to the other. Surely they'd seen all there was to see during their last trip!

In frustration, Cam tossed the note across his desk and began to pick through a stack of unopened letters. Perched atop of the heap was an envelope covered with the barely recognizable penmanship of his Aunt Belmont. From the wildly scrawled direction on the front, it would appear that her temper had not lessened. Another harrowing thought!

Cam resolved to deal with it later. Abruptly, he shoved the stack away and pulled back Helene's note, all thoughts of Mrs. Belmont vanishing away on another wave of anxiety. How odd it seemed that Helene would leave him such a message—and a rather coolly worded one at that—when he had not been expected home until the following day. And yet, she had apparently said nothing of her plans to those who should have been told: the servants. It was most unlike Helene, who was exceedingly thoughtful.

Impatiently, Cam turned the note toward the open window and skimmed it again. The words seemed innocuous enough. The paper was the ordinary sort of foolscap kept around the house in any number of places. It was, however, rather crumpled, and it had been folded and refolded several times. Again, it seemed quite out of character for Helene. Without knowing precisely why he did so, Cam rose with the letter in hand and retraced his steps into the hall.

In the center of the hall stood Milford, unfurling a filthy drab coat from Bentley's shoulders. Bleary-eyed and rumpled, the boy had obviously returned from his adventures with Will Wodeway a little worse for the wear.

His brother barely lifted his gaze to meet Cam's, almost wincing as he did so. "Morning, Cam," he managed to mutter.

Cam absently returned his greeting, then stalked toward the butler. "Look here, Milford. Do you know anything at all about Miss de Severs going off to Fairford again?"

Milford seemed to stiffen. "My lord, as I have said, she merely drove off with Mr. Lowe. They may have been headed to Singapore for all that she told me of it."

Bentley, assiduously engaged in brushing horsehair off his boot tops and onto the floor, jerked his head up in sudden attention. "Helene gone off to Fairford again? What the devil for? There's naught to see but an old church full of glass and carvings."

"As I'm well aware," snapped Cam, still unable to suppress his aggravation when Bentley showed any interest in Helene. "Yet according to this note, she certainly has gone. She and Ariane left with Lowe about a half-hour past."

"Well, they didn't go to Fairford," returned Bentley as he studied a thick clot of mud on his boot. "Not unless our angelic rector sprouted wings and flew over Aldhampton on his way."

"Why?" Cam and his butler spoke at once.

Bentley tossed them a look of mild disdain. "*Because,*" he said, pronouncing the word as if he doubted their intelligence, "I've just this moment *come* from Aldhampton. It's on the way to Fairford. Recollect, if you will, that there is no other reasonable way to travel from there to here."

Cam felt inexplicably sick. "And would you have noticed Lowe's equipage had you passed it?" He spoke in a rush, his unease growing. Had there been an accident of some sort?

Bentley elevated one brow and surveyed his elder brother with barely veiled disdain. "Give a little credit where 'tis due, Cam. I know every farm gig and mail coach from here to Bath."

"Indeed, my lord," interposed the butler, "no one could have missed the rector today, for he was traveling with four horses, not the usual two."

Bentley turned on the butler with a look of amazement. "A foursome? Pulling old Thomas's rig? By God, the man means to make some time, does he not? Perhaps he did fly over Aldhampton, after all!"

A stricken silence fell across the three of them. Both Milford and Bentley stared at Cam, as if wondering what next to do. But the butler spoke first, his voice odd and unsteady. "There was . . . something else odd, my lord. Just prior to their leaving, I saw the rector exiting your study. It struck me as a little unusual, but I assume one of the downstairs maids showed him in. And Miss de Severs met him coming out."

Cam swallowed hard. On the face of it, there was nothing terribly odd in Lowe's action. The study was on the main floor, and open to anyone who cared to use it. Indeed, the rector had been there often. He had even borrowed books from time to time. But not lately.

"I believe," Cam managed to answer, "that I must ride toward Fairford. There are two inns and a smithy between here and there. Perhaps they pulled off the main road to mend a thrown shoe or some such thing."

"I'd best come along," insisted Bentley, obviously suspicious. "Look—there's Shreeves now, coming 'round to fetch both our mounts. I'll just have him shift our gear to fresh horses."

Mutely, Cam nodded.

Still talking over one shoulder, his brother headed for the door. "Oh, Milford? Be so obliging as to stuff some bread and cheese in my bag. I'm hungover as all hell, but I'll bloody starve without my luncheon."

For a long moment, Cam stood silently in the hall as activity burst forth all about him. Finally, he forced himself to go upstairs for a fresh shirt, pausing just long enough to toss a little cold water onto his face and chest. As he lifted his head from the basin, however, he glimpsed his own bloodless reflection in the mirror above and hesitated.

Good Lord, what was the matter with him?

There was no reason to suspect that anything was amiss. No reason at all for the sick sensation in the pit of his belly. No intelligent explanation for the sense of urgency that held him in its grip.

Helene had simply taken Ariane out for a drive with the rector, a man he knew well—and for the most part, trusted. What did it matter where they had gone, whether she had left a message, or whether or not they had been seen? Helene loved *him*.

Violently, Cam yanked on his shirt and tied a fresh cravat into the most simple of styles, insisting to himself that nothing could be wrong. This was Gloucestershire, for pity's sake, not Whitechapel, where people often disappeared without a trace.

Abruptly, he turned from the basin and jerked on a waistcoat and heavy surtout, then rummaged through his wardrobe until he found what he sought. With the near-silent *whisk* of steel against leather, Cam drew the glistening knife from its sheath to test its sharpness. Satisfied, he resheathed the blade and shoved it hard into his boot.

Inexplicably, the action comforted him, even more so when he recalled that in his saddlebag he still carried a brace of pistols, since fetching Helene's ring had required that he travel armed. And Bentley still carried his bird gun, and probably a pistol or two himself.

Cam realized that he should have felt like an idiot for being armed to the teeth merely to go in search of a parson's lost curricle. But inexplicably, he did not.

19

The Grand Panjandrum

In the early afternoon, a flock of sleepy Wiltshire quail were startled into flight as the Reverend Mr. Thomas Lowe's carriage plowed through their midst and went flying past the turn to Cricklade. Without so much as hesitating at the intersection, the horses barreled onward, past the streaking hedgerows, and down the road toward Swindon.

Under normal circumstances, Helene might well have failed to notice the tilted and weathered signpost that jutted from the roadside, since she had but a passing acquaintance with the geography of southern England. But today, other than the flushed quail, there had been no excitement whatsoever, except for the fact that Thomas had driven as if the devil were at his heels.

All conversation since leaving Chalcote had been desultory and trite, in marked contrast to his usual habit of chattering effusively about each village and spire—and indeed, very nearly every cow byre—they might happen to pass.

Lightly, she laid a hand over his driving glove, noting as she did so how tightly he grasped the ribbons. "I say, Thomas. Was not that the turn to Cricklade we just passed?"

Thomas sat silently, prodding the horses to go faster still. Their pace seemed almost unsafe, and yet the rector showed no sign of slowing. Indeed, they had paused but once to rest his horses. Initially, Helene had excused his behavior by telling herself that he wished to speed the journey for Ariane's sake, but in the face of his silence, even that charitable excuse began to fade. She felt suddenly ill-at-ease.

"Thomas?" she repeated, a little tightly. "Is something amiss? Are we not to go to Cricklade after all? I do believe we've passed the turn."

Abruptly, Thomas turned to face her. His expression could only be described as one of bleak desperation. "We are going, my dear, to Southampton," he said, his voice barely audible.

When Helene's mouth flew open, Thomas thrust one hand inappropriately around her shoulders, squeezing his fingers into her upper arm until it hurt. It was not an affectionate gesture.

Something was wrong. Terribly wrong.

"We shall be in Southampton by tomorrow, Helene," he whispered across Ariane's head, "and you will be still about it, lest you unnecessarily alarm the child."

But it was too late, Helene was certain. She looked down to see that Ariane's hands were knotted into the fabric of her cloak, the knuckles white and bloodless. The child sat still between them, rigidly staring across the horses' heads, her expression unfocused. It was a look which Helene recognized all too well, though it had been some weeks since she had seen it.

"Sir, you will stop this carriage at once," she said, keeping her voice lethally soft. Thomas's only reply was a bitter half-smile.

Tremulously, Helene extended her arm to point at a small copse of evergreens just ahead. "You will pull up this carriage now! *Ma foi,* I shall have an explanation from you! And I will have it in the privacy of those trees, or I cannot answer for my actions."

Withdrawing his arm, Thomas transferred the reins, then coolly pulled open his greatcoat. A pistol protruded heavily from an inner pocket. "Very well, Helene," he said, his tone impassive. "As long as we clearly understand one another."

A pistol! Her heart raced. Her vision clouded. She barely noticed the dark sidelong look Thomas cast in her direction as he slowed up his team.

What was going on? Who was this man? Surely not the amiably handsome rector, who had so openly befriended her? This was someone else altogether, with his jaw set at a cruel angle, and his eyes so coldly narrowed. With great care, he eased the curricle alongside the copse.

The hedgerow along the roadside faded from her vision. After that, Helene had no distinct memory of walking deep into the copse, then whirling on him in a fit of temper, though she must have done so.

Vaguely, she was aware of Ariane, who stood on the verge near the horses. Her only clear recollection was of facing down Thomas Lowe, and willing herself not to fly at him with her fists.

Ruthlessly, Helene dug her nails into her palms, reminding herself that any display of panic might distress Ariane. "Now just what is the meaning of this, Mr. Lowe?" she demanded, willing herself to breathe. "What wickedness are you about that you must thrust a gun into my face like a common highwayman? *Mon Dieu*, you are a priest!"

Slowly, Lowe paced toward her. "My former profession not withstanding, Helene, we are en route to Southampton. Regrettably, you left me little choice when—"

Viciously, she cut him off, stamping her foot into the stiff, wintry grass. "Indeed, sir, you must be mad if this is your idea of punishing me for refusing you. What manner of man drags an innocent child into his grievances?"

"Do not flatter yourself, my dear," he laughed lightly. "Whilst it's true that I must take control of you, one way or a—"

A sharp crack rang through the canopy of evergreens.

Helene did not know she had struck him until the blood began to trickle from one corner of Lowe's mouth. With his eyes narrowed to lethal slits, the rector balanced forward on the balls of his feet, as if he burned to leap forward and choke the life from her. But something, perhaps a gesture from Ariane in the distance, forestalled him. He stepped back a pace.

Gingerly, Thomas tilted his head, dabbing at the blood with the back of one hand. "Listen to me, Helene," he said icily. "And listen with the utmost care, for I do not mean to repeat myself. If you challenge me, I will hurt you. And very badly. Do not place us in such an awkward position again. The result would be exceedingly unpleasant for the girl."

"Why—how utterly *vile!* You would not dare to harm an innocent child by—*oh!*"

"I would prefer not to harm her, and I hope you do not force my hand by doing something rash or brave, my dear."

An angry, bone-deep tremble ran through Helene. "I swear to God, Thomas Lowe, when Camden Rutledge catches up with you, you'll pay dearly for frightening his daughter! Take her home this instant, do you hear me?"

Almost thoughtfully, Lowe rubbed the side of his mouth where her blow had caught him. "Well, there's the problem, Helene. The child isn't his. She's mine."

Helene felt the breath being dragged from her body. *"Yours?"* she managed to whisper weakly. A wild array of thoughts went tumbling through her head. She tried to make sense of what he was saying, but the pieces would not fall into place. She shook her head as if to clear her vision.

Thomas laughed almost sadly. "Come, Helene! You are a woman of the world! Surely you can see there's no resemblance between Treyhern and that girl. And he has to know Cassandra played him false. Though in truth, I suppose I admire the man for holding to his pride and giving the chit a home."

Helene stepped forcefully toward him. "A home from which you have ripped her, you deceitful wretch! You claim she is yours? Well, given the depravity I see before me now, I do not doubt you capable of such an evil," she hissed. "But tell me this, *rector*—is it not enough to lie with a decent man's wife, to commit fornication behind his back? Must you then snatch from him his child? And she *is his child*, sir. In the only way that signifies to God. Or to me."

For a moment, it seemed his face might crumple, but Lowe's composure held. "My, my," he said softly. "You really are taken with the fellow, are you not? I feared as much. Then Lady Catherine's veiled gossip sealed your fate."

Helene tossed him the most disdainful look she could muster. "Explain yourself, sir!"

In the sunlight, Thomas Lowe's blond good looks made him look like an archangel of evil. The effect was further heightened when he crooked one elegant eyebrow and smiled sardonically, as if laughing at her naiveté. "Treyhern had a devil of a time finding a good governess, did he not?" His expression turned bitter. "But then you arrived. I saw the risk at once. You were both smart and patient. Nonetheless, as long as I could observe you, I saw no need to panic."

"Panic?" cried Helene. "Good God, Thomas! What did I know of your perfidy? Or Ariane either, come to that?"

Thomas ignored her. "I had to befriend you, perhaps

even court you." Appreciatively, he eyed her up and down. "And it was no great sacrifice, Helene. Indeed, I'm exceedingly anxious to get you into my bed, once we are far from England. And far away from Treyhern, cold, inhuman bastard that he is. And I am tired of watching my child from afar, worrying about what she might say or remember."

"You . . . you mean to kidnap us?"

"Such harsh phrasing, my dear!" Lowe looked hurt. "I'm merely offering you and Ariane a better life, far away from the rigid class structure of England. Canada, America—just think of it!"

Abruptly, he paused to stare at her stricken visage, then threw back his head and laughed. "Oh, come now, Helene! Surely you are not as romantically stupid as Treyhern's sister! She cannot have convinced you that he will offer you marriage! Oh, he may well bed you—if he hasn't already. But that self-righteous blue-blood will never make a Parisian trollop's daughter mistress of his beloved Chalcote. He will never deign to do for you what I will—make an honest woman of you."

With a measure of arrogant disdain which only the French seem to possess, Helene spit vehemently at Lowe's feet. *"Pourceau!* Filthy swine! I shall never marry you!"

Thomas did approach her then, seizing her chin tightly in his hand and jerking her face ruthlessly into his. Helene could feel the heat of his breath against her cheek. She fought to turn away.

"Make no mistake what I am offering you, Helene," he whispered silkily, "before you so carelessly cast it aside. I may lust for you, but I am in no way enamoured of you, my lovely. And so my choice is a simple one: I will marry you, or I will kill you. Either ensures your silence. But for all that you may think me—sinner, adulterer, liar, and yes, I am all of those—I would prefer not to murder you in your bed. And I would prefer not to distress or hurt the child. But if I must, I will."

"Camden Rutledge will see you hanged for this, you fool!" she insisted. "If he doesn't shoot you where you stand!"

Grimly, Lowe smiled and released her face. "Again, your intelligence fails you, Helene. If I stay, he will most certainly hang me. It has become inevitable."

"I do not understand you. I think you have lost your reason."

Thomas shot her a withering look. "If Treyhern has cast off his fiancée to keep you in his bed, it means that you are fixed at Chalcote indefinitely. I cannot risk it. You are too clever. Already the child has begun to change. Eventually, she'll talk. And I have no way of knowing what she might say."

Absently, he stared down into the sweep of valley where a thickset farmer struggled to secure a shock of corn in the breeze. "Indeed, I am not even certain she remembers," he murmured.

Helene gasped, sudden intuition flaring. But Thomas was still speaking. "If I take you from Treyhern, not only do I evade the hangman, but I shall have a beautiful wife to warm my bed; one who can make my child well again." His mouth twitched with wry humor. "In short, you're the best end of a bad bargain, m'dear—better than the end of a rope."

"You killed her," whispered Helene hoarsely, drawing back from him. "That is the secret you fear, is it not? You murdered Cassandra Rutledge! And you did it in front of your child! Admit it, you fiend!"

Violently, Lowe shook his head, and for the first time, he looked wild with grief. "Oh no, Helene," he whispered. "Never that! Cassandra killed *herself!* And she did it the way she did everything in life—with pure, unmitigated spite." The rector blinked rapidly. "Oh, I was there, yes! I lit the candles, and waited just as usual. But she'd been growing distant. Avoiding me. And so I had to pressure her. I had a right, you know, to see her. And the child. But when at last she arrived, I saw at once that something was amiss. She was so cold. So aloof. And she said things. Terrible things."

"You fought with her?" asked Helene, disbelievingly.

"Just a quarrel at first," Thomas admitted hoarsely. He looked perilously unsteady as the words poured out. "She no longer wished to continue meeting me! She said she would no longer bring Ariane to me; that the child had grown old enough to talk, and had begun to chatter. She said that no matter how carefully she cautioned the child, that sooner or later, Ariane would tell her father—*Treyhern,* she meant—about our meetings."

Distracted by Thomas's grief, and amazed by his story, Helene watched his face in awe, never stopping to consider that she might seize the weapon from his coat. The rector heaved a deep, ragged breath and continued. "She said that I had become boring. That she was removing to Treyhern's house in town. That the country was crushing the life from her—and that she meant to leave all of us—even Ariane—at Chalcote. *But I did not kill her."*

"I . . . I believe you, Thomas," said Helene quietly. "I do believe you. Cam will, too."

He was staring straight at Helene now. "What an utter fool I was to love her so." He laughed bitterly. "She said it had been such a lark to seduce a rector! A temporary solution to her *ennui,* when she had no one else. I know now what I could not see then—that she was a test. A test of my faith. I failed it miserably, and what's worse—God help me—I'd do it all over again. Because Cassandra could entice a saint with the devil's own words."

"I am sorry, Thomas," whispered Helene. "I am so very sorry. But now, we must do what is best for Ariane. Please! We must think only of her welfare."

Something seemed to snap inside the rector at that,

and he lifted his gaze to hold hers, its cold intensity slowly returning. "Oh, I am fond of the girl, Helene. But I bloody well won't hang for her."

"But it was an accident," pleaded Helene, trying to convince herself. "You said it was just an accident, Thomas! Ariane will remember that, will she not?"

Firmly, Thomas shook his head. "Oh no, Helene. I dare not risk it. And as to what Ariane remembers, who knows? Oh, she has impressions—terrifying ones, to be sure. But can she testify that Cassandra swung the candelabrum at me? I cannot take that chance."

"She . . . she attacked you?" asked Helene, suddenly resolved to get to the truth, and to delay Lowe's flight as long as she dared.

"Oh, yes! The bitch meant to kill me, and to silence the truth of my words! I told her that I loved her. That I would never let her leave me. And I told her what I would do if she tried. Then, in her usual fit of temper, she swung the candelabrum at my head, and sent half a dozen candles flying. Then she came at me with her hands, scratching me, choking me."

"Thomas," she interjected plaintively. "Lord Treyhern will understand."

But Thomas was beyond listening. "I did not see—I swear to God, *I did not see* that one of the candles had rolled into a rubbish pile. Soon, the old window curtains had burst into flame, and still she fought me. Until her skirts caught fire. It was as if the whole room burst into flame.

"I barely got Ariane to safety, and that's the truth of it. Anyone witnessing such wrath would be hard-pressed to explain how it happened. But a terrified child?" He shook his head violently. "No, I dare not risk it. Even if I should be exonerated, Treyhern would ruin me. He is a hard man."

His tone was again implacable. Suddenly, Helene felt

her knees weaken from incessant fear and fatigue. "But Thomas, you cannot mean to take us on to Southampton! Why do you not simply go on without us?" she begged desperately. "You have no need of us. We shall do nothing but hinder your pace."

The dark, narrow gaze had returned. Slowly, very resolutely, Lowe shook his head. "You'll not plead your way out of this one, Helene. Nor will you delay us any further. I'll not leave the whole of my life behind without recompense. Treyhern has everything, but he shan't have my child—the only thing left of Cassandra on this mortal earth. Nor shall he have you."

Helene gasped aloud. "Oh, yes," he said softly, a wicked light in his eyes. "You will help my child. You will repair all the damage that her beautiful whore of a mother has done, do you understand? And from now until we leave England, we are . . . we are *Mr. and Mrs. Smith!* How droll! And if you give me a moment's trouble, Helene, you may depend upon one thing. It shall be your last." Roughly, he shoved her toward the carriage.

Cheston-on-the-Water was deadly quiet. The two horsemen reached the village in a few short minutes, and discovered nothing. There, in the interest of time, Cam set off alone in the direction of Fairford, sending Bentley to check the roads leading west and south.

It took the better part of an hour for Cam to confirm that no curricle matching the description of Thomas Lowe's had been seen along the road from Cheston to Fairford. Given the unseasonably warm day, he had had no trouble finding farmers clearing hedgerows and housewives scrubbing doorsteps. All of them knew the rector, and all were confident that he had not passed in their direction.

At the fourth cottage, instinct kicked in, and Cam felt sure he was wasting his time. With a jerk of the reins, he wheeled his mount around in a tight circle of dust, then headed back down the hill toward Cheston. He was suddenly very thankful that he had listened to Bentley, and had sent him out to check the other roads.

His confidence was doubly rewarded not five minutes later when he met his brother, riding fast uphill, his finely boned face set into stark, angry lines. Bentley drew up in a clatter of hooves, his horse whirling, pawing, and anxiously working the bit. Cam knew just how thwarted the horse felt.

"On the post road," Bentley panted as soon as Cam reached him. "An ostler at the King's Arms saw 'em. Headed south, not two hours past. Flying, he said. Seems they never went toward Fairford at all."

"You were right. And I bloody well don't like the smell of it," said Cam. "I don't like it one damned bit." And then, with a swift and certain jerk of his head, both horses set off at a furious pace. It was a given that they would follow Lowe until they found him, and that they would do it together.

Later, Cam was unable to say at precisely what point in their long journey the gnawing anxiety in his belly shifted to outright panic. Maybe it was when they discovered that a speeding curricle had all but overturned a farm cart near Latton.

But by the time they paused near the Cricklade crossroads to speak with a farmer who was wearily reshocking his corn, Cam was seeing blood. Specifically, Thomas Lowe's blood, for after a bit of cautious prodding, the farmer told an alarming tale of having seen a curricle and four pull off beside his copse of trees, and he made mention of the fact that he had seen the woman backhand the gent with a fair right arm.

It had to be Lowe, the fiend. And it was Helene who had struck him, Cam had no doubt. He knew perfectly well that under the right circumstances, she would do it without hesitation.

But how could Lowe be the villain in such an escapade? Perhaps he had merely taken an improper liberty? Were the circumstances not so despicable, it would have been laughable. If the pious, self-confident rector had tried to steal a kiss and been smacked for it, so much the better.

But it was worse than that. Cam felt it in his bones. And there would be no resolution to the mystery until they caught up with Lowe. After five minutes, they were back in the saddle and on their way again. It took but a few short miles before Bentley gave voice to Cam's fears.

"If that bastard has hurt Helene or Ariane," said Bentley grimly, "I swear I'll unman him with my bare hands."

His temper already in a lather, Cam snapped. "You'll damned well do nothing of the sort, Bentley! If Lowe is to be dealt with—*and he is*—then I'll not be denied the pleasure." Cam focused his determined gaze on his brother. "I mean to marry Helene, you know, as soon as this nightmare is over."

"Oh, bloody hell, Cam!" muttered Bentley staring down at the reins clutched limply in his riding gloves. "I know that."

Cam continued to stare at him, yet barely seeing his brother through his anger. "You knew that? You *knew* that? And yet, you dared to touch her? You pawed my wife-to-be like one of your tavern wenches? And do not dare hide behind Helene's skirts on that score, for I'll have the truth from her sooner or later!"

"Blister it, Cam! I didn't know it then," his brother mumbled, now addressing his wilted neckcloth. "It's one thing to fly in the face of one of your arrogant commands. But it's another thing altogether to trifle with a woman for whom you feel a real *tendre!* What kind of scoundrel do you think me? My God! Cat just told me the whole of it yesterday." He scowled bleakly. "Warned me off, good and proper. And told me about Joan, too."

"What do you mean—*told you about Joan?* Did you not believe me when I said our betrothal was ended?"

"Oh, damn me for a fool—!" said Bentley, jerking up his head, his expression stricken. "You just got back from town, didn't you? You've likely not even heard . . ."

"Heard what?" asked Cam suspiciously. This day was getting more unpleasant with every passing mile.

Bentley stared sightlessly over his horse's head and down the road, blinking rapidly. "Well, I daresay you'll not believe it. Indeed, I know I scarce can. But Cousin Joan has been . . . er, trifling with Lowe's curate. In the vestry. And now she's—" he cast his eyes down at the roadway. "Well, suffice it to say that we shall soon be welcoming two new members into the bosom of our family."

"No!" breathed Cam. "It cannot be!" Slowly Cam shook his head, and then he remembered his valet's carefully veiled hints. The old man had known—or at least suspected. "Crane," he muttered irascibly, "you old devil!"

Bentley shot him a cynical, sidelong glance. "No, I'm pretty sure it was Basil. Joan would never trifle with servants."

Staring straight down the road, Ariane sat quietly upon the carriage seat, never so much as twitching, though once or twice, her nose tickled madly. From long experience, Ariane knew that the quieter she was, the less grown-ups would notice. Certainly, they would not ask questions.

But she knew, too, that the quieter she was, the more she could hear. And today, she had heard plenty. And guessed even more. Ariane was quite good at guessing. She had suspected all along that the rector was a bad man. The baddest sort. He had always made her feel bad in her tummy. But other people did, too. So until now, it had meant little.

But now, she realized that the rector was the watcher. She was almost sure of it. In fact, she could almost remember . . . *something*. Something wicked.

Miss Helene was angry. Angry that the rector was taking them to Southampton. Why they must go there, Ariane did not know. The rector's horses were very tired. Miss Helene had begged him to change them out. But the rector had merely whipped them harder.

In the distance, she could see something high and silvery, almost shimmering against the late afternoon sky. Could that be Southampton?

No, this was *something she knew!* Forgetting to be still, Ariane slid closer to the edge of the seat, watching the sky as another farmhouse flew past. And then another, and another. Yes, this *was* it. Her favorite place in all the world. There was no mistaking the spire of Salisbury Cathedral, soaring high against the southern sky.

Papa had said that the spire reached up to God, and Ariane thought that if she could just get there, if she could just climb up it, maybe God could look down and find her papa. Then he would come and fetch them. It was silly, she knew. But it was something to pretend. And she was very, very good at pretending.

Soon, the rector's carriage had taken them deep into the town. Often the spire was hidden behind tall houses and shops. Then they would turn a corner, and the spire would peep out at them, like Boadicea peeping around the furniture. On some of the corners, she saw things that looked familiar. A house with a blue door. A shop with teapots in the window. Perhaps she had been to these places?

Perhaps not. Perhaps she was merely a stupid little girl. She shook her head, and fought back the hot press of tears. She would not let him see her cry. No, not him. Not never. He was very bad. She must never, ever talk about him. He had made her mama cry.

Had he? The memory flashed, and then was gone, just like the spire.

"Here we are," the rector announced at last, pulling up his horses. They had stopped in a wide but quiet marketplace, with shops all around. In the center sat a market cross, and across the lane was a narrow inn. She tried to read the sign, mouthing the words behind her scarf.

"The Haunch of Venison," murmured Helene in her governess voice, as if it were something important. Something, perhaps, that she should remember? Ariane was not sure, but she knew she could remember it. She tried very hard to remember *everything* nowadays.

But the rector was pulling out a portmanteau, and handing the horses over to a dirty little man who had crossed the street toward them. "It's a decent enough place," the rector said, still smiling at them, as if nothing at all were amiss. As if they were off together on a pleasant journey, instead of a very bad one. "The rooms above are quite small, but the food is excellent. I do not think you will be uncomfortable here."

Miss Helene gave the rector a very angry look, but said nothing.

"Ah," said the rector cheerfully, taking Ariane by the hand and proceeding across the lane. "I see that Mr. and Mrs. Smith are to play the squabbling couple. Come! Let us act out our little farce for yon innkeeper."

With one hand lifted to shield his eyes, Cam turned in the saddle to look past Bentley's shoulder and into the setting sun, now burning an uncharacteristic shade of crimson against the western horizon. The late afternoon chill was seeping into their clothing, and it had become increasingly clear that time was of the essence. It would be full night by the time they reached Salisbury, from which a half-dozen roads departed. That would surely complicate their search.

Cam now had no doubt that Helene and Ariane had been abducted. An innkeeper in Boscomb had reported seeing all three of them pass through little more than an hour before Cam and Bentley. His description of the carriage and occupants fit too well to be a mistake.

Cam shook his head. The fellow had described Lowe's horses as being *in a fair way to floundering,* which meant that he had pushed his team too hard. And why? Surely Helene would not . . .

No! She had not. Cam had doubted her once. He'd be a damned fool to do it again.

Thomas had seized Helene and Ariane against their will. The thought was wildly preposterous, yet Cam reminded himself that the man was smitten with Helene. But to kidnap her? And Ariane? It made no sense.

Yet that was just what had happened. And Cam meant full well to kill him for it. Gingerly, he bent forward to withdraw the knife from its sheath in his boot cuff. It was there, safe and sound, its newly sharpened blade glinting in a low shaft of dying sun.

Bentley's words cut into his thoughts. "If you were an abductor, Cam, why would you take this road?"

"What?" Cam twisted about in his saddle to face his brother.

His brows drawn together, Bentley stared almost blindly down the road before them. "What I mean to say is—just supposing that old Thomas has lost his wits and snatched Helene in a fit of jealous rage—why this road? Where would he be headed?"

Cam shuddered at his brother's spoken musings, so horribly parallel to his own. "If he has taken them," he answered grimly, "then he must be mad, and madmen have no logic."

Tactfully, his brother cleared his throat. "Now there's

where our opinions diverge, brother. And I daresay I've come across a few more desperate characters than you—no insult intended."

Cam elevated his brows and shot his brother a vaguely amused look. "None taken, to be sure! Have you a point?"

His eyes narrowed against the sky, Bentley nodded. The boy looked far more serious, and far more mature, than he'd ever seemed before. "Why go south?" he asked. "Why not set out for London, if one has no wish to be found? Or head north to Scotland? If Lowe meant to ask a ransom—or God forbid, to . . . to injure them—he'd have done so ere now."

The words hung in the falling dusk for a long moment. Cam willed his voice to be steady. "You have a theory?" he asked sharply.

"I believe the bastard's trying to make the port."

"*Southampton?* Surely you cannot think that he would . . ." The thought was too terrifying to comtemplate.

Solemnly, Bentley nodded. "Every day, a dozen ships put out for the four corners. But we will catch up to them in Salisbury, Cam. I am as bloody-minded about it as you. And I've more experience dodging the bailiffs." The boy's jaw was set at a grim angle. "Lowe's horses are nigh to dead. He must either change 'em, or rest 'em. There are but four small coaching inns from here to there, all easily checked as we go."

Implacably, Cam stared across the narrow lane to meet his brother's determined gaze. Suddenly, it dawned on him how very much they shared. In looks, certainly, but also, it would seem, in temperament. "And if the bastard makes Salisbury, how many liveries can supply him with fresh horses?" Cam asked.

The boy squinted. "At least three, possibly more."

Cam nodded. "Aye, we'll split up, then, and meet on the south side of town. If Lowe has the will to re-harness and move on, we'll do likewise. Otherwise, we'll rack up and begin anew before dawn. He'll not make it far if he's bound for the port. There's naught but one main road."

"That's as may be," muttered Bentley, spitting out a mouthful of road dust. "But one never knows which way a snake may slither."

Cam grunted his agreement, and the weary horsemen lapsed into a watchful, pensive silence. Other than the occasional barking dog or passing gig, the farms and villages of lower Wiltshire were dishearteningly quiet. As mile after mile passed with no sign of the curricle, Cam gradually slipped into a brooding silence.

Only one small thought consoled him. His daughter would be safe with Helene. As safe as she could possibly be. That was one thing of which Cam was certain. He had every confidence in Helene's judgment and vigilance, and he knew that as long as it was within her power to protect Ariane, Helene would do so. Or die trying.

Oh, God! That was just the sort of thing Helene would do—break her neck or get herself shot trying to protect his daughter. That painful realization, and the sudden understanding that followed it, brought tears to his eyes.

Had it taken a crisis such as this to make him acknowledge what he had long known to be a fact? Helene might be rash, yes. But she would never be reckless. Not when it truly mattered. Not when someone's well-being was concerned.

Cam swallowed hard, and admitted the truth that had nagged at him for weeks. There was nothing wrong with Helene. Nothing at all. She was a spirited and passionate woman, it was true. And an unabashed hellcat between the sheets, he had learned. But the vivacious, imprudent girl she had once been had matured into a woman who had a good head to match her good heart, and whose glowing character remained intact.

The problem was not Helene. It was him. It was his own duality of character, his own passionate nature that so desperately frightened him. Had he not proven that when he all but assaulted Helene in her own bed? Dear God! His fear and frustration had had nothing to do with Helene. She was merely the key that unlocked his own aching hunger; indeed, his very soul. And she always had been.

With Helene, there could be no pretension, no hiding from the truth of himself. Cam knew it was time he admitted that there was a large part of him which simply could not be controlled. Until now, that had been something he'd been unable to accept.

When Helene had been taken from him, it had served only to prove his mother's point. And then, driven by an irrational fear of becoming like his father, he had somehow repressed all emotion, all pleasure, and almost all of his love. Until he had become something worse. Perhaps much of what Bentley said was true. To much of the outside world, he had begun to look like a despotic, cold-hearted bastard. Only his love for Ariane was proof he was still human.

What a waste he had very nearly made of his life! He'd been afraid to give love unreservedly, out of fear that such giving would somehow diminish him. Yet Helene embraced her emotions, her zest for life, and yes, her capacity for lust and love.

And yet, Helene was never rash or reckless, or any of those other foolish words he had so flippantly ascribed to her. Despite all that she'd been through, and all that she had made of her life, her passionate spirit was intact.

How fortunate he was to know and love such a woman. How fortunate he was to have found her, the better half of himself, a second time. Before it was too late.

And now, he had to find her yet again.

20

And a little child shall lead them

Ariane awoke to find that the silence of the night had seeped into the room. But it was not the sort of silence that surrounded Chalcote. It was a quiet filled with waiting, with the creak of people climbing up the stairs and the rumble of carts rolling down the street.

Once a man strolled beneath the window singing a very loud and naughty song. Ariane knew most of the words, though, because Bentley often sang it. And just as badly, too.

With great care, she sat up and studied the bed which was shoved securely against the wall on her side. The headboard and footboard were high, requiring Ariane to carefully crawl along the foot, then slither off the lower corner.

Lightly, she stepped over the trundle, watching to ensure that *he* didn't wake up. Then she crept toward the window to peer down into the street. It was far, far down. In the moonlit marketplace below, she could see the stone market cross, with the booted legs of a man protruding from it—the singing man, most likely. Bentley slept a lot after singing, too.

The rector had told the innkeeper to give them one

large room on the top floor. "And a trundle bed for my wee one," he had added. So she had kicked him very hard in the shin. The rector had jumped, and muttered a word she did not think rectors were supposed to say.

I am not your wee anything! she had wanted to scream. In fact, she had opened her mouth, but Miss Helene had picked her up, laid her glove across Ariane's lips, and carried her across the room. Miss Helene had wanted her *not* to speak. And so she didn't. And then, *he* had called outside to the dirty little man who had taken their horses.

The man had come into the inn, and the rector had given him a gold coin. "My wee one tends to sleepwalk," he had said. "And my sweet wife and I are near dead with fatigue. Sit outside our door tonight, if you please, and shout out loudly if you hear anything at all. Just to be sure. Of course, there shall be just another such coin awaiting you tomorrow morning—*if* my beloved family is still snug in their beds." The rector gave a hearty wink.

The man winked back, and the rector added, "And you carry a knife, do you not, my good fellow? I daresay Salisbury has become a most dangerous town, eh?"

The dirty man nodded, bit into the coin, and patted his coat pocket.

Well—! Did they think she was such a fool as to not figure that one out? Miss Helene certainly was not. She had seen it too. She knew why the rector had done it. What he had meant. Miss Helene had spun about to face the wall, still holding Ariane tight, shaking as if she were angry.

Now, in the distance, a bell tolled. One. Two. Three. Four times. Ariane turned from the window to face Miss Helene. The rector had left the lamp turned down very, very low. In the pale light, she could see the slow rise and fall of Miss Helene's chest. She was asleep, then. But for a long, long time, she had lain awake beside Ariane, patting her on the leg and saying nothing, just staring up at the ceiling and wrinkling her brow as if thinking of a plan.

Yes, that was just the sort of thing Miss Helene would do. *Think up a plan.* But what sort? A plan to run away and hide? Ariane was very good at hiding. No one ever saw her. But Miss Helene would be afraid to take her. And Miss Helene would never leave her alone with the rector, who now lay snoring loudly on the trundle bed.

And Miss Helene had most likely never been to Salisbury. It was very far away from France and Bavaria and Vienna, and all the other places Miss Helene seemed to know about. But Ariane *had* been to Salisbury before. She knew where the cathedral was. She knew how to look for the spire. And she had stayed at another inn, larger and much nicer than this narrow little place *he* had brought them to.

Ariane closed her eyes and thought very hard about her previous visit. She could see the inn's sign swinging bright in the breeze. She had not been able to read the words, but her papa had read it to her, and pointed out the red lion above the words. *"The Red Lion* in *Milford Street,"* her papa had said.

And then, he had laughed, and thrown her high into the air. "When we return to Chalcote, Ariane, we must tell Milford that we slept in his street on our journey. He will be mightily impressed, will he not?" And when they got home, Papa had indeed asked Milford if he owned Milford Street.

"Oh, indeed, Mr. Rutledge," Papa's butler had said somberly. "Every cobbled inch! But alas, I anticipate selling it soon, in order to purchase a villa in Tuscany for my retirement years."

Papa had laughed and laughed and bounced Ariane on his knee. She was pretty sure Papa and Milford were having a jest. She did not think Milford would ever leave them to go to live in a villa, whatever that was. But she had worried about it just enough to remember it. She really did not want anyone else to leave Chalcote.

Across the room, the rector made a funny, choking-wheezing sound.

Just maybe, Ariane thought, *he was dying.* On tiptoe, she crept around to Miss Helene's side of their bed, and peered into the trundle. Ariane had already figured out that he had placed it just so, in order to keep Miss Helene from getting out of bed. But the rector lay perfectly still, breathing very, very quietly. She could see the pistol protruding from the bearer of his trousers, just beneath his waistcoat.

He drew another breath, quietly this time. Well! So he was not dead, then. That was just too, too bad! Maybe he should be dead? Just maybe she should lift up the lamp and pour the oil right over him and set him on fire!

Oh—! Wherever had that come from? Such a bad, wicked thought!

Ariane shut her eyes, then put her hands over her mouth, just in case some words came out. But they did not. And *he* kept sleeping. And making almost no sound at all. But someone was still snoring. She could still hear it, and quite loudly too. Miss Helene certainly did *not* snore. That could mean only one thing.

Slowly, oh-so-carefully, Ariane crept to the door, shuffling quietly over the threadbare carpet. *Yes!* The dark man was asleep. She could hear him snoring in the hall. Cautiously, Ariane lay down on her belly, and pressed her cheek to the floor. Intently, she studied the thin shaft of light, looking for feet, legs, anything—but in the flickering light of the wall sconce outside the door, she could see straight across to the opposite baseboard.

So . . . he sat either to the left or to the right. Not directly in front of the door. Suddenly, a deep, rumbling sound ripped through the air, sort of vibrating against the floor. At once, a horrible odor drifted through the crack and into the room.

Ughk—! That rather settled it, Ariane thought, pressing her nose to the carpet to shut out the stench. The small, dirty man sat to the left. The direction of his wafting stink was uncertain, but his nasty rumbling—that had definitely come from the left. She lifted her head and listened.

He still snored. The rector still breathed.

Slowly, carefully, Ariane got up from the floor, pulled on her cloak and hat, then, with her boots in hand, returned to the door and gingerly lifted the latch. In the corridor, the dirty man sat to the left, his legs stretched across the floor, his head lolled to one side. Testing each board as she went, Ariane stepped carefully over him and continued down the hall. It was just that simple. It often was, especially with adults. They never paid her any mind.

Ariane did not know how far she had walked after leaving the inn. At first, it had seemed very like a hiding game. She had crept down the narrow flights of stairs, paused in the big room filled with tables just long enough to pull on her half-boots, then she tiptoed through the kitchen. All was silent, even the latch on the back door, which had opened onto a musty alley.

But after wandering about a bit, and turning here and there, she had ended up right back in the market square where the singing man still slept! And so, afraid that the rector might be peeping out the window, she had run fast in the opposite direction, terrified at the thought of being caught.

But now, she was completely lost. The buildings looked bigger in the dark. Nothing seemed familiar. To make matters worse, there was no way to use the spire. It was still too dark to see it. How foolish not to have thought of that!

So, this was not a game at all. Things were very bad indeed. Yes, she had escaped *him*. But having escaped, she had no notion what she ought to do. Indeed, she had done something Miss Helene would never have done. She had run away with no plan at all! How she longed to crawl back into bed with Miss Helene. But now, she doubted she could find her way back to the inn. How foolish she had been to run away.

Ariane did cry in earnest then, and trying to look past her tears, she had turned about and headed down another cobbled alley, which after a few more twists and turns, led into a street whose name began with "Q." That was all she could read! Just "Q!"

This was bad. Very bad. Oh, how she wished she had tried harder with her lessons. Feeling very small and stupid, Ariane snuffled back her sobs and tried to think. Should she turn left or right on the Q street? The buildings were growing taller and darker all the time.

Suddenly, a loud rumbling noise echoed off the adjacent storefronts. She looked up to see a heavily laden brewer's dray rattling down the cobbles. Panic struck. Instinctively, she knew she must not be seen wandering alone. Retracing a few paces, Ariane ducked into an alley, just as they dray rumbled past.

At once, she knew she had made a big mistake.

"Well, well," cackled a voice from the shadows.

Ariane tried to run, but a strong hand dug into the folds of her traveling cloak and dragged her backward into the darkness.

"Come 'ere, me pretty, and let's 'ave a look at you, what?"

Ariane dug in her heels, but it was no use. She wanted to scream, but no noise would come out. *Did she even know how to scream?* It did not seem to matter.

After peering at her in the dark, the woman pulled her into Q street, where the half-moon shed a little light. "My, you're a fancy little thing!" the lady purred, like a warm cat saying words. "And finely dressed, I'll say. What's yer name, sweeting?"

Fear still threatened to choke her. Ariane stared up into the woman's face and tried not to cry. The woman was rather pretty when she smiled, showing teeth that looked just a little dark. Heaping ringlets of elaborate hair spilled over both shoulders, and even in the dim light, Ariane could see that her bosoms were very grand. And despite the wintry air, they were poked up high and sort of . . . well, falling out of her gown. Across the woman's arm lay a tattered cape. Had the lady come out of one of those dark, narrow doorways which gave onto the alley?

"What's yer name, me pretty?" repeated the woman, bending closer to her face. Ariane swallowed a sob.

"Ah, come on, ducks! You can tell old Queenie." She lifted a long, thin finger and pointed at the street sign. "This is my turf, d'ye see? Everyone in Queen Street knows me to be a fair-minded game gal. And I knows everyone hereabouts. But I *don't* know you, ducks. And such a turned-out lass as you has got no business in the streets afore cock-crow!"

A tremulous sob rocked through Ariane's body then. With a determined jerk, she tried to pull away but the woman—Queenie—still held her fast. Suddenly, the woman was kneeling in the dirty street, and staring her in the face. "Lor, I ain't never seen a one quake like you, dearie."

With one hand, the woman stroked the hair back from Ariane's face and made a little clucking noise. "Look ye, my girl, I'm on me way 'ome—and I'll bet you've run away from yours, eh? Caught yerself a whipping, I dessay. Fancy I know the signs." She gave Ariane a little shake and narrowed her eyes shrewdly. "Gar'n now! Tell me where yer from, and I'll see you safely back, eh? A strapping's better 'n starving any day."

Warily, Ariane hesitated. The lady seemed nice enough. What should she do? What would Miss Helene do? The town had seemed far safer from up high. But she had gotten lost. She could not go back there, could she?

Somewhere else then? She had escaped with some vague notion of going to Milford Street, to look for the Red Lion. Was that not a good plan? Eventually, her papa would come, and he would stay at the Red Lion, because he always did. She remembered him having said that.

Yes, Papa would find her. And then, they would go to—to *Southampton*. And there they would get Miss Helene from the rector. It was, she supposed, the only plan she had.

The woman called Queenie sighed deeply. "Now look 'ere, lass—" Her voice was rough and serious again. "I've 'ad me a 'ard night, and I'm going on me way now. Queenie ain't got time for them wot don't want it. D'ye need some 'elp er not?"

"M-M-Milford," Ariane stuttered, almost inaudibly.

"Eh?" said the woman, leaning forward in a cascade of yellow ringlets. "Milford's yer name?"

"M-Milford St-street," replied Ariane, a little louder.

Smartly, the woman nodded. "Right on me way 'ome, ducks!" Queenie hopped up from the cobblestones, grabbed Ariane by the hand, and dragged her down Queen Street. "And whereabouts in Milford do ye live, lass?"

"Th—the *Red Lion,*" she finally whispered. "P-p-papa always stays at the Red Lion."

"Coo!" said Queenie, jerking to a halt and looking worried. "The Red Lion, is it? *Hmm—!* Well, I can see you as far as the courtyard, dearie. But after that, yer on yer own. Old Queenie's got a little unfinished business with the tapster at the Lion."

Helene shook her head, trying to clear the fog. Somehow, she'd become trapped in the garden maze, unable to go forward or backward. Unable to find Ariane, who was lost deep inside the jungle of greenery. The child's terrified cries rang through the air. But every turn brought Helene face to face with yet anther challenge. A thicker patch of fog, a blazing fire, or a man with a pistol waited around every blind corner.

At last, she came upon a shallow puddle, narrow enough to leap across. But as she gathered her skirts and began to jump, she saw that it now swam with fierce, snapping creatures with jaws big enough to swallow her whole. But it was too late. Her feet had left the ground. She went sailing through the air just as a pair of hot, hungry jaws swallowed up her left leg. Inexorably, the creature began to drag her down, down. Down into the teeming puddle of wicked creatures and terrifying darkness.

Helene awoke with a start, sitting bolt upright in bed, and blinking uncertainly. The room was dark, the silence broken by the soft sound of someone breathing. She tried to pull herself higher in the bed, only to find her left leg was tightly ensnared in the bedsheets. Slicking a hand back through her hair, she discovered her forehead was beaded with sweat.

Where was she? Where had she been?

A dream. It was just a dream. She had been searching for . . . *for Ariane.* Her eyes darted through the room, and the memories of the preceding day came rushing back as well. Stripping back the bedcovers from her legs, Helene tried to shake off the last vestiges of the nightmare.

It was only then that she realized that wakefulness held a far greater terror. Something was wrong. But what? Stretching across the bed, Helene put out a searching hand, and patted her way across the mattress. There was nothing but a wall to her right. She was alone. Ariane was gone.

In the pale moonlight which seeped into the room, she could see that the door to their bedchamber stood open. Lowe's incompetent henchman lay sprawled asleep in the corridor beyond. Her sharp intake of breath roused Thomas Lowe, and he sat up with a muttered curse.

After crawling into bed long after midnight, Cam was almost immediately roused by a brisk young chambermaid who knocked upon his door with knuckles made of Sheffield's best steel.

When he groaned in protest, she look it as a greeting, swishing into the room with a lamp turned far too high, and bearing a bucket which made a god-awful clatter when she set it down. Then, with a cheerful good morning, the girl set about sweeping the hearth.

Rolling out of bed with a manly grunt, Cam sat on the edge of his bed, watching as she tipped steaming water into a porcelain basin. "The time—?" he managed to rasp, scrubbing his hand down a day's growth of stubble.

"Why, 'alf past five, m'lord, like you asked last night." The buxom young maid turned from the washstand, looking momentarily confused. "The potboy already woke old Stokes to open the kitchens early. You'd still be wanting breakfast, aye?"

Cam rubbed his palms over his eyes, which felt imbedded with a day's worth of road grit. His memory of the previous night's events began to return. "Yes, thanks," he finally mumbled, managing to smile at the girl. "Now go wake my brother. And miss—mind his hands! Whack him on the sconce with that bucket if the scamp missteps."

With another bright smile, the girl swished back out. Hastily, Cam stripped to the waist and washed as best he could, then dressed and jerked open the door just as Bentley stepped into the corridor. After an exchange of terse greetings, they reviewed the morning's strategy, then clattered down the twisting staircase, crossed the vestibule and entered the dimly lit common room.

Behind the wide oak bar, polished to a high sheen, a

burly man set down a stack of thick crockery plates. The smell of strong coffee wafted from the kitchens. In the cavernous hearth, a fire roared, and on the settle nearby lay a lump of rags. Spying a narrow trestle table near the hearth, Cam moved toward it, Bentley following close behind.

Just then, the bundle of rags sat up. A tattered quilt fell away to reveal a small, wide-eyed child. Cam stopped so abruptly, his brother felt flat against him.

"What the devil—!" muttered Bentley, gingerly rubbing his nose.

But Cam was already on his knees, pulling Ariane into his arms, and turning her toward the fire. "My God, my God," he murmured, letting his eyes drift anxiously over her, even as he skimmed assessing hands over her face, her arms, and finally her tiny ankles, to reassure himself that she was unhurt.

"Ariane—! Ariane, my precious! What has happened? Where is Helene?" Fretfully, he studied the child's pale face, her eyes, which blinked uncertainly. Her presence here seemed a miracle, but it was not enough. Abruptly, Cam looked about the room desperately searching for Helene.

Bentley stood back as the innkeeper circled around the bar, hastening toward the commotion.

"The lass is well enough, I daresay," announced the man, hands set stubbornly at his thick waist. "And I'll thank you to keep yer 'ands off, if you please."

"Good God!" roared Cam, leaping up from the settle as if he might throttle the innkeeper. *"Keep my hands off?* Let me tell you, my good fellow, I shall have an explanation for this! Someone will tell me just why my daughter—a mere *babe*—has been left to sit here unattended. And in *this—!"* He jabbed a finger at the ragged quilt. "She looks to have been scared nigh witless!"

Cam lunged toward the innkeeper, a wide, barrel-shaped man, but from behind, Bentley grabbed his brother's arm and yanked him sharply backward. The innkeeper set his hands at his hips and glowered at the earl.

"Now you look here, my fine fellow! If that's your chit, where've you been? That's wot I'd like to know! I'm Stokes, the innkeeper here—an honest man, too! I come to me back door this morning, minding me own business, an' there she lays! A sleepin' on my doorstep—pretty as you please!"

"Asleep on the doorstep?" echoed Bentley incredulously.

"Just so," muttered the man, cutting a dark glance back and forth between them. "And I weren't been born yesterday, sir!" he said, settling his glower on Cam. "Any fool can see that one's no urchin. And 'tis plain enough she's run away. And from some overbearing family, belike."

Cam growled again, but Bentley jerked hard on his arm. "Thank you, sir!" Bentley said. "We've been looking high and low for this child. Can you tell us anything more? Have you any idea how she got here?" He paused for a moment. "But I suppose, given her inability to speak, that you—"

"Eh? Wot's that?" interjected the fellow loudly, drawing back suspiciously. "I wonder if you know this child a'tall! No great talker, but she told me plain wot she wanted!"

"She told you *what—?*" asked Cam and Bentley at once.

"She told me that she was come to wait on her papa," explained the man slowly, as if he addressed idiots. "She told me she was come from somewhere else—what d'ye call it? Something like . . . Cow-cot."

His woolly brows drew together for a moment, then he nodded. "Aye! And then, she sits herself down right prettily, and said as how she would wait until her papa come to fetch her. And from that moment to this, she's spoke nary another word. Not her name, nor nothing else would she say. So there—! Wot's a fellow t'do? Send 'er to the magistrate?" The burly man sneered at them derisively.

His mouth still gaping, Bentley continued staring at the fellow, but Cam dropped down to embrace Ariane again, a strange mixture of relief and fear coursing through him. Behind him, he heard the man still complaining to his brother.

"Aye, I 'ad to feed her too, poor wee thing! Ate like she'd been left to starve. Give her a nice bit o' beef stew and bread with warm milk, which'll be two shillings tuppence, if you please, sir."

Behind him, Cam heard money changing hands, a great deal more than two shillings, from the sound of it. It was the least of his concerns. "Ariane, sweet," he said gently, clinging desperately to her little hand. "You must tell Papa what has happened! You must! Now, begin by telling me how you got here. Surely you remember that much? Surely you can squeak out a word or two for poor Papa, if you can talk to this big fellow here, eh?"

Ariane seemed to screw up her face in thought. "*Q-q-queenie*," she finally whispered. The one softly spoken word was like a balm to Cam's soul.

"Wot's that?" asked the innkeeper, stooping down with his fist full of coins. "Wot's she said?"

Cam tore his eyes away from his daughter to glance up from the settle. "Queenie? Does the term mean anything at all to you?"

The innkeeper's eyes narrowed. "Aye, it might, at that! There's a doxy called Queenie, works out o' the Cock an' Crown in Queen Street. I chased her out of here once or twice. We run a good establishment." He dropped to his haunches next to Cam and looked Ariane in the eye. "Was it Queenie wot left ye 'ere, miss? If it was, just say the word, an' I'll send me ostlers 'round to fetch 'er!"

The little girl stared back, her face pinched with despair.

"Yes," said Cam coldly. "Do that. I'll see her in Newgate for her trouble."

"Right!" said the innkeeper cheerfully, grunting as if he meant to stand. "I'll 'ave the constable on 'er in a trice!"

"Nooo!" Ariane wailed, her face crumbling into tears. "I like her!" she sobbed, flinging one booted foot forward to catch the innkeeper soundly beneath the kneecap. "She finded me! And I like her!"

The innkeeper was on his feet now, rubbing his knee and obviously biting back a curse. Cam stood also, and looked at him.

"Fetch her," he said ruthlessly. "Now."

It took but a quarter-hour for the Red Lion's minions to roust the woman known as Queenie, and then drag her, all but kicking and screaming, into the inn's dark interior. Unfortunately, it took twice as long to convince the woman that all Lord Treyhern wanted was information, for she had hurled herself onto the proffered bench with a righteous indignation, a seething mass of bright yellow hair, dingy pink satin, and huge, heaving breasts.

While awaiting the woman's arrival, Cam had tried to gently question Ariane, but she was either too tired or too traumatized to answer clearly. Other than a few whispered words about coming to Salisbury in a carriage, Ariane could say little that was helpful.

Now, Queenie seemed even less forthcoming. After ten minutes of futile interrogation, Cam tore his eyes from the obstinate woman and jerked out his watch with a violence. It was almost half past seven now. *Damn it—!*

How could he make the woman see that they had no time to waste! Where the devil was Lowe? More importantly, where was Helene? Cam knew she would never willingly have parted from Ariane, and driven by a moment of panic, he hardened his glance in the whore's direction.

Fear and cynicism was still evident in the anxious shift of her narrow gaze. "I don't know no more than what I told you, m'lord!" the haggard woman protested, slapping her hand palm down onto the tabletop. "I found 'er in the alleyway beside the Cock. I 'ad me a late night—if you knows what I mean—and when I come out, in she run. Right out o' Queen Street, looking like old Scratch's 'ounds was after 'er. That's all I know!"

Cam stared across the table at the woman who, in her day, had obviously been a beauty. That day, however, was some years past. Cam winced at the terror he had instilled in one less fortunate than himself. It gave him no pleasure.

Abruptly, he softened his tone. "I thank you, madam, for seeing my daughter to safety. But forgive me if I fail to comprehend how a six-year-old child can end up wandering the streets of a large town alone. Nor do I understand how you knew to bring her here?"

Queenie stared at him as if he had taken full leave of his senses. "Why, she tol' me 'er papa was staying at the Lion! 'Ow else would I know such a thing?" With an insolent gesture, she tossed a mass of dirty blonde hair back over one shoulder.

Bentley shoved himself away from the table and looked at her in misgiving. "She *spoke* to you? Very little, I suspect!"

Queenie must have missed the veiled insult in his words. She tipped up her narrow chin and stared at the ceiling thoughtfully. " 'Twas precious little, sir, to tell you truthfully. At first, she said nary a word, then all of a sudden-like, she pipes up and says *Milford!* Which I took to be 'er name, see? But she said no, 'twas Milford Street she wanted. And that her papa was staying at—no, *stayed* at—the Red Lion."

Slowly, the remaining few details spilled out. Cam studied her carefully, increasingly certain she spoke the truth. Indeed, she'd been found in her boarding house, asleep in her own bed. She admitted to who and what she was. At no time had she denied finding Ariane. And twice during the last five minutes, Cam had seen her cast a worried glance toward the settle near the fire, where Ariane lay swaddled in Cam's coat.

Glancing in that direction himself, he felt a moment of relief despite his unabated fear for Helene. Helene had been right all along. Ariane *could* talk—at least a little, if one could but persuade her to do so. Obviously Helene had also been correct in surmising that Ariane's speech was hindered by fear, and Cam was beginning to suspect that it had a great deal to do with Chalcote's erstwhile rector.

Tentatively, Queenie spoke. "Look, m'lord, why d'ye not bring the child over 'ere? Mayhap a woman—" Abruptly, she jerked backward, as if anticipating a blow, but when it did not come, she relaxed. "No insult meant, m'lord, but what I mean is, mayhap she'll talk t'me? She took a liking t'me. Why, I couldn't say."

Cam had to admire her courage. Many of her class would not have cooperated, no matter how much pressure had been exerted. With a curt nod, Cam left the table to scoop Ariane up into his arms. The little girl yawned, and scrubbed at one eye with a fist.

Gently, Queenie turned her gaze on Ariane as Cam sat down with her on his knee. "Lookee 'ere, sweet—tell yer papa where ye'd been when old Queenie found you in the alley this morning. D'ye remember?"

Ariane shook her head. "L-l-lost," she said breathlessly.

Queenie sighed softly. "Lor, you're one worrit little thing, I reckon. Try to tell us what 'appened, and yer papa'll put it to rights, see?" Obviously, the woman was no fool. She had already surmised from their questions that Ariane had been kidnapped.

Cam nodded his approval and the woman continued. "Who brought ye 'ere to Salisbury? D'ye remember that?"

With jerky motions, Ariane nodded. "The r-r-rector."

Queenie gasped indignantly. "Well, I never! Called 'imself a rector, did 'e? 'E oughter burn in 'ell for that, to be sure!"

"It's true," said Cam softly, suddenly deciding to trust the woman. "Though why a rector would do such a thing is not entirely clear. We believe he kidnapped Ariane. And my—her governess. We have been trailing them since yesterday."

"Gorblimey!" said the whore, her eyes wide with loathing. She turned her full focus upon the child. "Kidnapped by a rector? Then piked off alone?"

Mutely, Ariane nodded. She looked increasingly anxious, and in response, Queenie shot her a mischievous wink. "Gave the blighter the slip, eh? Now, how'd ye do it? That's what I'd like ter know! Reckon I can guess?" she asked, screwing up her face quite comically. "I s'pect as how you must 'ave . . . jumped out of a speedin' carriage, right? No, no! That ain't it. Then you must 'ave sprouted wings and flew out a window—?" She looked at Ariane expectantly, and softly, the girl giggled.

Queenie drew back, crossed her arms and narrowed her eyes. "Well, if ye didn't jump, and ye didn't fly, then how—?"

"A door," whispered Ariane conspiratorially.

"A *door—?*" repeated Bentley and Cam at once.

Queenie cut them a quelling look. "Aye, just walked out, hmm? Well, wee 'uns don't catch much notice, do they? But what manner o' door, I wonder . . . ? Was it an inn?" She squinted one eye mightily. "I guessed that one aright, didn't I?" she boasted. "Shall I guess which inn it was? Hmm . . . 'tweren't the Cock. That I know. And ye was walking south, so . . . it must be The Haunch, eh?"

Ariane's eyes grew round, and suddenly she began to nod as if some memory had stirred. *"The Haunch of Venice,"* she whispered, awe-struck. "H–h–he took us there. A man watched us—" Abruptly, she stopped and stared at her father.

"Go on, Ariane," he said softly, drawing her a little closer to his chest. "You are very smart to talk. Indeed, it is what you must do now, if Uncle Bentley and I are to find Miss Helene, and get her away from Mr. Lowe."

Ariane nodded and swallowed hard. Slowly, rather uncertainly, she began to explain what she had seen. It was a simple story, all borne out by the few facts Cam and Bentley already knew. She ended by explaining that she had believed her papa would eventually come and find her in Milford Street.

"And what a brave, smart girl you were, too!" said Cam, dropping a kiss atop her head. Then, eyes shut tight, he asked the one question he was sure he knew the answer to, but nonetheless feared. "Ariane, was Miss Helene frightened of the rector? He did not . . . she does not wish to go with him, does she?"

Emphatically, she shook her head. "She *hit* him," whispered Ariane in a dark little voice.

Abruptly, Cam rose, his arms still wrapped tightly around Ariane. It terrified him to realize the horrors his daughter had suffered. But he still feared for Helene. Silently, he sent up a prayer, then cast a determined look toward his brother. "Are the horses ready?"

Bentley jerked his head toward the door. "In the courtyard." His expression grim, the young man stood, hefted up his heavy saddlebags, and tossed his shotgun resolutely over one shoulder.

Sick with fear, Helene paced up and down the narrow lanes of Salisbury, pausing only to glance toward the east where the sky was beginning to brighten. At almost seven o'clock, it must be apparent even to Lowe that they had no hope of finding Ariane quickly. Another shaft of terror knifed into her belly, and she squeezed back the tears which threatened to overcome her.

The day, which had begun with a nightmare, seemed destined to end with one as well. After hearing Helene's fearful gasp, Lowe had awakened, his wrath soon palpable. He had crawled from the bed to look about the narrow chamber in disbelief. But Ariane was gone, and someone would pay. Helene looked at the rector and wondered how she had ever seen sanity—let alone kindness—in such a face.

After tugging on his boots, Lowe had stalked into the corridor to deliver a swift, rib-shattering kick to the man who lay sleeping outside. The ensuing racket had brought the indignant innkeeper flying up the stairs, but a gold sovereign had quickly sent him back down again, where he had immediately set about searching the inn from top to bottom. Half an hour later, they had moved on to the streets, with Helene working as diligently as anyone. But all efforts were in vain. Ariane had vanished.

Now, her hand tightly captured in Lowe's, Helene despondently retraced her steps back up Fish Lane to see that the rector's curricle had been brought 'round to Minster Street. Four fresh horses stood in harness amidst the chaos of what looked like the beginnings of market day.

Roughly, he all but dragged her through the marketplace, jerking his head toward the carriage. "This is bloody hopeless," he said roughly. "Get in!"

"Get *in—?*" she cried. *"Mon Dieu!* Are you mad? Do you mean to leave your child to fend for herself in the streets? What if she has fallen into the hands of some villain?"

"A villain?" sneered Thomas, pulling her inexorably toward the carriage. "I believe, madam, you applied that same term to me yesterday, so what is one villain to another? The child is willful and disobedient. I dare not wait any longer."

Helene was aghast. Lowe now looked wild with anger, more desperate than ever. He truly intended to abandon Ariane! His fear of Cam must be deep indeed. Roughly, he shoved Helene up into the carriage. But Helene resisted. She could not—*would not*— leave a six-year-old child alone in such a place! Perched halfway onto the seat, she swiveled about to stare down at him, one fist balled in anger, willing herself not to hit him.

Lowe's eyes were almost black with rage. The mouth she had once thought handsome had drawn into a thin, cruel line. When she refused to budge further, he exhaled on a sharp hiss, and moved as if to shove her legs into the carriage. Terrified for Ariane, and incensed by his callous disregard, Helene simply snapped. *"Non!"* she cried, lifting both feet and slamming her heels down into Lowe's chest.

Lowe's fingers slipped from the carriage, and he tumbled backward onto the cobblestones, landing with a loud grunt. Everything that followed was a blur.

As Lowe levered onto one elbow, a man in a long drab coat crept silently around the corner just behind him. Dimly, Helene saw sunlight glint off polished wood. Bentley—swinging a firearm deftly down from his shoulder. He was circling behind the curricle.

At once, she saw Cam. He strode across the street and bent down to ruthlessly grasp Lowe's collar. In one smooth motion, he jerked Lowe up, yanked him against the wall of his chest, and drew a glittering knife to his throat.

Only a quick upward glance of Cam's eyes acknowledged Helene, still perched atop Lowe's carriage. "Get out on the other side," he softly ordered her, his voice dark and hard.

Willing her limbs to respond, Helene scrabbled backward as if to obey. Just then, a flash of motion caught her eye. She did not know how or when Lowe had jerked the pistol from his coat. She knew only that it was leveled at her heart. After that, everything happened in slow motion.

"I'll kill her, Treyhern," Lowe rasped, his aim wavering wildly. "I swear it."

The merest flicker of alarm lit Cam's face, swiftly replaced by a look of cold resolve. With another flick of his wrist, he drew his blade fractionally across Lowe's throat.

The rector jerked, his eyes wide, as one perfect drop of blood trickled down onto his cleric's collar.

A reverberating crack of thunder nearly knocked Helene off the carriage seat. She watched in horror as Lowe slid from Cam's grasp. He collapsed onto the road, the single drop of blood became a gush of red. It surged from his shirtfront and trickled from his mouth.

Despite what had been a burgeoning market crowd mere seconds earlier, utter silence fell over the street, broken only by the faint rumble of a farm cart departing in the distance. Then, from a window above, a woman screamed, her voice piercing the unearthly quiet.

Cam let his hands drop to his sides, staring down as the life flowed from Lowe's body to run in rivulets though the cobblestones. Gingerly, a crowd began to gather.

Only then did Helene see Bentley step from behind the curricle, a pistol clutched limply in his right hand, his shotgun held low in his left. He stood over the body, boots spread wide, the hem of his drab greatcoat splattered in bright red. Slowly, he lifted his eyes from the grisly view to hold his brother's stark, questioning gaze.

"Better me than you, brother," Bentley said softly. Then he tossed the shotgun back over his shoulder and calmly walked away.

21

My ring encompasses thy finger as thy breast my heart

In the private parlor of the Red Lion, the hiss of the fire had long since died away, wholly unnoticed by either of the occupants. Now, the only sound within was the incessant rhythm of the mantel clock as it ticked off the mind-numbing minutes.

Randolph Bentham Rutledge sat alone by the window, tipped away from the table in a ladder-back chair, and sipping pensively on a glass of Mr. Stokes's best brandy. He looked exhausted, unkempt, and far older than his years.

Unsteadily, Helene rose from the armchair by the hearth, paced toward the table, and seized an empty tumbler from the pewter tray.

Bentley cast her the merest flicker of surprise, then reached across the table to shove the brandy bottle toward her. After sloshing the glass half full, she looked at it disdainfully, then nudged it away again with the back of her hand. She sank into the chair beside him.

"Why, Bentley?" she said softly, her voice piercing the uneasy silence.

He refused to look at her. "Why what?" he asked dully.

"This morning, why did you do it? Shoot Lowe, I mean? Did you doubt that your brother would . . ." Lamely, she let her words trail away.

Bentley put down his glass with a thud and gave a harsh laugh. "Oh, not for one moment," he answered. Suddenly, his gaze snapped toward her, and his chair clattered forward onto all four legs. "Indeed, I watched him fondle that damned dagger of his all the way from Marlboro!"

Helene winced, and Bentley smiled sardonically. "Oh, admit it, Helene. Between the two of us, my brother is by far the more ruthless. And he was but a hair's-breadth from proving it. He *wanted* to slit that bastard's throat." His voice was hollow, even a little haunted, but there was no accusation in it.

For a moment, his fingers hovered over the glass, trembling. Despite his youthful bravado, Helene knew that Bentley was badly shaken. "Then why, Bentley? Why bloody your hands with a man's death?"

"A dozen reasons," he said dismissively. He tipped back the chair again and took a generous pull from his glass.

"Such as?" Helene leaned intently forward, staring at him.

He shrugged ambiguously. "Perhaps I saw his trigger finger flex? Perhaps I feel I owe my brother some pathetic sort of restitution? Or mayhap I just found Lowe annoying. Have your choice, Helene! I daresay there's truth enough in all of them."

Helene reached across the table and snared his trembling hand in hers. "I think you meant to take the burden of killing a man from your brother's shoulders," she softly challenged. "That was it, was it not? You know—as do I—that Cam would never willingly harm anyone. But he was going to kill Lowe because he had no choice. Because of me."

Bentley jerked his fingers from hers and pressed the heel of his hand to his forehead, as if his head ached. "I think it possible that Lowe could have gotten off a shot first," he finally responded, staring out the window.

"Do you really believe that?"

Bentley's head whipped around again, his flat, black stare catching hers. "Damn it, how do I know? But I do know that the guilt would have eaten at my brother. *Saint Camden—our brother of perpetual responsibility!*" Bentley gave a soft, humorless chuckle. "Yes, *he* is perpetually responsible. And *I* am infinitely unreliable. So what is one more sin on my slate, Helene? Damned little, I daresay." He ran his hand through a shock of dark, disorderly hair, then leaned across the table to refill his glass.

Helene smiled a little bitterly. "I think you are unfair to yourself, Bentley. However, we shall reserve that fight for another time, and another place." Smoothly, she rose from her chair and turned the corner of the table to stand behind him.

Her heart ached for the boy he should have been and was not, the boy who had never known a mother's love. Just as she hurt for the man who had struggled to be both a mother and a father to him.

Lightly, she set her hands on his shoulders and bent to drop a kiss on top of his head. "I thank you for saving my life, Bentley. There is no question that you did so."

"Helene—" Bentley crooked his head to look up at her uncertainly. For a long moment he hesitated, his jaw set at a tight angle. "Look here—there is something else. Something I know but Cam does not—not yet." He swallowed hard, his eyes bleak with surrender. "It has to do with why Lowe took Ariane. I daresay you've guessed what I mean?"

Mutely, Helene nodded, and Bentley continued. "When Ariane grows up, her life may not be easy. She may . . . hear things. Cruel things. But there is one cruelty that she should never have to hear—" He shook his head, unable or unwilling to say the words.

"That the man who loved her and raised her as his beloved child also murdered her father? Is that what you mean?" Helene's sudden comprehension left her knees weak. She sat back down abruptly. "My God, I never thought of it. How exceedingly wise you are, Bentley. Not precisely what I would call *infinitely unreliable.*"

Before Bentley could utter another self-deprecating remark, the parlor door swung wide. Cam strode in, his heavy boots thudding slowly across the wooden floor, his weary gaze holding Helene's as he came toward her. Low in his right hand, he carried a bulging saddlebag, which he promptly dropped onto the table.

Bentley moved as if to rise. Still looking at Helene, Cam laid a staying hand on his brother's shoulder. "The magistrate has gone," he said quietly. "An inquest must eventually take place, but I am assured that it will be a mere formality. There will be a few papers to sign later today, and then we may all go home tomorrow. Together. To Chalcote."

Helene exhaled on a sharp sigh, and laid a reassuring hand over Bentley's. The young man still stared blindly down the length of the table. Softly, Cam spoke again. "Go upstairs, Bentley. Take the bedchamber next to Ariane's. You need some sleep. Soon this will all be over."

Helene tore her gaze from Bentley's face to look anxiously up at Cam. "Miss—er—Queenie is still watching Ariane?"

With a crooked smile, Cam nodded.

At that moment, Bentley shoved back his chair with a harsh scrape. "Indeed, I believe that I will leave you," he said, with feigned nonchalance. "I could do with a bath and a nap." Without another word, he strolled casually from the room, seeming very much his old, arrogant self.

As the door clicked shut, Helene rose from her chair, only to find herself dragged up into Cam's powerful arms. And yet, she could feel him tremble inside as the dam of his emotions cracked, then collapsed. "Oh, God," he whispered hoarsely, burying his face into her hair. "Oh, God, Helene! I feared I'd lost you."

She pushed away a little, looking up into his eyes to see that every pretense, every layer of tight control had been stripped away, leaving him vulnerable and desperate. It was a look of unguarded pain, one which she had not seen since the night they had been torn apart by their parents.

On that dreadful night, they had been inexorably joined by a parting gaze which had been rich with need and fear and the promise of undying love. And that love had not died, had it?

Had she harbored any doubt about Cam's feelings for her, they were crushed by his lips which came down hard upon her own, drawing her into a kiss which was both bold and unyielding. Eagerly, Helene let her hands slide beneath his coat and up the taut, powerful muscles of his back, reveling in the intoxicating strength of him.

For long moments, Cam kissed Helene, deeply, thoroughly, and in a way which claimed her as his own, brooking no opposition. And when he had finished, he set her gently away, turned to the table, and began to unbuckle one of the bulging leather bags.

Carelessly, he jerked out a parcel wrapped in brown paper and ripped it open. A length of emerald silk slithered across the table, cascading into Bentley's empty chair.

Helene was confused. "What on earth—?"

"I meant it for your wedding dress, Helene," he answered, his voice grim and stubborn. "I always wished you to have green silk, you know. And it will look particularly splendid when worn with this." Quietly, he lifted her left hand and slid an ornate band set with a half-dozen emeralds onto her finger.

Helene knew it at once. The fine, filigreed pattern was as familiar to her as a dear friend. Slowly, she wrapped her fingers about his hand, staring at the ring.

Cam curled his thumb over her fist and lifted it to his mouth. The lines carved into his face and around his eyes were deep with fatigue. "If you no longer have the necklace, Hellie, don't fret, for we can have a copy made at—"

"I have it." The interruption came swiftly, but with a tiny, choking sound.

Cam sighed with obvious relief. Undoubtedly, the significance was not lost on him. The necklace would have roofed her ramshackle cottage a hundred times over. "I've also brought a special license from London, Helene," he added softly. "I know I said I would not press you, but I lied."

Helene lifted her gaze to his, trying to see past her misty eyes.

"We're to be wed at once," he firmly continued. "Before we leave Salisbury. I won't wait. I cannot bear the strain. So we're to do it tomorrow morning in the cathedral. I've already made the arrangements, do you hear? My mourning bedamned. The green silk—well, I'm sorry. You'll simply have to wear it later."

The press of tears only increased. Forcing them away, she opened her mouth to agree.

But Cam hushed her with another kiss, and curled his arms about her waist. "No more words, Helene, do you hear?" he said gruffly, lowering his forehead to touch hers. "I'm just too bloody tired to argue over something which was writ upon our hearts long ago. Our only mistake was to doubt one another. Do not doubt me now, Helene. Whatever new challenges life may fling at us—and I daresay there are going to be a few—we will go forward together. And you will have the protection of my name. So just be quiet about it."

"Am I to say nothing, then?" she asked, tucking her head beneath his chin. "No more words at all?"

Softly, he laughed, a low, resigned rumble above her ear. "I am not to be obeyed for one instant, am I? Very well, Helene! Say it!"

"Yes," she said softly. "There! One word only."

Epilogue

Here we come a-wassailing!

In the Great Hall of Chalcote, the servants and tenants gathered amidst thick garlands of greenery and row upon row of trestle tables laden with a sumptuous buffet. On the balcony above the grand staircase, a quartet of musicians from the village fiddled out country jigs and Christmas carols, while in the peaceful world outside, two inches of newly fallen snow lay like a luxuriant white carpet across the fields and forests of Gloucestershire.

On the table nearest the entrance, an assortment of gifts—warm woolen scarves, sturdy leather gloves, and all manner of toys and sweetmeats—lay in neatly arranged piles. Behind the table stood Milford who, with Ariane's assistance, was engaged in rummaging through the piles in order to present just the right gift to every new arrival as they came through the door, laughing and chattering and stamping the snow from their boots.

To Helene, it felt as if she had truly come home at last. Two old Tudor chairs had been dragged from the yellow parlor and placed upon a hastily constructed dais near the conservatory door. From this lofty vantage point, Helene and Cam had been exchanging season's greetings with their visitors for the better part of two hours. But throughout the whole of it, Helene noticed that Cam's watchful gaze had never left Ariane.

Helene felt herself glow with contentment. Ariane stood at Milford's elbow, smiling shyly at all who approached her. Though she said little beyond the occasional timid greeting, pleasure shone in her eyes as she passed the packages across the table.

Cam leaned back in his chair and lifted his goblet of mulled wine, gesturing discreetly in her direction. "Look at Ariane," he said softly. "She seems so . . . happy. So *normal*. My dear Helene, you cannot possibly know how grateful I am to you."

The crowd had drawn away from them to stare up at the musicians who had begun a rousing version of "The Twelve Days of Christmas." Seizing the privacy of the moment, Helene turned to kiss him swiftly on the cheek.

"Oh, Ariane is normal," she quietly agreed. "But Cam, my dear, you must know that I had little to do with it. Ariane was never truly ill, simply confused and frightened. She was just a worried little girl trying very hard to do what she believed to be was the right thing. She was trying to keep her mother's secret, as she'd been asked to do."

Cam was silent for a long moment. "Helene . . . do you think Ariane remembers?" His voice was laced with just a hint of his old pain.

Slowly, Helene shook her head. "No, Ariane has nothing but vague recollections. I believe she remembers that there was a fire, and that it had something to do with Lowe. But the only clear memory she seems to have is that she was forbidden to talk of it—and indeed, she hardly understood what *it* was."

"You refer to the relationship between her mother and Lowe?" he said grimly.

"Yes. I'm sorry."

"Do not worry, Helene," he whispered reassuringly. "It does not trouble me. Not in the way you mean. I merely hope that all of Ariane's memories will someday fade away."

Gently, Helene patted him on the knee. "They very nearly have, Cam. And together, we will ensure that they never return to trouble her. We will provide her with a family that is a bastion of strength and comfort."

"Dear Helene!" Cam reached out to cover her hand with his own, squeezing it tightly. Suddenly, a ghost of uncertainty passed over his face. "But do you not think that Ariane has seemed a little solemn these last three weeks?" he asked. "I confess, it has worried me."

Lightly, Helene laughed. "Oh, Cam! You are determined to worry, aren't you? Ariane is just moping over Bentley. You must know that she misses him dreadfully."

"Good heavens, you are right!" Cam seemed to relax in his chair. "And speaking of Bentley, I wonder where the devil that boy has got to."

"Oh, he is still in Paris, I do not doubt! I know he meant to go on to Italy by New Year's, but I do not think he will give up Paris quite so easily once he has seen it." Helene squeezed her husband's hand again. "But Bentley is very much on your mind, is he not?" she asked softly. "Perhaps, my dear, you miss him as much as Ariane does?"

At that, Cam threw back his head and laughed. "I cannot fool you for a minute, can I?" he complained again. "Yes, I miss the scamp. But mostly I just worry for him." His voice dropped to a more solemn tone. "It was bad enough, Helene, what he went through in Salisbury. And I know why he did it, too. And what did I do to reward him? I gave the living of Saint Michael's to Basil! It is a wonder Bentley does not hate me for that. Indeed, perhaps he does."

"Your brother does *not* hate you, my love," Helene

softly insisted. "And in truth, Bentley has grown up a vast deal. Still, we simply cannot expect him to live with Joan on his doorstep. Not until his heart has mended just a bit."

Cam turned fully to face her, lightly brushing the back of one hand across her cheek. "I did do the right thing by old Basil, didn't I? I mean, I know it was a hard one for Bentley to swallow, but I must take care of Joan."

Slowly, Helene nodded. "Yes, love. You did precisely the right thing, and Bentley understood. This trip abroad will be just the thing, you shall see. No doubt he will fall in love with some pretty mademoiselle before the year is out."

"Now that I can heartily recommend!" said Cam softly, his gaze rich with meaning.

"I love you, too," she returned. "And I always shall. Moreover, just look at all we have to further bless us this Christmastime." Helene lifted her hand to gesture at the crowded room. "Our dear friends, our healthy family. And trust me, Cam, when I say that Bentley, too, will make something of himself someday soon."

"Yes," Cam said slowly. "But precisely what that something will be, I dare not guess. I merely pray he does not die in a horse race or dawn appointment betimes."

"Really, Camden!" Helene gave a light laugh. "I think you have no faith in Bentley at all. Besides, he's quite a good shot."

The reminder was not lost on Cam. "Well, we've not heard a word out of him these last two months," he returned, shifting uncomfortably in his seat. "So I suppose we must assume that no news is good news."

Suddenly, Helene smiled, looking uncharacteristically shy. "Well, as to news, my love, I have some. And it is very good indeed!" She drew her hand away, and lightly brushed it down her belly.

Cam stared at her for a long moment, and then suddenly, his face lit up with joy. "Oh, my dear! You cannot mean it! I mean, I had hoped—that is to say, it is my fondest wish—but I had not expected this so soon."

"But do you know, my dear, I think it could not have happened soon enough for me. Indeed, we have wasted so many, many years. For my part, I do not mean to waste a moment of those we have left." And then, very gently, Helene bent forward to brush her lips lightly over his cheek.

But Cam's strong hands went around her shoulders, and at once, the kiss on the cheek turned to something just a little different.

Long moments later, the lord and lady of the manor were roused from their diversions to find that the crowded room had lost complete interest in "The Twelve Days of Christmas" somewhere near the "ten lords a-leaping."

Then Camden Rutledge, the terribly solemn and oh-so-proper Earl of Treyhern, blushed three shades of red as his Great Hall erupted into a thunderous round of applause.

POCKET STAR BOOKS
PROUDLY PRESENTS

ONE LITTLE SIN

LIZ CARLYLE

Coming in October 2005 in paperback from
Pocket Star Books

Turn the pages for a preview of the first
book in Liz's new trilogy
One Little Sin . . .

MacLachlan nodded, then turned to Esmée as if she were next on his list of Catastrophes-to-be-Dealt-With. "You," he said decisively. "Come with me into the study. We've a little something to settle, you and I."

Esmée must have faltered.

MacLachlan's eyes narrowed. "Oh, come now, Miss Hamilton!"

The doctor had already vanished. MacLachlan seized Esmée by the arm, and steered her almost roughly down the corridor. He pushed open the door, urged her inside, and slammed it shut.

"Good God" he said, exhaling sharply. "What a bloody awful nightmare this day has turned out to be!"

"Oh, aye, d' ye think so?" asked Esmée, her voice tart. "Then how would you like to have your womb up tied in knots like poor Mrs. Crosby, with your life's blood leaching out, and your child all but lost? *That*, MacLachlan, is what a nightmare feels like."

The muscle in MacLachlan's too-perfect jaw began to twitch. "I am not insensible to Julia's anguish," he gritted. "I would bear it for her if I could, but I cannot. All I can do is to try to be a good friend."

"Oh, would that every woman had such a friend!" she returned. "You are off gallivanting about town with a brandy bottle as your boon companion, whilst she is all but miscarrying your next child!"

Esmée had not sat down, a circumstance which MacLachlan either did not notice, or did not care about. He had begun to pace the floor between the windows, one hand set at the back of his neck, the other on his hip.

His jaw was growing tighter and tighter as he paced, and his temple was beginning to visibly throb, too.

"Well?" she challenged. "Have you nothing to say, man?"

Suddenly, he whirled on her. "Now you listen to me, you spite-tongued little witch," he said. "And listen well, for I mean to say this but once: Julia Crosby's child is none of your business—nor any of mine, either, come to that."

"Aye, 'tis none of my business if you sire a bastard in every parish," Esmée returned.

"You're bloody well right it's not," he retorted. "And perhaps I have! But whilst I'm defending myself from your hot-headed notions, let me say that I have *not* spent the day idly drinking, either."

"Oh, faith! You reek of it!"

"Yes, and yesterday I reeked of coffee," he snapped. "Neither you nor Lord Devellyn possess a modicum of grace, it seems. He slopped brandy down my trousers."

Esmée didn't believe him. "Oh, aye, you've been gone all day, and when at last you come home, you smell as if you spent the afternoon in the gutter. What's anyone to think?"

He stabbed his finger in her face. "Miss Hamilton, had I any wish to be nagged, insulted, or upbraided, I would get myself a wife, not a goddamned governess!" he roared. "And besides that, you do not get paid to *think!*"

Esmée felt her temper implode. "Oh, no, I get paid to . . . to *what?*" she shrilly demanded as he resumed his pacing. "Satisfy the master's base instincts when his itch wants scratching? Remind me again. I somehow got muddled up over my duties."

He spun about, and grabbed her by the shoulders,

shoving her against the door. "Shut up, Esmée," he growled. "For once, just shut the hell up." And then he was kissing her, brutishly and relentlessly.

She tried to squirm away, but he held her prisoner between his hands. The harsh stubble of his beard raked across her face as he slanted his lips over hers, again and again, his powerful hands clenched upon her shoulders.

She tried to twist her face away. His nostrils were wide now, his mouth hot and demanding. Something inside her sagged, gave way, and she opened her mouth to him. He surged inside, thrusting deep. Her shoulder blades pressed against the wood, she began to shudder. There was no tenderness to his touch now, just a black, demanding hunger. Esmée began to shove at his shoulders, and then to pummel them with the heels of her hands.

As abruptly as it had begun, he tore his mouth from hers, and stared her in the eyes, his nostrils still wide, his breathing still rough and quick. And then, his eyes dropped shut. "Damn it all," he whispered. "No, damn *me*."

For a moment there was an awful silence. Then Esmée broke it. "I ought to slap the breath of life from you," she gritted. "Don't ever touch me again, MacLachlan. I am *not* Mrs. Crosby. I am not even my mother, lest you be confused. Now take your lecherous hands off me, or I'll be kneeing you in the knackers so hard you heave."

Catch a glimpse of
Liz Carlyle's Previous
Bestselling Devil Series
Available from Pocket Books

A DEAL WITH THE DEVIL
THE DEVIL YOU KNOW
THE DEVIL TO PAY

From

THE DEVIL YOU KNOW

In a matter of minutes, a flash of sapphire blue floated across the landing, and turned down the darkened corridor. He recognized Frederica's tense whisper, and strained to make out the words.

A masculine voice responded. "But how can you marry someone else, Freddie?" he complained. "I've arranged everything! Even Papa has come round."

"Take your hand off my arm," Frederica hissed. "Life is not so simple, Johnny, as you make it out."

Abruptly, the footsteps stopped, mere inches from Bentley's hiding place. "Aye, you're bitter now, but I swear I'll make you forget that," whispered Johnny hotly. "I swear it. Just let me—"

Bentley heard a soft, strangled gasp. "Why, how dare you!" Frederica cried.

His every muscle suddenly jolting, Bentley lunged. Seizing Johnny Ellows's coat collar in one fist, he jerked the lad off his feet and gave him a shake which rattled his teeth. Slinging his victim aside, Bentley looked at Frederica.

"Hello, Freddie," he said quietly. "Careful in the dark, love. You never know who you might run into."

Ellows had staggered to his feet. "See here, Rutledge," he growled, planting one hand on Frederica's shoulder. "This is none of your concern."

Gently, Bentley lifted his hand away. "I'm afraid, Johnny-Boy, that I've just made it my concern." His voice was lethally soft. "Touch her again without her express request, and the next thing you'll be touching is the trigger on a dueling pistol. And if those clever Cambridge dons of yours gave you any grasp of ballistics, physics, or the laws of probability, then you'll be pissing down your leg and praying to your Maker when you do it. *Because I don't miss.* Now take that bit of wisdom back to Essex, Ellows, and stuff it up your priggish Papa's arse."

Ellows's face had gone white. Anxiously, he looked from Bentley to Frederica and back again, then scuttled away. Bentley waited for Frederica's expression of gratitude, but none came. Instead, she tried to slip away. Bentley caught her elbow. "Whoa, Freddie." Their bodies were just inches apart. "Going somewhere?"

Her expression froze. "None of your business, Rutledge," she coolly answered. "And I appreciate your help, but I can manage Johnny."

Her indifference was like a slap in the face. On a stab of anger, Bentley yanked her hard against him. "Can you now, sweetheart?"

She tried to wrench away. Ruthlessly, he tightened his grip. He didn't know what he'd expected, but it wasn't this. "Let go of my arm!" she snapped. "Why are you even here?"

"Maybe I've come to kiss the bride, Freddie."

"Are you and Johnny both run mad?" she hissed. "Get out, before you're seen."

"How the warmth of your welcome touches me, Freddie." His voice was a cold whisper. "Are you this hospitable to all your invited guests?"

Frederica tried to look disdainful as her eyes swept over Bentley Rutledge. But more than six feet of accursedly handsome and thoroughly outraged male glowered back. And this male would not be so easily dispatched as the last. "You w- were invited to the ball?"

Rutledge cocked one of his arrogant eyebrows. "Now why is it, Freddie, I begin to wonder if someone forgot to scrape the *rough edges* off Rannoch's guest list?" His hand tightened on her elbow. "What a bloody shame. Does that mean I won't be invited to the wedding?"

"No—I m- mean *yes*."

"By the way, Freddie, what was that date?" he gritted. "I'd like to get you penciled into my social calendar—assuming I can wedge the happy nuptials in between my rampant bacchanalia and my debauching of virgins."

"Bentley, please! I cannot be seen talking to you."

His hard, sour smile taunted her. "Now, that's a strange one, Freddie. I mean, we're such old friends. And you were more than cordial last time we ran into one another."

"I don't understand," she whispered. "Why are you doing this?

His eyes glittered maliciously. "Well, now, I'm not perfectly sure, Freddie. Maybe I don't have anything better to do than waste an evening with people who are over-dressed, over-fed, and overly self-important. Or maybe I'm just trying to understand how a woman can make such passionate love with me one day, then marry someone else the next. Yes, by Jove. I think that was it."

Frederica turned her face from his. "Please just go, Bentley. What we did was a dreadful mistake."

"By God, it was no *mistake!*" he growled. "We did it quite deliberately."

"Please." Her voice trembled. "Don't make trouble."

"Then answer me, damn it!" He seized her chin and jerked her eyes back into his. "Tell me, how could a woman do that—do it *twice*, actually—then turn around and announce her betrothal to someone I never heard of? Perhaps you could explain? And if you can, why, I'll leave on your next breath."

From

A DEAL WITH THE DEVIL

Aubrey could not believe it when Lord Walrafen stepped back inside her sitting room. Had the man no shame? Hadn't he caused trouble enough? Apparently not. All long legs and masculine beauty, the earl strode across the floor as if he owned it. Which, of course, he did.

She jerked from her chair at the worktable and watched him warily.

He tossed his folio down with aristocratic disdain. "I spoke to Jenks," he said coolly. "You won't have any trouble from quarter."

"Oh, you *spoke* to him—?" she hissed, circling from behind the table. "Why, how very *lordly* of you, sir. And just what did you tell him? Never to interrupt you whilst you're debauching your staff?"

He looked at her in some surprise. Surprise which swiftly shifted to something else. He stalked closer, so close she could see flecks of ebony in his silvery gaze. "Madam, were I intent on debauching you, I'd have had your drawers round your ankles ages ago," he returned. "All I did was kiss you—and not entirely without your consent."

"Why, how dare you!" Aubrey had quite forgotten her plan to keep her mouth shut. To do *anything* to keep her job. "How dare you lay the blame for your lapse at my door!"

The earl shrugged. "I'm sorry you were embarrassed," he answered. "That was never my intent."

"Oh, but you found me irresistible, so all must be forgiven?" she suggested cynically. "I suppose you were overcome with lust at the sight of my exceptional book-keeping skills. Or was it my extraordinary way with the linen press?"

"Actually," interjected the earl, "it was your arse, Aubrey. Your skirts cling to it most invitingly when you reach upward."

Much of her color drained. "I see," she whispered. "And like some ripe apple, my lord, I am to be yours for the plucking?"

Walrafen lifted one brow at her analogy. "Forgive me, my dear, but you did give that impression," he answered. "But perhaps I was confused. Perhaps that was someone else's tongue in my mouth?"

Instinct seized her. Aubrey drew back her hand to strike him.

The earl's hand came up, quick as a cat on its prey, snaring her wrist and dragging her against him. "Don't even consider it, my dear," he said, his voice low and ominous. "I've put up with a vast deal of insolence from you already."

"Well put up with *this*, Lord Walrafen," she whispered darkly. "*I* choose who shares my bed. No one commands it."

Walrafen no longer looked so civilized. His eyes were dark, his mouth hard. Aubrey drew in a jagged breath, and with it came the scent of hot, angry male. His expensive cologne didn't smell quite so refined now. "As to your bed, Aubrey," he whispered hotly against her ear, "perhaps you'd best remember who owns it? And as to commands, yes, you are free to choose. So choose very, very wisely."

"And I thought you were a gentleman," she hissed.

He drew back, his gaze running over her face. "A politician," he corrected. "A real gentleman wouldn't know what to do with you."

"Oh, and you do?"

Challenge fired his eyes. Walrafen jerked her fully against him. "I think I'm catching on," he said, right before he kissed her.

She fought him, beating her hands against his shoulders and twisting her face away. When that yielded nothing, she tried to bite him. He caught her by both wrists, and forced them against the tabletop, pinning her with his body. Aubrey felt the evidence of his desire, hard and unmistakable. For an instant, their gazes locked.

Walrafen was trying to catch his breath. "Don't fight me, Aubrey," he growled.

Her breath, too, was short. "Let me go," she hissed.

But something in his eyes shocked her. She saw in him a ferocity, a wild, hot madness she could never have imagined. But there was pain, too. She had hurt him. Still, he looked like a man who got what he wanted. Good Lord, she'd been playing with fire.

"Just let me go," she whispered again.

But even as his grip was loosening, his lips were moving toward her again, and her eyes—her treacherous eyes—were slowly closing in surrender. "Are you sure that's what you want?" His voice was like sin and silk. "*Are* you, Aubrey?"

Her body went limp against the wood. Oh, God! That was the trouble, wasn't it? She *was not sure.* It had been years since she had felt so fully alive. Any human contact, any sort of emotion—yes, even lust and anger—felt better than the nothing she'd been living with.

The moment's hesitation was her undoing. The earl kissed her again, his lips soft and warm, melting over her own.

From
THE DEVIL TO PAY

Devellyn came suddenly awake to a sound he did not recognize. Someone was rummaging about in his room. *Honeywell? Fenton?* But he saw no candle. Even the one he'd been reading by had guttered. He lifted his head from the back of the chair where he'd foolishly drifted off, and laid aside his magazine. Cool night air swirled through the room. The window. It should not have been open.

At the foot of his bed, a slight figure loomed. Metal jangled softly on his dressing table. *A bloody thief?* Yes, and a young one, too, by the look of him.

By God, not again! Noiselessly, he rose to his feet. He wished to the devil he wasn't wearing a white nightshirt. In the gloom, he could barely make out the slender figure meticulously pilfering his things. *A mere boy.* He'd likely break both his arms before the rascal realized what had got hold of him.

Devellyn was unsympathetic. He lunged, taking the lad down in the narrow space between the bed and dressing table. Something metallic clattered across the floor. The boy grunted when the marquess landed, but strangely, he made no other sound. Still, he was quick. And deadly silent. He kicked and flailed viciously, then gave Devellyn a good elbow to the ribs in a blind, backward shot.

"Umph!" grunted Devellyn. "Hold still, you thieving bastard!"

For an instant, they rolled and tumbled across the rug, arms and legs entwined, elbows flying. Devellyn slammed the lad's head into the bed's footboard. But the lad was tough. He cursed softly, and caught Devellyn this time with an elbow to the throat. Devellyn choked. The lad tried to drag himself across the carpet toward the open window, and bloody near made it.

Devellyn scrabbled after him, snatching one ankle. "By God, I'll see you hanged!"

Another grunt, and the lad almost squirmed away, clawing his way along the carpet between the footboard and dressing table. Devellyn grabbed him around the ankle, then the knee, hauling him ruthlessly back inch by inch. When he had him, he rolled him over and slung a leg over the lad's body, weighing him down.

For a few seconds, the thief fought like a tiger, clawing and scratching, and doing his best to squirm from beneath Devellyn. It was then he made a near-fatal mistake. He tried to knee Devellyn in the knackers.

"Why, you bloody, snot-nosed shite!" the marquess roared. He tried to grab the lad around the waist again, but the boy was onto that trick. He twisted violently, but he wasn't quite fast enough. Devellyn caught him. But not by the waist.

"Well, damn me for a fool!" he said, his hand full of warm, plump breast.

The thief stopped wiggling and twisting. He—no, *she*—lay splayed beneath Devellyn's body, panting for breath. He opened his mouth to bellow for Honeywell to bring a lamp when the thief cursed again. This time, something about the sound made Devellyn freeze.

"What the bloody hell?"

"Look 'ere, gov'," whispered Ruby Black. "Let loose, awright? It ain't wot yer thinkin'."

Understanding slammed into him. Ruby's lissome body was round and warm beneath his own. He didn't know what the hell was happening, but he had no intention of letting her go. Especially not her breast. He squeezed it roughly.

In the darkness, she gasped. "Now, it ain't wot yer think," she whispered again. "Let me up, awright?"

Devellyn snapped. "Why, you bald-faced, light-fingered little bitch!" he spat. "Of all the unmitigated gall—"

Ruby twisted impotently. "I didn't nick nothing," she hissed. "Let me up, and I'll be on me way."

Devellyn tore the hat from her head, and slicked his hand over her hair, as if that might disprove what his aching, itching body already knew. It did not help. It was Ruby, right enough. But this time, her hair was drawn back tight, coiled up high like some prim, proper governess. He fisted his hand in the coil of hair, and forced her face into his.

"Let me go," she whispered. "Please."

"Oh, no, Ruby," he answered. "You've the devil to pay this time, remember?"

"I brought yer goods back, gov. Let me go."

But Devellyn had ceased, really, to hear her. His brain had seemingly disengaged. He heard only her breath panting in the darkness. Felt only the warm, full curves of her body. And there was the rage; that simmering anger and frustration which had boiled down to a sort of nasty black pitch in the bottom of his soul.

Suddenly, she tried to jerk free.

"Oh, no you don't, darling," he hissed, pressing his lips to her ear. "We've unfinished business, you and I."

With all of his seventeen stone bearing down on her, Devellyn thrust one hand beneath her arse, and lifted her hips against his cock. She squirmed desperately, a foolish thing to do. Devellyn felt the anger and lust course through him. He wanted a lamp. A candle. *Anything*. But he knew better. She was too fast. Too smart. So instead, he tightened his fingers in her hair, tilted back her head, and raked his teeth down her throat.

Devellyn felt like he was going to explode. His hand went to the fall of her trousers, and roughly jerked. A button gave, flew off, and landed softly on the carpet. He had to have her. Had to be inside. He forced away the fear that she was not willing. The fact that they were on the floor, wedged between the table and bed. And, most importantly, that he had no clue who the hell she really was. He wasn't about to slow down and ask.

Her baggy trousers gave way easily. Too easily. He set his hand flat on her belly, and felt her warm skin quiver as he skimmed down. Suddenly, he halted. "Good God Almighty," he choked.

Nothing but her bare flesh lay beneath, soft and inviting. Devellyn tore his mouth from hers. "You don't have a stitch on under here."

Ruby twisted her face away. "Well, I didn't plan on 'aving me trousers off, did I?"

Ruby gasped, and writhed beneath him. But Devellyn's nightshirt was already twisted around his waist from their wrestling match. Her desperation merely served to rub the fall of her trousers back and forth against his hardening cock.

Roughly, he massaged her breast, rolling it back and forth in his hand, then plucking at her nipple. She wore nothing beneath her coarse frieze shirt. He was sure of it. He wanted more. Wanted to touch her. Impatiently, he moved to jerk her shirt free, only to find it already loose.

"Don't," she whispered. "Oh, don't. Let me go."

"Oh, no," he hissed, skating one hand underneath the shirt, up her bare, shivering flesh. "I mean to take what I paid for, you hot-blooded little bitch."

She trembled when he settled his bare hand over her breast. "I brought yer money back," she insisted. "On that table. *Look.*"

"And leave you to dive out the window again?" he whispered. "Not bloody likely."

She whimpered beneath him as he inched his hand up her body, but her breath seized and her nipple peaked hard as soon as his bare palm brushed it.

"You like that?" he rasped.

"No."

"Liar," said Devellyn.

"Please. I'm begging you."

He chuckled, and lowered her mouth to hers. "Oh, Ruby, I do love to hear you beg," he said. Then he kissed her roughly, opening his mouth wide over hers and thrusting deep on the first stroke.

He felt her exhale, felt her warm breath on his cheek, and then he felt her hips rise. Lust surged through him, stronger than ever. He drew his tongue from her mouth, and thrust again, shoving her head back against the floor.